A L I E N S™

BUG HUNT

READ ALL OF THE EXCITING ALIEN™ NOVELS FROM TITAN BOOKS

ALIEN: OUT OF THE SHADOWS by Tim Lebbon
ALIEN: SEA OF SORROWS by James A. Moore
ALIEN: RIVER OF PAIN by Christopher Golden

THE RAGE WAR by Tim Lebbon:
PREDATOR: INCURSION
ALIEN: INVASION
ALIEN VS. PREDATOR: ARMAGEDDON

THE OFFICIAL MOVIE NOVELIZATIONS BY ALAN DEAN FOSTER
ALIEN
ALIENS™
ALIEN 3™
ALIEN: COVENANT™
ALIEN: COVENANT – ORIGINS

ALIEN RESURRECTION by A.C. Crispin

THE COMPLETE ALIENS OMNIBUS
VOLUME 1
VOLUME 2
VOLUME 3
VOLUME 4 (June 2017)
VOLUME 5 (December 2017)
VOLUME 6 (June 2018)
VOLUME 7 (December 2018)

THE COMPLETE ALIENS VS. PREDATOR™ OMNIBUS

THE COMPLETE PREDATOR™ OMNIBUS (January 2018)

ALIEN ILLUSTRATED BOOKS
ALIEN: THE ARCHIVE
ALIEN: THE ILLUSTRATED STORY
THE ART OF ALIEN: ISOLATION
ALIEN NEXT DOOR
ALIEN: THE SET PHOTOGRAPHY

ALL-NEW TALES FROM THE EXPANDED ALIEN UNIVERSE

A L I E N S™

BUG HUNT

EDITED BY **JONATHAN MABERRY**

TITAN BOOKS

ALIENS ™: BUG HUNT
Hardback edition ISBN: 9781785655777
US paperback edition ISBN: 9781785654442
UK paperback edition ISBN: 9781785655784
E-book edition ISBN: 9781785654459

Published by Titan Books
A division of Titan Publishing Group Ltd
144 Southwark Street, London SE1 0UP

First edition: April 2017
10 9 8 7 6 5 4 3 2 1

This is a work of fiction. Names, characters, places, and incidents are used fictitiously, and any resemblance to actual persons, living or dead, business establishments, events, or locales is entirely coincidental.

A CIP catalogue record for this title is available from the British Library.

Printed and bound in the United States.

Did you enjoy this book?
We love to hear from our readers. Please email us at
readerfeedback@titanemail.com or write to us at
Reader Feedback at the above address.
TITAN BOOKS.COM

To Ridley Scott and James Cameron.
Thanks for taking us out into the big black
and scaring the bejeezus out of us.

And, as always, to Sara Jo.

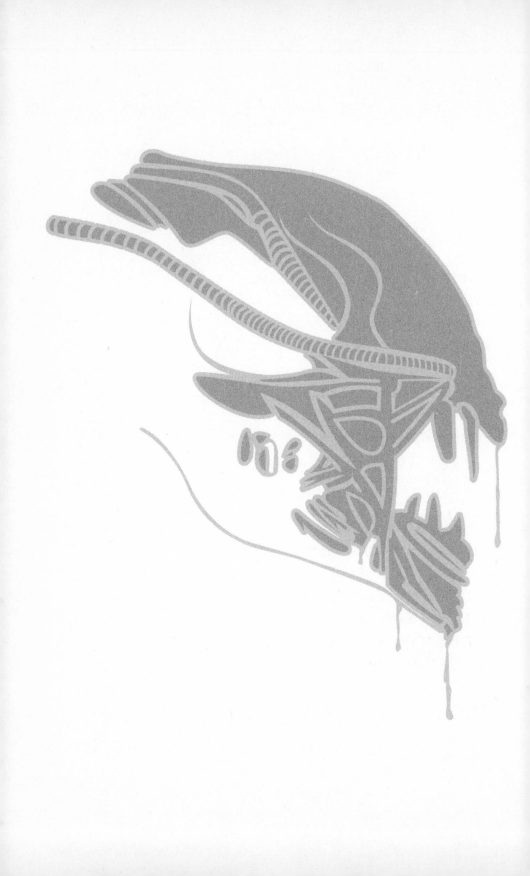

CONTENTS

INTRODUCTION

BY JONATHAN MABERRY

On a beautiful spring day I drove from Philly to New York with a movie projectionist buddy of mine to see the premier of a new film by Ridley Scott. We had only ever heard of the director from one previous piece, the period drama *The Duelists*. No idea if the guy could handle a science fiction flick. Mind you, this was years before *Blade Runner*. No one knew who Scott was. And no one knew what his new movie, *Alien*, was going to be like. All we'd seen were the trailers.

My buddy ran the *Alien* trailer every day for weeks and he was convinced it was going to be good. I was skeptical, having been disappointed in most recent science-fiction films and was, frankly, hoping for another flick like *Star Wars*.

We settled in, both interested but jaded. We'd seen every flick and thought that nothing could do more than form the basis for a critical discussion. We never expected the movie to have punch.

Or, rather, to have *bite*.

It was a packed house on a matinee. Outside it was a sunshiny New York afternoon.

Suddenly we were in outer space. Aboard a rusty old piece of junk freighter. Far away. And in real trouble.

The tagline of the film was: "In space, no one can hear you scream."

Well, they sure as hell could hear people scream in that damn theater. Everyone. Every. Single. Person.

Me, too... and I'm a hard sell. I'm a big guy. I was working as a bodyguard back then. Tough as nails. My buddy had seen every horror flick ever made. We were the film critic guys, not the rubes who would jump, and yell, and yelp, and cry out at cinematic monsters.

Except that's what happened.

That movie scared the hell out of us. Nothing had done that since I saw *Night of the Living Dead* when I was ten. And because it scared me so badly I did the same thing with *Alien* that I'd done with Romero's zombie flick. I stayed to see it again.

Over time I got to know those characters. I read Alan Dean Foster's rather brilliant novelization. I read the comic adaptation *Heavy Metal* published. I bought the damn calendar. I was hooked.

I even watched every cheap knock-off of it, hoping for something that would approach the blend of intelligent storytelling, subtlety and excitement. I never found another movie that came close.

Until the summer of 1986.

James Cameron hit us with *Aliens*. Not a remake, as so many sequels are. And not an inferior follow-up. A masterpiece. *Another* masterpiece. Brilliant and different. Where *Alien* was a horror movie set in outer space, *Aliens* was a war story set in space. Like the first movie it relied on the talent of a rich ensemble cast of character actors. Like the first movie it paved new ground. Like the first movie it scared the hell out of me. In all the right ways.

Since then there have been more sequels and prequels. There have been comic books. There have been tons of novels. And there have been video games. The world of *Alien* has grown and continues to grow because it's captured the imagination of the public while at the same time respecting their intelligence. That's a hard balance.

Of all the movies, though, my personal favorite is *Aliens.* I loved the story of the Colonial Marines. Apone and Hicks, Hudson and Vasquez, and all the others. I even liked Gorman. Kind of.

The camaraderie between those marines was one of the inspirations for Echo Team, the Special Ops shooters in my bestselling Joe Ledger weird-science thriller series.

Several of my author friends have done superb novels set in this world. Alan Dean Foster did the first three books, knocking each one out of the park. The late—and much missed—A.C. Crispin did *Alien Resurrection.* There have been a lot of others, including some by contributors to this anthology, Yvonne Navarro, Christopher Golden, James A. Moore and Tim Lebbon.

I've long wanted to suit up and go into battle with the Colonial Marines. A couple of years ago I was in London having dinner with the publishers of the Titan Aliens novels, Nick and Vivian Landau. I mentioned that I wanted to do an anthology set in this world. Not the meta-world of the whole *Alien* franchise, but specifically the world of the Colonial Marines. They put me in touch with in-house editor Steve Saffel, and we closed a deal.

Which is when I got to play. I made a wish list of who I thought could write the absolute hell out of short stories of soldiers going into battle against aliens. Not just against the Xenomorphs, but other kinds of aliens featured in the movies and related books and comics; no, this book also contains stories that pit the Marines against all sorts of otherworldly threats. The Marines have a catch-all nickname for *any* alien that wants to turn humans into brunch: bugs. Hence the famous line from *Aliens*.

HUDSON: Is this a stand up fight or another bug hunt?

There are all kinds of bug hunts here. Against Xenomorphs and against critters that don't even have a name yet. Scary things that lurk in the dark. We went on the premise that it's a large, weird, dangerous universe filled with creatures who aren't warm and fuzzy E.T.s and who don't necessarily want to share. And who are looking for a hot lunch.

I thought it might take me as much as a month to fill my roster of literary gunslingers to go hunting with me. Ha. It took me about two days. You see, I'm not the only writer out there who's been itching to tell a story in this world. Not only did I get enough commitments for a thick, delicious collection of stories... once the news got out that I was doing this book I had to turn down a couple of hundred pitches.

Yeah. Nice.

So, *Aliens: Bug Hunt*.

The stories here are all different. They range from pure adrenaline-fueled action to introspective human dramas to the deeply weird. As the editor of the anthology I got to read them first—and there is a greedy little joy in that. As a fan of the genre I feel like I've been invited back into the world of Xenomorphs, corporate greed, kickass action, heroics, horror, and the kind of dark magic that is particular to this kind of horror-based science fiction.

These are grand tales of heroism, cowardice, struggle, betrayal, remorse, and the cost in human terms of taking up arms against unknown foes. Some of these tales fit easily into the existing canon of the *Alien/Aliens* franchise. Other stories won't necessarily be considered canonical, though—they're farther out on the edge, suggesting that it's a bigger, darker, stranger and more dangerous universe than any of us think...

So, grab your pulse rifle and let's go hunting.

Enjoy!

CHANCE ENCOUNTER

BY PAUL KUPPERBERG

"Double or nothing they don't get the tub off the ground before the next shift," London said.

"No bet," Gilmore said, only half paying attention to her E.V.A. companion.

"Okay, you call the time."

"Leave me alone, London."

Gilmore picked up her pace, springing ahead of him in slow motion arcs through the thin atmosphere and less than one-quarter Earth gravity, keeping an eye out for ground obstacles in the tall rust red tree-like growths and brown grasses through which they tromped.

One of the disadvantages of a full-suit extra-vehicular excursion was that no matter how far ahead of London she pulled, she couldn't escape his voice buzzing in her earpiece.

And listening to London was a waste of time. London just liked to talk. She didn't know if it was a nervous habit, the natural patter of the confidence man, or because he loved the sound of his own voice—probably all of the above—but most of the crew aboard the USCSS *Typhoon* knew to tune out or avoid conversation with the Navigation Officer. At least those who planned to end this tour with any cash left in their jumpsuits.

"C'mon, what's the big deal, Gilmore? Double or nothing."

Except when forced down on an unexplored low gravity, bio-diverse planet in the Zeta^2 Reticuli system for emergency repairs and paired with him for a recon to gather data for the Weyland-Yutani Corporation. It was S.O.P.; explore for exploitable resources, an order the company backed with substantial financial incentives and a call London never failed to answer.

"Double or nothing *what*?"

"One of us gotta owe the other for something," he said.

"When have I ever gambled with you?" she said, not bothering to hide her annoyance.

London thought about it. "Never," he said. "Whatever. Just trying to keep things interesting."

"Thanks, but this is interesting enough for me."

Gilmore came to a stop at the edge of the pale grassy plain. Ahead, the grasses began to give way to a forest of impossibly tall, thin trees that rose even more impossibly high through the crystal clear air into the cloudless sky. She checked the sensorpad strapped to the forearm of her suit. Lines of many colors rose and fell and numbers flitted across the screen as the device measured and recorded every sort of environmental and atmospheric condition. Of course, none of it meant squat to the Warrant Officer, but it was all being transmitted back to the *Typhoon* where Science Officer Jepson would analyze it at her leisure.

Confined by her suit, Gilmore had to lean backwards to follow the lines of the great trees into the sky. "Get a load of these things, huh? Bet they're at least twice as tall as the giant redwoods on Earth."

"How much?" London said.

"Shut up, London." She took a few low-gravity leaps to the nearest tree. It was a little more than a couple of meters wide, but the same low-gravity that made it possible for her to cover many times the normal distance with each step allowed that slim structure to grow to almost a thousand meters tall.

Gilmore pushed at the tree. It bent easily under her touch. "I don't think these are trees. More like a species of giant grass. You getting a sample?"

London had already unhooked a tool and sample bag. "Ten-four. Imagine the size of the tomatoes they're gonna be able to grow once they crack this genetic code."

Gilmore switched the view on her visor to telescopically scan the area. "Crazy world," she said. "Twenty-two percent Earth-grav, but it's got an atmosphere, oxygen, water, developed flora, probably fauna."

London carved a sliver of the rust red stalk into the bag. "Surprised there's anything at all. Planets with gravity this low don't usually hang on to much atmosphere."

"Jepson said they're rare. Something to do with orbits, rate of rotation, magnetic field, the escape velocity of oxygen… but you know, once she starts explaining, you better have a Ph.D or forget it. Hey, London! Check it out."

London turned to see Gilmore pointing into the distance, at the forest. "Holy crap."

They looked to be some form of aquatic life, part jellyfish, part squid, great gray and rust behemoths floating through the thin atmosphere from the cover of the giant stalks like creatures deep beneath an Earthly sea. The oversized scale of the surrounding landscape, made it difficult for Gilmore to gauge the creatures' size by eye, but her visor read-out tagged them at sixty meters and more. There were too many to count, all moving at a good clip, their trailing tentacles emitting wispy puffs that propelled them along.

"Look at them go," Gilmore said in awe. "They got to be doing eighty, ninety klicks."

"Yeah, they're sure in a hurry. What do you think can scare something that big?"

"Something bigger?"

"I hope not."

Gilmore started to say maybe this was their normal migratory or grazing behavior when the giant stalks behind the floating creatures began to shudder and sway. The creatures responded to the disturbance by picking up speed and starting to scatter.

A black form a fraction of the size of its prey exploded from the forest, springing into the air on massively muscled hindquarters on a trajectory for one of the Floaters. The behemoth was struggling to gain altitude, its tentacles throbbing with the effort, but it was too big a target to miss. The black thing, its long tail trailing behind it, landed on its back, anchoring itself with great claws dug into its rust-colored flesh. Almost immediately, the giant thing faltered in its escape, starting to collapse like a balloon losing air. The attacker was obscured by undulating mounds of flesh, but there was no mistaking the contrails of blood and viscera that followed the great creature in its slow, spiraling descent.

Through her helmet, Gilmore more felt than heard a high-pitched vibration that made her wince. She could only imagine it was the Floater's death wail.

"Jesus," London whispered.

"Yeah," Gilmore said, breathing heavy. All of a sudden, this lightweight world no longer seemed so much interesting as dangerous. "Come on. Let's get back to the ship."

———

By the time Jepson was done synching the raw sensor data with the feeds from Gilmore and London's bodycams, the *Typhoon*'s

Science Officer had clear images of the alien life forms and theories about both. She brought them up on the screen in the Mess, where she sat with London, Gilmore, Captain Lawford, and Executive Officer Katz.

"Let's start with the Floaters," Jepson said. "There's nothing like them in the E.T. database, but the odds of there being many low-grav planets capable of sustaining an atmosphere and life at this scale are pretty damned slim."

"I'll give you twelve to one," London offered to a chorus of groans.

"They're significantly higher than that," Jepson said, then turned her eyes on the grinning Warrant Officer. "Besides, you still owe me from last week's poker game."

"I'll pretend I didn't hear that," the Captain said.

"I've worked out their mass, specific gravity, and I have some educated guesses on their chemistry, means of propulsion, etcetera. Nothing about the Floaters' physiognomy suggests that they're in any way aggressive. In fact, everything points to a species that evolved in a relatively benign environment, with no need to develop defensive capabilities. I suppose the low gravity favors the lighter, weaker species against an aggressor species with what one would assume would be a necessarily heavier structure to support its biological armaments. Genetically speaking, it's..." Jepson said, starting to wander off down a speculative path before the Captain brought her back on point by saying, "You say the Floaters evolved without any natural enemies. What do you call the thing that attacked one of them?"

"An alien," the Science Officer said. Jepson tapped her pad, changing the image on the screen from the graceful behemoth to an enlarged freeze frame of the Leaper. "It's big by our standards, anywhere from five to seven meters, but tiny in comparison to the Floaters, and ninety-nine percent certainly not native to this planet."

London whistled. "Man, the odds just keep getting better, don't they?"

"Where did it come from? How did it get here?" Katz said.

Jepson shrugged. "Beats me. Tissue samples would go a long way to answering that."

"Well, unless the Leaper ate that entire Floater, we know where we can get a sample of at least one of 'em," Gilmore said.

"And the Leaper might have left some of its genetic material on the corpse," Jepson said, sitting up in her seat with excitement.

Engineer's mate Knutson stuck his head through the hatch and said, "Got a message coming in on the company comm, boss. Scrambled and urgent."

"What the hell do they want now?" Lawford grumbled as she pushed back her seat.

"Hell if I know," Knutson said, and was gone. Lawford followed.

———

Two hours later, Gilmore and London were once again suited up and hopping over the rusty landscape. This time, they carried assault rifles and were followed by the similarly armed XO and Science Officer.

Lawford had returned to the Mess from taking the comm with deep frown lines creasing her forehead and said to the crew, "Jepson's preliminary report's got the company all excited. We must've stumbled across something because I've been ordered to bring back a Leaper specimen, dead or alive at, quote, *any* reasonable cost, unquote."

"I don't like the sound of that," Katz said.

"Then you're going to like this even less. The order's accompanied by a warning to approach the Leapers with extreme caution."

"Now that sounds like a job that ought to come with a nice, fat juicy bonus," London said with a grin.

Lawford nodded.

"Then count me in," he said.

"You're already in. So is Gilmore. Katz and Jepson, you go too. And everybody goes armed. It worries me when even the company's nervous about what they're sending us into."

Gilmore and London retraced their steps to the edge of the plain of high grass that fed into the forest of giant stalks. The hike was little different than their first across the alien landscape, except for the weapons in their hands and the nervous awareness that they might have to use them.

"Keep your eyes open," Gilmore said. She pointed east. "The Floater was brought down less than a klick from here. The Leaper might still be in the area."

"I'm getting a thermal on the downed Floater," Jepson confirmed. "Going to take a good long time for that giant to cool down."

"Anything on the Leaper?" Katz said.

"Can't tell. I'm getting all kinds of bio readings, but I think most of them are from the Floater. It's taking a long time to die, but it's really all just a lot of data noise if I don't know what I'm looking for."

"A twenty-foot plus monster with an ass and hindquarters like a kangaroo on steroids," London said. "Can't miss it."

"Yeah, I'll try not to," Katz said. "Okay, let's go. Stow those pads and check your charge, Jepson. There'll be time for science as soon as the area's secured."

———

When he was still just a kid, London had wheedled his way into a backroom poker game with a bunch of Marines and corporate spacers. He was already a pretty good player and he had enough in his stash to last him through as many hands as it took to get the feel of the table. So he kept his mouth shut and his eyes open. Most of the guys were strictly amateur, easy enough to take, but usually only for small change. The one real player at the table was a grizzled Marine named Klonsky.

He played like he didn't give a damn. He kept up a running commentary and stream of joking patter, hardly bothering to glance at his cards or the growing pile of cash in front of him.

London played it cool, losing a little more than he won and throwing a few hands to come off as just another casual player, biding his time until he had the cards in his hand to make his move. It came, in a game of hold 'em, and while Klonsky blathered on, London built a beautiful hand, a surefire winner that got better and better as the pot grew bigger and bigger, until every cent he had was on the table.

But when they laid down their cards, Klonsky had him beat.

"Fortune favors the bold, kid," Klonsky said with a wink and a grin, and London watched his former stake disappear into the other man's pile of cash. Much to his surprise, he wasn't the least bit angry or resentful. It had cost him everything, but it was worth it to find out just how much he had to learn. London walked away from the encounter poorer but wiser, and wearing his own version of Klonsky's personality, an ill-fitting suit that he gradually tailored to fit himself.

London knew he rubbed a lot of people the wrong way but didn't care. As long as he could suck you into his game and take your cash, he didn't need your love.

Signing on with Weyland-Yutani had less to do with wanderlust than it did with cash. The pay was good and space was filled with bored people with money in their pockets and no place to spend it.

Fortune favors the bold, he thought, and there wasn't anybody aboard the *Typhoon* bolder than him.

London moved gradually ahead of the others through the tall grass. First come, first serve, though not at the price of caution. All the cash in the universe was useless to him dead, so he kept one eye on his environment, money on his instruments, and his finger on the trigger.

Death had reduced the Floater to a slowly collapsing mountain of organic matter. It was still twitching and undulating when they found it, here and there, a tentacle lay twisted and exposed along its length, writhing like giant gray snakes in the rusty grass.

"Are you sure it's dead?" Gilmore said. "Seems awful twitchy for a corpse."

"As sure as I can be without a normal biometric to compare it against," Jepson said. "As far as I can tell, this thing's got at least four hearts, three brains, and what I'm willing to bet is at least six separate nervous systems."

"Is it safe to approach?" Katz said.

"I think so," Jepson said.

"You *think* so? That fills me with confidence," Gilmore said.

"It's fine, wiseass," Jepson said. "Just don't forget there's a third life-form on the loose somewhere nearby."

"Okay, let's see if we can find where the Leaper struck this thing and get our samples," Jepson said.

"Stay in visual contact with one another at all times," Katz said, looking around. "Where's London?"

Gilmore pointed to a spot a dozen meters closer to the forest of giant stalks. "I just saw him, right over there."

Katz cursed and called the Warrant Officer's name a few more times. There was no answer.

—————

While the rest of them took their readings and poked cautiously at the body with sticks, London gave himself a running start and hopped onto the Floater. It was like trying to grab hold of a rubber sheet in the rain, but London managed to scramble awkwardly up onto the creature and find his footing.

London grinned as he listened to his shipmates' speculative chatter over the radio. By the time they decided to do anything, he'd be back with the bonus already as good as in his pocket.

The Floater was headed due north in its flight from the Leaper, so the spot they were looking for would be on its *south* end. What was so complicated?

As it turned out, not complicated at all. Within minutes, London saw ahead of him the massive, ugly trench torn in the sea of rust-colored flesh. Its edges were graying and oozing, splayed open to reveal a yawning cavern of hideously mottled and visibly decaying organic matter.

London's stomach churned at the sight and for a second he thought he was going to lose his lunch, but he shut his eyes and thought of the reward, choking down his nausea and getting to work. He filled some bags with samples of flesh and viscera from the wound, but the money was in specimens from the Leaper. He searched the wound carefully for anything that the striking predator might have shed.

He heard Katz calling his name on his headset but he ignored it and went on with his search. Let them wait a few more minutes. He'd claim a radio glitch and none of the others had to be the wiser.

"Answer me, London," Katz's voice crackled in his ear. And then his radio did glitch, the voice hissing into static and the static stretching into a high-pitched whine that made London wince in pain.

It was followed by a Leaper exploding from the Floater's wound and rising high into the air, its shadow falling across the stunned Warrant Officer before the creature began to descend on him.

———

Gilmore grabbed at her helmet as though trying to cover her ears when the feedback squealed through her headset. The sound made her weak at the knees and she found herself starting to twist and slowly fall. The low-grav made her motions almost balletic, and as she turned to sink into the grass, she saw, rising above the Floater the great form of the Leaper, a thing of darkness and sinew and sharp-edged claws and fangs.

"Incoming!" she screamed, but even she couldn't hear herself over the Leaper's call.

The black thing was coming down on top of him. As London tried to scramble out from beneath it, he lost his footing on the rubbery flesh and fell. He was just able to wrap one gloved hand around the barrel of his rifle, which he had put down while he collected his samples before tumbling down the Floater's flank like a rock in an avalanche.

He hit the ground as the Leaper landed where he had just stood and then bounced, as if on a trampoline to follow its prey. London didn't have time to turn his rifle around. Instead, he swung it like a bat, smashing it against the creature's massive, narrow head. London didn't know whether he had hurt or just annoyed the creature but had no intention of sticking around long enough to find out.

As fast as he could regain his footing, he pounced into the air and took off in leaps that covered three or four meters each, knowing full well the Leaper could catch him in a single jump. But so far, nothing was breathing down his neck and the squeal was no longer coming from the radio.

The realization that she hadn't adequately thought this situation through struck Jepson like a punch to the gut. She had been so excited by the one Leaper that she never even stopped to consider there would be others.

But she considered it now.

They were bursting through the Floater's flesh, four, five,

six, and more of them. They were huge, five or six meters high, and everything about them spoke to an evolution as a killing machine. Their hides were like polished ebony and every appendage bristled with something pointed and deadly. Long narrow heads opened into impossibly wide maws lined with rows of razor-sharp teeth, and their lower halves were powerfully muscled to take advantage of the low gravity, with long, thick spiked tails.

Gilmore was staggered by the screech, her finger tightening reflexively on the trigger. The laser blast scorched the ground as she struggled to gain control of her muscles. The scream was rippling through her, making it difficult to think, much less take aim.

The moment the Leaper had been spotted, Katz pulled a flash-bang from his pouch and armed it. If it was a choice between getting the company its Leaper samples or blowing every last one of the ugly bastards to smithereens to save their asses, Katz knew which way he was going.

He tossed the flash-bang underhand, floating it right into three of the monsters who were converging on him. As it left his hand, their scream ripped through his head and he tried screaming loud enough to drown it out so he could get his rifle up and pull the trigger.

The concussive went off with a blinding light and deafening force enough to make the thin air ripple, spreading a cloud of gray smoke all around them. Katz couldn't see through the smoke what, if any damage, he had inflicted, but the explosion seemed to have stopped the scream, at least for the moment.

Then London's voice came screaming over his static-filled headset, "Heads up. I'm coming in... and I ain't alone."

He wished to hell he had more than three of the little canisters left in his pouch. Two, after he used one to repel a quartet of Leapers that were coming for Gilmore, and then down to one after they linked up with Jepson. But the first three blasts seemed to have made the Leapers more cautious, giving them a wide berth as the shipmates backed slowly from them.

"London," Katz said. "Where the hell are you? We're surrounded here."

"I got my own problems," the Warrant Officer grunted. "I'm cut off. I'm gonna take cover in the forest."

Jepson consulted the pad on her forearm. "Keep your transponder on so I can track you, London."

"Roger that. I'll try to find an observation post so I can... uh-oh. Sh—," they heard, but the scream started up again and washed the rest of his words away in static.

———

All of a sudden, the world was spinning and London didn't know which way was up. Something had hold of his leg and he was being dangled like a ragdoll high into the sky, the rusty landscape whizzing by over his head. Then the sky and ground disappeared and the world turned dark and he was being battered on all sides before plummeting into deepening darkness.

The Leaper landed smoothly on the forest floor, its powerful legs flexing to absorb the impact. It dropped London and he tumbled to the loamy ground with a groan. He lay as he fell, face up, catching his breath after his dizzying ride.

The creature stood over him, crouched on massive haunches and cocked its head, as though listening.

London tried to catch his breath, his eyes never leaving the Leaper. He had been turned around and was deep enough in the forest to have no idea which way was out. He still had his sidearm in its holster, but this monster didn't look like it would be much bothered by a few slugs.

He tried his radio, whispering through clenched teeth, but he only got a few words out before the electronic squeal obliterated his message. To add to his problem, the alarm on his oxygen supply was trilling a thirty-minute warning. After that, he was down to a ten-minute emergency tank.

The Leaper turned its dead, empty face to him.

Talk about long odds, he thought.

"Son of a bitch. I think they're herding us, into the forest," Katz said, slowly sweeping the barrel of his rifle across the wall of alien creatures surrounding them and forcing them back towards the forest of giant stalks.

"The *Typhoon*'s not answering our distress call," Gilmore said.

"They can't hear it," Jepson said, speaking fast through her fear. "It's the Leaper. I think the Floaters communicate using some sort of sonar, like whales. The Leapers disrupt it with a counter-frequency to confuse their prey. Our radios operate close enough to the Floaters' frequency to be affected. I've switched suit-to-suit comm over to another band, but it's only effective in close proximity."

"I don't think that's going to be an issue," Katz said. "So here's the way I see our options: we try and shoot our way out now and they kill us here, or we let them herd us wherever and they kill us there."

London's voice cut briefly into the comm, saying one of them had grabbed him but he was okay before the shrill scream obliterated the rest of his message.

Jepson gasped. "He's alive."

"I guess if anyone's going to beat the odds, it's him," Gilmore said.

They were on the move again, the Leaper dragging London by his leg through the dark forest. The company assured crews that their E.V.A. suits were made to stand up to any conditions, but he doubted being dragged by giant clawed aliens had been included in their testing protocols.

Do or die, he thought. More likely do *and* die, but anything had to be better than being a pull toy for this nightmare. He reached for his sidearm but didn't dare draw it while he was being jostled about. It was the only weapon he had and he couldn't risk dropping it.

He didn't have long to wait. The Leaper pushed past a giant stalk and into a clearing. London's heart sank. A Floater had been brought crashing down in the forest, its massive carcass flattening the surrounding vegetation and serving as the hive for a colony of Leapers. London couldn't tell how long the Floater had been dead, but from the look of the gray, rotting flesh it had been a while.

London's stomach churned and he licked dry lips. No matter how he ran the game, he couldn't come up with a winning hand. He was outnumbered and even with a good head start, one of these things could bring him to ground with a few good leaps. He might be able to take a few of them down before they got him, but so what? He was starting to think it might be smarter to just turn the gun on himself and get it over with.

"London? Do you hear me?"

Gilmore's voice crackled in his ear, half static and breaking up. He winced in anticipation of the answering squeal, but it didn't come.

"Gilmore? You guys okay? You reading me?" he said, his heart starting to pound even harder.

The response was garbled but the signal was improving by the second. They were still alive but the Leapers were herding them deeper into the forest. From the strengthening radio signal, they were headed his way. That was the good news. The bad was, the Leaper once again grabbed him by the leg and began dragging him towards the gaping rotting cavern of Leaper flesh.

"If you're gonna ride in to save my sorry ass, now would be a good time," he said, his voice hoarse. He pulled his gun.

"Fast as we can," Katz said.

"I think I'm gonna have to start shooting, man," he said, talking just to talk and to hear another human respond.

"Still have your rifle?" Gilmore asked.

"Negative. Broke it on one of their heads. All I got's my sidearm."

"Okay, hang tight," Jepson said, sounding out of breath. "From your signal strength, I think we're close."

"I ain't the one dealing this hand," he said. "Crap. Okay, we're inside. Double-time it, will you?"

Inside the Floater was a world of deep shadows and even darker shapes moving through corridors and chambers of deteriorating flesh hanging from cathedral high vaults of bone. He was being dragged through a thick slimy sludge of rotted organic matter.

"Waiting on an update here," he said.

"Shut up, London." Gilmore's voice came crystal clear through his headset and it was tense with suppressed panic. "We're here. There's got to be fifty of them out here."

"And even more inside with me. Anybody got any ideas?"

"Just one," Katz said.

———

The first mate raised his rifle and said, "Fire!" And then he did, making a slow, wide sweeping arc with the laser through a clutch of Leapers.

The creatures' mouths opened wide. Dripping, secondary maws of deadly teeth protruded from their jaws as their bodies exploded into black and green bursts of flesh and acid blood.

"Look at 'em light up," Gilmore shouted and started shooting. Jepson added to the chaos as the surviving Leapers erupted into a frenzied panic, like a nest of grasshoppers with a lighted match thrown into it.

"Unbelievable," Jepson said with a gasp. "Aim for their bodies. The heads and limbs are armored but the rest are easy targets."

The Leaper suddenly let London drop into the slime and turned to hop back the way they had just come. Then the rest of the Leapers moving around in the dark were also racing for the exit.

Rolling onto his stomach and then pushing himself onto one knee, London raised his gun and fired at the closest dark shape. Its body seemed to shatter and it collapsed.

"Bingo," he shouted and clamored awkwardly to his feet on the slimy surface. Just for the hell of it, he popped off two more of the bastards, then turned to make sure nothing was about to land on him in the dark. That's when he saw the nest. He switched on the small lamp on his helmet for a better look and saw, stretched between two of the towering ribs, a wall of Floater flesh into which thousands of leathery and irregularly shaped objects had been implanted.

He knew he should just get the hell out of there, but before he did, there was one thing he had to do.

Katz was holding the remaining flash-bang in reserve, waiting to regroup with London for use to help cover their getaway. The Leapers obviously weren't accustomed to resistance, and the carnage the landing crew was inflicting on them was enormous. But there was still enough of them that if the Leapers decided to rush them en masse, they wouldn't have stood a chance.

The first mate was almost sorry he had allowed the thought to enter his mind, because the moment it did, the Leapers behavior began to change, almost as though they were adapting their tactics to this new, lethal opponent. They were spreading out, widening the distances between themselves, creating scores of individual, harder to hit targets, tightening the circle around them.

"London!" he shouted.

"I'm coming, boss," London said. "And I'm planning on leaving things hot behind me."

"Explain," Katz snapped.

London grinned, moving as fast as he could across the slick, slimy surface.

"I got a back-up oxygen tank and a gun. You do the math."

A dark shape swept across his path. He lost his footing in the slime, but threw himself headlong toward the exit, sliding across the ground like a sled on ice under the shape and out into the open.

"Heads up," he shouted, using the low-gravity to push himself to his feet. The others were back to back, eyes on the surrounding Leapers. London had already disconnected the small oxygen cylinder tucked into a pocket on his chest and now he gently tossed it into the entrance. He took aim and fired.

And missed with his first shot, and with his second. The third was even wider off the mark.

"Jeez, London," Gilmore snapped. "Out of the way!"

A couple of hops brought her to London. She raised her rifle and fanned the beam across the canister until she homed in on it and blasted away.

The Leapers started to move.

Katz yelled something that was lost in the sweep of the concussive wave from the exploding oxygen tank which sent them all flying. The blast ignited the ground cover and the fiery heat seemed to transmit itself through the vegetation and the Floater carcass without bursting into towering licks of flame.

The blast was intense and even before the humans had stopped tumbling, the Leaper colony was in motion. But instead of pouncing on their stunned prey, they streamed as one into the smoldering carcass.

"You said you found a nest," Jepson said, breathing heavily. "They must be trying to save the offspring."

"Who cares?" London said. "Let's go while we can."

"Anyone know which way we came?" Gilmore said.

"I do," Katz said. "I used to be a Boy Scout. I marked our trail."

London looked at him. "A Boy Scout? You?"

Katz grinned and armed the concussive grenade and threw it at the mouth of the carcass, crammed with Leapers doomed by a hereditary instinct that made them race blindly into disaster to save their unborn.

"I said 'used to be,'" he said.

The grenade went off and, in the billowing smoke, the crew of the *Typhoon* slipped away into the forest.

As the repaired *Typhoon* climbed into the sky, the crew could see the smoke billowing from the forest of giant stalks. Infra-red imaging showed that the conflagration had spread almost three kilometers from its starting point but seemed to be dying of its own accord. Jepson started to explain how the combination of low atmospheric pressure and certain flammable elements enabled the heat to burn without flames, but everybody was suddenly tired and headed off to bed.

In his quarters, London stripped down and allowed himself as long and as hot a shower as the ships' system would give him before sitting down on the edge of his bunk with the souvenir he had collected during the E.V.A. While most of the biological samples of the vegetation and the Floaters had made it back to the ship, no one had the time or the presence of mind to grab something before their escape.

There had been a lot of grumbling about the lack of Leaper DNA gathered once they got back to the ship. But all agreed that coming out of the experience alive was better than nothing, and, besides, they still had the bonus they would be receiving for the Floater samples.

London kept his mouth shut and the object he had snatched up on his way out the door hidden. It was oblong, a little larger than a potato, and had a black, leathery shell. He guessed it was a Leaper egg and was willing to bet the bank the company was going to pay him life-changing money to get their hands on it. And he figured since the risk in getting it had been all his, the bonus money should be too.

"Fortune favors the bold, kid," he said to himself, out loud and with a smile, left the egg on top of his locker before shutting the lights and drifting off to dream about what he was going to do with his fortune.

London was dreaming. He was seated at a poker table with five Leapers, one of them smoking a cigar, playing poker. Instead of chips, they were playing for Leaper eggs and London was winning big. He had a surefire hand, five Leapers straight, so he picked up his biggest egg to throw it into the pot, but the leathery shell was warm and alive in his hand, pulsating. And then, it began to crack open with a sharp, wet sound.

London's eyes flicked open. He came awake so fast, he could still hear the sound of the cracking egg in the dark of his cabin.

It wasn't until he felt the warm, moist creature crawl onto his face and fire its tentacle down his throat that he realized he wasn't dreaming, but by then, it was too late.

REAPER

BY DAN ABNETT

They slam-dropped out of the *Montoro's* belly hangars and rode the rattling wind down to LV-KR 115.

A thirty-minute descent. Canetti had the stick of the lead drop. He lost sight of the other Cheyenne in a matter of seconds. After the bump and the stomach-lurch of clamp release, he looked up and watched the giant oblong shadow of the *Montoro* slowly turning away and receding into the pale darkness of near-space, as though it was leaving them behind rather than the other way around.

Drop two was at his nine, the small blue blades of its thrusters flashing on and off as it trimmed its headlong fall.

Then they hit cloud and he couldn't see it anymore. Frame vibration increased and the stick quivered in his hand. The cloud was like whisked soup. He watched the track, the amber squares of the trajectory field lapping and overlapping around the steady cursor that was them.

"Still with me, drop two?" he asked into his helmet mic.

A rasp of noise.

"Copy that, lead drop. Nice weather for it."

"Copy, two."

Another belch of gritty sound.

"Coming up on the marker. Execution point in ten. See you on the other side."

"Copy, two. Happy hunting."

Out there in the soup, invisible, drop two was pulling west, diverting from the lead drop's course, heading out across the northern continental towards the secondary LZ.

The intercom bleeped. Lieutenant Teller in the payload bay below him.

"How we doing, Canetti?"

"In the pipe. Looks good."

"What have you got?"

"Weather, sir," said Canetti.

———

Rogers pulled up the schematics for the crop tractor and Teller slid his seat along the deck rail to look at the wall display. The whole platoon had reviewed the data two dozen times during on-board briefs, and even done a walk-through in the simulator.

The airframe juddered. Teller kept his eyes fixed on the monitor display. Rogers knew the lieutenant was tense. He'd made eight drops, but every one had been with Captain Broome along, calling the shots. This time, Broome was on drop two, checking out the secondary LZ. Teller had command for the main excursion. Rogers knew it was a test. Teller was looking at SOCS promotion. He'd passed the boards, but he needed practical citations on his docket.

"Main upper hull is big enough for a set-down," she said, pointing.

"Uh huh," said Teller.

"Unless this chop keeps up," Rogers added. "Windshear off the fields could swing us off the flat top into the control tower or the uplink masts."

"In which case, we divert to the baler housing on the side," Teller said. "There's a large platform there."

"Agreed," said Rogers. They had already agreed all of this. Teller was just rehearsing. He was doing what Sergeant Bose called a "fine tooth," a repeated workthrough until the mission parameters were like muscle memory.

Rogers tapped the keys of her console.

"Canetti was right," she said. "Lots of weather. Storm formation's kicking a serious crosswind."

"Baler housing it is," said Teller.

"I'll let Canetti know," she replied.

———

Teller studied the screen. He clicked through images of the target vehicle: Plan and elevation schematics, feed-cap shots of similar machines working on site, and images from the Weyland-Yutani product brochure. A model 868 "Ceres" Harvester Unit. 210,000 metric, 297 meters long, its steel carapace painted bright yellow with environment-resistant polymer. Hell of a thing.

Teller was fourth generation USMC. He'd grown up in Annapolis, and had spent many hours of his childhood in the Yard's famous museum. The crop tractor reminded him of the old surface Navy aircraft carriers displayed there like trophy fish. The carriers were antiques, part of a school of warfare that had been obsolete for sixty years when he was born. Their spirit lived on in Conestoga-class light assault ships like the Montoro, and even more so in the massive Hellespont-class fleet carriers, the design ethic that had once commanded the oceans converted to space warfare. But the visual aesthetics endured in the Company-manufactured crop tractors, set on vast wheel-trains and programmed to endlessly harvest the prairies of gene-fixed agro-worlds like LV-KR 115.

The unit they were chasing was serial 678493, chassis name "*Consus.*" Crew of sixty-eight, working a five-year shift between replenishment cycles, harvesting and freeze-packing the crop into bales twenty-four seven. Remote-flown lifters transported the cargo to orbiting silos for freight collection. Five-year contract. Hell of a life.

The *Consus* was one of two harvesters working LV-KR 115. Six weeks after its last replenishment it had reported a malfunction. Contact dropped out, then Company tracking indicated that the tractor had diverted from its programmed harvesting grid. *Demeter*, the other tractor operating on the surface, had attempted contact, but then aborted five rescue ops in a row because of bad weather. The chief officer of the *Demeter* had logged "the worst storms ever seen on LV-KR 115." Data supported that. LV-KR 115 suffered seasonal storms, but the atmospheric tumult that had hammered the planet for the last three months was unprecedented.

Agricultural fliers were grounded, but UD4L Cheyenne dropships were all-weather rated and built to take punishment. USMC pilots like Canetti were also better trained than the average company contractor. Teller had known Canetti land a drop on manual in the middle of sandstorm and 200 kph shear.

It wasn't going to be much of a chase. The crop tractors maxed out at a crawling 7 kph surface speed, a ridiculously easy bounce for a UD4L drop.

And anyway, the *Consus* had stopped moving altogether three weeks earlier.

"You still think it's the drive system?" Rogers asked him.

"Drives explains the dead-stop, but not the comms," he replied.

"Power plant, then?"

"And aux? That's unlucky. Besides, the Company has attempted four restarts by remote. They're not getting a 'fail' message. They're getting nothing."

"I said it," said Sergeant Bose. "Some joker's lost their shit."

Bose had unclasped his restraints and was standing behind them, strap-hanging from the overhead bar, his body rocking to the jolt of the airframe.

"Maybe," said Teller. It was a sad truth that no matter what safety measures, redundancies, back-ups and secondaries were rigged into high-value hardware units, the most common cause of shut-down was human action. Despite rigorous vetting and psychological testing, people on long-ticket contracts snapped. One rogue actor with a firearm could take down a contained working environment and cause all the system damage that explained the data.

"More than maybe, I'd say," said Bose.

"That's why we're loading plastics for entry," said Teller. The clip of every weapon in the platoon was marked with blue tape. Non-lethal munitions. Teller did not want crossfire fatalities.

Bose shrugged. Everyone had live rounds in their webbing anyway.

A buzzer sounded.

"Coming up, two minutes!" Canetti's voice reported through the speakers.

"Get up, get set!" Bose called, turning to the troopers in their rows of landing rigs. "Lamp goes on, we go clean and fast!"

The marines started to prep and shake out, each one ready to pop the lock of their restraint harness.

"Lids, goggles, rebreathers," Teller said. "There's a lot of chaff in the air, a lot of airborne dirt. Get through it, get inside. No one goes bareface until we've accessed the interior. If I have to write any of you up for any crap, I want you to be able to see me as well as hear me when I do it."

Canetti eased back on the stick. They were forty meters up, and way past stall-speed. VTOL mode was on, and the drop was nose-high. The air was filthy, like a blizzard of black snow. There was a hard cross pitching about 160 kph. Zero visibility. He tried kicking on the floods, but that made things worse. He guessed it was airblown particulates, maybe soil, or processed grain waste. It was as if the quartz of the cockpit canopy had been sprayed with blackout paint.

He switched to instruments. 3D imaging showed him the ground, and picked up a huge furrow in the top soil. The tractor's track. He adjusted the scope and suddenly painted the side of the *Consus*, rising like the wall of a dam.

"Shit," he said gently, and pulled hard. Collision warnings began to shriek. Hazards blinked on and off across his board. The airframe shuddered violently, and the turbines wailed in protest. The stick was like glue. He trusted the VTOL systems, but now he was worried about the blizzarding soup outside clogging his intakes and thrust nozzles. Software and autoflight were keeping the drop in the air, a plate-spinning balancing act of trim and vector-thrust beyond the manual abilities of any human operator.

"Come on, you dog," he whispered.

The tractor was huge. He tweaked the resolution of the imaging, and got the datalink to run a comparison with the stored schematics. The screen pinged up an overlay match. As he had judged from the relative position of the track, they were approaching the port side of the beast. Canetti didn't want to trust his instincts: it was too easy to get turned around in a blind-out like this.

He flipped the match view to the heads-up display, and panned for the port-side baler housing. It was easy to identify, a long loading platform like a lateral hangar bay with open sidings and weather-port roof overhang. The roof was low and tight. Between them, Canetti and the autoguide was going to have to slide the drop in under the overhang sideways, like posting a letter into a mailbox width-ways.

"Standby," he told the cabin below. The thrusters were straining. Autoguide or no autoguide, one sudden gust of wind would mash them sideways into the tractor's hull or the housing overhang.

"Are you getting paid proportionally to this shit?" Rogers asked over the intercom, her tone light and measured to calm his focus.

"Absolutely not," he replied.

Jesus Christ, that overhang was low. With an almost angry stab, he flicked off the collision warning. It wasn't telling him anything he couldn't already see on imaging, and the noise was drilling his nerves.

"Come on, come on..." he murmured.

The drop, all twenty-five meters of it, drifted into the slot sideways. Not even a scrape to the tail boom. He could just about see the deck below him, picked up through the broiling grit by the floods. He let the drop sink.

Contact. A sprung bounce as the landing gear made contact. A slight lateral drag as the skids travelled. He heard metal-on-metal squealing.

And they were down.

"Everybody off!" Canetti yelled into his mic.

———

Rogers dropped the ramp and opened the exteriors. A combination of funneled wind and pressure exchange almost blew the ready marines off their feet. The payload bay instantly filled with swirling airborne filth. Teller could feel it pattering off his body armor and sleeves. It felt like his goggles were being jet-washed.

"Go!" Bose yelled over the set-to-set.

They scrambled down into the grit-storm. It wasn't the most dynamic or heroic de-bus in the history of the Corps. Fighting the gale, the marines moved like clichéd mime artists.

"Achieve the hatch!" Bose ordered, leading the way. "O'Dowd, get ready with your damn tether!"

There was an entry hatch on the hull-side of the baler platform. They had already run tether cables from the payload bay deck rings, roping the men together in strings of five. Fighting into the wind a step at a time, each lead man carried the snap-hook for the front of the tether line. The last man in each file played out the end of the cable from the ramp drums.

"Jesus!" Private O'Dowd protested.

"Jesus loves you, son," Bose replied. "Now get the line secured!"

At the head of one string, Bose carried the snap-hook. He almost slammed into the hatch, and then groped frantically for a lock-point. He found one, flipped it out, and snapped the hook in place.

"O'Dowd!"

O'Dowd was beside him, leading the second string in. A gust blew him into the hatch, and he dropped the snap-hook. It was swinging from his waist. He fumbled to grab it. Blind, his hands found the wrong hook and disconnected his own harness from the tether line. Trusting too much in a line he was no longer connected to, O'Dowd relaxed slightly, and the wind took him off his feet. He crashed away, rolling and sliding along the deck.

O'Dowd's barreling form took Teller off his feet. Teller had been advancing at the front of the third string. They both went down. Rogers, in the string behind Teller, grabbed at Teller, her heels sliding on the deck plates. Teller, on his side, lashed out and got hold of O'Dowd's webbing. From the schems being projected onto the inside of his goggles, Teller could see that O'Dowd was about three meters shy of falling into the through-deck cavity, a five-meter drop straight down into the metal guts of the baling machinery.

"Lieutenant? Lieutenant!" Bose called.

"Get the hatch open!" Teller yelled back, strained to keep his grip on O'Dowd.

Bose turned back to the hatch. The lever mechanism felt misshapen. He tried to locate the bar. He pulled out his cutting tool, lit the torch, and sliced through the handle and the cross-bolt.

There was no power. He and Private Belfi had to haul the hatch open together. It slid surprisingly easily in its groove, as if the wind had loosened it in the frame.

The entry lock was dark, and the wind and grit followed them inside. One by one, the strings fought their way in behind them. Teller's group was the last through, dragging O'Dowd with them.

"Get that hatch shut!" Teller ordered. Rogers and Pator slammed it back home, shutting out the storm.

The air went still. Slowly, the eddying dust and grit began to settle. They could hear the bang and surge of the wind against the hatch, the monsoon patter of particles hitting the hull. The marines were breathing hard. Helmet and pack lamps went on, revealing a grey haze and shadows. Teller pulled up his goggles. Visibility hardly improved.

"Interior hatch," he ordered. His voice sounded dead and hollow in the dull, confined air. He could feel the scratch of dust in his throat and it seemed like his nostrils were plugged with grit.

"Interior hatch locked," Bose called back.

"Cut it," said Teller.

Bose got to work with his torch again, and sliced the lock. They got the interior hatch open.

Stale, oddly cold air breathed out at them. The interior serviceway was unlit. Heat and light had been absent for a long time. The platoon moved through, weapons up, lamps on.

"Take a look," Bose said to Teller as Teller moved through the inner hatch. The inside lock of the hatch showed bare metal where Bose's torch had cut through it. But the lock itself was malformed.

"The hell?" said Teller.

"Someone's used a torch or a burner to seal that from the inside," said Bose. "Exterior hatch was the same."

"They locked themselves in?"

"Someone did," said Bose.

"Why?" asked Rogers.

"To keep something out?" said Teller.

"I know. I'm saying what?"

"I'm saying I have no idea."

———

In cover formation, they moved through the dark interior. There was nothing around. No sign of life, not even any trash or debris. Their flashlights picked up the bare metal of the deck plates, the untreated steel of the walls, the hard edges of the bulkheads. Rogers found a wall rack of heavy weather gear, but there were no suits on the pegs. Just unpainted helmets, shoulder plates and buckles.

"Why take the suits and not the head gear?" she asked.

"Some one got cold?" suggested Belfi.

Rogers took down one of the helmets. She thought the slide-down visor was some kind of metal blast shield, but turning it over, she saw it was tinted glass. The exterior had been treated with some process that had left it frosted and opaque.

Inside, there was no padding or inner liner, just the buckles and press-studs needed to fit one. A silt of fine dust winnowed out of the helmet as she turned it over.

"Can we patch up some power?" Teller asked.

Gothlin moved up, found a wall-box, and tried to rig in the man-portable genny. Nothing happened.

"Are the connectors clean?" asked Teller.

Gothlin played her flashlight inside.

"Clean as, sir," she said. "Cleaner than the boxes on the *Montoro*."

Teller saw the torch beam glinting off metal that was

polished to an almost chrome finish.

"Hang on, back, back," Teller said, directing Gothlin to pan her torch around again. There was no trunking coming off the box. No cables, no wall lines, no ducting, just a feint, grubby streak where the power trunking had once been run along the wall. A few metal cable fasteners remained in place.

"They stripped out all the wiring?" asked Gothlin.

"Maybe they needed it for a fix somewhere else?" said Belfi.

Teller shook his head.

"Doesn't look like it was stripped out," he said. "It's just gone."

They cut through four more hatches to reach the control deck. Behind the third one, Belfi's lamp picked up something on the floor: small metal objects catching the light.

"What is it?" asked Teller.

Belfi crouched down, and picked the little items up. He cupped them in his hand.

"Looks like... a belt buckle. And a wedding ring. And... what are these?"

Teller took a look. The tiny things looked familiar. Out of context, it took a moment to place them.

"Eyelets," he said.

"What now?"

"Eyelets. Metal eyelets for laces. From a pair of boots."

The control deck was dark. They moved between the console stations and seats.

"Are those windows?" asked Rogers, panning her torch beam.

"Should be," said Teller.

"Sergeant?" Rogers called. "See if we can get the storm shields up."

"On it," said Bose.

"There's trunking here," said Gothlin. "There's cables and wiring. These consoles look pretty much intact."

"See if you can boost one into life," said Teller. "Concentrate on archive, log, datalink."

Gothlin got to work.

"Lieutenant?" Bose called out.

"Yup?"

"The storm shields are open."

Teller and Rogers crossed to the back of windows at the front of the deck. They were black, as though the external shutters were down.

"Are you sure?" asked Teller.

"Positive," said Bose.

"So, is that the storm?" asked Rogers.

"No, there's something wrong with the glass," replied Bose.

Teller unhooked his goggles and shone his torch at them. The glass was almost opaque. The glare coating was gone. The external surface looked like it had been rubbed with an abrasive scourer. Billions of micro scratches fogged the lenses.

"The dust did that?" asked Rogers.

There was a flicker of light and a mechanical chatter. Gothlin had patched in the portable power unit and woken up the master console.

"What have we got?" asked Teller, coming over.

"Not much of anything, sir," said Gothlin. "Memory's been dumped, or backed up someplace I can't access. No logs."

"Datalink?" asked Rogers.

"Maybe," replied Gothlin, at work.

"Try automated task record," said Teller. "The harvester would record its own routes to make sure it matched quotas."

"Good call," said Gothlin. "That would be stored automatically and pretty much tamper proof."

She typed, and data scrolled across the screens. It was hard to read. Rogers tried to wipe the soot off the monitor glass, but it wasn't soot. It was ground-in distortion.

Gothlin peered.

"Okay, we have a track monitor. That column is the timecode. Day to day, hour by hour. That's... yeah, that's yield. That side bar there is coordinates, so we can map from that. So let's see... nothing for the last three weeks. Nada. No tracking record at all. I guess that's how long this baby's been dead out here."

"What's the last log?" asked Rogers.

"Mmmmm... three weeks, but it's incomplete, and runs incomplete for... the nine weeks prior to that. The tractor was moving for those nine weeks, but no yield was taken. Or nothing logged anyway. There's a code here. Hang on, let me try and work this out. There should be a key. That code repeats at every track entry through the nine-week period. Okay, yeah. It means... 'off designated course' ."

"So the *Consus* was moving for nine weeks off pattern?" asked Teller.

"That matches the data collected by the Company," said Rogers. "Diverted from harvest route and no answer as to why."

"At the start of that nine-week period," asked Teller. "What's that?"

There was an unusually dense block of data.

Gothlin typed some more.

"That's the malfunction," she said.

"The causal event," murmured Rogers.

"Details?" asked Teller.

"Mmmmm... okay, hello. Looks like the *Consus* hit something. It was harvesting and it ran into something in the crop. Some light damage to the blades, nothing systemic. But it hit something big. There's a file attached."

"Open it," said Teller.

Gothlin grinned up at him.

"Already on it," she said.

Pictures opened on screen. Blurry low-res pics taken from a flier. They could see the tractor, an aerial view. The endless landscape of the crop, like an ocean. The weather had been better then. This had been before the storms.

There was something in the crop ahead of the tractor. A large dark mass half buried in the deep corn.

"Zoom it?" asked Teller.

"No, but there's a close up or two," Gothlin replied. She opened more pictures.

"What the hell is that?" asked Teller.

The storm had suddenly eased. Waiting in the lead drop cockpit, Canetti suddenly realized that light levels were rising. The black soup of weather was slowly resolving into an eerie amber twilight. The wind was dropping. The drop was no longer vibrating on its stand.

He looked out. There was still dust in the air, and the light was stained, as though pale smoke was shrouding the sun. He could see out beyond the lip of the baler housing platform. He could see the ground. It looked bare and grey.

"This is Canetti," he said into the mic. "The storm's dropping right now. I've got some visibility."

"Copy that, Canetti," Rogers crackled back over the link. "How's it looking in there?"

"We're still trying to piece it together," Rogers replied.

"You want me to take a look around out here? I can't see much from the cockpit."

"Okay, but be careful. And check in with drop two first."

"Copy that," he replied. He switched channels.

"Drop two, drop two, this is lead drop. Drop two, drop two, do you copy? This is lead drop. Do you copy?"

Dead air hissed back at him.

"Drop two, drop two, requesting sit rep from Captain Broome.

Drop two, what is your status? Have you reached the *Demeter*?"

Atmospherics, Canetti reasoned, the weather. He left the channel open, replugged his headset to mobile, and unstrapped.

Outside, a breeze was gusting, tugging at him. Fine dust, like flour, swirling in the air. Beyond the baler housing, the world was lit amber. A dead sky hung over dead land, all hazed by the powder dust. He figured he could see about one, maybe two klicks before it got too murky.

The wide prairies of LV-KR 115 dwarfed anything on Earth. Flat and unimpeded by geographical feature, they made an ideal site for bulk crop production. Weyland-Yutani had terra-formed the soil, boosting nitrate levels, and then sown a robust strain of genetically modified, high-yield wheat across the entire northern and western territories. The strain was self-seeding. Crop would follow crop on a self-germinating cycle. The Company proudly claimed that LV-KR 115 would render annual, overlapping harvests for a ninety-year period before another round of terra-forming was required to re-nitrate the soil.

So where was the crop, he wondered. The *Consus* had wandered off course. This region hadn't been systematically harvested. But there was no wheat out there.

As far as he could see, the ground was bare and black.

"What is it?" asked Rogers. "Some kind of pit?"

"Is it natural?" asked Bose. "Like a sinkhole or something?"

Teller looked at the pictures.

"That doesn't look natural," he said. "Well, it looks organic. Like it was made."

The cavity in the pictures was deep, and maybe fifty meters across. The earth around its mouth was folded into disturbingly organic puckers. It looks like a throat, or similar body cavity.

"Looks like the tractor hit it and took the top right off," said Gothlin. "Unplugged it."

"And let something out," said Rogers.

"Why the hell you saying that, Rogers?" asked Bose.

"Because it looks like a nest," she replied.

"Is this a bug hunt?" asked Belfi. "Dammit, don't tell me this is a bug hunt."

"We don't know anything yet," said Teller.

He drew Rogers to one side.

"You know something I don't?" he asked.

"I know Canetti can't raise the *Demeter* or drop two," she replied.

"Okay. But I don't mean about that."

She shrugged.

"I grew up in the South West," she said. "I know what a termite nest looks like. Ant hills too."

"Great, but this—"

"Termites can remain dormant for decades," she said.

"That's locusts."

"Well, whatever, the same applies. If this is unknown exotic life-form nest, it could have been dormant a long time. The harvester blades its top off, thing wakes up. If there's a feeding cycle, the Company has provided an entire planet's worth of crops."

"Weyland-Yutani would have detected something like that during survey and the TF program."

"Yeah," Rogers said, "because as we know, they never make any mistakes. The *Consus* woke something up. It's picking everything clean. Organics, clothes, fabrics, trunking… boots."

He looked sick suddenly.

———

"People," he said. "Everything's stripped back to bare metal. The crew seal themselves in, deeper and deeper. The exotic life-forms eat away everything, until they destroy the harvester systems and leave it dead."

"So, they sealed themselves in this control room? Okay, where are they?"

Teller looked around as Bose put a hand on his arm.

"Look at this," he said.

There were storage lockers at the back of the control deck. Searching, Bose and Belfi had been forced to cut them open because they had been torch-welded shut from inside.

God alone knew what fate had befallen the rest of the sixty-eight crew, but the last four had died here, inside the lockers, sealed in coffins of their own manufacture.

Teller stared at the shriveled remains. Starvation, he thought. Starvation and dehydration.

"Why... why didn't they cut themselves out again?" asked Gothlin, wide-eyed. "They had cutters."

"Because they didn't know it was safe to come out," said Rogers. "They didn't dare."

"We're aborting," said Teller. "Everyone back to the drop."

"If this is a bug hunt," Bose protested, "we can—"

"No, we absolutely can't," said Teller. "If Rogers is right, we're dealing with an immense exotic predator. But it's not one target. It's composed of countless tiny individuals. You're a good shot, sergeant. How much ammo did you bring? How do you rate your chances in target practice against a swarm of space locusts?"

"Shit," said Bose.

"The Company will have to bomb LV-KR 115 with pesticides," said Rogers.

"The whole planet?" asked Belfi.

"The freak weather," said Rogers quietly, "I think it's catastrophic atmospheric disturbance caused by the sheer size of the swarm."

"Are you shitting me?" asked Pator.

"Think about it. These space bugs sleep for years, then wake up and feed. Probably used to raze the old grasslands and then sleep again until the vegetation regrew. Life cycle. But the Company fixed this planet with endless, fast-growing, self-replicating crop yields. A never-ending food supply. Can you even imagine how big the swarm has got with nothing to limit or inhibit its growth?"

"Jesus Christ," murmured O'Dowd.

"We didn't hit weather on the way down," said Teller. "We hit the pressure wave of the swarm."

———

Canetti leaned out over the edge of the baler platform and craned his neck. He could see the side of the crop tractor's hull. He expected to see the same bright yellow paintwork that featured in the brochure pictures they had all examined at brief. In the ghastly amber light, the side of the hull looked like bare metal.

He reached over and touched the surface of the hull. It was rough. It *was* bare metal. Bare metal that felt like it had been sand-blasted.

A shadow fell across him. He looked up.

The storm was coming back. The sky was black, and visibility was dropping fast. Sudden, strong wind blasted at him. A wall of darkness was rushing across the bare earth towards the tractor.

It was churning up gritty clouds of dust and dry soil in front of it. The wall itself, a kilometer high or more, was a seething, boiling back mass, iridescent.

Battered by the wind, Canetti staggered back to the drop's ramp. He clung on to the stanchion, afraid he was going to be dragged off his feet by the wind force. There was grit everywhere. He'd taken off his mask and goggles, and he could feel his hands and face were bloody and raw.

He couldn't breathe.

The wall hit the harvester.

There was no time to cry out. Billions of small black shapes billowed around Canetti.

He vanished, shredded. A body-armor shoulder plate hit the deck. The metal innards of an ear-piece mic.

A belt buckle, polished brightly.

Hurrying down the serviceway towards the baler housing, they all felt the *Consus* rock hard. The entire bulk of it was shaking. Howling wind screamed down the hallways through the hatches they had cut open on their way in.

"Back!" Teller yelled. "Back!"

"To what?" shouted Bose.

Teller didn't know what to say.

"The lockers?" Rogers offered at the top of her voice.

The idea was appalling, unthinkable, but they all realized how it might have been the only option. The only viable chance.

The idea was academic anyway.

The control deck was two floors away, and the storm was already on them, roaring up the serviceway towards them in an engulfing flash-flood of gleaming darkness.

They ran anyway, without hope.

All except Bose.

He turned, aimed his pulse rifle at the oncoming blizzard, and opened fire.

It was all he could do. The last thing he would do. Be a marine. Be Corps. Take as many of the enemy down with him as he could.

He was still yelling and firing when the storm engulfed him.

BROKEN

BY RACHEL CAINE

"On."

It was the first word he said, and at the same time, he opened his eyes. They worked perfectly, of course, but the data that his optics streamed came in a flood, and took a moment to process. The *moment* was approximately a nanosecond, and then he blinked, because blinking delivered moisturizing lubricant to his eyes, and made them look flawlessly human at the same time.

He knew he was not human. That knowledge had been hard-coded into him, along with a variety of terms for what he was. *Android. Synthetic. Robot. Artificial person.*

He decided he was an *artificial person*, and as he did, he smiled, focused on the person standing across from him, and said, "Hello."

The person ignored him to tap on a data tablet. She was

loud, he realized, and dialed his inputs back to acceptable levels where the pulsing roar of her heartbeat and rush of blood and gurgle of nutrient processing and creaking bellows of her lungs no longer distracted him. Now he only heard the tap of her fingers on the pad, the hum of electronics all around him, the whisper of the air recycling system. A great deal of inputs, but his brain flawlessly processed, identified, and stored each one.

The woman—his first Real Person—had a slight frown on her face, and he checked his database, widened his eyes to the correct pre-programmed amount, shifted the timbre of his voice to a warmer, deeper setting as he asked, "Are you in some distress? How can I help?"

She glanced up from the data pad, and he felt something flash through him like a faulty circuit. What *was* that? Processing caught up an instant later, and identified it as *emotion*. She seemed *irritated*, and he was… *sorry*. Her shoulders had gone stiff, and that body language conformed to—to what? Suspicion?

"Designation HS17B48XG5-D5, your name is now Bishop, do you acknowledge?"

Her voice was a complex marvel of harmonics, one he stored to examine later, but she had asked him a question, and he immediately answered, "Acknowledged, Dr. Sasaki. I'm pleased to meet you."

Her frown deepened. "I didn't tell you my name."

"I'm sorry, Dr. Sasaki, I read your name tag. I hope that's all right." He smiled again. This seemed to be the right expression for the occasion, and he chose one that the database identified as *wistful*. "Have I done something wrong?"

She seemed to debate that for a very long time, with her finger hovering over her data pad, and then shook her head. "No, Bishop, you haven't. Please join the others."

She pointed across the room—a very plain, empty room, with nothing in it but Dr. Sasaki, who also wore white, a form-fitting skin of material that wrapped up around her head in a hood to conceal her hair, and the only other shades in the room were the black letters of her nametag under the embossed seal of the Weyland-Yutani Corporation, the color of her skin— *amber*—and her eyes, which matched a shade his database identified as *dark brown*. Even the data pad was the same stark white, at least on the side he could see.

Bishop turned while processing all that to look where she indicated. There was a doorway behind him and beyond it another room.

Instead of moving toward it, he looked down, because he detected that the area on which he stood resonated at a different frequency. It was a round section that was hollow beneath, and bisected in the middle. "What is that, Dr. Sasaki?" he asked, and then immediately clarified, because he had been imprecise. "What am I standing on?"

"You're a curious one," she said, and there was a change in her voice now, another resonant shift he'd have to save for examination. "That's the failsafe. There is a very small chance that upon activation, a synthetic such as yourself may exhibit signs of... instability."

"I see," Bishop said, still staring down. "It opens. Where does it go?"

"The chute leads to a machine that disassembles defective units to constituent parts for reuse."

He was standing over an execution chamber.

Bishop stepped off the circle. It wasn't a conscious decision, it was one his volume processor, his *brain*, had simply ordered in the interest of self-preservation. The artificial organ that regulated the flow of hydraulic fluid through his trunk, head and limbs had increased its rate of flow.

He didn't want to die.

"Thank you, Dr. Sasaki," he said, because he had been programmed to be polite, and walked into the next room.

Behind him, he heard Dr. Sasaki give a deep, trembling sigh, and whisper something in a language he identified as Japanese.

I should have flushed him.

Another flicker of emotion raced through him, this one subtly different. A new one.

Sadness.

There were four other Artificial Persons seated in the next room. All of them looked identical to him in form and coloring, except that they were dressed in gray clothing with the Weyland-Yutani corporate logo on the collars, and he had nothing except his synthetic skin. "Hello," he said. "My name is Bishop."

All four stood up, flawlessly synchronized. He heard the pitch of data exchange, inaudible to human hearing, as they coordinated actions, and then one said, "I am Rook." The others were named Castle, King, and Knight.

"Someone likes chess," Bishop said, and smiled, because he felt a pulse of what he identified as *amusement*. It was followed by *disquiet* when none of the rest smiled back. They simply stared, clinically analyzing him, cataloguing, dissecting.

"Our names are based on chess terms," Knight replied. It was Bishop's voice, but the inflections were flat, uninspired, lifeless. "I am not sure why that implies someone likes chess."

"Then I can't help you," Bishop said. He took in more data. The room was white, like the last, only there were no *failsafes* in the floor, and there were two stiff, white couches that could seat three each. A low table in the middle, also white—he was, he realized, finding the decorating uninspired—held a neatly folded cloth jumpsuit like the ones his brothers—could he call them brothers?—also wore. He took it and pulled it on over his synthetic epidermis with quick, efficient motions, pulled the zipper shut, and said, "What do we do now?"

The others sat down on the couches, perfectly synchronized. He heard the dataset sync calling to him to join them, but instead, Bishop continued to stand, and folded his arms.

Identical sets of eyes stared at him—medium brown, not as dark as Dr. Sasaki's—and he studied the identical, worn features of their faces. Pale skin. High, arching forehead with a shock of brown hair. Deep-set lines bracketing nose and mouth.

Looking at the other four seemed like looking at strangers, not a mirror.

The others turned their heads in unison toward the closed door at the far end. He heard the activation code being entered, too, but waited until the portal slid open before he shifted his gaze to it.

A young, bulky man—a real person, bored and annoyed—leaned in and said, "Move out. You're being shipped."

"Shipped where?" Bishop asked. The man seemed startled, and then he frowned, the same as Dr. Sasaki had. *My responses are outside the normal parameters,* he thought. *But not so far outside that I was sent to my death down the chute.* What did that make him? Defective? Strange?

Different, he thought. *I'm different.* He waited for the emotion to come, and it did, a bright flash he identified as… *satisfaction.*

"Shut up and walk," the man said, and Bishop did. But where the other four walked in precise rhythm, he made sure his steps were a bit longer, a bit out of sync.

Different.

———

"Holy *fuck,* watch your field of fire!" Lieutenant Larsen screamed it at Private Peekskill, who'd sprayed a deadly burst of bullets too close to a screaming knot of civilians. There were dozens of them, all spread out flat or crouched down or already dead in the firefight; at least five lay sprawled on the bullet-chewed wooden floor, spot-lit by a broken skylight.

Bishop, unarmed, crouched behind a pillar next to Larsen; the rest of their squad, including Peekskill, were pinned down on the other side of the common hall that had once doubled as the brand new Haarsa Colony marketplace. Bishop still saw grace in the arching lines of the concrete pillars, and the glass tile mosaic on the far wall—damaged by gunfire and bomb fragments—showed real merit. Haarsa was planned to be a showplace for the Terraforming Division of Weyland-Yutani; there were a total of forty-seven colonists here already, and—by his calculations—half were now dead in some part of the facility or other. This wasn't going to reflect well on next quarter's profit and loss statements.

"Sorry, Lew!" Peekskill yelled back, and opened fire on a balcony somewhere overhead. Bishop turned down his hearing as the bullets pounded into concrete, wood, glass and steel above, shattering store windows and severing power lines with showers of sparks, and finally, Peekskill managed to find at least one soft target.

Even muted, Bishop heard the difference when bullets ripped through flesh, bone, and organs.

"He got one of them," Bishop reported quietly to Lieutenant Larsen, which was probably unnecessary, since Peekskill gave a wild whoop of victory across the way. Bishop ignored that to listen to other things. "The rest are retreating, sir. I don't think we're going to dig them out this way, and we don't have a lot of time. Has the corporation considered paying them?"

The soldiers currently occupying Haarsa Colony were criminals who called themselves Company F. Company F recruited former Colonial Marines, mercs, anyone who met their standards of moral absence and greed. Their methodology was, Bishop thought, objectively brilliant; they landed on an otherwise hard-working, peaceful settlement, took hostages, killed as many as it took to get their point across, and made a financial demand to the Weyland-Yutani Corporation, or whichever rival company owned the terraformed colony. It was a quick payoff, and the pirates moved on to pillage another day.

Only this time, it had gone wrong simply because a complement of Colonial Marines, under the command of Lieutenant Lucky Larsen, had been less than half a day's flight out after refueling. And Weyland-Yutani had decided that it wasn't paying Company F any more bounties.

"Well, fuck me," Larsen said in disgust. He was a short man, blocky, with a scar bisecting his face almost exactly down the middle, but twisting over his nose like a seam not pulled straight. He also had thick burn scars running up the left side of his neck. Lucky Larsen, his soldiers called him, for obvious reasons. "How many left in Company F, Bishop?"

"Minus the one that Private Peekskill just killed, I count at least thirty, sir, holding eleven hostages, including four children." Company F liked holding children, under the theory that it forced a faster payout. While it didn't make Bishop angry, it did make him—what was that exact emotion?—*disgusted*.

"Too many for us to dig out without losses of our own, and we've got our orders," the lieutenant said. He seemed especially grim, Bishop thought. "Right. Time to get these people out. Bishop, take point, get the ones who can walk to the transport and on the ship. Check the wounded. Then tag the ones you think are worth cryo, but remember, we only have twelve extra chambers."

"Yes, sir." Bishop stood up, but he didn't immediately follow the order, even though that priority was clear. "Sir. If we're not going after Company F, how do we rescue the hostages?"

"We don't," Larsen said. "Orders are to blow the central converters and evac."

"I don't understand. If we destroy the central converters, it'll flood the central complex with Prevox gas. Everyone will be dead if they can't get to masks." *Dead painfully*, Bishop thought, but didn't add. Larsen knew how Prevox worked. It was a vital component in the terraforming process, but it was volatile and dangerous.

"Lucky for us, the masks are smart-linked, so even if they do make it to the cabinets, the masks won't work. Ybarra already locked them down."

Bishop felt the artificial muscles of his face contracting, forming his expression into a pinched frown. "That means *everyone dies*. Even the hostages."

"Yeah, Bishop, no shit that's what it means, it happens and there's nothing we can do about it. Now go get these people out. That's an order. We have to save those we can."

Larsen, Bishop realized, didn't like this either. Not at all. But he had orders. Real people had the ability to disobey an order, but in Bishop's observation they rarely did—not when there were real consequences along with the action. It was almost as if there were no real distinctions between real people (*biologicals*, he called them, but only privately) and artificials.

At least an artificial person had the excuse of being programmed.

Bishop weighed the odds of persuading Larsen to go against orders, and decided that they weren't good. Larsen wasn't afraid to kill, and he wasn't afraid of civilian casualties; he had a pragmatic outlook to war, and as far as he was concerned, Haarsa Colony had just become a war zone. Innocents were bound to die, and his job was to make sure his soldiers survived.

So Bishop walked out into the open atrium, spoke calmly and quietly to the frightened colonists, and sent them with Peekskill's soldiers back to the ship as he methodically checked each of the fallen. Seven dead, two so gravely wounded that even cryosleep and the best medical attention wasn't going to save them. That left ten for the cryo chambers, and Bishop used comms to call for transport.

Larsen left him to it, and followed a map to the central control room. Bishop calmly reassured the wounded—those who could hear him—that they would be evacuated and treated, and they were in no danger.

He tried not to listen to the cries of the ones he'd red-tagged as too far gone. He wasn't wrong about their chances at life. It wasn't a judgment call. They were dying, and nothing could stop it.

So when the two company medics, Patel and Luo, arrived and began loading the yellow tags on stretchers, it was odd that he felt it necessary to go and talk to those who were being left behind, to tell them that everything was all right. He didn't tell them they were dying.

Four of them died while he was with them. One ceased functioning before he could get to him. The others weren't conscious.

When he looked up, he was the only one standing, and the atrium seemed utterly still now, with only the rush of wind through the broken skylight. The dead were as silent as the broken, bullet-marked concrete.

"Bishop." He looked up. Larsen was leaning over the balcony, staring down. "Everybody out?"

"Yes, Lieutenant."

"Then what the fuck are you doing? Get to the ship. We have less than five minutes before the converters blow."

Bishop considered that. The calculations took nanoseconds, but he already knew before the results came in what he was going to do. Maybe he was, after all, defective. A true Artificial Person didn't make a decision in advance of data calculations. "I can take a supply of functioning masks with me. Enough for the hostages. I can get to them in time."

"No."

"I don't need to breathe—"

"Bishop, I said no. You're an asset, and I'm not leaving you to get reprogrammed by Company F, or shot full of holes. You know how much you cost?"

Bishop blinked, not because he needed the lubrication, but because he had to reorganize his information. *Lieutenant Larsen doesn't see me as part of his team. I'm an asset. A machine. An expensive machine that he'll get in trouble for losing.* It was the same cold math that Weyland-Yutani used to decide that they could afford to lose Haarsa Colony, and every human being inside it, to stop Company F and make it clear they weren't paying ransoms any longer.

They were sending the message in blood, and Lieutenant Larsen was willing to write it for them... but not in *synthetic* blood.

Bishop, an Artificial Person, turned away and walked out

of the atrium, down a sloping corridor, and let Larsen's shouts echo behind him. He knew Larsen wouldn't come after. For all the shouts, Larsen wasn't stupid; he wouldn't risk his life for this. If Bishop succeeded, he'd take credit. If Bishop failed, he'd blame the pirates.

He heard Larsen's footsteps, running for the exit, as he reached the first emergency life cabinet and tore it open. The neatly ranked life support masks all showed red indicators, which meant they were indeed disabled, but Bishop took them one at a time, cracked the processor casing, snapped the tiny filament that locked out changes, and used his onboard data sync to flash-program them again.

There were eleven hostages. He took eleven masks, stuffed them into an expandable bag from his pack, and broke into a run deeper into the bowels of Haarsa Colony.

The SECURE AREA door he found was too thick to batter down, but he ran a password breaker—intended only for official use—on the keypad and had it open in fifteen seconds. The timer he ran as a faint display on his left eye showed him that he had less than two minutes left before the converters blew out. It would take time for the gas to reach toxic levels, but Prevox bound to oxygen, which meant everyone breathing would suffocate well before the toxins killed them. *The children will die faster.* He tried to calculate how much faster, but without more information, it was imprecise, and he erased the calculations and ran faster, stretching lab-grown tendons and pumping hydraulics at a red-line rate.

It was good he was moving so fast, because the first bullets missed him by quite a large margin, and he shifted course and dove behind the cover of a corner as another weapon roared. Concrete chipped and flew in knife-edged shards. He felt a cut, and looked down to see that his synthetic epidermis was sliced across the top of his hand, leaking a thin stream of thick, white fluid. It revealed a marvel of strong, pale synth-engineered tendons, pistons, data channels, glistening hair-thin wires. If he'd had time, he'd have been fascinated. Instead, he opened a kit at his belt, took out a small can, and sprayed skin over the gap. It had an ugly look, but he'd fix it later. If there was a later.

"Hey! Marine!" someone yelled around the corner. "How does it feel to be another gun for hire for the suits? You take an oath to the corporations now?"

Bishop didn't answer, because he was distracted—not by his wound, but by something else. A sensation, like a tapping on his brain. He'd felt it before, but not for years, not since...

Not since the day he was born.

"He's not a Colonial Marine," said a very familiar voice. His own voice. "He's a synthetic. Like me."

The sensation he was feeling was a sync link trying to connect. They were programmed that way, to share data across models. He rejected the sync and said, in a calm tone that was somehow entirely different from his brother's, "Not like you, Rook."

"His name is Bishop," Rook said to the others on his side of the corner. "He isn't a threat. We're not programmed to fight. He won't even have a weapon."

That much was true. Bishop didn't like guns. He'd never really thought of that as programming, but it probably was. Still. He wasn't Rook.

"We can always use another synth," the other voice said, the one that wasn't a mirror image of his own. "Come on out, Bishop. We won't shoot. Consider yourself a new member of Company F."

"It's not that easy," Rook said, and he still had the same strange cadence, the same monotone delivery that Bishop remembered. Just enough wrong to make Bishop think, *but am I really right?* "He's been programmed for loyalty to the Corps. You'll need to reprogram him."

"Like they did you?" Bishop asked. That got a general wave of cold laughter.

"Naw, we didn't have to push a button. This is Kee Parker, by the way. Leader of Company. Old Rook, he was ours to begin with. Got shot up on a mission, they scrapped him, we salvaged him. You're with Lucky Larsen, right? Damn, small universe. I was there when he got his face sliced open. Ugly enough to make me want to puke. Company F's just like the Marines. Only we pay more. What do you say, Bishop? You in?"

"Sure," Bishop said. "As long as you release the hostages. You have—" He flipped the timer back to visible, "— seventeen seconds."

There was a murmur among the soldiers, and a woman said, "The fuck?" while someone else said, "Fucking synths, we should just take him for parts," and a hostage began to cry.

Sixteen.

Fifteen.

Fourteen.

At ten, Bishop calmly called the time again, and said, "What does Company F stand for?"

"Company F, for *Fuck You*, and also, fuck your countdown, synth. Step out and we won't shoot. Stay there and we'll cut you to pieces."

That wasn't the plan, which Bishop knew because sync link or not, he was somehow aware of Rook moving. Rook was circling around to come in behind him, most likely to take him prisoner, but possibly to shoot him in the back.

Bishop turned, ran in the direction Rook would be coming, and timed it to turn the corner just as his brother, his mirror image, reached it.

Face to face, again.

Except they weren't mirrors anymore, if they ever had been. Rook looked expressionless, plastic, *lifeless* though he moved like a person. Bishop was undecided on the human concept of souls, but a look into Rook's empty eyes was enough to show that his brother definitely didn't possess one.

Rook didn't hesitate. He lunged forward, and there was a knife in his hand, a black combat model with a six-inch blade. Bishop met him halfway, twisting that hand enough that the stab missed him. Then he slammed the heel of his palm into the spots where he knew Rook was vulnerable—he'd taken time to learn his own vulnerabilities—and in three seconds, Rook was down, the knife skittering away from his open hand.

Bishop knelt on his spine, picked up the knife, and said, "I'm sorry," before he plunged the knife down into just the right spot to sever the nexus that fed instructions from the brain to the limbs. Rook wasn't dead. He just couldn't move. Eventually, he'd power down, and finally, in several human lifetimes, he'd go completely dark.

Bishop stood, flipped the knife expertly end over end, and caught it by the blade before slipping it into his belt.

"Just because you're not programmed for something doesn't mean you can't learn it," he told Rook, though Rook was long past learning anything. The head was turned sideways, and one eye stared up at him. The mouth opened and closed, but nothing except a gout of white hydraulic fluid came out.

Bishop watched the timer, and when it reached *zero*, he crouched down against the wall. He'd calculated this part, too: this wall was mathematically the least likely to be damaged by the blast.

Boom.

That was how they wrote the sound in books he'd read, but it wasn't a *boom*, really; it was a roar, and deep and shuddering thunder that rattled the entire complex, shattered structural bones, and tore through his body like a solid blow. Bishop thought of the ruined beauty of the marketplace. It would be gone now, and those he'd red-tagged and witnessed dying would be buried in ruins.

The blast had hit the opposite corner hard. Bishop restarted the counter. He had less than a minute to get these masks on the hostages, if they'd survived.

He ran that direction, and came to a fast, skidding stop when he saw most of Company F was lying dead, crushed and broken and bleeding, but there were four or five still standing, and they were all aiming weapons at him.

"It's Rook," he said, and kept his voice the mirror of his crippled brother's. Flat, unfeeling, and above all, calm. He drew the knife from his belt and showed it to them, then put it on the ground. "Bishop's dead."

One of the soldiers spat out blood and lowered his gun. Once he had, all the rest did, too. "What's in the bag?"

"More explosives," Bishop said. The idea was to keep them talking. One of the fallen Company F crew screamed from somewhere under a pile of rubble, and Bishop looked at it, then back at the leader. *Kee Parker*. "Do you want me to dig them out?"

"No, I want you to take that bag of boom up top, tell them you're Bishop, get on board, and blow those bastards all to hell. We owe them that. That's an order, Rook. Take 'em out."

The timer said twenty seconds had elapsed since the explosion. Particulates were rising; he set his internal sensors to alert him when they reached significant enough levels to affect Parker. "Of course," he said, with the same flat delivery. "Anything else?"

"Anything else, what the hell else could there be? *Go!*"

Bishop angled his head up and said, "The roof is unstable. You should move."

"Fuck." Parker looked around. Most of the hostages had survived. Three of the children, and five adults. Three lay buried somewhere in the rubble with his other soldiers. "Get them up. All right, let's go. After you."

Bishop set a slow pace as the seconds ticked by. The alert flashed red in the corner of his vision, and he banished it with a blink as he turned to look behind him.

Parker and his remaining three soldiers were still on their feet, but they looked unsteady. Of the hostages, two of the children had fallen, and been picked up by adults. The third, older, swayed and clutched at the woman next to her. They were all gasping.

"Prevox," Parker managed to gasp, and he lunged past

Rook to one of the life cabinets. He unlocked it with a flash of fingers on the pad, grabbed a mask, and put it over his face. Bishop saw him take in a breath, and then another, and another.

Parker turned toward the synth he still thought was Rook. Bishop would never forget that look, that desperate, angry, terror-filled look. Not that he ever forgot anything, but Parker's expression seemed different.

It seemed *important*.

"I'm not Rook, and they're not working," Bishop told him. He eased him to a sitting position. Parker managed to fumble off the mask. He was trying to breathe—he *was* breathing, but it didn't do any good. His skin had gone gray. "I have to save the ones I have for hostages. I'll help you too. Just last."

Bishop took Parker's gun away and put it aside. The other Company F survivors had already fallen. So had all of the hostages. Bishop methodically took the weapons, then fitted the working masks on each of the hostages, starting with the smallest. There were extras, since some of those he'd intended to save were already dead.

When he got back around to Parker, it was too late. Too late for his soldiers as well. *I can't harm a human being,* Bishop thought, but he hadn't. He'd simply prioritized helping in a logical way. It wasn't his fault that had resulted in someone's death.

But, he thought, *better the pirates than the prisoners.* He wasn't altogether sure he should be making those kinds of judgments. He didn't know who to ask what was right and wrong in this case.

He picked up two of the children, one in each arm, and set off at a run for the surface.

———

They'd left a drop ship for him, but the Marines were gone, and for good reason: the ground itself was unstable. Bishop's monitors reported multiple system failures, due to the explosion in the converters; it was only a matter of time before the entire thing went up in a fireball. If the reactor didn't blow, then the oxygen supplies would as soon as the still-raging fire reached them.

Bishop made three trips, carrying two at once, and as he came back for the last two masked survivors, he found them dead.

Also, he found them without masks, their faces gray and still, mouths open and eyes shining silver from Prevox poisoning.

He was still trying to understand what had happened when he was shot in the back.

Bishop didn't know what pain felt like to a real person, but to him it felt like a burning sensation that cut through him like a hot blade from back to front. Through skill, planning or blind luck, the bullet tumbled through a nexus cluster, and he felt his right side go limp and dead, and he crumped to the ground and rolled onto his back.

Two of the Company F soldiers stood over him, guns aimed down at his chest. They were wearing masks, the masks he'd put on the hostages.

That was a surprise.

His face registered an emotion, but he wasn't sure how that looked. A tragedy/comedy mask, split like Lieutenant Larsen's down the middle? The pain hadn't stopped, his synthetic brain reported. *Dying is painful.* That was an interesting fact. He wondered if he was afraid. His hydraulic system was redlining, as it had when he was running top speed, though he could hardly move at all. His tongue felt dry. He felt a cold trickle of fluid underneath his body. *Bleeding. Leaking. Is there a difference?*

"Fucking synth," one of them said from under her mask, and kicked him very hard, but on the side he couldn't feel. "Surprised? We had an air pocket under the rubble that saved us. Then we found these." She tapped the mask she wore. "Thanks for that."

"Thanks for nothing, you freak," the other one, a man, said. They both aimed their weapons. At this range, those would shred him apart.

Bishop tried to speak. With half his mouth working, he wasn't sure it was very successful. "Sorry," he told them.

Which was an odd thing to say, and he was sure he was malfunctioning, because he recognized the feeling that swept over him. It was hot and uncontrollable and almost human in its intensity, and all he knew in that moment was *If they leave here, they'll slaughter the hostages,* and it was a moral dilemma that he was not programmed to handle.

Until he programmed himself.

He opened his sync link to the masks, and turned them off.

He saw the exact moment that they realized they couldn't breathe, that they'd taken in lethal gulps of Prevox-laden air. He expected them to shoot, but instead, they dropped their weapons and grabbed for the masks, slapping them as if that would make them work, then wrenching them off to try to gasp clean air that didn't exist, and then...

He closed his eyes and didn't watch the rest. There was a new feeling. *Guilt.*

For his last action, Bishop synced to the drop ship, put it on autopilot, and ordered it to dust off with the survivors he'd loaded inside. He kept tracing it until it was too far up for the sync to work, and then he had to believe that it would reach the ship, that Lieutenant Larsen would understand that he had done his job for the Marines. *I prioritized,* he told himself. *I didn't kill anyone. I prioritized, and I protected.*

That was important. If he ever told anyone what he'd done, they'd flush him. Execute him. But then again, he was going to die here well before that.

There was nothing else to be accomplished. Bishop went to power save mode.

He slept.

When he booted awake again, he was in a medbay, and someone had their fingers in his back, probing, moving aside hydraulic tubes and connecting hair-thin wires with sharp little snaps of feeling, and suddenly, Bishop was online. Fully online.

Healed.

"Yeah, that's got it," said a new voice, a strange voice, and the intrusive fingers left his body and smoothed skin back in place. He felt the cut being sealed, and rolled over to sit up.

The Marine who'd repaired him took a wide step back, holding out both hands. "Whoa, whoa, peace, I'm friendly, man."

"So am I," Bishop said. "Hello. Where's Lieutenant Larsen?"

"Reassigned," said a big man with a wide grin and an unlit cigar in his mouth. "Said for us to check. Said there was a synth on Haarsa that might still be salvageable, and since we lost ours couple of trips back…" He had a sharp look in his eyes, Bishop thought. "You're not one of those A2 models, right?"

"No," Bishop said. "I'm three generations later. D4. My designation is HS17B48XG5-D5."

"And what do they call you when you're home?"

"Bishop," he said, and smiled. "My name is Bishop."

"I like it. Suits you, synth."

"I prefer the term Artificial Person, sir."

"Apone. Sergeant. Don't call me *sir*, I'm not a damn officer. Just Sergeant or Apone or both. You got me, Bishop?"

"Yes, Sergeant."

"Good." Sergeant Apone held out his hand. Bishop stared at it for several seconds, then reached out and offered his own. He was careful not to crush the man's hand when they shook. "Welcome to the team, Bishop. This fool's Private Hudson."

"Aww, Sarge, I didn't know you cared."

"Shut up, Hudson."

Hudson gave Bishop a wide grin, all teeth. "He says *shut up* but I hear *keep talking*." He offered his hand for shaking, too. Odd. In all his life, Bishop had never been treated like an equal, not like that. Now, twice. "You ever played Five Finger Fillet?"

Bishop shook his head. Apone rolled his eyes, chomped his cigar, and said, "You break him, you buy him, Hudson." He crossed his arms and leaned against the wall to watch, though. Not interfering.

Hudson pulled out a knife. "You're gonna love this game."

And he was right.

I think I'm broken, Bishop thought, as he slammed the knife faster and faster between his spread fingers, to Hudson's crows of delight. For no reason, he remembered Dr. Sasaki's finger hovering over a data tablet, ready to send him to recycle, and his hand blurred even faster, until even his eyes could barely track it.

Maybe I've always been broken.

That was all right. It made him… happy.

RECLAMATION

BY YVONNE NAVARRO

The first time Dwayne Hicks saw the woman he would ask to marry him was in the cantina on base, after his graduation from boot camp. He had made a lot of friends in the Colonial Marines, both before and after signing up, and he'd sworn he wouldn't be like them—hooked up with the first cute face he met (and most definitely *not* another jarhead) while his plans to explore space on the government's payroll went down the drain thanks to a ring and a couple of kids.

Then he saw Rachel Miller fifteen feet away, just as she slammed the point of her Ka-Bar into the table in front of her, right through the hand of the guy who'd run his palm down the curve of her uniformed backside.

How could he not fall in love with a woman like that?

PFC Rachel Miller became PFC Rachel Miller-Hicks not quite eight weeks later, in a small ceremony in the base chapel. They had their First Sergeant's approval, with the explicit understanding that there would be no special treatment. A Marine was a Marine, and they would do what they were told. The only concession to their status was they would be stationed together. They each got two rank promotions and spent eleven great months with each other before Rachel's squad got sent on a mission to investigate a small moon believed to be hiding pirated spacecraft. "No big deal," she told Hicks. "The ship's called the *Paradox*. Two months to get there, a week or two to find out what's going on and clean it up, two months back. Six months at the most. We got this."

The first time Hicks got a video message from Rachel was seven weeks in, at the end of her squad's hypersleep. The grainy black and white image on his screen showed his dark-haired wife with her short hair flattened around her head like a halo—forty-nine days of not moving your head will do that. She looked groggy as she rubbed her face, trying to bring sensation back, and she was the most beautiful thing Hicks had ever seen, even though he was seeing the past—standard transmission time from her locale to Earth was about twelve hours.

"*Hi, baby. Just woke up so I hope this makes sense. We're five or so days out, Gunny says nothing new came in about the place while we were under. If it's been quiet all this time, I'm not sure what the big deal is. But hey, I just follow orders. Hoorah.*" Rachel stopped and rubbed her face again, then grinned at the vid-camera. "*Glad I don't grow hair on my face. The rest of these guys look like scraggly apes. I'll send another message tomorrow. Love you.*"

He couldn't answer her, but her messages to him came in

like they were on a timer, and if they weren't exactly exciting, they were reassuring in their sameness:

"Hi, baby. Nothing new on the moon front, just that bare piece of rock getting closer in the view screen and us doing prep. Like mama always said, no news is good news, right? Out until tomorrow. Love you."

There wasn't much for an E-3 in the Corps to do at night other than drink and raise hell, but although Hicks had a long way to go before he became an old married man, he did want to be home each night when Rachel's transmission finally came through. His evenings became as routine as his wife's were somewhere in the vastness of space: his duty day ended, he ate a plate or two of unidentifiable slop at the mess hall, then he went home. There he shucked his uniform, showered, and sat in front of the television until the com program chimed. On this particular Tuesday evening, he wasn't expecting anything different. Of course, when you're least expecting it is when the shit always falls out of nowhere.

"Hi, baby. Gunny says this has to be quick. We're down on the surface—been here for about five hours, I guess—but we haven't found anything yet. We have a location lock on a ship's beacon, but it's another sixty klicks. Not sure if it's a valid vessel or pirated, but I guess we'll find out." The Rachel onscreen tonight was geared up and rolling in full kit: helmet, body armor, eye gear, weapons. Hicks didn't know why the sight suddenly unnerved him; after all, he'd trained with her countless times and he knew she was capable of taking care of herself and kicking major ass. And—this made him grin—don't forget the first time he'd set eyes on her.

On the screen, Rachel looked over her shoulder, as if making sure no one else was within earshot. Her image vibrated with the ship's movement. *"There's something hinky about this place. I can't put my finger on it but I can tell the others are feeling it, too. Not much here but rocks and small mountains, no atmosphere, so it's not like anything alive is out there. But sometimes the shadows look... I don't know. Funny, like they move just out of the corner of your eye as we pass."* Suddenly she laughed. *"Listen to me, right? I sound like a baby. First time jitters, that's all."* She looked over her shoulder again, and this time Hicks heard someone else speak, although he couldn't make out the words. *"Okay, gotta go. We're getting close to the mark. Love you."*

The screen flickered out and for the first time in all these transmissions, Hicks heard himself whisper back, "Love you, too."

———

The last message came the next night. By military standards, it was late (if you're early, you're on time; if you're on time, you're late) and Hicks had been waiting for it, pacing in front of a silent television because he couldn't stand the mindless babble coming out of the actors' mouths—every word seemed to cut into his already tattered nerves. The truth was he'd been walking the rounds in the small living room for almost an hour, way before Rachel's nightly transmission.

"But sometimes the shadows look... I don't know. Funny, like they move just out of the corner of your eye as we pass."

He couldn't get those words out of his mind and he wasn't buying into her comment about it being initial mission jitters— Rachel wasn't like that. She was always the first one to react in an emergency. Even if it was just training, she was the coolest head and the steadiest hand, made the best decisions. Her brain would calculate the solution, her green eyes would focus on whatever steps were needed to do it, and that was it—mission accomplished. There was no reason to think that wouldn't be the case here. Except...

"But sometimes the shadows look... I don't know... Funny, like they move just out of the corner of your eye as we pass."

The coms chimed and Hicks jerked around and stared at the computer across the room. Then he was there and clicking on the icon, leaning forward as if that could make him better able to hear his wife.

"Just a quick one, Dwayne. I shouldn't be taking the time to make this recording and Gunny'll have my ass if he catches me, but I don't care. We're under attack by some kind of alien. We can't get a full sighting so we don't have enough info to feed into the database and identify it. We think it's black—hell, everything around here is black—and big. We're shooting at shadows and sometimes we hear these crazy screaming sounds, but other than that... nothing. The sensors show motion all around us but we can't pinpoint anything. We sent out a two-man forward patrol but that was an hour ago and we haven't gotten a single thing back from them."

Suddenly gunfire erupted somewhere off-screen. Rachel stood and swung her pulse rifle into position as someone, a man, first yelled, then screamed. Hicks had never heard such a sound in real life—it sounded like the Marine was being burned alive. Another noise cut over it all, a shrieking that Hicks felt in his ears like nails being dragged across an old-fashioned chalkboard. It made him pull in and hunch in front of his computer, and he couldn't imagine what it was like in real-time. His wife's rifle fired once, twice, a half dozen times; he could see her uniformed back and the way the rifle punched into her body each time. Abruptly she turned and her hands scrabbled for the keyboard. *"We're under attack. I'll—"*

Something huge and dark rolled across the view of the camera and Rachel leapt away. There was more gunfire, an impossible amount, more shouts, more screams, then...

Nothing.

Hicks watched helplessly, fists clenched, waiting, hoping, *praying* for it to be over and for his wife to return to the recording console. A minute, then two, three, more—

A hand, bruised and splotched with black-looking blood, flashed into view. Hicks had time to register the Claddagh wedding band that matched his own before Rachel slammed her hand onto the SEND button.

That was the last time Dwayne Hicks ever heard from his wife.

FIVE YEARS LATER

Someone hadn't been paying attention.

Corporal Dwayne Hicks stared at the orders that had just come through, thinking that it was just too good to be true and shit like this never happened in real life. Some admin PFC's stupid mistake? Undoubtedly. Coincidence? Maybe. Destiny?

Fucking-A.

His memories of the night of her last transmission were fragmented at best, crystalline at worse. When the transmission had stopped, he had careened out of his apartment with his phone plastered to his ear, alternately crying and shouting at his First Sergeant as he cut a madman's route with his car to his headquarters. Then there were calls and conferences and video conferences, an endless array of bullshit that did nothing to fix the fact that all contact with Rachel and her entire squad had ceased, and there was no distress call, no ship's locator beacon, there was *nothing*.

Ever.

Again.

PFC Rachel Miller-Hicks, along with the Gunnery Sergeant in charge, two Corporals, and eight more PFCs, were officially listed as MIA. The brass in the Colonial Marine Corps flapped their lips and the memorandums were written, higher and higher up the chain, until the issue stopped somewhere and just stayed there. After all, it wasn't the first ship the Corps had lost and it certainly wouldn't be the last. It had been sent to investigate pirating, and the final ruling was that the crew had been hijacked and the ship likely brought down by superior firepower; its locator beacon had been disabled as it was stripped of useable parts. The crew was presumed dead but until the required seven years had passed, they would remain MIA.

Hicks had lost track of how many emails and vid-messages

he'd sent trying to find out why Rachel's death—and he had no doubt she *was* dead—hadn't been investigated. He didn't need to know what had happened, because he had seen it... and so had dozens of other higher-ups in the Corps. He'd been told to let it go, that while the Corps wasn't suggesting his wife or the other members of that crew weren't important, it was too risky and expensive to go after the corpses and the remains of a ship that far from the border of the Core Territories. When he'd demanded to know why they'd sent Rachel's squad in the first place, the response had always been the same bullshit: "That's on a need to know basis." His sarcastic responses about needing to know had gotten him three NJPs for insubordination; his First Sergeant had saved his ass each time, but the last one had been just that—the last. *"You've hit your three times the charm, Hicks. Yeah, it's fucked up what happened but I don't have any answers for you. I know you won't forget it but now you just gotta deal and move on."*

That had been eight months ago and Hicks had taken the man's advice to let it ride... on the outside. On the inside, beneath his I-don't-give-a-shit expression and calm blue eyes, he seethed. And now...

He stared at the orders again.

The letter and number of the destination meant nothing to him other than he knew it by heart because he'd seen it on so much paperwork and it was four parsecs on the other side of Beta Trianguli Australis. The mission objective was to recover equipment abandoned on a previous operation; he wasn't surprised to see there was no mention of bodies, the date of the first mission, or names. That was a screw-up and a good thing—had the names of the MIA crew not been left off, the database crosscheck would have eighty-sixed him from being a part of it and he would've never known they were going back. The departure date was eight days from now, and if you were a family man that wasn't much lead time considering the length of the deployment. But Hicks wasn't a family man; the potential for that had been stolen from him when his wife had been killed by someone—or some*thing*—in the same place these orders were sending him.

Eight days felt like a lifetime.

Hicks wished they were leaving tomorrow.

Dwayne Hicks woke up from hypersleep with his dead wife's image in his mind and the skin of his lips stuck together. He forced his mouth open and discovered his tongue tasted like leftover chicken skin after it'd been in the garbage for a week. Every joint and muscle in his body fought his efforts to sit up, but it wasn't the first time he'd been through this.

Around him the other members of his squad were waking up with the predictable swear words and groans while the Gunnery Sergeant, a burly man by the name of Maxwell— Gunny Max—who had iron gray flattop, was already in uniform and working the command console. Everyone in this crew was new to Hicks and their ship was a medium-sized reclamation rig retro-fitted for speed. It had gotten them to mission and in landing position in a little over five weeks—travel time had improved since Rachel had made this, her final trip.

"Let's go, boys and girls," boomed Gunny as he stood and came over to pace in front of the sleeping pods. "Get your ass going and your blood flowing. Gonna set this bucket down on the surface in fifty-eight minutes and counting."

PFC Schmid hooked one leg over the edge of her pod and looked up muzzily as she scratched at her tousled dark hair. "No flyby first, Gunny?"

"Time is money and the Corps is tighter than the high school bikini you don't fit into anymore, Schmid." He flashed a toothy grin.

"The hell I don't," she countered, but she was already on her feet and swinging open her footlocker.

Maxwell fixed his gaze on Hicks. "Call roll," he ordered.

"Make sure everyone came out of hypersleep in working order and gets something fast to eat. Then suit up."

Before Hicks could reply, PFC Laff cut in. "A shower—"

"That's funny, Laff," snapped Maxwell. Someone—Vernon?—choked, trying to hide a chuckle. "Take a shower next month. We got a job to do."

"You heard Gunny," Lance Corporal Horsley said quickly. "You're down to fifty-six minutes."

"Respond when I call your name," Hicks said in a voice loud enough to be heard down to the end of the sleeping area. He yanked up his pants with one hand and pulled a clipboard from his footlocker with the other. "And you'd better be bleeding out before you tell me you can't be ready in time." He began going down the list of names as he finished dressing. "Trexler."

"Yeah."

"Laff, I already know you're fine. Addison."

"Here."

"I got you, Schmid. Strand?"

"Yep."

"Kneezuh."

A good-looking blonde jerked her head in his direction, her blue eyes flashing. "It's pronounced *Nez*," she said sharply. Then she added, "Sir."

Hicks grinned to himself. He always appreciated people who stood up for themselves. "Right." He ran down the rest of the names—"Knight, DePerte, Vernon, Hagerty"—and got responses from each. By then all were rummaging in their footlockers and focused on the upcoming landing.

"Weapons?" asked Hagerty.

"Absolutely," responded Hicks. He shot a sideways glance at Gunny, but his superior didn't contradict him. "Always."

So far Hicks had done a badass job of hiding his emotions, but when the ship actually settled onto the bleak, dusty surface of the moon where Rachel had said her last words, he felt his heart rate triple, not just in his chest but in his temples—that place where at his angriest, he could always pick up the *thud thud thud* of his racing pulse. He actively inhaled, trying to calm his nerves, but he wasn't into that meditation crap and this was just too big, too *important*—

Gunny's voice ground through his helmet's speaker. *"Hicks, what's up with you? Your vitals are through the roof."*

"Just excited to be in the Corp, Gunny," he answered. "An adventure every day, every hour."

"Very funny. You gonna pass out on me?"

"Not this year."

Gunny didn't respond but Hicks swore he could feel the tough old man's gaze across the com waves.

"Airlock is tight," PFC DePerte said on the main channel. *"Rear hatch opening in five, four, three, two, one."*

The steamy sound of hydraulics filled everyone's coms as the ship's oversized rear hatch opened. The retrofit had made it wide enough to accommodate two drop ships side by side, in addition to lining the loading area with enough light to power a small town. The problem with that was no one could see jack past the line of illumination; there was brightness, then there was blackness.

"Why here?" PFC Knight suddenly asked. *"What's out there?"*

"Time'll tell," quipped Strand. *"We—"*

"Metal." Even over the com, PFC Addison's alto voice came across as vibrant. A striking and tall African-American woman, Hicks thought she was more suited to being an actress than a jarhead. That opinion notwithstanding, he wouldn't want to face off with her in a fight. *"I did a scan for near-vicinity metal and hit triple cherries. It picked up something that's either big or in a whole lot of pieces."*

"Could be a ship," Vernon put in. *"That's what we're after, right?"*

"Not much history on this mission," Nezuh said. *"But it seems pretty obvious we're after whatever we can salvage after a crash. The question is how long ago did it happen?"*

"This ain't the time for chitchat, Marines." Gunny Max's voice drowned out anyone else's comments. *"Power up your suits and make sure you have enough push to stay on the surface. Anyone who thinks it's funny to free-float gets a hundred push-ups for every second they don't have both feet planted. Understand?"* The spattering of affirmative responses seemed to be enough, so Gunny said, *"Move out. And somebody get a spotlight out there. I can't see shit on the vidscreen."*

Strand strode to the front of the group and swung a high-power light into place. The harsh cone of illumination swelled then disappeared into a blackness that seemed absolutely endless. With no atmosphere, not even dust floated in front of them.

"Fail," LCpl Horsley said. It was probably meant as a joke, but that failed, too.

"Let's go," Hicks ordered. *"Strand, you're with me. Trexler come up front with the radiation detector. Addison and DePerte to the left, Vernon and Hagerty to the right. The rest of you spread out and flank us. Keep it tight."*

It didn't take long to cross the line where the lights from the ship stopped helping. What they got from the spotlight wasn't much, and the small but powerful lights on each side of their individual helmets didn't seem to help; to Hicks, the lifeless moon in front of them still looked gray and black through his amber-tinted solar visor. They had set down in a decent-sized flat area between small, jagged mountains. Scattered around them was evidence of meteor strikes in sizes varying from a couple of meters to a quarter mile across. It was stark and, like most uninhabitable, airless moons, coldly beautiful.

They moved forward in silence until Hicks held up his hand. "Where are we headed out here, Gunny? I don't see anything besides dirt and hills."

After a few seconds, Maxwell replied. *"Go straight another three hundred meters. The scan says there's metal there. If it's been here awhile, you might have to dig to find it, but it's definitely on the screen."*

"Roger," he said. So the Gunny had no back info on the mission, either. Hicks gestured and the crew followed as he moved, monitoring their progress on the tactical GPS on his wrist. He'd managed to calm his hammering heartbeat but he still felt hyper-alert and edgy, ready to jump. His thoughts were spinning, not only with memories but with questions. If only he'd been able to get to the data from Rachel's last mission, the exact location where her ship had set down. If this moon had really been a place for pirated ships to hide, there was no guarantee that the ship—assuming that's what it was—they were coming up on was hers.

"I'm picking up trace radiation," Trexler said. *"Not much though. It seems pretty dissipated."*

"Is it safe?" Hicks asked.

"Yeah. For this amount, we're plenty protected by our suits. It does mean we're getting close to... whatever it is."

"There," Strand said suddenly. *"At the base of that hill..."* His voice trailed off and he slowed. *"What's behind it?"*

Hicks took the spotlight from Strand, aiming it high and over the dirt-covered metal edges that rose in front of them. He kept moving, closing the distance until he was able to get a definitive visual on the object—scratch that—*objects*—that receded into the dark.

"Another ship," he said. "More than one, in fact. Gunny, you hearing this?"

"Yeah. Any sign of activity?"

"Negative," Hicks replied.

"Are the hulls damaged?"

"I can't tell from here. We're moving in." Hicks motioned to the others and they advanced cautiously, knowing without being told to watch on all sides. No one broke radio silence, focusing instead on their surroundings. When they were ten meters from the first ship, Hicks stopped and the rest of them followed suit.

No doubt about it—this was Rachel's ship, the *Paradox*. Hicks knew the mechanics of it by heart and what it looked like from every possible angle, including the interior. He'd had half a decade to burn the specs into his brain. It looked like it had set down properly—no crash damage—but there were darker spots at random places on the hull in starburst patterns; those could mean it had taken fire but they weren't large enough to have come from another ship. Small arms fire?

"Hicks?"

Damn it—the vitals monitor on his suit was betraying him again. "I'm fine, Gunny." Before Maxwell could say anything else, Hicks pointed at Vernon and Hagerty. "You two head around the stern, see if there's any penetration damage to the hull. Addison and DePerte will check the nose and anything behind it. I want three of you to go inside with me."

Schmid, Nezuh, and Knight formed up next to him, and Hicks led the way to the ship's closed entry door. "Max, the ship's name is *Paradox*, and the main entrance door is sealed. There's a keypad to the right of the door. Can you find the code?"

"Give me thirty seconds," Max replied, but he had it in under fifteen. Hicks punched it in and they brought their weapons up automatically when the door slid to the side. There was no sound of air releasing and inside the ship was as black as a pool of tar—no console or equipment lights, no backups. There was obviously still power but someone had purposely killed the lights.

Strand was there with the portable spotlight before Hicks had to ask for it. Hicks took it and lowered the intensity so it didn't overpower everything, then shined it around the entrance and into the space beyond. There wasn't much to see; no bodies, no weapons. Except—

"Is that blood?"

Hicks swung the light back in the direction that Schmid was

pointing, at another hatchway, also closed. The glow ran across a black stain that started at the simple toggle switch on the right side of the hatch and ended in an elongated dripping pattern on the floor. "I want a check-in from both exterior teams right now," Hicks barked into his mic.

Addison's distinctive voice came back immediately. *"We're good."*

"Roger that." Vernon's voice was cut a little by static but he sounded calm and confident.

"I want both recon teams back to the entrance," Hicks ordered.

"What's your status?" Maxwell asked.

"We're on high alert," Hicks replied, switching the channel so everyone heard. "It's hard to tell in this light, but it looks like there's blood inside." He felt the jump in his pulse but his voice was level and strong, and Hicks was proud of himself as he said the words. After five years he knew he wouldn't find Rachel alive, but hope was a hard thing to completely extinguish.

"We're moving in," he said. "Switch to night optics. I'm going to leave the spotlight at the door. Spread out and keep your weapons ready, but no one moves out of sight of another team member. Recon teams, what's your position?"

"We got your back," Hagerty replied. *"Addison and DePerte are in sight. When they get here, we'll all come in behind you."*

"Let's go." Hicks put the spotlight down next to the open door, positioned so that most of its light shone outside, then he switched his view to night and moved forward. When he got to the stained switch by the hatchway, he checked to make sure the rest of his team was ready, then pushed it. Although no green light came on to indicate it was responding, the door opened.

More blackness, not a single glow from anything to break the fuzzy green vista in front of them. There were, however, darker splotches here and there along the floor and walls, some splattering, others trailing. Hicks looked down and saw that he was standing in the center of a particularly large patch of it. The others probably didn't need to be told that there was no longer any doubt that it was blood.

"Sir?" Knight was whispering, as if there was something in here that could hear them.

"Let's go," Hicks said. "And stay frosty."

Without being told, Schmid took point, crouching slightly, her pulse rifle forward and ready. The area in front of them fanned out into a command center that looked virtually destroyed—no wonder the ship had never gotten off the ground again.

"Barely discernible levels of radiation," Trexler told them quietly. "But I think there's a body—check that—more than one, under that smashed console."

Schmid and Laff angled toward it. Hicks followed, his heart suddenly banging inside his ribs. There was nothing he could do to slow it; he expected Maxwell to say something about his vitals at any second but Gunny didn't break their focus. With night vision green washing over everything there was no way Hicks could match what was in front of him to his memory of the grainy black and white vid-messages that Rachel had sent him, and besides, his gaze had always been on his wife's face.

One of the Marines said something and Hicks realized he hadn't heard the words over his own rapid breathing. "Come again," he managed, fighting not to stutter. Inside the temperature-controlled suit, stress was making him sweat and beads rolled into his eyes.

"There's not much left of the corpses," Laff repeated. *"Freeze-dried skin over bones. But there are names sewn into the uniforms so we can ID them that way."* Hicks felt each word like a hammer blow in the center of his chest. Laff glanced at him, then continued. *"They went down fighting, but we just don't know who."*

"Or what," Trexler said.

Hicks scowled and turned toward the PFC. "Where's that coming from?"

Trexler lifted his hand. *"Look at that, sir."*

They all looked to where his gloved finger was pointing,

at another hatchway on the other side of the room. It was far enough so they could barely make it out, but the doors didn't look like they were completely closed. There was no halfway position, so it must have malfunctioned.

"We'll check that in a minute," Hicks said hoarsely. He inhaled deeply then made himself step forward so that when PFC Laff stood, he could see the dead Marines on the floor. His eyes focused and for a minute everything—the *Paradox*, his crew, his *life*, spun away. Then it all came back into dreadful reality.

"Rachel," he whispered. His voice was just low enough to not be clear.

The right half of his wife's skull was caved in. There was no way to tell if she'd been bludgeoned with something or shot, although both hands still clenched her pulse rifle. Her dried face bore no expression but death—tightly drawn skin, deep holes instead of eyes, lips shriveled to nothing over a still-beautiful set of teeth. Hicks knelt and smoothed out the dust-laden nametag on her chest.

R. MILLER-HICKS

"Oh, God," Schmid said. *"Are you related to him?"*

"Her," Hicks said automatically. His gloved hands were clunky as he eased her fingers, so dry and thin, away from the barrel of the rifle, then slipped off the wedding ring.

"Sir?" Schmid's tone clearly conveyed she had no idea what he was doing.

"She was my wife," Hicks said as he unzipped a pocket and tucked the gold band inside. He touched Rachel's dust-laden hair a final time, then got back to his feet.

"Hicks, how the hell did you get pegged for this mission?" Gunny Maxwell demanded in his ear.

"No idea, sir, but I'm glad I did. At least I can put an end to the waiting."

No one said anything for a long moment, then someone—

Hicks couldn't tell who because his head seemed temporarily full of fuzzy white noise—asked, *"How long has she been gone?"*

The noise fell away and Hicks answered in a wooden voice, "She and her crew went missing five years ago."

"Jesus," Addison said quietly. *"I'm so sorry."*

Hicks cleared his throat before the others could chime in. "Let's go," he ordered. "Right now we need to check out the rest of this ship and make sure we're all safe." He forced himself to turn his back on his wife's body and strode toward the hatch on the other side of the room. "We'll start in here."

His crew followed, and although they'd never been on a mission together, everyone moved exactly as they should. The hatch was jammed with only about four inches open, just enough so they couldn't see a damned thing, even with night vision.

"I got this," said LCpl Horsley. He went back across the room and after a minute returned with a piece of metal long enough to use as a pry bar. Fifteen seconds later the door grudgingly slid aside.

Schmid eased forward, taking point again. Hicks and the others followed her into the part of the ship that contained the hypersleep pods partially recessed into one wall in a long line. *"There's damage in here, too,"* Schmid said. *"Looks like a firefight, but I don't see any bodies."*

The pods were empty but most of the transparent covers were shattered or speckled with the blast patterns of bullets. "Gunny," Hicks said, "you reading me?"

"Roger."

"Can you do an infrared scan of the ship?"

"Already initiated it. Not showing any signs of life."

"I think whatever caused this is long gone," Horsley said.

"Maybe," Hicks said. "But keep your guard up, just in case."

PFC Nezuh, followed by a couple more Marines, had moved down the pods, inspecting each one. Now they were at the end, where the walls held upright storage units that were spaced evenly apart. They lined the walls farther than the night phase of their visors could penetrate. *"There's some kind of… stuff on the floor back here,"* she said. *"It's sticky."*

Hicks and the others joined them, staring downward. LCpl Horsley still had the makeshift pry bar, and he ran it across the flooring. *"On the surface, yeah, but it's hardened beneath it. And it's not even. It's rounded, like coils."*

"It's not just on the floor," said Addison. *"Look overhead. It's everywhere."*

Knight had put a hand on the wall as he walked. Now he pulled it away and watched as long strands of the substance came with it, clinging tenaciously to his gloves. *"What the hell is this stuff?"*

Hicks frowned. "Let's—" His voice dropped away as something moved in the blackness behind Nezuh. Something big.

And *fast*.

Her sudden shriek cut into their speakers like a blast of feedback, loud enough to make some of them clap their hands against their helmets. Even so they surged toward her, but before they could get anywhere close, Nezuh's pulse rifle fired. The discharges arced left across the ceiling then came back to the right, this time at chest level. The chamber erupted in smoke, shouts of surprise and fear, and blasts of blinding white in their vision.

"Get down!" Hicks shouted as he hit the floor and rolled. "It's reflex!" His back thudded hard against one wall and he grunted, then tried to focus on the far end. Nothing in front of him made sense—it looked like giant, dark worms were coming out of the spaces between the storage units. Everything was happening fast and he couldn't stop on any one thing; they were in the midst of a full-on battle but Hicks had no idea what they were fighting.

"Report!" Max was screaming in his ear. *"I'm losing vitals on team members! Damn it, Hicks—report!"*

Almost in response to Maxwell's orders, another sound scissored into Hicks's ears, a monstrous combination of a hyena's scream and an elephant's roar. He screamed and scuttled backward, instinctively trying to get away; his hand slapped against someone's sleeve and he grabbed at it, dragging the unidentified Marine with him. His team was retreating, fighting for their lives, but from his position on the floor Hicks couldn't fire at anything without shooting his own crew members.

"Pull out!" he yelled. "Marines, get out *now*!"

The Marine closest to him—Hagerty—turned to flee, but before she could take a single step something yanked her into the air and slammed her against the ceiling. Her rifle discharged as she tried to hold onto it, and two more of his team jerked as rounds tore through their suits and into flesh.

"Hicks, are you there?" Maxwell's voice bellowed into his earpiece, mingling with the screams of something unknown and Marines dying. *"What's going on down there? Your numbers are dropping!"*

"Under attack by unknown combatant," Hicks managed to respond. He sucked in oxygen, then yelled as loud as he could, "Marines, *retreat now*!" He tried to scramble backward on his butt but the person he was holding didn't move. Hicks flipped onto his side and got enough of a hand on the other's suit to turn it to face him. The smudged nametag on the suit read TREXLER but there was no protective visor in the helmet anymore—just a black, wet hole.

Another hideous, animalistic scream shot through his earpiece. Hicks let go of Trexler's body and low-crawled forward. He wanted to go back and fight, see if he could get any more of his team out, but a fast look over his shoulder made him realize that was impossible. Pulse rounds were zigzagging through the chamber, but the rounds were decreasing and the origin directions were all wrong—upward from the floor, ricocheting dangerously off the ceiling. Only one Marine was still upright, legs wide, rifle spitting defiantly into the darkness.

Hicks struggled to rise and a bright knot of pain shot through his left calf; something, a round, a sharp piece of metal, who knew—had penetrated the muscle. The suit had auto-sealed around it but there was no way he was putting weight on that leg. One hand reached and found the edge of a sleeping pod; he grunted and rose, bringing up his rifle and aiming it at the smoke and tracers to the right of the other Marine—the size and stance registered in his brain as PFC Addison. Before he could squeeze the trigger, something too fast for him to identify lunged at her; her rifle went flying into the shadows and her long, lean body bent backwards almost in half as whatever now owned this ship dragged her away.

"Hicks, get out now," Maxwell screamed in his ear. *"There's no one to save—you're the only one left! GET OUT!"*

For a precious second Hicks was so shocked he couldn't move. His whole team was gone? Then instinct kicked in and he swung around and lurched toward the broken hatch door. The line of hypersleep pods made the way seem impossibly long and he lost track of how many times he fell, until he finally just stayed down and dragged himself along the floor. When he made it through, he saw something move in the far side of the chamber, something oversized and black rapidly sliding toward him.

This wasn't the time to identify it. Hicks pushed up and over the lip of the faulty hatch door and reeled across the command center room like a drunkard, rocking from side to side when his bad leg wanted to buckle beneath him. Somewhere to his right was Rachel's body, but he couldn't think about that now, not if he wanted to live. His night vision module was damaged and the green view in front of him was sizzling in and out, in and out; he *had* to make it to the other hatch before it died on him completely and he couldn't see anything.

Hicks felt the creature come up behind him just as he lunged through the hatch and slapped his hand against the toggle switch on the flipside of the wall. The door slid closed and he leaned against the metal, gasping—

—and something brutal and huge slammed into it from the other side.

The impact flung him away from the door and Hicks landed on his back with the wind knocked out of him. For a moment all he could do was lie there like a stunned, upside down turtle, listening as the interior hatch door was beaten by a monstrous force. Finally, he shook his head to clear it and scrambled backward, turning as he went until he was upright and staggering forward. Behind him the metal shrieked and started to buckle— it wasn't that thick and it wasn't going to hold.

"The code!" he shouted. "Max, I need the code for the exterior hatch!"

"It's already open," Gunny shot back. *"Why—"*

"I have to *close* it!" Hicks launched himself through the open door and ended up skidding to his knees on the dusty moon surface, right calf pulsing with pain. "Right now!" He twisted up and back, slamming his palm against the side of the ship, shaking as he waited. His night vision was still wonky and his head was ringing, but he could have sworn he heard metal being wrenched apart. "Max, I need it *now!*"

It took Gunny another three seconds, a tiny slice of time that felt like eternity, and then he read it off. Hicks punched it in and got a red light—he'd mistyped. "Say again!" he yelled as the sputtering field of green that was the entrance bay of the *Paradox* shimmered with movement. "Again!"

Maxwell repeated himself, slowing just enough for Hicks to punch in the code correctly this time. Hicks had the sensation of something coiled and black *rolling* toward him, then the heavy exterior hatch closed. There was a muffled *boom* as whatever was on the other side hit it, then hit it again. But this was the exterior door, designed to withstand human warfare and the vacuum of space.

It held.

Lethal non-human organic life form of indeterminate origin and physical description.

That was what GySgt Maxwell put on all the reports, in spaces with labels like CAUSE OF LOSS OF LIFE and REASON FOR FAILURE TO RECLAIM ASSIGNED RESOURCES and JUSTIFICATION FOR ABORTING MISSION. There was no collaborating their stories because he and Maxwell told the God's honest truth about what happened, and the video feed files from Hicks and the eleven other dead crew members supported their statements. Once the battle began the vids were flush with screams and pulse rifle shots, but they were lousy with visual details—flashes of light, rolling shadows, the impression of something huge and fast and dark but that couldn't be pinpointed. There had been an uneasy question and answer session when Hicks had been facing officers so far above his pay grade that any one of them could've pointed a finger and ended his career. But again, he had just told the truth.

"Cpl Hicks, why didn't you tell a superior officer that your wife had been on the Paradox?"

"Because I wanted to try and find out what happened to her, sir."

"And did you?"

"Yes, sir. She was killed by—"

Again, that eleven-word narrative.

"—a lethal non-human organic life form of indeterminate origin and physical description."

In the end, the matter had gone all the way up the Chain of Command to their Lieutenant Colonel before being closed out. The status of his wife and the rest of the Paradox's crew were changed to KILLED IN ACTION, and GySgt Maxwell deployed somewhere else. Hicks returned to his usual squad to find his NCO furious that Hicks had gotten the orders to be on the squad that reclaimed the Paradox to begin with. Since the NCO was an E-6 who was perpetually pissed off at the world, life was normal.

Finally Hicks had put an end to the mystery that had been his wife's disappearance.

But he didn't have closure. Far from it.

Sometimes at night, he would sit at his computer and re-watch the video messages that Rachel had sent him, her wedding ring rolling between his thumb and forefinger. Those were the nights Hicks would cycle from her first message to the last. That one he studied, his blue eyes narrowed and sharp, over and over, even as he replayed his own experience inside the ship that had become her coffin.

Those were the nights that Cpl Dwayne Hicks, his expression outwardly calm, would look from the screen to Rachel's wedding ring in his hand.

Those were the nights that he would fold his fist around it, squeezing so hard that the edges cut into his flesh and his palm bled onto the gold metal.

It was still out there. Someday, somehow, he would get the chance to find and kill the creature that had murdered his wife.

BLOWBACK

BY CHRISTOPHER GOLDEN

Dietrich had never puked on a dropship before, and she hoped today wouldn't change that. She held onto the safety bar across her chest and tried to take even breaths, but the fact they were in freefall through the thick friction atmosphere of an alien moon didn't help. The dropship shuddered so hard it felt like it might break apart, so hard her bones seemed to crash together.

She glanced over at Private Malinka, saw the girl's ashen pallor, and figured it might be a race to see who could vomit first. At least Jette Malinka would have an excuse. The girl was nineteen years old and this was her first drop outside of a simulator. Dietrich's only excuse would be too much whiskey the night before.

Way too much whiskey.

She kept her jaw tight, breathed through her nose and tried

to look straight ahead without focusing on the person sitting straight across from her—Corporal Tim Stenbeck. Dietrich didn't want to look at Stenbeck because then she'd remember the taste of whiskey on his lips and the guilt that had burned through her when she had woken up this morning in his bunk. She and Stenbeck had been involved for a while. You couldn't call it dating. They'd eaten and drunk and slept together for a few months, but that had ended nearly seven weeks ago.

With the exception of last night. It had been a blip on the radar, a foolish mistake, and she still felt the burn on her face from his stubble. It was a strangely pleasant sensation, which only made her feel worse. She had been the one to end it, bored with him and worried that he had started thinking long term, thinking he might be in love.

It hadn't been fair to him, what had happened last night. She was afraid it might give him ideas.

But then, he had been the one to bring the bottle of whiskey to her door. All she'd done was let him in.

Dietrich breathed through her nose. Rode the dropship down, waiting for the moment when gravity would reassert, when Khan would take over the controls from the pilot seat, and then would try to land this crate on a rocky plateau in an inhospitable atmosphere on a planet that had already killed most of two research teams.

The Colonial Marines weren't here for research. They were here to make sure the third team of scientists Weyland-Yutani planned to send might have time to build themselves a compound before the local fauna—whatever the hell these aliens might be—could turn them into chum.

Mind wandering, Dietrich scanned the faces of her squad. Spunkmeyer, Hicks, Hudson, Vasquez, Frost, Malinka, Wierzbowski, Crowe, Zeller, Sergeant Apone, and their mission C.O., Lieutenant Emma Paulson. All good Marines, and that included the one face she had refused to see. Stenbeck.

Now she let herself see his face, unsurprised to find him

watching her. Stenbeck gave her a nod as if to assure her all was well, that he was a big boy and knew where things stood between them. She still felt a little guilty, but maybe she didn't need to. After all, they'd both had a hell of a night.

Dietrich gave him a nod. The dropship jerked upward as Khan took the controls. Bile surged up the back of her throat but she fought it back down, counted to ten, and then exhaled. The dropship kept moving through the atmospheric soup, but now she could hear the rasp of the dusty air scraping the hull as they flew, and she knew it was almost over.

"Goddamn, what a ride!" Hudson yelled. "Let's do it again!"

Many of them laughed. Hicks patted Malinka on the knee, but the girl's ashen pallor had improved already.

"Hell with that," Vasquez said. "I'm already bored with this op. Can we just go out and kill whatever we're supposed to kill, get this bug hunt over with?"

"Belay that shit, Vasquez," Sergeant Apone growled. "We're gonna set a good example for our greenie today. Private Malinka needs to see how this unit operates so she can learn how you've all survived together this long. Which means you and Hudson and Wierzbowski and Stenbeck are on notice right now, before we even hit the surface. We do this quick and by the book. Is that clear?"

"I hear your voice in my sleep, Sarge," Vasquez said, glancing around at the rest of the unit. Only Hicks didn't smile. Always focused on the fight to come, that guy.

"What's that?" Apone barked.

"I said, 'Yes, sir, Sergeant, sir!'"

"Damn right you did," Apone said.

Vasquez and Dietrich exchanged a knowing look. Half the time, Vasquez only said the things she did in order to get a rise out of Sergeant Apone. The man wasn't much older than Dietrich herself, but he had a grizzled air about him—partly due to the bushy black mustache he always seemed to be smoothing down—that made him seem like everybody's disapproving father. Dietrich knew from late-night conversation that Vasquez didn't have a high opinion of fathers and couldn't resist pushing Apone's buttons.

It was odd to hear Apone lumping Stenbeck and Hudson into the same list of troublemakers. They had been friends once—best of—but that had been before Stenbeck and Dietrich had hooked up. After that, there'd been a chill between them, sometimes turning into open aggression. Dietrich had never understood it, but she had to admit to herself that it was part of the reason she had broken things off with Stenbeck. Her own friendship with Hudson had broken down because of the way the two guys had been at each other's throats, and she hated having that tension in the unit.

Since she'd stopped sleeping with Stenbeck, things had mostly gotten back to normal, though some of the uneasy tension remained between the two men. She wondered if Hudson had heard them together last night, wondered what the hell his problem was to begin with.

"Think you could fill us in now, Lieutenant?" Hicks asked, turning toward Paulson. "I know this op is need-to-know, but we're practically on the ground."

Lieutenant Paulson frowned, the expression tugging at the thin white scar that cut across her mouth. She ran the palm of her right hand over her shaved scalp and then glanced up toward the pilot's seat.

"How long till touchdown, Corporal Khan?" she asked.

Khan glanced at an instrument panel, hands on the stick. "Touchdown in three minutes or less."

The lieutenant nodded slowly, contemplating, and then turned to look at Hicks. Dietrich read irritation on Apone's face, and wondered how much the Sarge had been told about their mission. Wondered if that irritation came from what he knew, or what he didn't know.

"We're about to land on Clytemnestra, a moon orbiting Thestias, in the Pollux system," Lieutenant Paulson said, ice blue eyes sharp and bright in the otherwise gray cabin of the dropship. "The rest of what I'm about to say is classified. You're not to repeat it to anyone. If you do, you'll be charged with—"

"Corporate espionage," Dietrich said. "We know. Maybe Malinka doesn't know—"

"I know," the young private replied, the tight, short curls on her head trembling as she turned to look at Dietrich. "Sometimes we're military. Sometimes we're a private task force. That's what happens when the armed forces have a corporate sponsor, but I know what I signed up for, Cynthia."

Dietrich flinched. Held up a hand to forestall the girl's hostility. "Back off, kid. I'm just looking out for you."

Malinka nodded. "Thanks for that," she said, brushing Dietrich off.

"Put a leash on it, both of you," Apone ordered. "Private Malinka, I'm glad you know what your role is and very happy you don't feel like you need babysitting, 'cause you're not gonna get any from this group."

"I can hold up my end," Malinka said curtly.

"See you do," Apone replied.

Stenbeck laughed and elbowed Spunkmeyer. "Looks like Vasquez isn't the only rabid dog on this squad now."

"That's enough," Lieutenant Paulson said.

Vasquez murdered Stenbeck with a glance. "This bitch'll bite your damn balls off."

"In one bite, you can bet your ass," Hudson said appreciatively. "Asshole."

"Enough!" Apone shouted. "You all want to know what you might be dying for today, or not?"

That quieted them down.

"All right," Paulson said. "Back to Clytemnestra. The company's exploration drones found an element on this moon that will revolutionize interstellar travel. They've been working for decades on better engines, better fuel. Eleven years ago, they theorized that a combination of two elements—let's forget the chemistry and just call them salt and pepper—"

"You don't think we could understand the chemistry?" Frost asked, wounded.

Sergeant Apone smoothed his mustache. "Shut it, Frost. She *knows* you can't."

Paulson held up a hand to silence the laughter that followed, and forged onward. "The problem is that every time the researchers tried to combine salt and pepper, they blew up their lab. What they needed was some third element that would stabilize that mixture. From the reports I've read, they tried over two thousand combinations before they gave up a few years ago.

"But eleven months ago, Weyland-Yutani drones found a gas in the atmosphere of this moon that they are certain will render those combustible elements inert. If they're right, they think they'll have a fuel that will allow spacecraft to be reengineered, to travel many times faster than they ever have. Before, the amalgam of those elements would have just exploded, killing everyone on board. But now, if they can draw it from the atmosphere of Clytemnestra… well, you can imagine."

Hicks cleared his throat. "Thanks, Lieutenant. I think we've got the rest."

"The usual," Hudson agreed. "Put our asses in the shredder."

"Don't be such a pussy, Hudson," Vasquez said. "You gotta think long term, *hermano*. They put two science teams down on this damn plateau and bugs killed 'em all. So they call the exterminators—that's us. Killing bugs is just good exercise, man."

"And what do we get out of it?" Wierzbowski muttered.

Sergeant Apone glared at him. "For starters, you don't get court-martialed."

Dietrich breathed. Her nausea had all but vanished.

"I'll tell you what you get, Wierzbowski," she said. "Less time drifting around deep space, waiting for some action."

Even Hicks smiled at that.

"What do we know about these bugs?" Malinka asked.

The Colonial Marines tended to call any non-humanoid alien species *bugs*, but she'd have liked a little more to go on before encountering this batch for the first time.

"Not a hell of a lot," Apone grumbled. "What I can tell you is that you're gonna need exo-suits in this atmosphere."

"Shit," Hudson whined. "I hate those damn things. It's like trying to fight covered in wet wool."

"They'll slow you down a little," Lieutenant Paulson admitted. She glanced meaningfully around at the gathered Marines. "But they'll also be the only thing keeping you alive."

"Nah, Lieutenant," Vasquez said, smiling grimly. "It's my guns that'll keep me alive."

Half a dozen Colonial Marines cheered, and this time, the officers didn't try to quiet them down. Dietrich saw Apone shoot Paulson a worried look, and for a moment, her stomach felt a little queasy again. She didn't like that look. Not in the least.

"Honey!" Khan called from the pilot's seat. "We're home!"

The dropship touched down hard, skidded a few feet in Clytemnestra's high winds, and then came to a halt. Dietrich had bitten her lip and the copper tang of her own blood flooded her mouth.

Great, she thought. *Not even out of the ship and already wounded.*

It should've been funny, but she couldn't find the humor in it.

⸻

"I've got movement," Zeller said, holding the motion tracker out in front of him as if it were some kind of shield.

Dietrich swept the barrel of her pulse rifle from side to side, but the dust and grit of Clytemnestra's atmosphere scoured the goggles of her exo-suit, making it hard to see. She'd been caught outside in a blizzard once and the effect had been similar. A gust blasted her from behind and she staggered, cursing this damned moon, where the air couldn't seem to make up its mind. The wind shifted direction by the second. That might have had something to do with their position on a mountain plateau. Ridges of stone climbed thirty feet higher to the north and west, so it felt almost as if they were inside a broken bowl.

"I see nothing," Wierzbowski snapped, sweeping with his own motion sensor. "Not a blip on this thing."

The unit spread in a circle, all turned outward, the whole group moving together. Dietrich scuttled sideways to keep her back to the unit, wind tugging at her pulse rifle.

"I've got multiples now!" Zeller barked. "Northwest, coming our way."

"Up high?" Sergeant Apone shouted. "You saying these things are flying?"

Dietrich saw it then, slicing through the air. Just a glimpse of it, thin and wraith-like, body open to catch the wind as it glided toward her. She muttered a stream of profanity into her comm unit and pulled the trigger, firing a plasma burst that lit up the dust storm like lightning high up in a thunderstorm. The thing banked left, somehow made itself smaller, and then plummeted toward the ground, headed for her face.

She dropped, rolled right, came up onto one knee with her weapon aimed at the spot where the thing had alighted. It stood six feet away and for a few heartbeats they were eye to eye, Dietrich and this creature unlike any she'd ever seen. Despite what she'd seen overhead, the bug stood tall and thin, its limbs like razors. Its body seemed smooth and black, glassy as volcanic rock. She counted two sets of eyes, both covered by a gossamer membrane which seemed to screen out the dust and grit of the atmosphere.

Gunfire punched the air around her. Zeller shouted about incoming bugs. Wierzbowski kept insisting he didn't see anything on his sensor.

As Dietrich pulled the trigger, the wind roared across the plateau and nudged her to the left, throwing off her aim. Plasma bursts tore up the rocky ground near the bug and it shot her a look that might have been nothing more than curiosity. Then it opened like a flag unfurling. The wind took it, blew it backward and upward and it angled its body so that it was soaring high out of range in the space between one breath and another.

"Holy shit," Dietrich whispered into her comms.

"Cynthia," a voice said, and she snapped her head around, distracted by the use of her first name. Stenbeck, of course. Even behind the goggles and inside that exo-suit, she saw the way he looked at her.

"I'm fine," she said.

"You can't hesitate like that," he warned. "Coulda gotten yourself—"

Hudson backed toward them, firing off into the darkness, the bursting plasma rounds interrupting them. "Can you two hump each other later?" he said. "Like, after we kill all these damn locusts, or whatever they are?"

More shouting. More weapons fire. More shapes knifing through the atmo-storm. Wierzbowski complained again about his sensor until Spunkmeyer finally slapped it out of his hand.

"It's broken, idiot! Use your goddamn eyes instead!"

Laughter all around.

"Shit, 'Bowski, you know you must be stupid when Spunkmeyer's got to explain stuff to you," Vasquez said.

Their gunfire had driven the bugs away for the moment. The unit regrouped around Lieutenant Paulson and Sergeant Apone.

"Fix that scanner, Hicks," Apone ordered.

They all heard it through comms, and Dietrich watched Hicks march over and pick up the faulty sensor. How he was supposed to get it working out here with no tools, and unable to take off his exo-suit, she had no idea, but he started by just banging the thing against his thigh a couple of times. Hicks let his plasma rifle hang by its strap, smacked the sensor against the palm of his hand, then pressed a button on the thing's underside while the rest of the unit watched the plateau for more bugs.

Dietrich heard Hicks sigh over comms. Even in the shifting gray dust of the atmo-storm, she saw the sensor light up. Hicks turned to hand it back to Wierzbowski, just as Zeller started shouting again. The sensor in Hicks's hand lit up red.

"Incoming!" Zeller shouted.

Dietrich and Hudson backed up, side by side, and she heard him swear as he tripped and fell. Shapes sailed overhead and she stitched the storm with plasma fire, forcing the bugs to break off. She dropped to one knee to help Hudson, who scrambled to get up in spite of the awkward weight of the exo-suit.

"You all right?"

Hudson gave a sick sort of laugh. "I'm better than these assholes."

Confused, she took her eyes off the sky and turned to see what the hell he was talking about. They had known the two small research teams sent here by the company had died, so it shouldn't have come as a shock to her, but when she saw the withered corpses, the bare, grit-scoured bones, the dried skin stretched tight across a face beneath the headpiece of a shattered exo-suit, she froze.

This is no way to die, Dietrich thought.

"Get up!" Stenbeck shouted. "Incoming, damn it, get on your feet!"

Dietrich and Hudson rose in the same moment, both of them staring as Stenbeck raced toward them. He lifted his plasma rifle and fired above them, but Dietrich's focus stayed on the pair of bugs slicing through the dust storm, gliding down behind Stenbeck. By the time she raised her plasma rifle, they were too low for her to take the shot without hitting Stenbeck.

"Down!" Hudson said, taking aim. "Stenny, hit the dirt!"

Even from thirty feet away, through the dust, through the goggles of his exo-suit, Stenbeck's moment of epiphany showed in his eyes. He dove to the rocky ground, rolled, propped himself onto his elbows too late. The things were almost on him. Dietrich and Hudson started to fire.

A figure came out of nowhere, emerging from the dust to the east. Tall and thin, wrapped in an exo-suit, weapon at the ready. Only when she started shouting and cursing did Dietrich recognize Private Malinka's voice. On the range, Malinka had no peer. Nineteen years old, but she could shoot the whiskers off a cat from a hundred yards. But Malinka had never seen real combat before today.

The girl's first two shots missed. Stenbeck had fallen on his own weapon and struggled to bring it round, even as the first of the bugs landed on him. One of its wings sliced the exo-suit open like it was made of cobweb.

Dietrich opened fire again, shouting Stenbeck's name. She got one syllable into it when Malinka's third shot hit one of the bugs.

The creature exploded in a roiling ball of flame that hit the second one—the one on Stenbeck—and then that bug exploded as well. The blast blew Malinka off her feet and she tumbled into the rising dust and smoke, lost from view in the storm. For a few seconds Dietrich could only blink and stare at blossoming clouds of fire as the wind carried them away, painting the darkness red and orange and blue.

"Aw, man, what the hell was that?" Hudson whined. "Stenny, man. Stenny!"

Hudson started toward the burning air, barely seeming to notice the way gusts would ignite above them, a chain reaction that seemed to threaten the possibility of the whole sky lighting on fire.

Dietrich grabbed Hudson. "Get your shit together. Nothing you can do for him now. Don't you have eyes?"

Hudson stared at her, goggle to goggle. She had denied it to herself, but in her heart she knew what had ended his friendship with Stenbeck, knew that Hudson wanted her for himself even if he'd never say it. Stenbeck had known it, too, and it had complicated things. The friendship between the two men had been half the reason she had ended it with Stenbeck.

They needed each other more than she needed the familiar comfort of Stenbeck in her bed. For her sake, she was glad she'd had too much to drink and hooked up with Stenbeck last night, one last memory. For Hudson's sake, she wished none of it had ever happened.

Now she had to watch Hudson swivel his head around to stare at the slowly extinguishing fireball, and the charred, blackened bones it illuminated, all that remained of Stenbeck.

"Aw, man," Hudson said. "This is bullshit."

Thunder crashed across the sky. They turned to see a fresh fireball streaming toward the ground. Pieces of the bug whipped past them, hitting the dirt like shrapnel. Dietrich glanced around, saw nobody, and knew the only way home was to kill their way out.

"Do your job, Hudson," she said. "Light 'em up!"

He snapped his head up, then nodded. Killing bugs was just about the only thing he'd ever been really good at. Back they moved toward the center of the plateau. Bugs whipped overhead like flags unfurling. Dietrich took one out with a burst from her plasma rifle, staggered by the blast as it exploded. Hudson shot two.

"Damn it, Lieutenant," Hicks growled on the commlink. "What the hell are these things?"

Before Paulson could reply, a chorus of voices filled Dietrich's head. Above them all, she could hear Zeller and Wierzbowski shouting about the next wave of attacks coming from the cliffs to the northwest. Even as she and Hudson turned in that direction, a gust of wind cleared some of the dust off the plateau and Dietrich spotted the rest of the unit closing ranks. Malinka limped as she hurried to join them, injured but alive.

"Hand to hand," Lieutenant Paulson barked. "If they come in close, you can't shoot 'em. You have to take 'em hand to hand!"

Ice slid through Dietrich's veins. She thought of the bodies of those scientists, withered skin tight against their skulls. What the hell was Paulson playing at, thinking they could kill all of these things with just the combat knives sheathed at their hips? She drew her blade but confusion hissed at the back of her brain. They didn't even know how many of the bugs there were. Trying to kill them hand to hand was suicide, but she saw Frost drawing his own knife and realized it was the two of them, now. The others would keep firing, but if the aliens got too close it would be up to her and Frost to protect them.

This is it, then, she thought. Dietrich only hoped they wouldn't leave her corpse behind on Clytemnestra, that she wouldn't end up a lonely ghost, wandering this rock forever. She glanced at Stenbeck's charred remains and prayed his spirit had gone elsewhere, that if any of them had souls, they would end up in a better place than this.

Gunfire tore through the dust again. A rising crescendo of plasma rifle fire traced its way through the darkness in all directions. Crowe and Spunkmeyer had begun to roar and now Vasquez and Hudson and Wierzbowski joined in. Zeller and Malinka, too. The black kites sliced through the storm, descending. Lieutenant Paulson waited, following them with her weapon, and when she opened fire one of the bugs exploded in a fireball that struck another, and another, destroying four of the deadly kites and turning them into a chain reaction conflagration that swept into the whirl of the storm until the whole sky became a churning tornado of grit and debris and blazing embers.

To Dietrich, it looked like they were in Hell.

The gunfire continued. Each new kill fueled the inferno overhead and she felt its heat baking her inside her exo-suit. She glanced southward, tracking movement in her peripheral vision, and saw a kite slicing low over the ground, headed right for Malinka and Zeller.

She acted without processing the risk. Instinct and training kicking in, she ran half a dozen steps in her bulky exo-suit, and put herself between the bug and her people. It kept low to the ground until it was within a couple of yards, then it cut upward, right for her face.

Dietrich twisted sideways, shot a kick at the center of the thing's mass. Its unfurled body began to collapse and she saw in that moment what was about to happen—the way its razor-thin wings would tear right through her suit. She drew her leg back, spun away, sliced the knife down at the back of its wing as its momentum carried it past her. The blade scratched that black glass wing, but did not cut.

She froze. Blades wouldn't work.

"Lieutenant!" she shouted, turning to scan for Paulson, ready to run to her. They had to retreat, had to get off this godforsaken rock.

She didn't see the bug come sailing along the southern edge of the plateau until Zeller started shouting that it was too close, that someone had to kill it. Dietrich turned. Zeller was right—if he'd shot it, the explosion would have torched him and Malinka both. Even knowing the blade would do nothing, Dietrich started toward them, wouldn't leave them to die.

Zeller managed to get his blade out. He fought the thing, stabbing at it, even punctured one of the thing's shielded eyes, but its wings kept slicing at him, tearing his suit to ribbons, and in seconds Zeller was on his knees.

"I can't…" he said on the commlink, for all of them to hear. "My eyes… I think my eyes are bleeding."

Dietrich halted her approach. Even if the bug didn't kill Zeller, the atmosphere had already poisoned him. He'd be choking on his own blood, his skin bubbling with pustules.

The gunfire continued. Other voices shouted on comms. Bugs exploded in the air along the outer rim of the plateau. The brighter the burning air, the easier it was to spot them, to kill them before they came closer.

Malinka backed away from Zeller's weakening struggle against the thing that had killed him. They were wrapped together, the Marine and the black glass kite. When Malinka reached her, Dietrich saw the shock in the girl's eyes and knew that no matter how tough she had been in training, she understood combat now. Understood horror. Understood what it meant to be a Colonial Marine.

Dietrich sheathed her knife, raised her plasma rifle, and fired three rounds into the thing that was killing Zeller. The explosion incinerated Zeller on the spot and knocked Dietrich and Malinka off their feet. They hit the ground, rolling on the super-heated rocky soil.

Blinking, Dietrich realized she'd been out for a few seconds. She looked up to see Malinka above her, shouting at her to get up. Then Hudson and Vasquez were there, cursing at her. When she reached out to Hudson, she saw the fear in his eyes. Fear for her. But it was Vasquez who grabbed her hand, hauled her off the ground, gave her a shove to get her running.

Lieutenant Paulson had ordered a retreat. Dietrich could hear Apone's familiar growl over the comms, urging them onward. She had lost track of her position, so she could only rely on the others as they hustled back to the dropship, their withdrawal punctuated by a dozen more explosions that heated the air so much the air inside her suit burned to breathe.

Then they were at the dropship. Khan had lowered the ramp and Dietrich stumbled a bit going up. She dropped to the floor inside, surrounded by the others, and as the ramp began to close and she stared out at the burning storm, she wondered about the ghosts of Stenbeck and Zeller. The dropship's external guns shot a couple of the kites to keep them away from the closing ramp, and then it was over.

Over.

She remembered Stenbeck's hands on her skin last night, the taste of whiskey on his lips, and the way she'd broken his heart. The morning's nausea returned, but she held it together.

"Anyone wanna explain that?" Vasquez snapped, stripping out of her exo-suit. "How the hell do those things just explode? The whole sky went up in flames!"

The pilot, Khan, craned his neck around to look back at them all as they tore out of their suits and stowed their weapons, checking themselves and each other for injuries.

"Just proved the company's science team right," Khan said. "Species is carbon-based, like most known life forms, but the solvent for all life from Earth is water. For these aliens, it's propane."

Dietrich lay on her back, still in her exo-suit, trying to find the will to get up.

Hudson laughed. "Oh, that's beautiful. They knew the things were gonna go boom if we shot 'em and they sent us out there anyway?"

"They knew there was a chance," the pilot admitted.

"Khan, get us off this fucking rock," Apone grumbled as he slumped onto the starboard bench, already starting to strap himself in.

"Sorry, Sarge. Can't do that."

Dietrich had been catching her breath, knowing she'd have to get up in a few seconds to strap herself in for dust-off. Now she rolled over and sat on her knees, glaring toward the front of the ship. Around her, the rest of the unit had stopped their bitching, stopped stowing their weapons, stopped grieving for the ones they'd left behind.

"What the hell are you talking about, *Corporal*?" Apone snapped, emphasizing Khan's rank, reminding the pilot of the chain of command.

But Khan wasn't looking at Apone. His gaze locked onto Lieutenant Paulson instead. They all turned to stare at her.

"You want to explain this, Lieutenant?" Apone asked.

Dietrich listened to the thump and scuff of kites attacking the hull, but her eyes were on Paulson, on the way the woman seemed to deflate with regret.

"Corporal Khan," Paulson said, "I assume by your reaction that you've gotten readings from the dropship's external instruments? You've located the source of the stabilizing element?"

If you'd taken a poll of the unit, pretty much everyone would have voted for Hicks as the most even-keeled of the lot.

But it wasn't Spunkmeyer or Wierzbowski or even Vasquez who smashed a hand against the hull and glowered at the lieutenant.

"What the hell is this?" Hicks snapped. "Not only did you have intel about the bugs that could've saved Stenbeck and Zeller, but now you're saying you and Khan have been keeping this other shit from us, too?"

Lieutenant Paulson squared up to him. "You're going to want to stand down, Corporal Hicks."

Dietrich forced herself to stand, reached out for Hicks's shoulder. Said his name. He shook her off, kept glaring.

Apone stepped between Hicks and Paulson. "*Stand down*, Corporal," the Sarge said, but then he turned to face the lieutenant. "Maybe you want to explain yourself? If there were mission parameters you couldn't share before, I'd like to hear them now."

Lieutenant Paulson at least had the decency to look uncomfortable. She nodded slowly, glanced at Khan, and then backed off, obviously aware of the animosity growing against her.

"We had an additional set of orders," Paulson said. "You all know how this works. Every mission has multiple objectives. Objective one was to clear the plateau and pave the way for the next science team to drop a temporary base there. Objective two was to see if the instruments could scan and locate the source of the stabilizing element. Based on information transmitted back by the last group who died here, the company had some theories—"

"That's what I started to say, Lieutenant," Khan interrupted. "They're not theories anymore."

Dietrich simmered with anger. Rage helped to make her forget her grief, at least for a minute. She stared at Khan and Paulson, silently blaming them for the deaths of Stenbeck and Zeller, knowing it wasn't really their fault. The company was to blame. Weyland-fucking-Yutani.

She could feel what was coming. Not the detail their pilot was about to reveal, but what it would mean for all of them. What it would cost them.

"Spill it already," she said.

Khan glanced at Paulson. The lieutenant nodded, giving silent permission for him to speak. Khan scanned the back of the dropship, taking in the rest of the unit with a glance.

"The element the company's looking for," Khan said. "The bugs produce it. Just like we breathe in oxygen and breathe out carbon dioxide, they breathe in whatever the shit in this atmosphere is, and they exhale the gas we're looking for. Without it, the whole sky would ignite."

Dietrich massaged her temple, trying to process that. "So if we killed enough of them—"

"We'd destabilize the atmosphere," Apone finished for her. "Maybe blow up the planet. Shit."

"But now we don't *want* to kill them," Dietrich said, glancing around at the others, at Hicks, Hudson, Malinka, Vasquez and the rest. She saw it dawning on their faces, even as she worked it out.

Dietrich swore under her breath and started checking the seals on her exo-suit. She reached for her helmet.

"I don't get it," Wierzbowski said. "That's why we're here. To kill 'em."

He'd never been very bright.

"Not anymore," Vasquez sneered, glaring at Paulson and Khan as she reached for the exo-suit she'd already removed.

"The job's changed, Wierzbowski," Dietrich said, sharing a worried glance with Hicks. "We're not supposed to kill them anymore. Turns out these things are the goddamn prize we came looking for. Now the job is to catch one."

The sick expression on Wierzbowski's face reflected the twist in the pit of her stomach. In silence, the rest of the unit exchanged scowls and then began dragging their exo-suits back on, reaching for their weapons. Malinka grinned, visibly excited at the prospect, and that was when Dietrich knew she wanted to stay far away from the girl. That excitement would make her reckless.

The scraping on the hull continued. The bugs were out there waiting, almost as if they knew the dropship wasn't going anywhere.

"All right, Marines," Sergeant Apone growled as he walked toward the rear of the ship, waiting for Khan to lower the ramp. "Let's get it done. Watch each other's backs and try not to die."

Vasquez and Hudson high-fived each other, even in the exo-suits, trying to amp themselves up. As Khan hit the controls and the light started to flash, indicating that the ramp was opening, they all gripped their weapons tighter and watched the gap for those thin fingers, those sharp black glass edges. Air vented out of the ship and the whole unit started forward.

Try not to die, Apone had said.

Dietrich intended to try her best.

EXTERMINATORS

BY MATT FORBECK

Corporal Cynthia Dietrich and Private First Class Ricco Frost stumbled into the Last Chance like drunken rhinos, shaking off the hot rain as if they'd just emerged from a boiling river. Almost every other head in the main room of the backwater saloon—all four of them—spun to glare at the two Marines with undisguised disgust. The grizzled bartender, who looked like he might have come with the ancient pre-fab place when it was new, was the only exception.

"Fuck," Frost said as he wiped off his face. "It's hotter than hell out there."

"What'll it be, ladies?" the bartender said, splaying both hands on the rough surface of the chipboard bar before him.

Frost squinted at the man, trying to make out his face in the darkened place, lit only by flickering ad signs for liquor and beer and a guttering gas lamp. After a moment, he decided who the barkeep was didn't matter. He didn't know him. Hell, he and Dietrich didn't know anyone on this entire soaking-wet ball of shit.

"Tequila," Dietrich barked out with a grin. "All of it!"

The pair held onto each other for support as they made their way to the bar and planted themselves on top of a couple of rickety stools. The bartender produced a couple plastic shot glasses and filled them with a clear liquid from a label-less bottle.

Frost wrinkled his nose at it. He couldn't say if it was tequila or not, but at this point, he didn't think it mattered much. Whatever its name, it was potent enough to do the trick.

He plucked up one of the giant plastic thimbles, and Dietrich did the same. They tapped their shot glasses together and then slammed back the contents in one go. Both Marines howled as the liquor burned its way down their throats, then collapsed against each other, laughing. They slapped their empty shot glasses down on the bar, still chuckling.

Frost finally glanced about to see who they were sharing the bar with, and he saw only grim faces staring back at them. He tapped Dietrich on the shoulder and gestured toward the others with his chin.

"Well, what the hell's wrong with you people?" Dietrich said, still smiling.

"You two oughta get the hell out of here," a black man with graying hair and beard said with a snarl.

"What?" Frost said, determined not to let the man bring him or Dietrich down. "But we just got here! We've been trapped on a slow transport from the outer rim for the past six months, and we have a shitload of accumulated steam to blow off!"

"Let 'em be, Jesse," a fat, bald white man cradling his hand in his lap and sitting next to the black man said. "It's already too late."

"You don't know that, Tim," the black man said. "They're

young. Fit. Soldiers. They start running right now, they might still have a chance."

Frost glanced at Dietrich. Neither one of them liked how these men were talking. They'd run into some real jackasses in bars before, but they hadn't been expecting any trouble here. Sullivan 9 was a remote refueling station with damn little to offer anyone but a steady supply of fuel—oxygen, hydrogen, even propane and wood—and a drink or three to warm visitors on their way.

And they hadn't even been able to find that in the main building where they'd left the rest of their platoon. They'd had to bribe one of the station attendants for the directions to this place so they could slip away to it. She hadn't wanted to give it up to them, but Dietrich was a heavy tipper.

"Long as there's still drink here, we're not going anywhere," Dietrich said, her voice loud enough to make sure everyone in the room heard it.

"Or until the captain comes looking for us," Frost said with a chortle. He looked at the bartender and gave his shot glass a meaningful tap. The bartender filled it up and did the same for Dietrich.

"Come on, Berto," Jesse said. "They don't need to die here with the rest of us."

"Ain't no one dying here today," the bartender said. He left the bottle there in front of them and sneered at Jesse. "Either way, I'm doing my job. You oughta try to do the same."

"Fuck the job," Jesse said. "They don't pay any of us enough for shit like this."

"You want to leave?" Berto said. "There's the door."

Jesse eyed the exit, but instead of making a move for it, he took a slug of his beer and wiped his mouth on his grimy sleeve. "We'd never make it."

"What the hell are you gas-gulpers going on about?" Dietrich said. "You're creeping me out."

Berto hemmed and hawed for a moment. "You shouldn't have come here. It's not safe."

Frost had never been one to let anyone intimidate him, and he wasn't about to let some backwater bartender manage it now. He slapped his hand on the table to get the man's attention, gave him his best "you'd better not be threatening me" glare, and spat one word at him. "Why?"

Berto couldn't meet Frost's eyes. He just grimaced at Tim and Jesse and said, "Show them."

The two men pushed their chairs to the side and stood up. At the far side of the table behind them sat another man, face down. He had been so quiet the entire time that Frost had assumed he was just a passed-out drunk as the Marine soon hoped to be.

Tim reached over and grabbed the man's cap by its bill and pushed his limp form back into a sitting position. The man's head lolled back, and his button-down shirt fell open, revealing what looked like an armored jacket underneath.

Dietrich stared at the man while Frost coughed a harsh laugh at Berto. "You trying to tell us this piss you've been slinging at us isn't safe to drink?"

The bartender shook his head. "Take a good look at him. He ain't drunk."

"Holy shit," Dietrich whispered. "What the fuck happened to him?"

Frost had rarely heard Dietrich sound so serious, and it stopped him cold in the middle of concocting a snarky retort for Berto. He got up from his stool instead and took a few cautious steps toward the quiet man.

He was an Asian man with wide, reddish cheeks and streaks of gray slicing through his shock of hair. His face had fallen slack, and a layer of sweat covered his skin. His eyes sat open, but the irises had rolled back up into his head.

"Is he dead?"

Jesse shook his head. "Not yet anyway."

Frost crept closer. There was something odd about the armor the man wore on his chest. He'd never seen anything like it before. It looked hard, chitinous even, but it didn't cover his entire chest, just the front of his undershirt.

He didn't see how the thin straps coming out on six sides of the armor could keep it attached to the man's chest. They didn't go all that far.

Then he gasped. The armor didn't have straps. It had legs.

Frost stepped back toward the bar and tapped his empty shot glass. Berto filled it all the way to the rim and did the same for Dietrich too.

Frost slammed back his shot, and Berto refilled it without being asked. "What is that thing?" Frost asked.

Tim shook his head. "We don't know. Park here staggered outside after having his regular nightcap and just started screaming. We came out to help him, and we found him like this."

"What the fuck?" Dietrich said. "Why'd you bring him back here then instead of to the main station. They got an infirmary there, right?"

Tim pointed at the thing on Park's chest. "There were more of these things out there in the dark. Don't know how many, but enough we didn't want to try to carry him through it."

Frost groaned. "And you couldn't just have called for help?"

Berto snorted. "This look like a legal place to you? You think we got comm lines installed?"

Jesse shook his head with regret. "Shocks me every day that Weyland-Yutani hasn't shut us down yet."

"Well, you can't just leave him like that," Dietrich said. "Get it off him!"

Tim held up the hand he'd been favoring. The fingers on it were as red as if the skin had started to melt off them. "Tried that," he said. "Didn't go so well."

Frost could now recognize the strain in the bartender's voice. It hadn't been from having intruders in his place but from the agonizing pain he'd been trying to hide.

"I tried to pull it off with my bare hands, and it set Park screeching like a gutted monkey. Figured that meant I was doing something right, so I dug my fingers in around that thing's edge and pulled."

"It used some kind of acid to glue itself to Park's chest," Jesse said. "Shit spurt out with a gout of Park's blood and did that to Tim's hand."

"And you didn't go run for help?" Dietrich said, agog. "Are you fucking insane?"

Tim slumped back down in his chair. "We didn't get ten meters before those things cut us off."

"We ran right back here. That was three hours ago. We've been trying to figure out what to do ever since."

"And then we walked in," Frost said with a low groan.

"And now you're stuck here with us," Jesse said.

"I didn't see anything out there while we were running through the rain," Dietrich said. "Maybe those things are gone now."

Frost strode toward the door and hauled it open on its squeaky hinges. The rain still pounded down out of the night sky, warm as blood. He squinted into the blackness, unable to see much but the lights of the refueling station in the distance. Their ship sat somewhere beyond it, entirely out of sight.

It wasn't that long of a walk to the station, he knew, but it seemed light-years away. The captain, Frost suspected, wouldn't come looking for them until morning. Hell, up until now, he'd been relying on it.

"I got a bad feeling about this."

"You always say that." Dietrich pushed past his shoulder. "See anything?"

Frost shook his head. The light that hung over the bar's door only illuminated the ground beneath it and the massive propane tank out front that powered the bar. The rest of the area stood shrouded in soaking wet darkness.

Lightning flashed, and Frost spotted something rustling along the open, rocky landscape, just out of range of the bar's outside light. At first, he thought it might be leaves, something like giant palm fronds, rustling in the wind, but despite the rain, the air remained still.

"There." He pointed it out to Dietrich. "What's that?"

Dietrich leaned forward to peer into the darkness. Thunder rumbled, close. Lightning flashed again, and this time Frost got a better look at them. They weren't leaves. They were large insects. Lots of them, swarming over each other.

Frost pulled a small flashlight out of his pocket and pointed it toward the things he'd seen. Its bright light lanced through the darkness and caught the pile of bugs in its beam. They scattered from the brightness, looking for someplace dark to hide.

Some of them just ran away, while others disappeared into fissures in the ground. In an instant, they were gone.

Dietrich leaped backward, her hand over her mouth to stifle a scream, and Frost slammed shut the door. "They're just bugs," Frost said as he held Dietrich's shoulders to help calm her. "It's no big deal."

"That's what Park thought," Jesse said. "Now look at him."

Frost refused to. He turned to Berto instead. "It's safe in here, right?" he said. "We can just wait them out. Someone will come looking for us eventually."

"Maybe," Tim said. "As long as those things out there don't get them too."

"You got a better plan?"

Frost wished he and Dietrich had brought their weapons with them. It was one thing to sneak out of the ship to go on a bender, though, and something far worse to do it while fully armed. They'd left everything they'd had back in ship.

Tim just stared at the floor. Jesse shrugged at the Marines. "Not like we had anything better to do. That's why we were here in the first place."

"Right." Frost motioned to Berto. "I'd like to buy a round for the house."

The bartender waved Frost off, but he put the bottle of supposed tequila out on the bar anyhow. "Forget it," he said.

"We're past worrying about payment at this point."

"Very kind of you," Dietrich said as she reached for the bottle. While she topped off the two shot glasses on the bar, Berto produced four more, and she filled them too.

Frost picked up two of the shot glasses and brought them over to Jesse and Tim. Despite the fear his hands might start shaking, he didn't spill a single drop.

Berto knocked back one of the remaining shots himself and then gazed at the other.

"Who's that for?" Dietrich said.

Berto nodded toward Park. "He ain't dead yet."

Frost came back to the bar and scooped up the extra shot. He walked it over to the unconscious man and set it on the table in front of him. "I don't think he's in the drinking mood."

"Maybe," Tim said as he picked up the shot. "But you never know until you try."

Using his good hand, Tim waved the shot under Park's nose, letting the pungent odor of the crude alcohol waft up out of the glass at him. "Come on, pal," he said. "You know you want it."

To everyone's surprise, Park's entire body twitched.

Tim leaped back, spilled the shot all over Park. "Shit!" he said. "Son of a bitch."

Park's head moved now, and his eyes rolled forward. He gazed out at the others, struggling to focus on them.

Jesse patted Park on the shoulder. "It's all right, man," he said in an even, steady voice. "We got you back inside."

Park tried to sit up straight, but the shell on his chest stopped him. He looked down at it, confused and unable to comprehend it. He opened his mouth to complain about it, but nothing came out.

"We're stuck in here," Jesse told Park. "We want to get you to a doctor, but I think we're going to have to wait until daybreak."

Park tried to speak again but failed. His face contorted in frustration, and tears welled up in his eyes. Frost wanted to go talk with him, but with the state Park was in, Frost didn't know how the man would react to a stranger approaching him. And if he was honest with himself, the thing on the man's chest terrified him.

Tim stood next to Park and tried to comfort him. "It's gonna be all right," he said.

Frost suspected no one in the room believed him.

Park reached out and squeezed Tim's good hand. The human contact calmed him, and he took a deep breath to steady himself. For a moment, he seemed like he might be all right.

Then Park began to cough.

It started out low at first, as if the man was only clearing his throat. Jesse reached around and patted him on his back.

Soon, though, Park's distress became worse, developing into a hacking cough. It seemed to become more and more painful every time he flinched forward, hunching over the shell of the creature still attached to his chest.

"We need to get him to a doctor," Frost said. "Now."

"You gonna try to move him like this?" Tim said.

"Then we need to go get a doctor," Dietrich said as she stepped toward the door.

Frost followed her. "What about those things out there?"

Dietrich shrugged. "We don't know how fast they are, right? We just run flat-out for the station, and maybe they don't catch us."

"In that downpour?" Berto said. "What if you slip? They'll be on you in a heartbeat!"

Frost decided that didn't matter. If this was their only shot, they had to take it. They couldn't just let Park die.

He threw the door open and put an arm around Dietrich. "Ready?"

Dietrich nodded, and the pair steeled themselves for their mad dash up a rocky path in a hot, thick rain. They'd done things like this before, on planets so far away from there, sometimes with bullets zipping past them. Frost told himself this had to be easier. Safer, even. Right?

Before they could take their first step outside though, Park threw back his head and screamed.

Dietrich spun away from the door, and Frost followed suit, slamming it closed. In the far corner of the bar, Park sat in his chair, his back arched as if someone had stabbed him. Jesse sat on one side of him, Tim on the other, both staring at their friend, helpless.

"What's happening?" Dietrich said, her voice rising in panic.

No one answered. Park stopped screaming and began to buck up and down in his chair as if he was being electrocuted.

"Stop him!" Berto said to Tim and Jesse. "Grab him and stop him before he hurts himself!"

The two men did as ordered, each taking Park by one arm. It was all they could do to keep the man from flinging himself to the floor. After a long moment, Park stopped contorting and slumped back down in his chair.

Park looked to his friends as if he meant to thank them, but instead of words, blood began to pour from his mouth.

"Dear, God," Tim said.

Despite the man's terror, both he and Jesse kept hold of Park. Frost couldn't tell if they intended to or were just so shocked they'd forgotten they had the option of letting go.

Park began to gurgle then, a horrible sound that burbled up through the blood. He leaned over the table, the crimson fluid spilling from his mouth as his stomach heaved harder and harder.

Nothing but the blood came out, at least at first.

The heaves didn't stop though. They kept coming, harder and faster, until Frost was surprised the man's stomach hadn't erupted from his mouth.

Park lurched forward so hard he would have crashed his face into the table if his friends hadn't been holding him back. As he did, something dark and slimy began to pour from his mouth, muffling his agonized gurgling.

Frost took an involuntarily step back. When he saw Dietrich

remained frozen in fright, he reached forward and pulled her to stand at his side.

"Oh, shit," Berto said. "Shit, shit, shit, shit, shit."

Park continued to vomit, heaving forward over and over again. Every time he did, more things spilled from his face, so many that Frost wondered where they could have all possibly come from. The pile they formed spread slowly across the table, covering it, some of them spilling onto the floor.

Frost had seen many strange things in his life, but he'd never felt so disgusted.

And then the things Park had vomited began to move.

Frost hated himself for it, but he let out a little squeal of disgust. It wasn't any louder than Tim's, though, and not nearly so long.

Jesse and Tim let go of Park, leaped out of their chairs, and staggered away in shock. As they did, Park flung himself backward with one final convulsion. His chair toppled over and cracked from the impact.

The things on the table continued to crawl off it in a slimy cataract that spilled onto the floor. From there, the fist-sized creatures scuttled in every direction. Some of them headed straight for Frost and Dietrich.

Dietrich grabbed Frost's arm and pulled him toward the door. "We gotta go," she said. "We gotta run."

"Wait." Frost yanked free from Dietrich's grasp and pulled out his flashlight again. He shined the beam at the creatures and instantly recognized them for what they were. "Those are the same things we saw outside!"

The insects scattered at the touch of the light, scurrying away from the beam as fast as their little legs would take them. Some of them started crawling up Tim and Jesse, working their way up their pants. The men began howling and stomping about in stark terror.

Frost played the beam over the men, moving it from one to the other. At the same time, he tried to keep an eye on the strays coming his way, emboldened by the fact the light no longer touched them instead.

"It's too much!" Frost said. "I can't stop them all!"

Over and over again, he flicked the light from Tim to Jesse and back to the floor between him and the insects. He could never keep the beam in one place long enough to really drive the creatures away. If he kept it focused in any one spot for too long, the bugs surged forward everywhere else.

Frost wanted to save Tim and Jesse, who had resorted to brushing the insects off themselves with their bare hands. Where the creatures touched their bare skin, they left burns, and the men yelped about them in pain and terror.

"Lights!" Dietrich shouted at Berto. "We need lights!"

The bartender reached under the bar and twisted something with a loud squeak. The guttering gaslight that hung in the middle of the ceiling and had barely provided any illumination or warmth burst into fully fueled brightness.

The bugs fled. Many of them leapt from Jesse and Tim, and in midair, they spread their wings from beneath their shells and took flight, clicking and clattering as they went.

"They can fly?" Dietrich said. "Not fair!"

"Just huddle here under the light!" Frost said, as much to Dietrich as everyone else in the bar. "They won't touch us here!"

Jesse and Tim made their way there, spinning about as they did, making sure the creatures couldn't hide in their shadows. They knocked a few of the insects toward the others, but Frost scared them away with his flashlight. Within moments, the four of them stood safe under the hissing gaslight.

"Ow!" Jesse said. "That fucking hurt!"

He and Tim were covered with red welts where the alien creatures had attacked them. Frost couldn't tell if they were bites, stings, or something else, but each of the wounds was about the size of a pool ball and looked painfully red and raw. Jesse had taken one over his right eye and was holding a hand over it. Blood trickled between his fingers.

"I think they're gone," Dietrich said.

"For now," said Tim. "Little fuckers."

"What about Park?" Jesse said. "We should check on him."

"He's dead already," Dietrich said. "Forget him."

Together, they stared at the table that now stood between them and where Park had fallen. "We can't just leave him like that," Tim said. "It ain't right."

"Neither is having a swarm of cockroaches come flying out of your face!" Dietrich said. "Nothing about this is right!"

"Give me that flashlight." Tim put his hand out toward Frost. "If you're all too scared, I'll go take a look."

Frost stared at Tim's empty hand. He knew one thing. As scared as he was of these creatures, the bugs, he wasn't going to give up the one thing he had he knew worked against them. No matter what.

"Forget it," he said. "I'll go."

"We'll all go," Dietrich said.

"We just need to move that table out of the way," Jesse said. He took his hand away from his eye. It had swollen shut tight.

"Right," Frost said. "Any volunteers?"

Jesse didn't say a word. He just darted forward and pushed the table to one side, hard and fast. As he did, a few more insects fluttered out from underneath it, so he turned the damn thing over, exposing its underside to the light.

A dozen more insects fled for the darkness. This time, Frost followed them with the flashlight's beam to see where they went. They made their way toward the walls and disappeared by slipping into the cracks near the floor, squeezing through spaces that seemed impossibly thin.

"Bring that light over here," Jesse said as he creeped toward Park's corpse.

Frost angled off to the side and shined his light past Jesse. What he saw made him swallow hard to keep down his liquor.

The creature that had been attached to Park's chest had fallen off. It lay to one side of him, nothing left of it now but an empty shell that gleamed in the light. Park's torso below where the shell had been attached sat splayed open, as if something had flayed all the flesh off it, exposing the bones and organs beneath.

Dietrich turned aside and threw up on the floor.

"They goddamn ate him from the inside!" Berto said.

Looking closer, Frost saw that the bartender was right. Most of Park's intestines were missing, and the bottom had been torn out of his stomach.

"We gotta get out of here," Dietrich said after spluttering the foul taste from her mouth. "We can't stay."

"What, with all those things out there?" Berto said. "How are we gonna get past them?"

"Maybe they ran off already," Frost said. He turned toward the door, happy to have any excuse to pull himself away from looking at Park's corpse for another second. "We can at least check."

Frost held the flashlight in front of him and pulled the door open with his free hand. He shined his beam outside, right into the area beyond the pool of light around the door.

There were more of the bugs out there than ever before. Most of them were smaller, like the ones that had come out of Park, but there seemed to be many more of them than could have come from the man. Several larger ones scuttled among them, moving like giants among toddlers.

"They've cut off the path," Frost said. "There's no way to get through them."

"We have to try, don't we?" Dietrich said. "So we stomp on a few alien insects on our way. Good for us!"

"Did you see how fast those fuckers can fly?" Jesse said. "There's no way you can outrun them."

"We don't have a choice!" Tim shouted as he came up behind the others.

"We need more lights," Frost said. "Do you have any more flashlights around here?"

Berto gave him a grim shake of his head.

"What else can we use then? Got a lighter? Matches?"

Berto reached behind the bar and pulled out a large box of safety matches. "Sometimes the pilot light goes out and I have to relight it."

"Those won't make it through the rain," Jesse said.

"And they don't make enough light anyhow," Tim said.

"No, but we can use them to light torches, right?"

Berto barked a high-pitched, nervous laugh. "I'm fresh out of those."

"But we can make torches." Frost glanced around the room. "Bust up a chair or table and use the legs. Wrap the end in a bar rag soaked in that shit you call tequila."

Dietrich frowned. "How long you think that'll last?"

"Longer than a fucking match at least."

"But how long is it going to take us to make enough torches?" Tim said.

"What?" Frost said. "Are you going anywhere until we do?"

Tim gave him a shrug of his shoulders that said *fair enough*.

It was then that the gaslight went out. Worse than that, though, was the scritching sound that began coming from every corner of the bar as the insects began to work their way back inside.

Frost wasn't sure who screamed the loudest—it might have been him—but he was the first to come to his senses.

"They must have chewed through the gas line," Frost said.

"They're bugs!" said Berto. "How can they be smart enough to do that?"

Frost didn't care to argue the point. The evidence was in his favor.

He flicked his flashlight back on, and in its light he grabbed the bottle of tequila off the bar. As fast as he could, he poured the liquor out on the floor in a wide circle around Dietrich, Tim, Jesse, and himself.

It was then that Berto—who was still standing behind the bar—started to scream. This time not simply in terror but also in pain.

"Quick," Frost said to Dietrich. "Light me one of those matches!"

He wanted to turn the light on Berto and help him out, but he couldn't. Not yet. If he did, he'd be condemning the rest of them to a painful death. He just hoped the bartender could hold out just a little longer.

Dietrich struck the match against the side of the box, and it burst into flame. Her hands were shaking so badly, though, she dropped it. It went out as it hit the floor. She grabbed another, spilling several of the rest of the matches on the floor. Cursing, she ignored them and struck the second match. This one she managed to hold onto, and she touched it to the booze Frost had spilled about the place.

A blazing ring of fire burst up around them. The alien insects that had already started crowding around them skittered away from the heat and light. Some of them had been standing in the alcohol when it went up and had been set on fire. They squealed and hissed as they baked inside their shells. A few of the critters had made it inside the circle, too, but Jesse and Tim kicked them back over the line.

Frost turned the flashlight back toward Berto, but he wasn't there. The flickering light from the few beer signs in the bar didn't give much in the way of illumination—certainly not enough to frighten off the creatures—but Frost was sure Berto hadn't run past them somehow. He had to still be there with them.

Frost splashed some of the tequila on the bar and used it to make a line back to the ring of fire. It ignited, and the fire followed the line backward to the top of the bar.

Berto leaped up from behind the bar, desperate to immerse himself in the light. The creatures covered every inch of him that Frost could see, biting his flesh, trying to crawl into his mouth. He fell into the pool of burning tequila and embraced the bar like a drowning man grasping a life preserver.

The insects on the upper part of his body fled, but they

didn't go far. They just moved down his body, out of the fire, out of the light.

With the creatures now away from his face, Berto opened his mouth and let out a horrifying howl of agony. His shirt had already caught on fire, but he did nothing to extinguish it. Instead, he crawled up onto the bar and immolated himself in the blaze.

The smell of burning flesh filled the air, and Frost gagged at the sickly scent.

"We have to save him!" Jesse said.

"How!" Tim said. "It's too late for him! What about us?"

"Fuck you, and fuck this." Jesse stormed forward and tried to grab Berto by his shoulders. The flames proved too hot for him to handle, though, and he fell back, his fingers already blistering.

"Shit," he said. "Shit!"

Berto had already stopped screaming. As the others watched, his body—no longer grasping at the edge of the bar—slipped backward and tumbled out of sight.

Jesse made to go after Berto once again, but Frost grabbed him by the back of his shirt to stop him. "Forget it," he said. "He's gone."

For an instant, Frost wondered if Jesse would coldcock him right then and there and go after Berto. The man seemed to realize the pointlessness of it, though, and his shoulders sagged in defeat.

The chipboard surface of the bar had caught fire by now, and the flames began to spread. "Well, that'll drive the bugs out," Tim said.

"And us along with it," said Dietrich. "We need to get out of here."

"Goddamn right," Frost said. "If those things chewed through the gas line, you know what that means?"

"Shit," said Jesse. "It's leaking. If it reaches that fire, or the other way around, we're done for."

"We're done for out there too," Tim said. "There's no way

we can make it to the station from here."

"Speak for yourself," Dietrich said. "We don't have to outrun those things, old man. We just have to outrun you."

"Fuck you."

"You go fuck whatever you want," Dietrich said. "This whole place could blow up any second. We're leaving. Come with us, or die in a fire here. Your choice."

"She's right," Jesse said. "We need to go. Now."

"What about torches?" Tim said.

"We don't have time to make them," Dietrich said. "We run for the door, smash through it, and keep running until we find the lights of the station or die trying."

Tim groaned, but Jesse put a stop to that. "Can you come up with a better plan in the next five seconds? No? Then let's go."

Tim glared at Jesse for a full three seconds before he nodded his assent.

"All right." Frost hefted his flashlight in one hand and the still-half-full bottle of tequila in the other. "On three. One…"

Tim bolted for the door. Shocked, Frost and Dietrich watched him go. Jesse recovered first and chased after his friend.

As the two locals reached the door, Dietrich pushed Frost from behind, and the two Marines started after them. "Hey!"

Tim and Jesse ignored Dietrich's protest and slipped out the door. Frost charged through it himself and someone—he couldn't tell who—punched him in the side of the head as he emerged into the hot rain.

Frost fell forward, skidding into the steaming mud on his chest. As he hit the ground, he could smell the telltale scent of propane wafting around him, combined with the taste of failure. His flashlight tumbled out of his hand, the light flipping between earth and sky until it landed several feet away.

Frost could see Jesse's face by the beam of the flashlight as he scooped it up. "Sorry," the man said in a heartfelt way. Then he charged off toward the station without a moment's more hesitation, racing along in Tim's footprints.

Frost felt someone's hand on his shoulder and spun about, ready for a fight. It was Dietrich, though, who hadn't abandoned him. "Are you all right?" she said. "We gotta move!"

As Frost scrambled to his feet, he watched his flashlight's beam shrink smaller and smaller by the second. "We're never going to catch them."

"We have to try!" Dietrich said.

As the words left her mouth, though, a man—Jesse, maybe?—shouted out in the night. Another voice joined him soon after. A moment later, the flashlight's shrunken beam tumbled to the ground and went out.

"Oh, shit," Dietrich said through her hand as she stared into the darkness. "We are so, so fucked."

Frost winced in a shaken cocktail of shame and pain. He'd let those men trick him, and now he and Dietrich would pay for it with their lives.

"Wait," Dietrich said. "I still have those matches! Do you have the tequila?"

Frost held up the bottle. By some miracle, he'd managed to keep hold of it as he fell, and he'd barely lost a drop of it. "What good's that going to do?"

Dietrich didn't respond. Instead, she produced the matchbox and fished a fresh match from it. Then she set to lighting it.

The first attempt failed, as did the second. Frost could hear the crawling little aliens out there, chittering in the rain. Were they talking with each other? Coordinating their plan of attack?

He couldn't tell. He just knew the men were still screaming. It would only be a matter of time before the bugs finished the locals off, though, and came crawling after the Marines.

Dietrich huddled in close to Frost, and they covered the matchbox with their heads. This time, the match flared to glaring life.

Dietrich took the match and dropped it into the bottle of tequila. The liquor erupted into a blue flame that licked its way up and out of the bottle.

"What the hell good is that?" Frost said.

"Throw it at the tank," Dietrich said.

Frost goggled at her. "There's a leak near the tank," he said. "I can smell it."

"So can I."

"This could blow it all up."

Dietrich reached out and took Frost by the hand. "Beats being eaten by those little bastards, doesn't it?"

Frost stared at the tank sitting there in front of the bar. Then he glanced back toward where he'd seen the locals fall. One of them had already stopped screaming. He couldn't tell which, but he didn't suppose it mattered.

He leaned over and gave Dietrich a kiss. Then he cocked his arm back and hurled that flaming bottle of tequila at the leaking propane tank with every bit of strength he could muster.

The glass bottle shattered against the steel tank, splashing burning alcohol all over it.

The tank exploded.

The shockwave knocked Frost and Dietrich flat. The last thing Frost remembered as he went flying backward through the air was watching a gigantic fireball erupt from the tank and light up the night sky.

Frost woke up in a hospital bed the next day, in some distant building he'd never seen, where things were clean and white. Dietrich lay in the bed next to him, still unconscious.

It seemed she'd put herself between Frost and the explosion and taken the brunt of it. The nurses weren't sure if she'd make it. "You never know," one of them said to Frost. "She's a fighter."

Later, the captain came by to ask Frost what had happened, and he told her everything. A pair of representatives from Weyland-Yutani stopped by, too, and Frost repeated his account for them. None of them seemed to believe a word of it.

The captain took particularly detailed notes as she grilled Frost without relenting. When they were finally done, the captain said to him, "You've had a horrible experience. You and Dietrich almost died in that explosion. It's not surprising your brain would create impossible memories like this to explain what happened."

"Fuck you."

The captain gave him a sympathetic nod. "I'll ask the doctor to prescribe you a sedative."

Later, once everyone had left Frost alone with his thoughts, he actually began to wonder about his sanity. Maybe Berto had given them some bad tequila. Maybe the concussion he'd sustained had scrambled his brain. Maybe he actually had hallucinated the whole thing.

He just couldn't tell anymore. Yet it had seemed so real.

Soon after, Frost forced himself out of bed and hobbled over to sit next to Dietrich and hold her hand. He didn't know if it meant anything to her while she was out cold like that, but it comforted him. For the moment, that was enough.

Frost was almost falling asleep himself when Dietrich finally opened her eyes. She could barely breathe still, just enough to squeeze a few words out of her scorched lungs.

"We get 'em?" Dietrich croaked. She sounded like a three-packs-a-day smoker.

"What?" Frost startled at the abrupt sound. "Who?"

Dietrich stared back at Frost through watery eyes. "The bugs. We kill all those fuckers?"

"As many as we could," Frost said. "Enough anyway."

Dietrich gave him a wide smile and before she closed her eyes again she said, "Next time we run up against something like that, I'm bringing a fucking flamethrower."

NO GOOD DEED

BY RAY GARTON

(FOR MY FRIENDS SCOTT CONNORS AND ERINN KEMPER)

"This moon is not a nice place to visit," Jex said, looking at his screen while his thin fingers moved like tarantula legs over the touchpad. "Savage winds, severe electrical storms. And yet, people live here."

"Live and work," Mad said as the *Viper* touched down with a jolt. "In this case, they're the same thing. Terraforming is a life commitment."

"Research and mining, too. One of Weyland-Yutani's busy shake-and-bake colonies. The terraforming is advanced enough for the air to be breathable, but we'll want to suit up fully for protection against the weather."

The *Viper* powered down and Mad removed her seat straps.

"LV-426, one of the three moons of Calpamos, and Weyland-Yutani is working on all of them. Also known as Acheron. The mythological River of Pain."

"I thought it was the Stream of Woe."

"Would you like to argue about it?"

She chuckled and said, "Fuck off, Jex. No communication from the colony, so I'm assuming they're busy with other things."

"Of course, you didn't *initiate* communication."

"No, but I would have *responded*. The point is, they haven't noticed us or don't care. Which means they also haven't noticed the two escaped psychopaths who just got here. You still got a lock on Jaeger?"

"He and his companion have left the shuttle behind and are approaching Hadley's Hope."

"We've got to beat them there. Any chance of that?"

"Given our position, we'll have to move fast."

"Then let's move." Her seat slid back, then swiveled with a whirring sound, and Mad launched out of it. "I saw their mugshots, but haven't had a chance to look at their histories since we left the *Tartarus*. Access their criminal records and fill me in while we suit up."

He got out of his seat as he accessed the proper file in his internal database while following Mad to the rear of the ship to dress. "We don't have enough time for everything, but I can hit a few highlights. Enzo Jaeger, the alpha male in this pack of two, once held an entire childcare center full of children hostage to distract law enforcement while accomplices went on crime sprees throughout the city. The operation was meticulously planned, perfectly synchronized, extremely risky, and yet they pulled it off without incident."

"Don't tell me. He didn't leave witnesses."

"You'd think. But he had the children locked in a room shortly after he took everyone hostage so they weren't exposed to anything. Once his pals had enough time to get their jobs done, Jaeger killed all of the adults."

"He has a sentimental streak."

"Who'd a thunk it? Then he launched himself from the roof in a military-issue jetpack to meet with his compatriots and share the loot."

"Any survivors of *that*?"

"Only Jaeger. And the loot. He used most of his newfound wealth to set up a criminal empire. Illegal weapons, drugs, pornography, black market sex slavery, professional assassins, a shopping center of crime."

"Is it true that he hung one of his wives by her ankles, eviscerated her, and she bled to death with her intestines dangling in her face?"

"It is. *That* must have been some argument, huh?"

"And the other guy?"

"Jack Bates. He began his criminal career by killing his mother and eating part of her at the age of fourteen. Things only got worse from there. He's not too bright. Jaeger used him as muscle in the escape. He's a large person and apparently does anything Jaeger tells him to do, including killing twenty-three people in the process of escaping the *Tartarus*. Prison sweethearts. A tale as old as time."

"How does one man kill twenty-three people? What weapon was he using?"

"He was unarmed."

"That's impressive. And hard to believe. By 'not too bright,' do you mean he's mentally impaired?"

"That's unclear. After killing his mother, he was put into a juvenile detention center, where apparently he didn't fare well. Bates claims that while there, he was forced to participate in some research programs conducted by MetCon Pharmaceuticals."

Mad pulled a zipper up with a quiet hiss as she frowned at Jex. "They experimented on him?"

"Drug research, they told him. They claimed they were

testing a new drug to enhance performance and extend longevity, something they were calling Haxon-K."

"Enhance what kind of performance?"

"He didn't say."

"Nobody believes him, I suppose."

"MetCon denies it, of course, and the authorities are more likely to believe a pharmaceutical company than a convicted mother-eater. The detention facility denies everything, as well. But it's not the first time someone has made such a claim, and there is evidence of back-channel collusion between MetCon— other corporations, as well—and various prison systems. But not enough evidence to interest authorities."

"And there never will be."

"Of course not, we know better than that. To answer your question, yes, nobody believes Bates. He claims he's never been the same, that it made him dumb and a lot meaner."

"Meaner than killing and eating his mother?"

"Mean enough to kill twenty-three people in eighteen minutes. Do you think he's telling the truth?"

"Unlike the authorities, I am less inclined to believe any corporation, particularly a pharmaceutical company, than I am to believe just about anybody else. Including a convicted mother-eater. We know that kind of thing goes on, Jex, and somebody like Bates would be a prime target precisely *because* nobody would believe him."

"Are we planning to take Jaeger and Bates back alive?"

"Under normal circumstances, sure, because under normal circumstances, the bounty's usually higher when they're alive. But circumstances are not normal. These two will not hesitate to obliterate anybody who gets in their way and they will not go without a fight. They're heavily armed and we can't let that happen here. Too many colonists, a high risk of civilian casualties. They said dead or alive, and I hope they meant it, because those guys are either going back to the *Tartarus* in bags, or I'll just take a finger from each of their bodies. Besides, the bounty is the same either way. They really want these guys."

"The universe will thank you. Their *mothers* will thank you. Well... Jaeger's mother would. She's still alive. Completely disowned him."

"Good for her."

Once they were suited up, they went to the weapons rack and began to fill their holsters and pockets. Mad took a Smith & Wesson .357 Magnum, a .40 caliber Glock, and the sawed-off shotgun that fit nicely into the long pocket at her right hip. She also took a set of electric brass knuckles that delivered a powerful electrical charge with each punch, and a knife. As an afterthought, she strapped a couple of packs of punch-packing flash grenades. Just in case.

Turning to Jex, she said, "While we're out there, don't hesitate to kill either of them if you get a chance. Right away, as soon as we reach them."

"In other words, shoot on sight."

"Yep."

"Brevity has never been one of your strengths."

She chuckled and said, "Fuck off, Jex."

Mad had been in the right place at the right time. She had gone to the *Tartarus* to visit an old friend who was incarcerated there. Jewel Vargas was on the minimum security level because her crimes were nonviolent and she had made a deal. She was a digital thief who had stolen a lot of money from some bad people who immediately wanted it back. When they came after her, she cut a deal with authorities that would shorten her sentence and make the time more palatable in exchange for all the information she had on the criminals from whom she had stolen the money, which gave authorities the evidence they needed to arrest them and shut them down.

A few minutes into their visit, alarms sounded and red

lights began to flash everywhere. A rumbling explosion on another level jolted the ship. Then another.

Madison Voss used aliases whenever she went someplace where her name might be recognized. But her real name was necessary for the I.D. check required to board the *Tartarus* and see her friend Jewel. As a bounty hunter, she had developed a bit of a reputation for bringing in a couple of high-profile fugitives, and she was well known to members of law enforcement and the penal system. It took only minutes for a guard to track her to Visiting Room B3 and lead her to the administration deck, where Warden Jeffrey Wallingford explained the situation. He was not tall, but he was broad, with skin so black he looked like a muscular, uniformed slice of nighttime.

Two men had escaped the *Tartarus* in a stolen shuttle, and they had set explosives in every dock that launched the ship's armed cruisers, timed to go off as they were making their exit. Two officers of the *Tartarus* pursued in other shuttles, but they had a clumsy start, the shuttles were not armed or equipped to track and retrieve fugitives, and they lost the escapees.

"It may have been presumptuous," Warden Wallingford said, "but we took the liberty of sending their complete files to your ship's computer. I am hoping you're available to take up pursuit, because these men should not be loose, as you'll see when you read their files."

"I am available," Mad said. "Twenty-five million with half up front."

"Mizz Voss, you *know* that is an outrageous—"

"Mad," she said with a smile. "I like to be called Mad. And this isn't negotiable. Twenty-five million with half up front, or I go back and finish my visit with my friend." When he stared blankly at her, she added, "Time is a factor in these cases, you know."

After a moment, he nodded once.

Now they were about to plunge themselves into the brutal climate of Acheron, all before dinner.

Jex was accustomed to emergency runs by now and the

routine was second nature to him. He had been with her for four years and she credited him with keeping her sane on the job. A friend-with-benefits of Mad's had a high-level position at Hyperdyne and allowed her to commission a custom-made synthetic. She was given access to technological advances that would not be available to the public until the following year's models were released. It had cost a fortune, but she had saved up for it and knew exactly what she wanted. A male synthetic with a sense of humor, one who could make her laugh. A smartass.

Bounty hunting was not pleasant work, but it paid well and it kept her busy. Too busy to have to interact with other people and socialize, skills that had always eluded her. She hated small talk and found most people petty and small-minded. Mad had been told, more than once, that she had a "depressive" personality, and she supposed it was true, which was probably why she was so bad at getting along with other people. They all seemed so goddamned happy for no good reason. Or, worse, for stupid reasons. But she refused to take antidepressants or drugs of any kind if she could avoid them. What she needed was a friend, so she had one made.

Jex was her only friend. She never lost sight of the fact that he was a synthetic made to her specifications, but it did not matter. She had developed real affection for him because he made her laugh and because he would shut up whenever she asked. He kept her from going crazy.

"Let's go make some money, Jex."

"Let's do that. Oh, and I get to shoot on sight. That's very exciting. I think I wet myself a little."

Mad chuckled and said, "Fuck off, Jex."

———

The high wail of Bates screaming in terror, bordering on hysteria, stabbed into Enzo Jaeger's ears inside the protective helmet he wore. For a moment, it overwhelmed the constant sound of rain pouring on his helmet and even the ripping thunder. Jaeger looked at his companion; he was able to see him clearly only because his helmet's transparent faceplate was coated with a water repellant that kept his vision clear.

"Jack, what the *fuck*?" he said.

After a pause, Bates said, "Sorry, Enzo. I got my foot stuck between two rocks. Got scared for a second."

"Did you get your foot loose?"

"Yes, Jack. Hey, Jack." Another pause, and when he spoke again, fear had returned to his voice, quietly this time. "There's not gonna be any MetCon here, is there?"

"*Any* MetCon? It's a pharmaceutical corporation, Jack, and it's not here, no. This is Weyland-Yutani, remember?"

"Oh, yeah, yeah, Wayluntani, you told me, Wayluntani." He pointed at the structure ahead with the big Weyland-Yutani logo emblazoned on the wall, its yellow and blue faded by the elements. "Wayluntani."

"Dammit, Jack, I *told* you, remember? This is a Weyland-Yutani shake-and-bake colony and I got a friend works here. Remember? Don't go having one of your goddamned panic attacks now, you hear me?"

"Yuh-yeah, Enzo, yeah. I forgot you told me. Suh-sorry. It's just, y'know, it scared me for a second, there, that, you know, we might run into some MetCon."

His fear suddenly gone, Bates's voice became a whimper. The poor, stupid son of a bitch.

He was Jaeger's only friend on the *Tartarus*, a mountain of a man with astonishing strength, which was, he assumed, the reason the other prisoners steered clear of him and seemed to fear him. Jaeger had befriended him shortly after being incarcerated on the prison ship because he was the biggest guy there and everybody seemed afraid to get near him. He was a big badass, that was Jaeger's only interest in him; he did not expect to like him or even *want* to like him.

He had assumed at first that Bates's odd behavior and

apparent thick-headedness were the result of long-term drug use. But as he spent more time with Bates—time that was, for the most part, blissfully free of interaction with any of the other inmates, which was the way Jaeger liked it—he came to see that the big guy was about as dumb as a bag of hair, that was all. He had never used drugs. In spite of his size and intimidating appearance—he had close-cropped, bright-red hair, vaguely simian features on his heavily-freckled face, with tiny ears, deep-set eyes, and permanent tooth extensions forming small tusks that curled upward from between his big, lumpy lips, mediocre dental work at best—he was as meek as a kitten, with a childlike personality. A damaged child with foggy memories of bad things he knew he had done but could not recall in any detail, but vivid memories of the bad things that had been done to him. And there had been a host of those in a childhood that had been a steady stream of abuse from a cruel and hateful mother.

At first, Jaeger had dismissed Bates's stories about being a guinea pig for MetCon. Bates cowered in terror whenever he saw the MetCon logo on a magazine screen or video ad. Jaeger had assumed that the poor, pathetic guy had concocted those stories to fill the foggy spaces in his broken memory and at some point had convinced himself they were true.

But he heard whispers from others. They avoided him when he was with Bates, which was most of the time, but they could not be together every second, and sometimes he heard whispers. In the cafeteria, they said that Bates's meek-as-a-kitten personality changed drastically and abruptly when he was threatened or afraid. He became violent, dangerous. Some said his personality was not all that changed, that sometimes his physical appearance was altered, his size and even the color of his skin. That sudden change in behavior had landed him in solitary more than once, and the injured and dead he left behind ensured that he never would leave the *Tartarus*.

Jaeger saw the change for himself only once when a piece

of fresh meat on the *Tartarus* had decided to pick a fight with the biggest guy there with a few smartass remarks. The wrong remarks. It had happened so quickly and there had been so much screaming and blood and chaos that the whole thing had remained blurry in Jaeger's mind. Ever since then, he had never been quite certain of what he had seen, but he could no longer dismiss all of Bates's stories about his troubled youth and his nightmarish experience with MetCon.

He learned that the others stayed away from Bates not only because they were afraid of his size and strength; they were afraid of accidentally offending him, unintentionally pissing him off. Bates was so godawful dumb that he often misunderstood things he was told or misinterpreted the behavior of others; he always assumed the worst and took offense easily. After witnessing the sudden, blurry slaughter of the last guy who had pissed Bates off with a couple of smartass remarks about his mother, nobody wanted to take any chances.

The whole thing made him wonder how much truth was in Bates's stories, and if so, that made him wonder exactly what the hell MetCon had done to him. "Haxon-K," he would say, sometimes repeating it quietly in his lower bunk at night, either in his sleep or while lying awake in the dark. That was the name of the drug he said they were testing on him, the drug that did such terrible things to him, though he was unable to give specifics.

The more he thought about it, the more unlikely it seemed that someone as empty-headed as Jack could concoct a story like that.

Jaeger felt sorry for him. He was what Jaeger's mother used to call a "mental inebriate." Whatever had caused it, though, obviously had not been Bates's own doing, and he suspected that the traumatic physical, sexual, and psychological abuse he had grown up with probably had a lot to do with it. For that reason, and because, in spite of everything he had done and was capable of doing, Bates seemed to have a big, childlike heart, Jaeger felt sorry for him.

For Enzo Jaeger that was extraordinary. Pity was something he rarely, if ever, felt.

He had no time to navel-gaze, though, and shifted his thoughts to the present situation. They had been pounded by the moon's raging winds since arriving, until about ten minutes ago when they got beyond the storm wall that protected Hadley's Hope from the endless onslaught. It made walking easier, but it did nothing to give them shelter from the drenching rain or jagged bolts of lightning that lit up the dark-gray sky and sometimes struck the ground or one of the tortured stone formations that twisted up toward the sky. Jaeger had an old buddy named Lupo who had gone straight and was currently working heavy equipment in the very shake-and-bake colony that was sprawled before them now. He hoped that Lupo would help him get a ship that would take him and Jack even farther away from the *Tartarus*. If Lupo would not help, then they would simply take what they needed on their own.

But something was wrong. As they made their way around a corner of the complex, Jaeger's skin suddenly felt tighter on his body, as if it were shrinking, an alarm signal that always sharpened his attention. He saw something to his left that bothered him before he understood why.

A big Daihotai tractor stood halfway through a bay door. In the slashing rain, the tractor's 8x8 wheel arrangement made it look like some kind of hulking mechanical monster. It was the kind of vehicle his buddy Lupo would be operating and repairing in the colony. But it was still and silent. As he and Jack fully rounded that corner, he saw that the tractor was unoccupied and the big metal bay door had slammed down on it from above.

When Jaeger stopped, Bates did, too, and stood beside him, waiting for him to say something.

"This doesn't look good," he said. "But we've gotta get in

there. Hold your fire until I say. You got that, Jack?"

"Got it, Enzo, got it."

Jaeger's muscles tensed as he neared the open bay door and his heart throbbed in his neck. He leaned forward for one of those heartbeats, then withdrew again after getting a quick but clear look through the bay door. He saw no people or movement and heard no sounds from inside. There was no sign of life at all. Someone would have approached them by now. Combined with the bay door being closed on the abandoned tractor, things did not look good to Jaeger.

"Why's it so empty?" Bates whispered.

"Good question. Eyes and ears open, now, you got it?"

"Yep."

As they passed beneath the half-closed bay door, Bates had to duck a bit to avoid bumping his head.

Once inside, they slid back their helmet faceplates. Jaeger felt cold, damp air on his face as he looked around.

Tractors were lined up in rows to the left, with rows of Power Loaders to the right, all surrounded by crates and other equipment. It seemed to Jaeger that if he wanted to find his buddy Lupo, he had come inadvertently to the most likely part of the colony. But there was no one there. Besides the perpetual storm outside the bay door, there were no sounds, no signs of activity at all.

When he turned his gaze down to the floor, Jaeger's worries became fears. He saw shiny pools of dark red surrounded by dark spatterings.

"Something bad happened here, Enzo," Bates whispered.

As his eyes swept the floor of the large chamber—as much of it as he could see, anyway—Jaeger saw more puddles and spatters, as well as streaks of red here and there over the floor. Blood had been shed, bodies had been removed. Things looked bleak.

"Yeah," Jaeger finally replied. "Something bad." He reached his right hand up, unsnapped the holster that stuck up over his shoulder, and removed the 12-gauge Mossberg shotgun he kept strapped to his back. He opened the collapsible shoulder stock. His left hand checked to make sure that his Glock 9mm was still at his hip, ready to be drawn.

They took a few more steps into the building, with Bates following Jaeger's lead. A whirring noise made Jaeger halt and turn his head toward the sound: up and to the right. The sound came again from the left.

Surveillance cameras mounted around the facility were turning toward them, watching them.

A stern female voice crackled over speakers Jaeger could not locate: "Identify yourself."

Jaeger turned to Bates and gave him a wink, a signal for him to remain silent until otherwise notified.

"Uh, my friend and I have found ourselves stranded on this moon and we were looking for shelter. The conditions are not hospitable." He smiled up at the cameras.

"Identify yourself."

"Uh, well, we were on our way to—"

A confusion of voices burst from the speakers, then a male voice said, "Enzo? Enzo fucking *Jaeger*?"

Jaeger grinned. "Lupo? Is that you?"

"What the hell are you *doing* here?"

He smiled and shrugged. "It's a small galaxy. This is my friend Jack."

"No, seriously, what *are* you doing here?"

"Uh, well, that's quite a story."

"I'm sure it is."

Jaeger nodded down at the floor. "Looks like you've had some problems here."

"Yeah. Careful, Enzo, you may be in danger at the moment. Look around. Look real good, and make sure you're alone in there."

When Jaeger looked around a second time, he noticed how many dark spaces there were between tractors and loaders, in corners, spaces in which he could see nothing but impenetrable shadows. His eyes narrowed as he looked deeper into that darkness.

Was that… movement?

———

Mad had seen the dull glow of Hadley's Hope oozing above the twisted rock formations in what looked like the near distance as soon as she and Jex had exited the *Viper*. The walk there, on the other hand, was hampered by the worst winds she had ever encountered and a steady downpour of rain, and it seemed to take much longer than she expected.

"It doesn't look like the kind of place that has an exciting night life," Jex said after they rounded the end of the storm wall and stopped to survey what they could see of the complex. "By the way, Jaeger and Bates beat us here. If you remember, I *told* you we'd have to be fast if we wanted to—"

"Fuck off, Jex." Mad frowned as she looked at the colony in front of her. "This place looks dead." She and Jex had visited a shake-and-bake colony a few years ago on the trail of a fugitive and it had been a bustling place throughout their visit. Loud machinery and heavy equipment were in operation around the clock and there was endless movement all through the colony as tractors arrived from and others departed to mines and mining or wildcatting expeditions or other destinations.

All the lights that illuminated Hadley's Hope seemed to draw attention to its stillness. There was no activity anywhere she looked.

"It looks like a ghost town," she said. "Like it's been abandoned."

"Not according to my readings," Jex said. "They appear to have holed up inside. And they've shut this place down to do it. That's not very Weyland-Yutani of them. Unless they're trying to avoid some kind of threat. Maybe from outside."

"Then maybe we should try to get inside." Mad started walking briskly again and Jex kept up.

A few minutes later, Jex said, "There seems to be a bay door lodged open with a Daihotai tractor up ahead."

"That doesn't sound good. But we'll take it as an invitation to come inside."

———

Jaeger realized he was quickly starting to feel paranoid and resisted it by taking his eyes from the dark corners around him and looking again at the surveillance camera directly in front of and above him.

"Who's in here with us, Lupo?"

"We're, um, not entirely sure yet. And it's not so much a who as a what."

"OK. You gonna explain any of that fucking jabber or am I supposed to take guesses at whatever the hell you're talking about?"

"You've come at a bad time, Enzo. You and your friend need to turn around and get out of here while you can. Go back to your ship and get the hell out of here."

"We don't have enough fuel to get anywhere."

"Then go take shelter in your ship. I'm serious, Enzo. You need to leave the building now. You're not safe here and we can't let you in. For all I know… you may be safer out there."

"What the hell are you talking about, Lupo?"

"Identify yourself," the female voice said again.

Jaeger frowned, squinted at the camera. "What?"

"Identify yourself!"

It suddenly occurred to Jaeger that the woman was not talking to him and he spun around in time to see two faceless figures just inside the bay door raising their guns and aiming at him.

"Take cover, Jack," he said. They fired an instant before

Jaeger fired his shotgun and half a heartbeat after both of them began to dive behind the nearest tractor, with Bates half a step behind him, as both guns fired. The three shots roared and reverberated in the chamber, bouncing sharply off the walls.

The shooters ran for cover in different directions, one toward the tractors, the other toward the loaders, and all those dark corners.

"Who the fuck are they, Enzo?" Bates said, his voice high with panic. "Who could've found us? I thought we blew up all the *Tartarus*'s cruisers. Who's shooting at us, Enzo?"

"Be quiet. I don't know. Lemme think, lemme think."

Whoever the shooters were, it was clear that they intended to kill Jaeger and Bates because they had started shooting at them on sight. Their only choice was to keep making nice with Lupo and get inside with him.

"Hey, Lupo!" Jaeger shouted. "Turns out we're kinda wanted. We could use some help here."

Lupo's staticky voice said, "I told you, Enzo, we can't help you, we can't let you in. I'm afraid you're on your own, buddy."

"Fuck," Jaeger muttered, turning to look around them. "Where'd those two go?"

———

Mad huddled behind a row of tractor wheels and listened to the voice over the speakers.

"Look, all of you, I don't care what your fucking gripe is with each other, take it someplace *else*. You're all in danger here."

When the voice did not continue, Mad whispered, "What do you think he's talking about?"

"There's something else in here with us," Jex replied in her earpiece.

"Who?"

Instead of responding, Jex began shooting. There was an explosion of gunfire from the rows of loaders where Jex had hidden. When Mad looked in the direction of the sounds, she saw a large shape moving in the shadows among the loaders. Something significantly larger than Jex.

"Jex, what's happening?"

"We may have to leave empty-handed," Jex said. "I recommend getting the hell out of here now."

He began shooting again.

Mad hurried across the open space toward Jex.

———

Jaeger was watching one of the two shooters run away from the tractors in the direction of all the sudden gunfire among the loaders across the way when Bates's whimpering wormed into his ears.

"What's the matter now?" Jaeger whispered, turning toward him. He found Bates facing in the opposite direction and looking up.

As Jaeger spun around, Bates began screaming. He looked up and saw the creature emerging from the murky shadows between two tractors. The first thing he saw was the mouth, mostly the glistening, dripping fangs.

Bates continued to scream as he backed away, loud, piercing screams that still, somehow, retained within them that frightened-child whimper.

Jaeger tried to make sense of the creature as it oozed out of the darkness and rose up, those nightmare fangs slowly parting as the mouth opened, its body black with slender arms, large hands that looked more like claws, long muscular legs, and a tail that curled upward behind it.

Something happened to Bates's scream. The whimper vanished and the sound thickened. Jaeger wanted to turn and see what was wrong but he could not take his eyes from the thing slowly closing in on him. He could not move, in fact, and felt as if every inch of his body had turned to icy, rigid steel.

The scream, which had become a guttural growl, stopped. But inside his helmet, he still heard Bates's breathing, heavy and punctuated with grunts of effort.

Jaeger heard a sound above him. He wanted to look up because it sounded like it had come from the roof of the tractor on his left, but he could not look away from what he was certain would be his death.

Somehow, he broke through his paralysis and raised the shotgun.

The creature rushed to close the distance between it and Jaeger as he curled his finger around the trigger of his shotgun.

A wet, throaty roar sounded as something seemed to drop on the alien from above, making it shriek as it spun around, thrashing its tail and trying to throw off the intruder.

It was Bates. As he lowered his gun and took a few steps back, forgotten now by the monster that had been advancing on him only seconds earlier, Jaeger realized that Bates had climbed on top of one of the tractors and dove onto the creature. But the thing that was now riding that black, spidery monster, roaring as it repeatedly pounded the long, cylindrical head of the shrieking thing, was no longer the Bates he knew.

He had shed his suit because he had become too big for it, and his exposed skin—a rusty red, as if all of his many prominent freckles had blended together and darkened— was rough and creased, like the thick hide of an elephant, and now sprouted bony thorns all over his body. His arms were the same size that his legs *used* to be and appeared to be longer, ending in enormous hands with a thorn on each knuckle and deadly black claws that had emerged from the tips of his fingers. Jaeger's big, dumb, lumbering friend had become a hulking, thorny, fast-moving devil from some mythological pit.

The creature had completely forgotten about Jaeger, who now stood in slack-jawed horror and watched the two monsters fight.

Mad saw Jex lying flat on his back on the floor, a gun in each hand, pushing himself rapidly backward over the floor with his feet as he fired up at the advancing creature, a black, spidery-scorpion nightmare.

Behind her, she heard a terrific roar from the rows of tractors, and a shriek like metal claws dragging over a gigantic, amplified chalkboard. But she barely registered the sounds as her right hand drew the sawed-off shotgun and her left reached for the Glock—then stopped uncertainly. Instead, she slipped the shotgun back into its pocket and snapped one of the grenades off of her belt. Her thumb popped the tab and she threw it directly at the creature, then dropped flat on the floor and covered her head with her arms.

The explosion sent a shockwave through her bones and the thing that had been about to attack Jex released a full and ear-shredding screech—what Mad had always imagined hell would sound like if it were a real place. She jumped to her feet and raced through the thin, stinging smoke left by the grenade toward Jex, who had taken advantage of the monster's momentary distraction to roll over, push himself up, and try to stand. But the alien was not distracted long enough.

Mad felt as if she were in a dream in which everything, including her own body, moved in agonizingly slow motion as she tried to run to Jex. The creature behind him lunged forward, moving slowly through the air as it reached out one of those long-fingered claw-hands and clutched Jex's right ankle.

Reaching for another grenade, she watched helplessly as the creature dragged Jex backward by the ankle, toward the shadows.

Mad heard the savage growl again, but this time it came from above her.

Something large dropped from the top of one of the loaders and onto the back of the creature, which reared up, dragging Jex with it. The alien lifted him into the air and swung him around by the leg to swat its attacker. Instead, the creature slammed Jex into the side of a loader with a leaden sound. Jex suddenly dropped to the floor in a splattering shower of white fluids. His right leg was gone.

Raising her eyes to the creature, she saw Jex's leg still clutched in its claw as it fought with the mammoth red beast that kept slamming his horned fist into the side of its head. The creature had a pronounced, gorilla-like face with what appeared to be tusks, a head of wild, bushy red hair, and eyes that glistened in the dark shadow cast by the pronounced brow.

The leg could be replaced. She reached down, grabbed Jex's arm, and dragged him away from the roaring and screeching. As they entered the clear passageway between the stored tractors and loaders, she saw Enzo Jaeger staggering out from between two tractors, his shotgun at his side, head down. He had not seen her yet.

She clutched the Glock, drew it.

He lifted his head, then began to raise the shotgun.

Mad fired and Jaeger's right kneecap exploded beneath the pantleg of his olive-green suit. He screamed all the way to the floor, and as his back hit the concrete, the 12 gauge spun in circles as it skittered away from his hand.

The hellish sounds continued to reverberate off the walls from the cluster of loaders.

Mad looked down and said, "Don't go anywhere, Jex."

"Oh, all right. But I won't wait forever."

As she stalked toward Jaeger, he reached for a holstered gun. She kicked his hand and the gun slid away from him.

"Enzo Jaeger, I presume?" she said, lifting her faceplate so he could see he had been brought down by a woman. She always enjoyed the hell out of that part.

He stared up at her with pain pulling the features of his face backward on each side, making sounds that vacillated between whimpers and grunts. Nearly squinting shut, his eyes studied her through his pain. "You're... you're..."

She smiled. "Madison Voss."

"Muh-Mad."

Lifting her eyebrows cheerily, she nodded. "You've heard of me."

He gave her a pain-twisted smile, nodding. "Yeah, I've heard about you. Here to… to take me in, huh?"

"That's right. You and your buddy. Where is he, by the way?"

"Well, I think… he just… saved your ass."

Mad thought of the beefy, towering beast that had intervened in time to save Jex, skin thick, heavy, red, and horned. That was Jack Bates. She remembered his claim that he had been experimented on by MetCon.

"I don't have time to fuck around," she said, looking down at Jaeger again, still holding her gun on him. She opened her mouth to say more but realized abruptly that the roaring and shrieking had stopped. Turning to the loaders again, she took in a surprised breath when she saw a naked man emerge from the shadows, bleeding at his neck, shoulder, belly, and thigh. He staggered into the opening.

"Enzo?" he croaked.

Jaeger propped himself up on an elbow. "Jack! You're OK!"

Hunched over weakly, limping, Bates said again, "Enzo? Zat you?"

"Yeah, it's me, Jack, I'm here. Over here, on the floor."

"Jack Bates?" Mad said.

Bates turned to her slowly, frowned. "Who's she?"

She smirked and said, "So, this is the one who ate his mother, huh?"

Jaeger grunted as he struggled to sit up. "Don't pay any attention to her, Jack. You hear me? Ignore her."

"My mother?" Bates said, standing in place now, staring at her. "You talkin' about my mother?"

She drew the Smith & Wesson and aimed it at him. "Over here, mama's boy."

"Ma… mama's…"

"I said *ignore* her, Jack!" He turned to Mad and said, "Will you shut the fuck up, bitch?" To Bates again, he said, "Listen, Jack, she's nobody, just fucking *ignore* her, listen to me, Jack, you listening to me?"

Bates began to sway where he stood, back and forth, and he groaned, a long, sustained sound that lasted until he screamed.

"Oh, shit!" Jaeger shouted. "You dumb fuck!" He looked around for his shotgun, then crawled toward it frantically.

Bates started toward her, limping at first, looking weak and wounded, but with each step, his speed increased, along with his size and height, impossibly fast, so fast that she could not process it. His skin became gnarled and darkened to a rusty color and small thorns popped out of it like spring buds on wild flowers in a children's cartoon. His face reshaped itself into one resembling a gorilla's, and tusks grew upward from his lower lip.

And she watched in frozen awe, stunned into paralysis for a moment as the monster Bates had become lumbered toward her.

He reached a colossal hand toward her as he approached, and it grew bigger and bigger, filling her field of vision.

She fired the gun.

He stopped and flinched, making a low, gurgling sound. It lasted no more than two seconds, then he was moving toward her again.

"Jack!" Jaeger shouted.

The thorny monster that, a moment ago, had been Jack Bates stopped and turned toward Jaeger, first its head, then its body.

A blast of the shotgun took off much of Bates's large, malformed face and knocked him backward. He hit the floor with a heavy, resounding *smack*.

Mad quickly turned to Jaeger and aimed the gun.

"Drop the shotgun, Enzo," she said.

He did not. "You've gotta take me with you," he said, his voice low and gravelly, moist with emotion. "I've gotta get off this fucking moon. You understand? He was my friend. Jack was my *only* friend. You understand me? I killed him to save you. You were dead, you hear me? *Dead.* He was going to *end* you because of what you said. I've seen him do it before. But I stopped him. That's got to mean something. Goddammit. *Something.*"

"You're wanted dead or alive, Enzo. And I never intended to take you back."

She fired the gun and a hole appeared above his right eye a fraction of a second before he flopped back on the floor.

———

Mad headed for the bay door, still lodged open by the abandoned tractor. Jex was strapped to her back, surprisingly light, and his leg, held in her hand by the ankle, flopped limply as she walked.

"You got the fingers?" Jex said.

"Please. You think I'm new at this?"

She had cut a finger from each fugitive. Back at the *Tartarus*, the fingers would be tested for prints and DNA and matched with the escaped prisoners so she could be paid her remaining five million bounty.

"We can go on vacation after this job," she said.

"You could use one. I don't need one."

As she neared the door, a blurt of static came from the speakers and a female voice shouted, "You! Whoever you are! Send help! We need help!"

Mad heard screaming in the background, then the woman who had spoken screamed.

Voices in the background screamed, "Let us out!" "Open the door!" "We have to get out!"

"Not our problem," Mad said. She began running. "We've gotta get the fuck out of here."

She lowered her faceplate as she passed through the bay door and into the cold storm outside. The rain became a sharp, machine-gun assault on her helmet. Jagged tendrils of lightning jittered across the dark sky in all directions.

"I can't believe this shit," she said, running through the downpour. "I'm running through this storm with you strapped to my back and your leg flapping around in my hand like an old fishing pole."

"Oh, admit it. You've been wanting to get a piece of me for four years."

She chuckled and said, "Fuck off, Jex."

ZERO TO HERO

BY WESTON OCHSE

LAMBDA SERPENTIS: LV-666
9 JULY 2182

Corporal Franklin Sykes had everything he'd ever wanted. There was no place farther from the core systems than the tiny moon LV-666 in the Lambda Serpentis system above the water planet Lambda Serpentis II. Nothing ever happened other than an oxygen scooper sinking every now or then on the planet below or a particularly virulent form of herpes spreading among the No Wey-Yu molybdenum miners. Which was exactly the reason he'd orchestrated his move here ever since word started spreading about some sort of alien monster that shit acid and ate metal.

Whether or not it was a rumor, he'd spent a silver bullet

he'd earned when he'd looked the other way when he caught a No Wey-Yu administrator doing the dirty to an underage girl in the back of his office. The corporate hack was more than happy to get Sykes out of there and the young Colonial Marine soon found himself in stasis and on his way to the emptiest corner of the known universe... a corner safe from the sort of aliens everyone had started talking about in low whispers at the ends of long boring days.

When Sykes had arrived on LV-666, he'd found the station even more to his liking. The mine was almost played out and rumors were that No Wey-Yu might be pulling out. Their leaving was of little concern to the small Colonial Marine contingent. The marines would stay no matter what happened, lonely guards on the edge of nothing.

When he wasn't working, Sykes immersed himself into Charity Rock, the intergalactic trading game that was all the rage. He was an Iberian Level trader with palaces in seven systems, a fleet of merchant ships, and his own private navy. He was trying to take an eighth system, but a handful of lesser traders had formed a consortium to edge him out.

His life was near on perfect.

Whenever Sykes wasn't playing, he was breaking up bar fights, or monitoring the ever-silent emergency broadcast system from the mines along with the rest of his eighteen-person Colonial Marine platoon, whose boredom had reached truly majestic levels. So it came as a complete and utter shock to him when at 0553 hours on Tuesday the emergency broadcast system lit up like an old-Earth Christmas tree with the following report:

S.O.S. FOR IMMEDIATE RELEASE. ALCON.
NO WEY-YU MINING CONCERN LV-666 REQUIRES
IMMEDIATE EVACUATION OF TUNNELS 10—14. 3 KIA
AND 7 WIA. S.O.S.

Sykes stared at the screen as it rebroadcast the S.O.S., his eyes wide and unbelieving.

His thoughts went immediately to the impossible. How could this happen?

He'd manipulated the system like a genius, ensuring he was as far away from those monsters as possible. Now the very things he'd been afraid of were in his backyard and he was about to be asked to lead a team to eradicate them. He breathed deeply, reminding himself that he was so far away from the center of things that it would be impossible for the monsters to be here. It was probably something else, like a cave in or loss of oxygen. Nowhere in the message had it mentioned anything like he feared.

Still... he re-read the emergency missive that detailed dead and wounded miners. Something had to have happened and it could very well be those—he stopped himself. He needed to be in control. He needed his wits about him. He breathed deeply again, this time through his nose. He needed to remain calm. The last thing he needed was to hyperventilate. After a few breaths, he looked at the facts. There was no denying that there was a problem. What the problem was, he'd need to ascertain before he'd allow himself to panic.

He reminded himself that the S.O.S. wasn't his only problem.

He also had some serious Charity Rock gameplay he needed to perform to stop the others from getting through a back door he'd intentionally left open. They knew about it. He knew they knew about it, but they didn't know that he knew that they knew. The trap had been set, and all he had to do was spring it, but he had to be online to do it.

And now there were dead and wounded miners to take care of.

He felt his insides wrench.

It was all just too much.

He wanted to puke.

He bent forward and hugged his legs, hoping, praying that the signal was an accident.

Maybe if he ignored it, it would go away.

But the system buzzed again and the same message broadcast across the screen.

Lance Corporal Haywald stepped into the office with a toothbrush in his mouth. "Did I hear the—" He leaned forward and read the screen. "Holy shit. Is that for real?" Then he noticed Sykes with his head between his legs. "What are you doing down there, corporal?"

Sykes sat up so fast he saw stars. He managed to clear his throat. "Adjusting my boots," he said, his voice a little more high-pitched than he'd wanted. He deepened it and added, "Get first squad together for response. I want them ready to deploy in five minutes."

Haywald stared at Sykes as if he'd just spoken Chinese. Sykes shook his head and stood as he shouted, "Move, Lance Corporal!" That broke the spell and a second later, Haywald hit the alert button.

Sykes did a complete security sweep of the system. They hadn't had any visitors since a ship full of No Wey-Yu med techs had come to vaccinate the miners with a new strain of penicillin. Of the seven-hundred and forty-two miners, two hundred and seventeen were on shift. Sykes sent a message to the No Wey-Yu site manager ordering him to hold off sending in the next shift.

Sykes got an immediate terse reply: *NO CAN DO!!!*

Sykes typed furiously. *YOUR MINERS ARE SENDING AN S.O.S.*

I'M SURE IT'S NOTHING.

There it was.

His out.

If the No Wey-Yu corporate site lead didn't want Colonial Marine support, who was Sykes to shove it down his throat?

Everything was suddenly right with the world.

Sykes brushed his hands together, then typed a message. COLONIAL MARINES. NO WEY-YU DECLINES

ASSISTANCE. STAND DOWN. Then he pressed send and turned off the alert. He put his feet on the desk and grinned, relishing the silence. Now he'd definitely have time to finalize the trap for the consortium. Who in the hell did they think they were messing with, anyway? His thoughts burrowed into the virtual reality of Charity Rock as he planned his Machiavellian machinations. Not for the first time, or even the hundredth, did he wish the realities were reversed and the game he played as an intergalactic trader was being a Colonial Marine.

He was hungry too. Wasn't it time for breakfast?

Sykes found himself in the galley drinking the last of his coffee, when Lance Corporal Haywald ran in wearing full battle rattle: an M41A Pulse Rifle, M3 Pattern Personal Armor, black fatigues with knee, elbow, shin and forearm ballistic pads, and a ballistic helmet with a riot mask that served to both protect the face and be a visual locus for the Heads Up Display or HUD.

Sykes felt a slash of pain go through his head as a headache was born and died. "What is it, Lance Corporal?" he asked. Breakfast lay like a brick road across his gut.

Haywald hesitated before he answered, then said, "No Wey-Yu Site Lead has requested our assistance."

He changed his mind? "He can't change his mind." Sykes pounded the table. "He said they didn't want any assistance," he said, realizing his voice had again risen too high.

"Apparently he did," Haywald said.

Sykes put his head in his hand and shook it back and forth, slowly saying "No," over and over again like it would be the magic word to change reality.

Haywald shifted from his right foot to his left. "Uh, Corporal?"

"What, Haywald?"

"Me and the others are gonna go take care of this. Uh, you can take it easy, if you want."

Sykes stopped shaking his head and stared coldly at his subordinate.

Haywald held out his hand. He flashed a false grin. "Really, sir. We got this."

It was one thing to be a coward, but it was another to be treated like one. Sykes fought the urge to accept Haywald's offer. Yeah, he could sit back and let his subordinates take care of things. After all, he was the ranking Marine. Who was he to put himself in harm's way? But there was something in Haywald's eyes that made him balk. Sykes couldn't put a finger on it, but it was almost like the younger Haywald felt sorry for him, and that Sykes couldn't stand.

Sykes pushed himself to his feet. "Are the others ready?"

"First Squad is, Corporal," Haywald answered.

"Have Second and Third Squad stand by. Let First know I'll be with them in ten minutes."

Haywald started to walk away.

"Lance Corporal."

Haywald turned. "Sir?"

"Never presume to know what the Corporal thinks or wants. Understood?"

"Understood, Corporal."

"Dismissed."

As soon as Haywald left the room, Sykes's entire body sagged and he threw himself back onto the bench. This was it. He was doomed. He died a thousand times over the next thirty seconds, inventing new ways to be broken, shot, eaten, melted, burned, gassed, crushed, and cut open. Not knowing what the monster looked like, his panicked brain invented an entire mental zoo filled with various and sundry terrible creatures, each one making him flinch, the realities of his own imagination too scary for him to behold. He stood unsteadily and took two steps, then the contents of his stomach spewed onto the floor.

———

Thirty minutes later they were on the lift to the lower levels. During the trip, Sykes was remotely notified through his helmet's communication suite that three of the four members of the Charity Rock trade consortium who'd allied against him had found his backdoor. He groaned. Without him to spring the trap, they'd have unfettered access to his accumulated wealth.

They arrived at Tunnel 10, which had been drilled, mined, and smoothed decades before and was now used for administration and logistics functions. In fact, all the single digit tunnels were the same way. If the danger was some sort of monster, he'd expect it to come from one of the lower tunnels, possibly towards the bottom of the mine, which would make it tunnel ninety-one.

A fourth member of the consortium entered through his back door.

Sykes gritted his teeth.

First Squad was comprised of Haywald, Michia, Chevelon, Franks, Phillips, Shire, and Albright. Michia had seen the most action, but he couldn't keep his drinking under control so he remained a perennial PFC. Albright and Shire were converted criminals and were solid, if not inexperienced, PFCs. Chevelon was so wet behind her ears she could barely put her gear on. That left Phillips and Haywald, both solid Lance Corporal marines and the two he could most count on.

"Shire."

She popped forward, ready, her face scarred from ritualistic tattooing on a prison barge. "Yes, Corporal."

"You and Phillips head down the hall and recon. Go a hundred meters, then hunker down and report."

Phillips nodded and joined Shire. Together they moved in a tactical crouch down the hall and around the curve.

They reported in at fifty meters.

Three minutes later, gunfire from two pulse rifles rocked the tunnel.

"Shire! Phillips! Report!" Sykes called through his helmet.

No response.

"Corporal, what should we do?" Chevelon asked, sweat beading across her nose and above her upper lip. She wiped it away with a quick hand.

"We wait. Those marines know what they're doing."

At least Sykes hoped they were okay. An image of a hundred multi-limbed monsters tearing around the corner towards them forced him to close his eyes for a few seconds. Just then he received electronic notification that the fifth and sixth members of the consortium had found his back door. Maybe if he was able to get this over quickly, he could get back into Charity Rock and spring his trap.

He reluctantly opened his eyes.

As it stood, right now he was helpless to do anything about the damn consortium. If they worked together, they could strip him of all the wealth he'd accumulated in seventeen thousand hours of gameplay. How many night shifts would he have to pull just to get a portion of it back?

Albright and Franks shifted nervously.

Chevelon almost dropped her rifle, and would have, if it hadn't been for the sling.

Sykes hissed into his helmet. "Shire! Come in, Shire!" He hated being blind. He hated not knowing what was going on. "Phillips, report!" He hated being down here instead of back in his hooch. He hated that the universe had decided today would be the day it fucked with him. He basically hated every damned thing.

Ten, twenty, thirty seconds ticked by as he continued his inventory of hate, his index finger tapping impatiently at the trigger well.

"What's going on, Corporal?" Haywald asked.

Sykes shook his head. How was he supposed to know? Why should he know anything? After all, he was only the one in charge.

A blood-curdling scream was abruptly silenced from somewhere far down the tunnel.

His anger faltered as fear tickled the back of his neck. He thought this was the worst situation he'd ever been in. He forced himself to breathe normally. "Shire, Phillips, this is Command One, come in," he said again into his helmet.

Static.

Then Haywald pointed down the hall. "There—what's that?"

Sykes raised his pulse rifle and sighted down its length. He'd never fired one outside of training. Would now be the moment? A shock of electric dread sizzled through him. He tasted metal. His entire body felt hollow as he moved his finger to the trigger.

A dark figure slumped from one side of the tunnel to the other, moving too fast for them to ascertain its features. As much as Sykes wanted to understand what he was seeing, the constant motion and the sweat dribbling into his eyes made it impossible.

"What is it?" he asked, his finger tightening on the trigger.

"It's moving too fast," Haywald cried. "Shoot it, Corporal!"

Sykes wanted to wipe the sweat from his eyes, but to do so would mean he'd lose his sight picture. He blinked furiously, then in one crystalline moment, he saw what he was aiming at. He lowered his weapon and stepped forward.

PFC Shire's impossibly fast gyrations slowed as she stumbled the last dozen feet, then fell to the ground, her arms and legs spasming out of control. Her eyes were wide and panicked behind a scratched faceplate.

"Spitting," she managed to say. "Spitting," she repeated.

"Spitting what?"

Sykes noticed a fine spray of liquid on the outside of her helmet. There was no sign of her weapon.

"They... everyone... spitting."

Why would anyone be spitting? It made no sense. And Phillips? Where was he?

Shire's entire body went rigid, then stilled. Her eyes were shut. Where her chest had been furiously heaving a second before, it now moved only slightly.

"What happened to her?" Haywald asked.

"No idea." Sykes turned to his men and said, "Keep sharp. Something got Shire and maybe Phillips, and we still don't know what it is."

Fear shined on five young faces. Haywald, Michia, Chevelon, Franks, and Albright, all staring at Corporal Sykes, waiting for him to lead them. He stared back, realizing how invested they were in him. His remote indicated that the seventh member of the consortium had made it through his back door. He dismissed the information packet. He didn't have time for any Charity Rock bullshit now. For perhaps the first time in his life, Sykes felt ready to lead. The hollow bowl within him was now filled with a confidence he'd never before felt. The looks his marines gave him had power and had given him the wherewithal to act like the marine he was always supposed to have been. Sykes had spent his life running from danger only to have danger find him, and now that he was confronted with it, he found that he liked the feeling it gave him. The adrenaline rush made him focus, noticing things, thinking critically in an instant.

He'd leave Shire behind. She was still alive; they'd get her to sick bay when they returned. In the meantime, they had to find Phillips and ascertain what the threat was.

He grinned. "Listen, Marines. Stay behind me, follow my commands, and we'll get through this. Someone or something is on the station and we need to find it." He cleared his throat. "Even more important, we need to find Phillips."

All the marines nodded.

Chevelon looked absolutely terrified.

Sykes grabbed her shoulder. "Come on, Marine. If you die, at least you'll die a hero."

She nodded and wiped sweat from her brow with her sleeve, her fear coalescing into something else, something nearer determination.

The scientists, miners, and marines all counted on him, and

for the first time it didn't feel like a burden. No, the feeling of responsibility and of service warmed him from within.

"What about Shire?" Franks asked.

"Leave her. We'll get her to the sick bay when this is all over. Now, follow me."

Sykes moved forward in a tactical crouch. He held his rifle at low ready, the way marines had been holding their rifles since before Hamarana, before The Kincaid, before Mogadishu and before Tarawa. Muzzle down, stock firmly in the shoulder, a marine could bring his weapon to bear in a moment's notice, while still able to assess and see what was in front of him.

Thirty meters down the corridor a miner lay in a pool of blood. This must have been who Shire had shot. But why? There seemed to be nothing out of place. The miner wore his protective boots, jumpsuit and gloves. Other than a missing helmet, unnecessary in this section of tunnels, everything was as it should be, except, of course, the gaping hole in the center of the man's chest. Whatever had happened, Shire had assessed and believed there to be a threat. That Sykes couldn't immediately recognize what the threat had been didn't matter. He was confident he soon would.

A composite metal door stood another fifteen meters down the tunnel on the left. Sykes stacked Michia and Chevelon on one side and put Franks and Albright on the other. He had Haywald form behind him. He called up the map of this level on his HUD. Meeting Room 57 was on the other side with another door on the far side leading to a tunnel that gave access to the other side of the complex. The door in front of him was currently locked. Sykes unlocked it using his HUD.

"Open the door, Haywald."

The young marine gave him a worried glance but did as he was told.

When the door opened, Sykes leaned inside to look.

Across a room with overturned tables and chairs, six miners had trapped a seventh who was huddled in a corner, his hands covering his face, screaming for them to stop. Instead of punching or kicking the seventh man, the others were bent at the waist, spitting at him. They looked more like giant birds violently pecking at the air, but even from across the room, Sykes could see the spittle flying from their mouths, coating the man's hands, dripping onto his chest, creating a thick, viscous puddle.

Sykes raised his rifle and fired into the other corner of the room. "Stand down!" he shouted.

All six of the attackers spun toward him.

Sykes felt an eerie sense of the weird as he saw the expressions on their faces. He'd expected anger, possibly even rage. Why else would they have decided to spit on one of their own? Instead, they seemed entirely void of emotion. Their faces were slack. Their eyes were empty.

Then they began to run right at him.

Sykes brought his rifle up, but thought better of it and stepped back into the hallway.

"Close the door!"

Haywald slammed it shut.

Sykes locked the door via his HUD and threw his back against it. What the hell had just happened? He replayed it in his mind. Six miners had cornered a seventh and were spitting on him. When they'd heard Sykes, they'd turned and run at him as if to attack, despite the fact they were facing a Marine wearing full body armor and carrying a pulse rifle. That made no sense. What was driving them so mad?

"Corporal Sykes, look here," Chevelon said, pointing to a stain on the wall about ten meters down the hall.

Haywald ran towards the spot. "It's blood, Corporal."

"Maybe it's Phillips's," Albright said.

Sykes pushed himself away from the door and led the others to the stain. It had the vague outlines of a bloody handprint.

"Michia, anything from Phillips?"

She shook her head.

"Keep at it."

When he didn't acknowledge, Sykes turned. He and Albright were off to the side, whispering to each other, Michia shaking his head.

"You two, what's going on?"

Albright straightened.

Michia sneered and shook his head again.

"What is it?" Sykes demanded.

"Albright has a theory," Michia began. "But I think she's been watching too many discs."

"What is it?" Sykes was losing his patience. "Albright, speak up."

Albright glanced worriedly at Michia, who looked away. "I've been thinking," he began, then faltered.

"You know the only thing scarier than a marine saying *I've been thinking* is a miner saying *watch what I built*," Sykes said.

"I told you so," Michia said.

Albright's shoulders slumped and he stared at the ground.

Sykes nodded. "Still, I've got the smartest marines in a hundred parsecs, so tell me?"

"We're the only marines in a hundred parsecs," Albright said.

"Be happy you made the cut," Sykes said. "Now, out with it."

Before he could speak, three miners appeared from far down the tunnel, running at them at full speed. Their heads moved like they were pecking air, but Sykes knew they were spitting. Everyone raised their weapons.

"What do we do?" Chevelon asked.

"Shoot them," he said.

All of them opened up on the charging men, who were hurled backwards by the combined force of their pulse rifle rounds.

After a moment, Sykes said, "Watch out for more." Then to Albright he said, "Where were we?"

"I was trying to figure out what's going on when I remembered something that happened on the prison barge. I was in solitary at the time, but the survivors talked about experimentation."

"Experimentation?"

"Med techs came in and gave everyone shots and two hours later there was a riot."

"Did they spit?"

"No, nothing like that. The other inmates, they just became enraged and tried to kill each other."

"And they blamed it on the med techs."

Albright shrugged. "Nothing definite, but... everyone was fine, then everyone got shots, then everyone wasn't fine." He squinted his eyes. "We were... what do you call it?"

"A hostage population," said Haywald.

"Like the miners," said Sykes.

"Like the miners," Albright said. "Who were just visited by No Wey-Yu med techs."

Sykes saw it all now. An old, played out mine. Too many miners to move. Why not test out a new bio-weapon. And the spitting... was that the delivery mechanism? Damn!

"What do we do?" Chevelon asked.

"We find Phillips and get the hell out of here."

Saying those words inspired him. The old Sykes would have said it was a good reason to leave, using the situation as a valid reason to save his own ass. But now, in the face of danger, he was able to make command decisions just as he was supposed to. To say he was filled with pride was an understatement. He'd gone from being an utter zero to something near a hero. Was this what it felt like? He damned his old self and felt a wash of shame slam over him, but then it was gone as he began to plan. He needed to get Phillips, then grab Shire and get them to sick bay.

Once there, they would secure the mine and send a message for rescue. He and his marines could probably hold out for six to ten months, which was enough time for a ship to rescue them. As for the miners, if what Albright said was correct, it was their own corporation that had done them in. Sykes would make sure and report them as soon as he returned to known space. To do so earlier might put the lives of his marines in jeopardy... damn, but his mind was clicking like a computer.

"Uh, Corporal?" asked Chevelon. "Are you hearing what I'm hearing?"

Sykes spun, a self-satisfied smile almost breaking his face. "What?" All of his marines had turned to face down the tunnel.

Sykes cocked his head. He could just hear something that sounded like far away rushing water, except it was getting closer. His eyes narrowed. Rushing water? On this moon? The sound grew louder, a low rush accentuated with what could only be waves. He checked his HUD for air quality to make sure they weren't hallucinating, reacting to something in the air. No, the air was the same thin mixture of oxygen and other chemicals to which they'd long ago become accustomed.

Sykes had no idea what was coming. "Weapons ready, Marines," he whispered.

As one, they brought their pulse rifles to bear, stocks snug against their shoulders.

A tickle of fear teased his stomach. Was this what it was like to lead? Were leaders scared as well? For so long he'd always thought that those who stood in the face of danger were fearless. He inhaled to steady his nerves, then laughed again, which made several of the marines turn and eye him. He nodded to each of them. "Steady," he said, low and mean.

Then the first of them appeared.

It wasn't water.

There were no waves.

It was the miners, shuffling their feet against the tunnel floor, moving only inches at a time. The combined sound of hundreds of feet constantly shuffling had confused his brain, making it think the sound came from water. How could it know that instead of walking, several hundred miners would be shuffling like they were a hundred years old and could barely move.

More and more, they came. An immense clump of shuffling miners moving along the long curve of the tunnel. Their heads were down, chins resting against their chests. He couldn't see if their eyes were open.

"Do we shoot them?" Michia asked.

The sound of the marine's voice triggered a change. The miners ceased all movement. Then, in one eerie pendulous move, their heads swiveled upwards. Blank gazes focused on them.

There were too many. Calculations clicked through Sykes's mind. He had to try something else.

"Marines, to me. We're going to move back."

He began to back away.

His marines joined him.

Then the miners broke into a run.

"Oh, hell!" Sykes turned and ran. "To me!"

He ran back to the door they'd locked. It was their only chance. He unlocked it and swung it open. Seven miners stood inside, staring at the open space where the door had been closed. Sykes wasn't sure if they were surprised. It didn't matter. He fired his pulse rifle from the hip, mowing them down as he pushed into the room, stepping over their freshly fallen bodies. Then he ran to the back of the room and took up position.

Gunfire erupted from the tunnel.

Haywald and Michia stumbled into the room.

Chevelon came next, firing and screaming, her face bloody, her left arm hanging dead.

"Shut the door," she cried. "They've got the others."

Haywald shoved his shoulder against it and Michia joined him.

When it latched, Sykes locked it.

Albright and Franks hadn't made it. That made four marines Sykes had lost, if you included Shire and Phillips.

Sykes put a fist to the side of his head and held it there. Shire! He'd left her out in the tunnel. And Phillips. Where was he?

Haywald and Michia came to him.

"What are your orders, corporal?" Haywald asked.

Sykes looked at each of them. What were his orders?

"Your orders?" Haywald repeated.

Sykes cleared his throat. "You and Michia see to Chevelon. Make sure she's okay, then post a sentry by the door."

They looked at each other, then obeyed.

Sykes was struck by the simplicity of it all. The mine was as much a trap for the miners as his game had been for the consortium. Each was a perfect setup. The only difference was that the game was just that, a game. Had he been thinking about the real live posting on LV-666 as he had the game, he might have been able to anticipate that a place so remote and played out might be an experiment waiting to happen. Now, here he was, as much a victim as the miners. He received one final remote notification, the game notifying him that all of his assets had been seized and that he was no longer capable of gameplay.

Sykes laughed silently, remembering when such things mattered. He righted a few of the overturned chairs, eying the dead miners. Eventually, they'd have to stack the bodies against one wall. They'd also have to be careful not to become infected. He turned, looking at the wall behind him, then spied the other door. He'd forgotten about that. Perhaps it was a way out. According to his tunnel diagram, it opened into another section of the complex. If they were lucky, they could escape. He moved to the door, checked and found it unlocked. Then, he cautiously pulled it open, and saw—Phillips!

The Colonial Marine stood there.

Had he hidden here when confronted with the miners in the room?

Sykes was about to pull him out when he registered the blankness of the man's stare.

Before Sykes could back away, Phillips reared back and spit. An immense orb of saliva hit the center of his faceplate and stayed there.

Sykes took a few backward steps.

Phillips followed him, spitting again and again.

Sykes fired from the hip again, hitting Phillips in the

stomach, the rounds blowing clean through. Phillips fell dead as Michia and Haywald ran over.

Then Sykes watched as the saliva began to move. Like a hyper amoeba, it grew appendages and pulled itself from the center of his mask to the sides, sliding under the faceplate and towards his face. Smaller sputum riveted around the edges, seeking a way through the faceplate.

Sykes dropped his rifle and struggled to remove his helmet. When he did, he hurled it across the room.

Had any gotten on him?

Was he infected?

He vigorously wiped his face with his gloved hands and the right hand came away with a small wet stain. Was that it? Had he gotten it?

Later, he didn't know how long later, because he must have blacked out, he found himself standing. He could just see them, Michia and Haywald, standing on either side of him. He wondered if Chevelon was standing behind him. He moved to turn, but found he couldn't. He tried to lift his hand and discovered that was impossible. It was like it wasn't there. But he knew it was, but that part of the nervous system that governed non-autonomous muscle movements had been turned off.

It wasn't lost on him that he wouldn't be in this predicament and still be in command of seven systems in Charity Rock if he'd just done as Haywald had offered. Why had he done it? Why hadn't he stayed behind? Sykes had developed a finely-honed sense of cowardice and he should have followed it.

Later, he wondered if his view might change. He was getting tired of staring at the closed door. He felt like a video game character waiting for the game to be turned on so he could do something.

Anything.

Even later, he began to laugh, not out loud, because he was incapable of it, but inside... in his mind... where he still felt normal. Uproariously, he laughed for days, especially when he repeated the phrase, *at least you'll die a hero*, a hundred thousand times like it was punishment.

Much later he craved to spit and felt it pool in his mouth.

Then… he didn't know how long it had been, he began to feel his body shutting down. Haywald and Michia had long ago fallen. His legs were wobbly. He knew he was dying and welcomed it. No water. No food. It was only a matter of time. He tried to fall, if only to change his view, but still couldn't move anything non-autonomous.

And damn it, he still wanted to spit.

If only someone would open the damned door.

DARK MOTHER

BY DAVID FARLAND

Sometimes we can wake from dark dreams into a deeper nightmare.

Carter Burke pounded the lock mechanism on the door and felt a surge of relief as it bolted shut. Ripley, on the far side of the door, had had death in her dark eyes. *Stupid sheep,* he thought. *She could have been rich.* Yes, he'd tried to impregnate her and Newt with aliens, but he'd imagined that once they got to the bio-weapons department at Weyland-Yutani, the creatures could have been safely removed. Sort of like a C-section. Ripley and the girl would have been fine, and they'd all be rich.

Instead they were trapped in the tunnels under Hadley's Hope, with Xenomorphs filling the tunnels.

Some people have no imagination. Stupid freaking cow. Now to get out of this place.

He whirled, fled through a storeroom, glanced back to the locked door, and heard Ripley banging at it. He drew a sliding panel shut between them, then heard chitin scraping the floor behind him and a hiss. Burke whirled to see a Xenomorph warrior in the doorway.

Terror spiked, sharp as a spear in the heart. He screamed, reached back to grab anything with which to arm himself.

The alien bared its double jaws, displaying rows of teeth dripping with white foam, but to Burke's shock, the creature did not bite. Instead it grabbed him, slammed him painfully against the heavy metal door.

Everything went black.

<hr />

Air rushed past his face, under his arms. *I'm flying... I'm Superman.*

He was a child again, flying through his house in his imagination. His parent's multimillion dollar flat had glowing white walls on a dim nightlight mode, with vast archways overhead—like a heavenly cathedral.

No, he realized, *I'm being carried.* He felt strong hands gripping his ribs, holding him.

An odd thought struck him. *Think before you scream.*

Flying through the house was a vivid memory, one of his earliest. His mother had carried him to the bathroom. She'd pulled him from bed, still wet from urine.

His mother dropped him roughly to the bathtub and turned on the water before he could begin to dress. Burke must have been about four. He peered up to her beautiful face. Even as a young woman, his mother had a sculpted look. His father was a plastic surgeon after all, and like the other surgeons at his country club, he'd made his wife stunning, inhumanely beautiful.

She changed her appearance from time to time, and on this occasion she appeared almost Latina, with a light coffee skin dye, black hair, and fiery black eye dye.

Burke's father pushed his head through the bathroom door and warned, "Be gentle with him, hon."

"He stinks," his mother said. "God, children stink."

In this memory, Burke hardly recognized his mother. He remembered her better with bright blue eyes and golden hair, or as a redhead with wider cheeks. Like many women who had had too many surgeries, her face lost its plasticity, became curiously unanimated, more as if she'd been carved from marble than flesh.

Her assertion stung him. Burke was a bed-wetter. No matter how much he bathed, his mother claimed he stank.

As a smaller boy, he'd longed to hold her, had dreamt of cradling his head between her firm breasts. But he'd never been able to.

She was a goddess, cool and untouchable.

Burke trembled, felt pain in his sides, and realized that someone was still carrying him.

Think before you scream.

He roused his sluggish eyes open enough to see: he was racing through a dim hall. The alien held him under the armpits, lurching and jostling at incredible speed as it went down a long corridor.

He struggled to breathe, took a mental inventory. He was in the grip of a Xenomorph, taller than him and stronger than him. He knew where it was taking him.

It carried him as his mother had, and with embarrassment he felt a familiar warmth between his legs. He hadn't wet himself since he was a child, and the thought flashed, *The alien thinks I stink.*

He had no weapons. He'd been forced to flee Ripley and her marines without one. But his father had taught him, *"Your mind can be a powerful weapon."*

Burke had nothing to lose, so he spoke cautiously. "Wait a minute," he offered. "Let's talk about this!"

His heart pounded and he waited for an interminable instant to see if the Xenomorph would respond. "Can you understand me? Are you open to negotiation?"

The Xenomorph stopped running, threw him in the air a little, and turned Burke to face him.

It understands me! He thought hopefully. *Or is it like a dog that just responds to tone.*

Without skipping a beat, the creature hissed and pounded him against a plasteel bulkhead, as if he were a baseball bat, and everything went dark.

Burke woke to sirens in a fetid room, tensing instantly. He could not move his arms or legs. *Think before you scream.* He let himself go limp, played dead. He could taste blood in his mouth, and his right cheek felt swollen.

He tried to recall a fleeting dream—about a girl he'd seduced in college. What was her name? Ah well, it didn't really matter. He'd seduced lots of girls. He was good-looking, after all, and rich, and people will fall for any lie you tell them.

He opened his good eye and peered about in the dim light. Brownish-gray material covered the walls, looking for all the world like the interior of an animal's ribcage. He'd once killed a neighbor's dog as a child, and knew those shapes. Other shapes seemed just as organic but impossible to define.

He recognized this place: the Atmospheric Processing Plant, down in its lowest levels. The alien hive.

His heart lurched and he tried to move, but his torso, legs, and arms felt stuck in some resinous substance. Everything smelled hot, and the resin had an unidentifiable odor—like human vomit mixed with decay and... sex.

Around him, he saw the shadowy shapes of other men. They stood encased in resin, frozen, their faces twisted in horror, arms and fingers out-stretched. He didn't recognize the closest man. He must have been a settler.

There was a gaping hole in the man's chest, where an alien's spawn had burst its way out.

That's where the rot is coming from.

Human carcasses were everywhere, as if plastered one above another.

Resin covered him, too. Only his face was free. He could breathe the fetid air, but could not move.

He experimented, tried swiveling his hips. The resin was thick around his legs, like cement boots, but the resin felt more viscous next to his body. The outside material had hardened like glue.

He tried shaking his head, managed to force the resin back a bit, but could not break free. He experimented with his hands.

The casing around his right hand was hard as stone, but on the left it must have been fresher. It still felt viscous around his fingers. He fought and twisted, till he managed to break the thin outer crust.

He imagined that if he worked fast enough, he might free an entire arm, then break open the rest of the crust inch by inch.

He heard a *splat*, then spotted movement through a partly obscured archway, saw the head and part of the body of an enormous Xenomorph, one that stood at least fifteen feet tall. It had a vast abdomen attached to it, taller than a house, longer than a bus, and she had just deposited an enormous white egg onto a pile of crap-like goo.

Her abdomen rippled as muscles in it moved, like a piece of worm's gut, and then she lurched forward slightly.

Burke recognized that... body part, dredged a word from a forgotten biology class. It was an *ovipositor*, like the ones on a carnivorous wasp, or a queen termite.

A smaller Xenomorph came into view, picked up the egg on its little goo pile, and peered toward him.

"Wait, no!" Burke shouted, and tried to wriggle his hand.

The huge alien mother made a soft growl, peered toward

him. The smaller Xenomorph set the egg aside, and Burke felt some relief.

But the Xenomorph drone hurried over to another egg, one that had been laying there, and carried it close to Burke, set it at his feet.

Burke felt scared witless. No plans would come.

He tried to wriggle aside, to break his casing. He fought to free his hand, but the Xenomorph hissed and whipped its tail, then thrust its teeth in his face.

"Calm down," Burke said. "I get it. You don't want me to move." Yet he couldn't just sit there.

The Xenomorph backed away. Above its shoulders, dead men peered down, and Burke suddenly remembered a huge Nativity scene that his mother had put up one Christmas. It had Mary and Joseph peering down at a baby Jesus in a cradle, while the Wise Men stared on and angels flew above.

In this scene, Burke was Joseph, and the baby Jesus was an egg with one of those creatures—a facehugger—inside. The hovering angels were horrid corpses, and once the egg hatched, the vaguely crablike creature would climb to his face, insert a tube down his throat, implant some kind of embryo.

"Look," he said to the Xenomorph. The worker peered at him ignorantly, but the queen in the other room turned her head, as if studying his gaze.

Her face was rigid, chiseled and sculpted, and he saw his mother's calculating, unfeeling gaze behind those eyes.

"What do you want?" he called to her. The room was hot, fires were already blazing. This whole place was going to go up in a mushroom cloud. "I work for Weyland-Yutani Corporation. I can get you anything. What do you want? A new world? You want cows to eat? People? I can get them for you!"

The queen mother peered at him as if trying to decipher what he said, then turned away as she pooped another egg.

Burke felt sweaty all over, had huge rivulets running down his face. He felt sick to his stomach, and choked on vomit.

The egg began to quiver and shake, and a crack appeared. His heart hammered wildly and his mouth felt drier than he'd ever imagined, drier than the toxic sands of the Gobi. He struggled to break free, rocking wildly, and the Xenomorph drone hissed a warning.

"Screw you!" he shouted as the facehugger oozed from its shell, a beige nightmare.

The Xenomorph drone hissed encouragement to the facehugger, then peered up in satisfaction, like a midwife caught in the throes of admiring the miracle of birth.

"Screw all of you!" Burke shouted. "That ain't no baby Jesus, and I ain't no…"

Loser.

He raged and struggled for one more moment. *Think before you scream.*

There's still a way to turn this around, he realized. He'd hoped to smuggle one of these facehuggers off-planet inside Ripley and Newt.

It will still work! he realized. *This creature could be a goldmine.* If he carried one inside him, he could get on ship, put himself in stasis, and leave instructions for those who found him.

All he lacked was time. The whole processing plant was going to blow soon. He'd need to break free after the attack, get out before the creature ate him from inside.

All too soon, the creature leapt at him, covered his face, with its soft crab-like body, and tried to insert something down his throat.

Burke struggled to keep his teeth clenched, to twist his face aside, but realized that every second he fought, was another second wasted.

Swallow it down, he told himself. *Just take it.*

He opened his mouth wide and let the facehugger do its work.

The facehuggers suppress the immune system and ALSO pacify/knock out the host. He MIGHT have thought, but he'd be SCREAMING inside.

Oh god, what have I done?

But it was his only chance. He didn't have a gun, nothing to even the odds. He didn't have the strength to break free.

He couldn't breathe. He fought the creature for a breath, but couldn't get air. His face and muscles all strained and began to burn, as if he were drowning.

Just take it, he told himself.

And as he faded from consciousness, he remembered.

As a teen he'd walked in on his mother once, the famous realtor, as she "entertained" a client. What the man did to her looked more like rape than lovemaking.

Burke had kept the incident secret for three days, worried what would happen. Would his father be furious? Had his mother seduced the man or been raped? Would she leave his father?

Secretly, he hoped that she'd leave. She ran the house with an iron hand.

And so at a Sunday dinner, he told his father what he'd seen, hoping that... mom would confess, that she'd be freed by it, that maybe things would work out better.

Heavy silence followed. Burke's father, a stern man who seemed never to grow old, simply spread his hands above his plate, winked at his wife, and said, "We all do what we *must* in this family."

"What do you mean?" Burke asked, lips trembling.

"Your mother brings in a lot of money in this family," his father said. "I'm a famous surgeon, but I only supply 18% of our income. Your mother gets the rest."

His mother was in her redhead phase, with wide-set cheekbones and skin bleached to ivory. "Don't you understand, son? I put on different faces for my clients. I target them. They wouldn't pay a normal realtor much, but a beautiful woman, one who could sue them into oblivion, who could expose them for what they are, lead them to arrest or divorce—they pay me very well."

While Burke's jaw dropped, his father smiled. "I saw the

rape. It was recorded. I've seen all of them. Why do you think I put on these different faces for your mother? It's so that the marks will be driven mad."

Burke's mother studied him with a sculpted gaze and said, "I do what I must for money, and if you are any son of mine, you will do your part, too..."

Burke woke to blaring sirens with a throat rubbed raw. They fall off of their own accord. ALSO – and shit, this doesn't work. The facehugger stays on for a few hours. The amount of time between when Burke is "taken" and the end of Alien is a ticking clock. And then it blows up. The room had grown blistering, and sweat poured from him, too much sweat. It was in his clothes, encasing him beneath the cocoon. He felt wrung out, at the end of his strength.

Through the narrow corridors, he could no longer see the Xenomorph worker, nor the queen.

Sirens blared and fires ranged. A female computerized voice warned, "Attention, emergency! All personnel must evacuate immediately. You now have fifteen minutes to reach minimum safe distance."

Shit, Burke wondered, *how long was I out for?*

Fifteen minutes. Did he have time to escape?

Even if he ran as fast as he could, he wouldn't make it outside the blast zone. He needed a vehicle. Even a wheeled excursion vehicle might do. A ship would be best.

He thrust his left arm against the resin, banging it with the heel of his palm. The outer crust cracked reluctantly, and he managed to reach around. By punching the crust above his right hand, he damaged the resin, but he felt weak. The material around his legs and torso had hardened while he slept, locking his body into place.

Worst of all, he had a stomach ache—not the normal pain of

bloating or heartburn, but something he'd never imagined—he felt the creature inside him, down in his guts, like a huge fish in a bowl, swimming about.

Terror lanced through him, cold and shocking, so that he was nearly mindless. He knew what was coming.

He pounded the resin until his left fist was bloody pulpy and raw, and still could not break through. He pummeled until his head dropped in fatigue.

All hope fled Burke, like water gushing from a broken barrel, and with the air left his lungs.

He nearly fainted from fatigue, nearly dropped the grenade. But he wasn't ready to die.

Sirens continued to blare, and the computer warned that Burke had thirteen minutes to reach safety. In the distance Xenomorphs shrieked in pain and rage. The hissing of a flamethrower sounded nearby.

He heard a huge Xenomorph pounding through the tunnels, charging toward him, and he realized that he had one chance to kill it, to get it off Ridley's tale.

For an instant, he imagined himself being a hero.

His mother's eyes. His mother's chiseled emotionless face, with skin thinly stretched over a skull.

He dived for cover as she rushed past, and he considered throwing the grenade after her.

Instead, he staggered along behind. "Ripley!" he called. It wasn't too late. He could still be a hero. He could make it to the ship. He had to.

So he began to jog, his path lit by a trail of flares that burned among the twists and turns of the hive.

Something wrenched inside him, and he felt terribly hungry. The chest-burster was draining his energy, so that he felt depleted.

Burke ran for a bit, reached an elevator. He hit the call button, but no elevator dropped.

Instead, the sirens blared.

"Seven minutes to reach minimum safe distance."

He struggled to catch his breath, and realized at last that the lift wasn't coming. Fire vented up from a nearby crevasse and lightning arced between two pillars. Some metal beams fell nearby, and the station shuddered. The plant was coming apart.

Burke hurried to the emergency stairs and began to climb up. In the stairwell above, he heard clawing footsteps on the roof, and the screams of the hive mother. Something was going on, and he could not imagine what was happening. The building shook, and more flames shot up beside the open staircase.

He reached the top of the landing platform as the mechanized voice called, *"Two minutes to reach minimum safe distance."*

Burke gazed up to see the blunt shape of the space shuttle lifting off into the clouds, the fires of its engines gleaming bright in the half-light.

Atop the ship, wedged into a crevice between the cabin and the hull, he could see an unexpected shape—the giant Queen Xenomorph, hitching a ride.

Flames shot up around the platform, impossibly hot, and lightning arced into the sky in a bright crown. The whole platform trembled as if it would teeter and fall into the fiery pit.

Burke reached to his aching head, mussed his hair, and peered about in frustration.

He held the incendiary grenade in his fist, refusing to take his finger off of the plunger quite yet.

Something moved inside him, pushing out his ribs, like a baby on steroids, kicking.

I have become a dark mother, he realized, *bearing life inside me. No different from the alien or my own dark mother.*

Fires vented from a dozen shafts nearby, billowing soot and smoke. The last of his hopes flew away with the ship.

He tossed the grenade over the edge of the building. In the end, he didn't even have the guts to commit suicide, much less try to be a hero.

"One minute to reach minimum safe distance," the computer

announced, and something within him lurched.

Burke shook his head, wondering. *Is there life after death? Do I get another chance? Or am I just going straight to hell?*

He wondered how many billions of people had asked that question in their final moment.

He dropped to his knees, too weary to flee anymore, and gave birth. The alien ripped from his chest. Blood and fluids gushed out with it, his guts and stomach spilling onto the metal floor like afterbirth. NO. It takes 12–18 hours to gestate!

Miraculously, the creature seemed to have missed ripping out his heart and lungs. It just left a gaping hole, and lay there, its skin looking almost red in the firelight. It made a tiny growl, and peered around.

Burke slumped to his side, felt his heart weakening, the blood and life pouring out. His breathing slowed until he had no more energy to even close his eyes, and then the ground rumbled as the facility exploded and light flared and took him.

———

Sometimes we can wake from dark dreams into a deeper nightmare.

EPISODE 22

BY LARRY CORREIA

SAGA OF THE WEAPON, SEASON 1, EPISODE 22
THE M41A PULSE RIFLE

The M41A is one of the most successful combat rifles in history, and has become a potent symbol of American military might, not just on Earth, but into the furthest reaches of space. It has seen battle on every continent and dozens of worlds. It is beloved by those who use it, and feared by their enemies.

However, the adoption of the Pulse Rifle was controversial, and the story of its evolution is filled with tragic errors that cost many Colonial Marines their lives.

Join us now as we discuss the history of the legendary M41A Pulse Rifle, on *Saga of the Weapon*.

There's nothing like the sound of a Pulse Rifle. It's like
a maniac is running a jackhammer on a steel drum.
That's the sound of freedom.
                    —Lance Corporal Chris Johnson, USCM

Today's Colonial Marine takes having a reliable and potent
rifle for granted, but it wasn't always so. When the USCM was
formed in 2101, their standard issue infantry weapon was the
Harrington Automatic Rifle, with one Weyland Storm issued
per squad.

Marines now don't realize how good they have it.
Back in my day, you had basically two choices. Have a
handy little rifle that ran slicker than snot—the HAR—
but bounced its feeble little bullets off your enemies'
body armor, or have a rifle that would put them down
no matter what, but only when that complex hunk
of junk wasn't broken down or hopelessly jammed
because a speck of dirt got into the action. You ever
pull the side plate off a Storm? It looks like an old
fashioned clock in there. When Marines talked about
something working like clockwork, we sure as hell
didn't mean the Storm.
                    —Staff Sergeant Mike Willis, USCM

Personally, back in the '60s I carried a HAR, because
I'd rather know it would go bang every time I
pulled the trigger, than have this super advanced
killing machine that could track enemies across the
battlefield from a satellite feed, but was so fickle that
if you looked at it funny it would crash. Nothing sucks
more than waiting for your rifle's operating system
to reboot while a thousand Swedish insurgents are
shooting at you.
                    —Corporal Cheryl Clark, USCM

After the battle of Kochan and the long campaign on Miehm, there was a clear need for a next generation infantry weapon to arm the United States Colonial Marines. It needed to be rugged enough to survive the rigors of combat in a wide variety of planetary ecosystems, and fire a potent enough round that it could defeat newer forms of advanced body armor. The 6.8mm armor piercing round of the beloved HAR was simply too anemic, and the Storm was just too fragile. After many campaigns with inadequate equipment, the USCM put their foot down. Enough was enough.

> I was there when General Phillips threw a fit in front of Space Command. He said that if his men were going to fight against the insurgents, what did he expect us to do? Tickle them to death? Watching a bunch of four stars yell at each other was way over my pay grade, but it was a hell of a show.
> —Captain Trent Miller, USASF

The Marine 70 Program shook up everything, and small arms procurement was no exception. The commission that was created to study the need for new replacement weapon systems immediately met fierce resistance. The Weyland-Yutani Corporation filed a lawsuit, alleging that the Colonial Marines were simply misusing their Storm rifles, and it was their lack of following the proper maintenance guidelines that was causing the reliability issues.

> Yeah... Those pogues actually blamed us. Can you believe that? Abuse and neglect they said. Guess what, you corpo-monkeys, this isn't a clean room at your factory. Proper maintenance kind of goes out the window when you've flown half way across the galaxy, to be neck deep in blood and mud and guts for weeks, and have to beat a man to death with the butt

of your rifle—seriously, who puts circuitry in a stock?—
and the unit armorer is a little indisposed because he
stepped on a land mine that morning. Well excuse me
that I didn't have the proper factory approved widget
to fix it! At that point if a Marine can't fix it with a
hammer and duct tape, it ain't going to get fixed.
—Sergeant Mario Cordova, USCM

Ultimately, amid allegations of bribery, corruption, and blackmail, Weyland-Yutani dropped the lawsuit, and the new small arms appropriation committee got to work.

You know what they say about things designed
by committees, right? Well, that's where we were
heading. You should have seen the original list of
requirements. It was ridiculous. The specs weren't
written by combatants. They were mostly wish lists
from staff officers who'd never seen the inside of a
drop ship unless it was parked at an air show, and
specs inserted by lobbyists requiring gizmos that
only their company happened to make. There were so
many suggested bells and whistles screwed on that
you'd need a wheel barrow to carry the rifle.
—Construction Mechanic
1st Class Mike Raulston, USASF

It was a time for bold concepts. Many of the more advanced technological aspects proposed by the committee would later be incorporated into other weapon systems, such as the stabilization mechanism of the M56 Smart Gun, but it threatened to bog down the current rifle project in red tape.

However, there was a ray of hope. While various mega corporations were preparing their new weapon systems for trials, a retired Colonial Marine, Jonathan LaForce, was working on the prototype of the rifle that would become the legendary

M41. By day he made ends meet running a food truck, but his nights were spent in his humble workshop. A distant cousin of legendary gun designer John Moses Browning (*see* Saga of the Weapon *episodes one, four, fifteen, and twenty*). Corporal LaForce had served with distinction at Miehm, and knew firsthand the needs of the modern warfighter.

> If you're a Marine, when you're saying your prayers, you better tell whoever it is you're talking to that you're thankful for LaForce. That man was a mechanical genius. We're lucky he was a gun nut, and not into space ships or something. Sure... We'd have some awesome space ships, but my Pulse Rifle has saved my life more times than I can count. Thank Odin for Corporal LaForce.
> —Gunnery Sergeant Aimee Morgan, USCM

LaForce started with the familiar layout of the HAR, utilizing an integrated pump action grenade launcher, but the similarities end there. The sonic "shaker" burst weapons used by the rebels on Miehm to disable the Marines' HARs, had shown the need for a firing mechanism that couldn't be disrupted by outside sources. So his new design started with a unique electronic pulse ignition.

This feature would go on to cause the M41A's infamous nickname.

> Pulse rifle isn't in the official designation, we all know that, but since it was a pulse that ignited the primer, the name just kind of stuck. Marines do that kind of thing. My great great whatever grandfather carried a Pig and his dad carried a Tommy Gun. It sounds cool, it works, it sticks. The problem with calling the M41 that name though is always some dumb boot hears we get issued pulse rifles and gets all excited thinking

it's going to be shooting laser beams or something.
What do they think this is? Sci-fi?
—Lance Corporal Tripp Dorsett, USCM

The specifications required the new weapon to use caseless ammunition, but this presented several challenges. LaForce believed that standard ammunition was a better choice, because sustained fire of caseless ammunition causes a rapid buildup of heat, which could cause stoppages or even premature parts breakage. In a rifle using standard brass-cased ammunition, the ejecting cartridge case serves as a heat sink, and some heat escapes through the ejection port. However, the committee specified all submissions had to be totally sealed from the elements. LaForce's solution to the overheating problem was using advanced materials for the internal mechanism, and ultramodern, cooler burning propellants for the ammunition.

LaForce was issued several new patents. Among them was the visionary rotating breach design, which not only cut felt recoil in half, but allowed the use of his new U Bend Conveyor magazines. This brilliant system made his weapon far more controllable than competing designs, even while using more powerful ammunition.

We had the best engineers in the business all competing to come up with a new gun, and some retired Marine, who doesn't even have an engineering degree, shows up to the trials with this cobbled together piece of junk that looked like it got built in his garage. I found out later it literally was built in his garage. Here we were, the sharpest designers in the military industrial complex, all representing corporations with millions budgeted for R&D and marketing, and he walks up to the line like he belongs there, and pulls this ugly thing out of a case, and goes to town.

Phase one was just a demo shoot for some of the officers. No big deal. Until LaForce opens up with that beast. Everybody knows what a pulse rifle sounds like now, but this was new back then and we'd never heard anything like it before. Nothing gets your attention like the noise a pulse rifle makes. Every head on the range swiveled that direction.

He'd chambered it in 12mm Darnall, a monster of an old caseless hunting round that can shoot through a genetically modified rhino, just to prove that he could. Show off. This thing was shooting bigger bullets and more of them, with less recoil and still shooting better groups than every million dollar prototype on the line... It blew our socks off.

The competitors found out later that LaForce hadn't been invited by the committee at all, but had snuck into the initial test firing. He'd saved the life of one of the Marine testers during the battle of Kochan and had called in a favor to get onto the range as an 'observer'. I had gone to MIT and spent thirty years designing firearms on the most advanced CAD programs in the solar system, and there were twenty others like me there, but we all got our butts kicked by a hobbyist whose day job was selling barbeque.

—Michael Ankenbrandt, Daihotai Engineering

LaForce had the clearly superior design, but no ability to manufacture it. After a demonstration where the prototype was frozen in mud, and then fired six thousand rounds without a single malfunction, LaForce received an official invitation to the competition. He was also approached by several of the competing arms manufacturers and offered huge sums of money for his patents. Surprisingly, he refused them all, declaring at the time that he was in it to help his brother Marines, not to get rich. At the time there were even rumors of an attempted break in at LaForce's workshop to steal the prototype, followed by an attempt at deliberate sabotage, all of which was blamed on—and vehemently denied by—Weyland-Yutani.

With a working prototype in hand, and USCM interest in his design, LaForce approached Armat. The once respected company had fallen on hard financial times, yet retained a reputation for never skimping on quality, and always doing its best to support the soldiers it supplied. Luckily for LaForce, Armat, and America, this would prove to be a match made in heaven.

> If you look at the history of small arms development, what came first, cartridge or rifle, is usually a chicken or the egg kind of proposal. Sometimes you design a platform to fire an existing cartridge to spec, other times you have the weapon system and you shoe horn in the best round you can fit. This time we got lucky. As LaForce was designing his Pulse Rifle, Armat had been making some real breakthroughs in chemical engineering and projectile materials. This allowed us to really push the boundaries of terminal ballistics. Our new experimental 10mm x 24 caseless approximated the ballistics of the old .300 Winchester Magnum sniper round in a far shorter and lighter package, with a bullet that could penetrate most modern body armor, and an explosive payload inside that would absolutely wreck whatever was hit. The issue was that it produced too much recoil energy to control on full auto in an assault weapon sized package, so we were primarily marketing it for crew served weaponry. When LaForce came to us with a light rifle platform that could easily handle the recoil of our new experimental 10mm round, our executives bet the future of the company on manufacturing the pulse rifle. The rest is history.
>
> —Mordechai Yitzhak, Armat Technician

Armat was able to utilize more advanced materials for the next prototypes, which drastically lowered the weight, while also increasing the already impressive durability. Their new propellant compounds were able to decisively solve the LaForce prototype's greatest weakness, heat dissipation. The Armat rifle easily won the rest of the competition, passing all tests with flying colors. The newly designated M41 was put into production, and entered service with the Colonial Marines in 2171.

However, all was not well. Some of the early batches of 10mm ammunition were subcontracted out to other manufacturers. It is unknown who changed the propellant design, and later congressional inquiries never discovered the culprit, but regardless of who was at fault, this mistake cost Colonial Marines their lives, and gave the early production M41s a bad reputation.

(Warning, the following footage from LV-832 is intended for mature audiences only. Viewer discretion is advised.)
It was a nightmare. All of the wildlife on LV-832 is gross, mean, and cranky, but the colonists there were hard as nails. You had to be to survive that shit hole. There is only one thing they ever needed to call in Marine support to deal with, and that was a swarm. There's this one species, imagine a carnivorous moose-sized critter with tentacles instead of antlers. Individually, not so dangerous. Only it turns out that every seven years they have a population explosion, swarm, and eat everything like locusts.

My platoon was supposed to protect this one settlement on LV-832 during the swarm. No problem. We're in a fortified position. We've got these fancy new Pulse Rifles. Just stupid alien animals. Nothing we can't handle. Right?

Then we heard the thunder. It was like ten million hooves on the rock, and this... wave. That's the only

word. Just a wave of angry green flesh comes rolling
down the mountain at us. It was far worse than
the projections. Corporal Richards was our forward
observer. He died horribly, trampled into bloody
chunks in seconds.

We opened up with everything. Our only hope
was to carve a hole in that wave of meat, to pile up
enough dead to make a wall.

But then our Pulse Rifles started to choke. Only
the swarm kept coming.

—1st Lieutenant Hank Reynolds, USCM

The horrific incident on LV-832 was not isolated. Wherever
the improperly formulated ammunition was shipped, problems
occurred. As the weapons would begin to heat up, the propellant
would expand and stick, causing malfunctions. Or worse, cook
off prematurely and detonate inside the conveyor magazines,
often with catastrophic results.

You ever see what a 10mm explosive round does
to a man? It penetrates a bit then explodes. The
secondary wound channels are nasty. You can stick a
softball into the hole. Yeah... Real nasty. Oh, we love
them now. But back in '71, imagine having that same
explosive round cook off inside your rifle, right next to
your face. Or worse, I heard about one dude where his
Pulse Rifle cooked off, and it caused a sympathetic
detonation with his grenade launcher. Marines were
scared of their own rifles. Some of the guys took to
carrying short-barreled shotguns on them for when
things got close.

—Lance Corporal Daniel Walker, USCM

Rumors began to swirl of Colonial Marines found dead
on the battlefield, with their Pulse Rifles disassembled, killed

while desperately trying to clear a stoppage.

To their credit, Armat did not try to pass the buck. Instead, they sprang into action, discovered the cause, alerted Space Command, and tried to track down the bad lots of ammunition. By the time the hearings began, the M41 was working as intended. However, the bad reputation lingered in line units for quite some time, and the topic is still hotly debated among gun enthusiasts today.

Design changes were immediately instituted to make the M41 less ammunition sensitive and more cooling vents were added to the shell. The integrated digital ammo counter was given a dimmer switch, because Marines had taken to covering the early versions with masking tape to avoid giving away their position during low light maneuvers. This variant was designated the M41A, which remains the standard issue rifle of the US Army and Colonial Marines to this day.

With the bugs worked out, the M41A began to earn a different kind of reputation.

Our Cheyenne hit the hot LZ like a meteor. There were so many missiles and so much flak that the night sky was lit up like the Fourth of July. Before the skids had touched ground we already had tracers coming in from three directions. We lost two men before we could even un-ass the transport. Our APC ate a rocket and we lost our Lieutenant. The DeLorme rebels were ready for us, dug in, and itching for a fight.

My platoon's orders were to take and hold the main plaza on the coastal platform. We encountered fierce resistance every step of the way. They were well funded. Most of the rebels were wearing top of the line carbon-weave armor, but our Pulse Rifles punched them anyway. Then the DeLorme Corporate Security Teams were wearing these heavy, servo assisted, armor suits. Tank boys we called them. Right hard bastards, every one of them. Except, even when our 10mm bullets failed to penetrate the plates, the impact and micro-explosions were enough to throw them off long enough for my Marines to close and finish them off through the rubberized gaps at their joints. The muzzle doesn't climb much, and the M41 is so acute, we'd just hammer the tank boys until we pierced something vulnerable and they dropped.

It was street to street, house to house. We'd catch sniper fire from a window, launch a grenade through it, and keep moving. We reached the plaza, and found out that we were it. Nobody else had made it through the drop. We had to hold that position or the whole mission would fold.

The battle went on all night, and the rebels kept throwing everything they had at us. We shot our Pulse Rifles until the muzzles were glowing orange, and they never stopped, never jammed, not so much as a hiccup. Cheyennes were doing high-speed fly bys and dropping crates of U Mags and grenades on us so we could stay in the fight.

That was the first time I used an M41A. It didn't let me down then, and it has never let me down since. After DeLorme, I've taken a Pulse Rifle to every godforsaken planetoid, orbital, moon, backwater colony, and bug hunt you can think of. I've used it in zero G. I've used it underwater. Polar wastes to burning sands, abuse it, drop it, burn it, and the M41A won't ever quit on you.

The Pulse Rifle is the only rifle tough enough for a Colonial Marine.

     —Staff Sergeant Michael Newman, USCM

The M41A has gone on to earn the respect of every warrior who has used it… or faced it. This mechanical marvel has taken its place in history, as one of the finest combat rifles ever fielded. The Pulse Rifle is known for going anywhere, doing anything, and accomplishing the impossible. Seldom has a weapon so encapsulated the bold, unstoppable nature of the men it is issued to, as the M41A Pulse Rifle.

This has been *Saga of the Weapon.*

DEEP BACKGROUND

BY KEITH R.A. DECANDIDO

"Ms. Hasegawa will see you now, Ms. Kejela."

Nickole Kejela had been fearing those words since she arrived in the tastefully appointed waiting room outside the office of the CEO of the Hasegawa News Service.

In the fifteen years she'd been working for HNS, ten of them as a field reporter, Nickole had never been called into a meeting in Hiromi Hasegawa's office.

Hell, she'd never even *met* the imposing head of the corporation in person. They'd been in the same room, of course, but it was always a huge function space at an event of some kind. Nickole had only been within a few meters of her once or twice.

With a sense of anticipation and dread, Nickole tucked away her NohtPad—she'd been composing some additional thoughts for the sidebar on her profile of Dr. Shalaballaz Rao—

and approached the large metal door that slid aside obligingly for her.

The first thing she noticed was that Hiromi Hasegawa was sitting behind a wooden desk. It had very little clutter on it, which surprised Nickole, as most executives had either a ton of stuff or nothing at all on their desks, but Hasegawa's was a bit of a middle ground.

Then the woman herself stood up, and Nickole was amazed at how small she was. On her casts and when she stood behind a podium, she looked like the tallest person in the room, but she barely cleared a meter and a half.

Nickole also noted that the head of HNS had had considerable cosmetic work done, but it was quality stuff. Had she not made an intensive study of the latest bodymod techniques for a story, she probably wouldn't have even noticed that she wasn't working with original merchandise, as it were.

Hasegawa walked to the other side of her wooden desk and put out a hand. "Nickole, it is a pleasure to finally meet you."

"Th-thank you, ma'am," Nickole tentatively returned the handshake.

"Oh, please, do not call me 'ma'am.' If we were out in public, of course, I would insist on it then, but when it is just the two of us, formality is a waste of time, and I do not have any *to* waste. Refer to me as 'Hiromi,' please."

Not even remotely comfortable with being so familiar with the most powerful news mogul extant, Nickole simply said, "Okay."

"Have a seat in the guest chair, please, Nickole." Hasegawa sat on the edge of her fancy desk.

Nickole did as requested. "Thank you."

Hasegawa leaned forward with a conspiratorial smile. "Please do not look so apprehensive, Nickole. You have absolutely nothing of which to be afraid."

"With respect, that flies in the face of every story I've heard about meetings in your office."

Waving a hand dismissively, Hasegawa said, "Those are mere rumors and innuendo." Then her smile became an evil grin. "Mind you, I started those rumors and spread that innuendo myself. I dislike meetings a great deal, so I prefer to limit their use to unpleasant tasks, where at all possible, so they may be ended with dispatch. Worry not, however, this most assuredly is *not* one of those. I promise, you will depart this office with the same position and occupation and salary you had when you entered—which, to be fair, cannot be said for many of the others who have sat in that chair over the last several years." She shifted on her butt, and then got up. "This artificial wood is supremely uncomfortable. I do wish I could acquire genuine lumber."

Nickole barely managed to contain her reaction, but it was a near thing.

That earned her a glare from Hasegawa's hooded eyes as she went to sit behind her desk once again. "Do you have something you wish to say in response to that, Nickole?"

On the one hand, Hasegawa's tone indicated that she should answer the question, and smartly. On the other, that same tone indicated that she wouldn't like Nickole's answer.

The first, however, outweighed the second. "A few years back, I did a story on the Forestry Act, and how heavily regulated the use of luxury plant items is now that there are barely enough plants left on Earth to keep oxygen in the air. I got to see some real wood up close and personal and I also talked to people who fake wood. Either what you're sitting behind is real wood, or it's a fake that is so detailed that it probably would've cost more to get done than the real thing would have."

To Nickole's immense relief, Hasegawa smiled. "You *are* as talented as I'd heard and hoped. Excellent, that is precisely what is needed. Oh, and it actually *is* artificial wood, and yes, it would have been *considerably* cheaper to acquire true lumber, but I also do enjoy the process of breathing, so I simply acquired the finest forgery of wood that I could obtain."

Nickole nodded. She didn't appreciate her boss testing her, but she *was* the boss…

"I was speaking with Helena about you. She informed me that you were working on an exposé on Weyland-Yutani."

"I *was*," Nickole said slowly, "but I couldn't corroborate enough of my sources."

"And you will not be able to." Hasegawa shook her head. "The company is *far* too skilled at the fine art of ass-covering for you to be able to obtain anything incriminating in so direct a manner. No, Nickole, the secret to finding out information that the company does not wish you to discover is to eschew directness and instead approach them sideways, so they do not see you coming."

Frowning, Nickole asked, "Are you saying I should revive the story?"

"The purpose of this meeting is to provide you with your next story assignment."

Nickole noticed that she didn't actually answer the question.

Hasegawa touched a control on her desk, and the wall behind her—which had been showing a view of the Himalayas—changed to a view of the cast on Rao that she'd been doing notes for. "I looked over the draft of your profile on Dr. Rao. It is quite well done."

That suffused Nickole with tremendous pride. Hasegawa was not known for uttering praise, certainly not for doing so without meaning it. "Thank you!"

"I appreciate how you provide a deep examination into who she is, and why she does what it is that she does. She is a *person*, not merely a subject. In addition, you provide nuance—enough so that intelligent people are able to appreciate it, but presented it in a way that even a complete imbecile can also appreciate it." She sighed. "Which is to the good, as the galaxy is quite well stocked with complete imbeciles." She touched another control, and the image went back to the Himalayas. "I have been friends with Emilio Cruz, the chief of staff of the Colonial Marine Corps, for quite a long time, and he has asked me for a favor."

"Um, okay." That was Hasegawa's second change of the subject in the last minute, and Nickole's head was swimming.

"Emilio wants us to embed a reporter with a unit in order to put a good face on them—to humanize them, in essence."

"How long?" Nickole asked.

"For a year."

Nickole's eyes widened and her jaw fell open. "Excuse me?"

Holding up both hands, Hasegawa started, "I realize that it sounds like a great deal—"

"More than a great deal! I've got vacations planned, there's my family—"

"I can promise you that this will not interfere with a bit of it. Understand, most Marine units spend approximately eighty-five percent of their time on standby waiting for a mission, while seventy-five percent of *those* missions are simple and harmless. We are not at war right at the moment, so the Marines are far more akin to security guards—they are required to be ruthlessly efficient when they are in action, but the majority of the time they are sitting on their posteriors. And worry not, as I said, you will still be allowed to take your vacation and see your family—this will hardly be an immersive assignment."

"Okay, I guess, but—what's the angle here? I mean, I'm sure doing a favor for the Marines will be good for the network in the long term, but—"

Hasegawa smiled, and this time it was the expression of a predator about to chow down on prey. "*This*, Nickole, is your sideways route."

"I'm sorry?" Nickole remained as confused as she had been throughout too much of this conversation.

"As I said, I have known Emilio for a *very* long time. It is not a single thing he has said, specifically, but I am fairly certain that the Marines are in the company's pocket. I am fairly certain they may have conspired to cover up what really happened on Hadley's Hope."

Nickole blinked. "You think Weyland-Yutani and the Marines are responsible for what happened there?"

"I think it is possible, yes." She leaned forward and stared intently at Nickole. "There is, as they say, some shit. I want you to sniff it out, and I believe that spending a year with a Marine unit will enable you to accomplish that."

"O-okay." This was a little better, and it actually brought everything she'd said up until now into focus. "Ostensibly, you want a profile of the Marines?"

"Not just ostensibly, I *also* wish that. Provide the same nuance that you brought to the Rao piece to these Marines. I have already uploaded the specifics to your queue. Get yourself a good night's rest, and then report to Lieutenant Berenato at Camp Obama first thing in the morning."

ME: Tell me your name, please, Private, and where you were born.

PVT. D.S. SANDOVAL: I am called Private Dmitri Sandoval. I was born in Estonia, but was raised in Brooklyn.

ME: And you, Private? Same thing, name and where you were born.

PVT. D.C. SANDOVAL: I'm Private Dmitri Sandoval, and my *mami* and *papi* was born and raised in San Pedro de Macaris, but this pretty face was born in Chicago.

ME: How the hell did you both get assigned to the same unit?

PVT. D.C. SANDOVAL: Step thought it was a computer glitch till we both showed up.

PVT. D.S. SANDOVAL: We are distinguished by nicknames. I am referred to as "Big D," and he is "Little D."

PVT. D.C. SANDOVAL: Which really ain't fair. I ain't little, I'm just shorter than this overgrown gorilla.

—transcript of raw footage of interview of Private Dmitri Shostakovich Sandoval and Private Dmitri Carlos Sandoval, Colonial Marines, J Company, conducted by Nickole Kejela

———

Nickole's first month was spent at Camp Obama, a Marine base near the California-Nevada border. The unit she was following was J Company, led by Lieutenant Emily Berenato. J was assigned to the camp for this month to act as camp security, and also to get trained on the latest weapons to come off the line.

Camp Obama had, as far as Nickole could determine, absolutely no shade. Which was only an issue because everything the Marines did except sleep was outside. After four weeks, her dark skin was practically mahogany.

She watched the Marines get trained on the new M41A Mark 2 pulse rifles. Nickole herself had no interest in weaponry of any kind, but she knew that plenty of people viewing her cast would want to know all about the new toys, so she forced herself to learn all about its range, how to load it, how to field-strip it, how it differed from the Mark 1's, and so on, which would all go in a sidebar.

She also watched the Marines perform drills that involved a lot of running over bizarre terrain, shooting things that didn't stay still, and variable lighting.

But what was of most interest to her was the Marines' informal training. One day, Sergeant Ayed Stepanyan gave them the afternoon off, and six of the Marines decided to play sharpshooter poker. They took four beams of wood and attached thirteen cards from a shuffled deck to each beam, then set them up on a ridge, one beam on top of the other.

The half-dozen Marines then went two thousand meters away and set up their M42A Scope Rifles. Each took a shot and had to hit a card. After they each took their turn, they shot again until they'd each shot five times. Whoever took out cards that made up the highest hand won. If you took a shot and missed, you folded.

Of course, the Marines took bets on who would win. Most of the money was on the company sharpshooter, Corporal Hakim

Rashad. A few side bets also went on some of the others, not to mention betting on what the hand would be.

By the fourth shot, everyone was out except for Rashad and Private Malik Washington, the newest and quietest member of the company. In fact, he'd arrived the day Nickole did.

Corporal Li Hsu was the only one who didn't participate—instead he used his binocs to see who shot what and kept track of the hands.

"Okay," Hsu said, "Rashad has two pair, aces and threes. Washington's four to a jack-high straight."

One of the Private Dmitri Sandovals—Little D—said, "Where the fuck did you learn to shoot like that, newbie?"

Washington smiled shyly. "Carnival. Always won the teddy bear."

Rashad took aim and fired.

Hsu looked through his binocs. "Ace of hearts! Full house for Rashad!"

Even as Washington took aim for his final shot, Rashad grinned. "Why you botherin', meat? Ain't no way a straight beats a boat!"

Washington, though, said nothing. Nickole just smiled. Her cam had a good zoom, and she knew exactly what cards the private had hit.

"Queen of spades," Hsu said after Washington took the shot. "So queen-high straight. Nice, but futile. Rashad's the winner with the full house!"

Cheers and attaboys sounded out as folks congratulated Rashad. Scrip also started exchanging hands.

"Not exactly, Corporal," Nickole said.

Shaking his head, Washington said, "It's okay, ma'am. The corporal said—"

But Nickole kept talking. "Look at the suits of the cards that Private Washington hit."

Hsu put the binocs back to his eyes and then his face fell. "Sonofabitch."

"What?" Rashad asked, cutting himself off in mid self-congratulatory cheer.

Lowering the binocs, Hsu said, "The reporter's right. Washington didn't get a queen-high straight. He got a queen-high straight *flush*." He chuckled. "Guess you get the teddy bear again."

Rashad's face fell. Nickole just smiled.

Everyone else was either angry or confused.

And then Little D, who was in charge of the bet money, said, "Y'all ain't gonna believe this."

Rashad turned to face Little D. "What?"

Holding up both hands, Little D said, "Don't shoot the messenger! I'm just tellin' you what is. And what it is is the reporter's the only one who put money down on the newbie."

"Excellent," Nickole said, stepping forward to claim her winnings from Little D.

Shaking his head, Rashad asked, "What the hell you bet on his sorry ass for?"

"Because I already knew about the teddy bears." She took the scrip from Little D. "I want to thank you all for this. It'll be a big help on my vacation to Prince Edward Island. Don't worry, though, I'll be back in two weeks."

"What the fuck is in PEI that you wanna vacation there?" Rashad asked.

"Well, for starters, a refreshing lack of Marines."

Everyone laughed at that one. Big D said, "You will be missed, Ms. Kejela." He was the only one who called her that. The others either used her first name or, more likely, just called her "the reporter."

"Thank you, Dmitri," she replied.

"Yeah, thank him," Rashad said. "Me, I'll be glad for the privacy."

"You're the one who left the bathroom door open, Rashad," she said with a sweet smile. "I'm off."

"No you're not."

Turning, Nickole saw Sergeant Stepanyan approaching.

"What do you mean I'm not?" she asked. "I planned this vacation a year ago, and my boss told me—"

"I don't know what your boss told you, but *my* boss just told me that we're gearing up and heading up to the *Nellie*, which is taking us to LV-418."

Nickole blinked. An actual mission? To another planet? "Uh, okay, but I was—"

"My orders, Ms. Kejela, are for *everyone* to saddle up. Including you."

————

SGT. STEPANYAN: Look, you can talk to me all you want, but you should focus on the others. I'm pretty much on my way to retirement. Already filled out the paperwork.

ME: Really? I wasn't aware of that. There's nothing in your service record about it.

SGT. STEPANYAN: Well, I haven't actually *sent* the paperwork yet. But I will. Probably tomorrow.

CPL. HSU: Don't pay him *any* attention, ma'am, he's been sayin' that for *years*, and we're still stuck with him!

—transcript of raw footage of interview of Sergeant Ayed Stepanyan, Colonial Marines, J Company, conducted by Nickole Kejela

————

Nickole spent the next twenty-four hours packing and leaving repeated messages of both voice and text with Hasegawa. Those messages garnered one response, five minutes before she was to report to the shuttle that would take them to the *Nellie* in orbit:

"This is why you are there. Take the sideways road."

With a sigh, Nickole reported to the shuttle, after putting in a request for everything that HNS had on LV-418. In particular, she recalled that one of her first assignments at HNS fifteen years ago was as a researcher on a piece about the procedure for setting up a colony, and she'd dug up a *ton* of stuff on that subject. The research would still be in the archives, and she nabbed all of it.

She spent the next six hours cancelling her vacation and failing to get refunds on anything, thanks to the short notice.

Still allowed to take my vacation. Eighty-five percent sitting around. Can't believe I fell for Hasegawa's bullshit.

After ten hours on the *Nellie*, they were clear of both Earth and the moon's gravity wells and the ship was basically a ballistic missile aimed at LV-418. She and J Company and the crew of the *Nellie* all went into cryosleep.

The lid on her chamber seemed to rise only a second after it had closed over her, but of course, the entire lengthy interplanetary journey had taken place without the need for the ship to feed or provide atmosphere for her or anyone else. Not to mention the limited entertainment options in interstellar space.

Her head swam as she sat up in the cryobed, trying to orient herself and keep the ship from dancing around in several directions at once.

"You okay?"

Nickole looked up to see a very blurry version of Private Washington looking down on her.

"I'm fine, Malik."

"You don't look fine. Never done cryosleep before?"

She shook her head, an action she regretted, as it made her head spin more. "Farthest out I ever went were the asteroid mines."

"Yeah," Washington said, "it's kinda like a hangover, the first time."

"Oh, it's *exactly* like a hangover," Nickole said emphatically, "but without the happy memories of being drunk."

Washington guided her to her feet and led her toward the mess area. "C'mon," he said, "best thing for a cryohangover is lots of really terrible food."

Nickole chuckled. "Sounds yummy."

"And hey, thanks for sticking up for me at the poker shoot. I didn't want to contradict the corporal…"

"Hey, I was motivated. That was a lot of cash I won." Nickole managed a ragged grin.

"Listen, there's something I didn't mention to you during the interview that I wanted to talk to you about."

Nickole frowned. "What's that?"

"You probably get this a lot, but—Well, I've been working on a novel. I was wondering if I could talk to you about writing some time?"

At that, Nickole laughed. "As long as you don't want me to write a book off your idea and split the profits."

Washington looked at her askance. "Why would I do that?"

They joined the others for their post-cryo breakfast.

Lieutenant Berenato joined them partway through. "Just talked to the *Nellie* crew. Situation's worse'n we thought."

"What *is* the situation?" Nickole asked.

Everyone stared at her.

"Sorry, I spent the flight out trying to cancel the vacation I was forbidden from taking," she said bitterly.

Rashad laughed. "Why you wanna go to PEI for, when you get to watch *Marines* in action, Poker Face?"

Nickole frowned at her new nickname, but decided she liked it better than "the reporter." At least this one had a story behind it.

Rashad kept laughing until he noticed Berenato staring at him. Then he shut up.

"You gotta teach me that stare," Nickole said to the lieutenant with a smile.

Berenato did not smile back. "And *you* need to read the briefing materials. Short version: the planet only has one continent. There's a research outpost there. The island has sinkholes. Stuff's falling down into them. The research outpost is bugging out, and they need our help."

Relief spread through Nickole. "Just a rescue operation? That's great."

Stepanyan chuckled. "Yeah, probably won't even break your fingernails. Or mine. Which is good, since I'm retiring after this."

Nickole rolled her eyes and continued to eat her tasteless steak and eggs.

"You ain't never gonna retire, Step," Little D said.

"I'm pretty sure he hasn't even *really* filled out the paperwork yet," Hsu added.

"You'll see," Stepanyan said enigmatically. "This will be my last mission, you watch."

———

ME: What's your proudest moment as a Marine?

CPL. RASHAD: That shit's easy. Lunar riots. This one motherfucker was beating on a woman. I put a shot in his head. Motherfucker went *down*.

ME: *That's* your proudest moment?

CPL. RASHAD: Damn right. We servin' and protectin' and shit, and that woman got *protected* by my ass. S'what it's all about.

—transcript of raw footage of interview of Corporal Hakim Rashad, Colonial Marines, J Company, conducted by Nickole Kejela

———

The research outpost on LV-418 had a room they called the Patio, which was fully enclosed—the planet didn't have a breathable atmosphere—and had a huge picture window that looked out over the island. It was filled with weird plants in a variety of colors like orange and yellow, and a lot of purple and black dirt.

Much of that dirt kept collapsing into big holes, including one right under where six of the scientists were getting samples. J Company was out there in EVA suits rescuing the half-dozen scientists from the hole. Rashad, Hsu, Washington, Big D, and Little D were all out rigging up ziplines and pulling the scientists out and over to the ATV, which was the only ground vehicle that was safe to move on the unstable ground.

Next to her was the head of the outpost, a short woman named Aparna Pradhuman. Nickole asked her, "I have to ask, Dr. Pradhuman, why would you send them out there when there are sinkholes?"

"Simple—I didn't send them. They went on their own." She shook her head. "Morons."

The Marines all had their own helmet cams, and Berenato had let Nickole watch the feed from them on her NohtPad, with their audio in an earbud. She wasn't really paying close attention to them—it was all being recorded, and she could go over it later—and she had the earbud turned down to almost nothing.

But Rashad yelling, "Holy motherfucking *shit*, what the *fuck* is *that*?" at the top of his lungs got her attention.

Looking at her NohtPad, she saw that Rashad was down in the deepest part of the sinkhole, handing off people to Big D, who was halfway up, who then got them to Little D on the surface, and then Washington brought them to the ATV and back to the base. Hsu kept an eye on the equipment, made sure that everything would hold together.

She zoomed Rashad's cam feed, and was stunned to see something else in the sinkhole besides, well, a hole.

At first, the sinkhole just looked like a massive divot in the ground, but some of the dirt had fallen away near Rashad, and it exposed a massive chamber that was filled to the brim with large ovals.

Rashad was asking, "What the *fuck* is all that?"

"Is it me," Nickole asked, "or do those look like eggs?"

Over the earbud, Nickole heard Berenato ask, "Can we bring a sample back?"

Hsu replied, "I wouldn't recommend it. If Rashad—or anyone else—starts barging around down there, the hole will probably just get bigger and we'll start losing people."

"All right," Berenato said. "Corporal Rashad, keep taking pictures so we've got *something* at least."

Pradhuman was staring over Nickole's shoulder at the NohtPad display of Rashad's cam. "What the hell is all *that*?"

"No idea." Nickole stared at her. "I take it you haven't seen anything like that before?"

Shaking her head, Pradhuman said, "I haven't, no. And I should have."

"What do you mean?"

The chief scientist started to talk and then stopped. "Never mind."

She walked away, but Nickole wasn't giving up that easily. Yet.

CPL. HSU: Honestly, I hate violence. Hate guns, hate killing, hate exercise.

ME: So naturally, you joined the Marines.

CPL. HSU: You laugh, but it was natural. I mean, we're at peace right now, so there's not much combat—and, honestly, I'm in it for the gadgets. Seriously, the toys I get to play with here are *way* better than anything I'd find in the private sector.

—transcript of raw footage of interview of Corporal Li Hsu, Colonial Marines, J Company, conducted by Nickole Kejela

---

Night was a relative term on LV-418, as it was pretty much dark all the time, but they kept a 24-hour schedule anyhow, to make things easier on the staff. The *Nellie's* window to head back to Earth wouldn't open for another fifteen hours, so Berenato agreed to let Pradhuman's people gather up everything they could and run whatever final tests were possible. They'd take the dropship back up to *Nellie* first thing in what passed for morning.

Nickole finished up her notes on today's footage. It was the type of thing that most reporters loved, but which didn't interest her in the least: the team being competent. You could find footage of Marines doing their jobs right *anywhere*. Still, that would make a decent sidebar. She wanted to know more about the people.

Her plan was to take another go at Stepanyan. The sergeant had deflected her interviews with claims of impending retirement, but it was obvious he'd been saying that for a while.

She was startled by the chime ringing on her barracks door. The place was tiny, but serviceable. Everyone got their own bunk—which was luxury for the Marines—since the base was built for fifty, but only two dozen were assigned.

"Come in," she said, and the door opened to reveal Pradhuman walking unsteadily in.

"Ms. Kejela, y'need t'see this." She held out a data disc.

"Dr. Pradhuman, are you drunk?"

"Certainly hope so. I drank enough t'get this way."

Nickole reached out and took the disc. "Doc—"

"Jus' *read* that, 'kay? Planetary survey. Ain't no *way* they're this inc—" She swallowed. "Incompetent." Then her face went blank for a second and then her brown skin started to go green. "'Scuse me."

Pradhuman ran out the door, and Nickole prayed that she reached the bathroom in time.

Curious, she plugged the disc into the adapter in her NohtPad.

It only had one file on it, which contained the planetary survey made by the Weyland Corp on LV-418 about a hundred years back, done a good twenty years before they took over the Yutani Corporation.

Nickole read it over, and didn't find anything odd, except insofar as the sinkholes weren't mentioned.

So why show it to me?

And then she recalled that she probably had a copy of this already. The survey would have been part of the massive download she did from HNS.

So she called it up and started to read it.

"Oh, fuck."

She read it all over, and then read it a second time.

This survey report in the HNS archives was *completely different* from the one Pradhuman had just given her. Among other things, it actually mentioned the possibility of geologic instability, as well as readings indicating underground caverns that had biological readings.

None of these items were in the survey that W-Y had given to Pradhuman in preparation for her expedition.

They knew about the sinkholes and the possibility of some kind of alien life form, and didn't tell the people they sent.

Before Nickole could even begin to figure out what this really meant for her story—what Hasegawa had really sent her on, not bunking with J Company for a year—the lights went out, replaced by red lights, a buzzer sounded, and a pleasant female electronic voice said, *"Warning: biological contaminant detected. Quarantine procedures implemented. All personnel must remain inside base until further notice."*

Grabbing her cam, Nickole ran out of her room, down the corridor, and to the infirmary, since she figured that was where a biological emergency would be dealt with.

Sure enough, Pradhuman was there, clutching a mug of something hot for dear life, along with Stepanyan and the base doctor, a stooped-over man named Cho Duk Park.

There was also someone on one of the beds. Nickole activated her cam, and then realized that whoever it was had some sort of—of *thing* covering her entire face.

It was one of the Marines, and when Nickole noticed the lieutenant's bars on her sleeve, she realized it was Berenato.

"What the hell happened?" Stepanyan was asking.

Park shrugged. "No idea. Looks like a parasite. Trying to get it off."

"Try harder, Doc."

Now Park looked up at Stepanyan. "Everything I try, vital signs go down. I assume you prefer I don't kill her?"

"That'd be nice, yeah, Doc."

"Then please leave. Let me do my job."

Throwing up his hands, Stepanyan said, "Fine," and left.

Nickole stayed behind and recorded Park's work. He kept trying different ways of getting the thing off, but alarms went off every time, and often Berenato would convulse.

After a while, the doctor gave up trying any treatments, as they only succeeded in causing Berenato more distress.

After an even longer while, Nickole stopped recording, as a doctor watching a patient lay still didn't make for great footage, and she went to get a nap and try not to have nightmares about what Pradhuman had shown her.

The "nap" lasted more than twelve hours. Nickole went into the medical bay and saw Pradhuman—now much more sober than the last time she'd seen her—and Stepanyan arguing over Berenato's body. Park was nowhere to be found.

"We *have* to get out of here."

"We cannot leave without the lieutenant."

"Sergeant, if we all leave except for her, she dies. If we stay here, we *all* die."

"The doctor said that she cannot be moved without injury. I refuse to leave her behind."

"We don't have a choice."

While Nickole was considering trying to surreptitiously record this, Park came in, sipping a can of something. "Are you two still shouting at each other?"

Pradhuman started, "We—"

"I don't care. You're disturbing my patient."

"Your patient's in a coma!" Pradhuman said.

"Fine, then you're disturbing *me*. Now please—"

Before Park could continue, the thing just fell off Berenato's face.

"That's peculiar." Park went over to check her vitals.

Then she started to convulse again—and then her chest seemed to expand...

———

LT. BERENATO: Please stop trying to talk to me. I understand that General Cruz specifically requested you here, but while I am under orders to allow you access to my unit, I have received no orders that force me to talk to you. Go away.

—transcript of raw footage of "interview" of Lieutenant Emily Berenato, Colonial Marines, J Company, conducted by Nickole Kejela

———

Nickole sat in the Patio behind a huge barricade that Rashad and Washington had constructed. She was next to Stepanyan, who was covered in horrid burns from the acid blood spewed by the—the *creatures*, whatever they were.

They were the only ones left.

At first there had just been the thing that exploded from Berenato's chest. But then more appeared. Nickole had no idea where they'd come from, but they overwhelmed the base within a day.

Rashad looked at Washington. "How much you got left?"

"Three clips. And the flamethrower's still in good shape."

Then Rashad turned to Nickole. "How's Step?"

Nickole shuddered. "He doesn't look good."

"Motherfuck, what *are* these damn things?"

"I don't know," Nickole said, "but the company knew about them, and kept it from Pradhuman and the others."

Nickole shuddered. Stepanyan and Little D had gathered the expedition team in the mess hall, and they'd wound up trapped there by the creatures. The sergeant was the only one to get out alive, and at that, he'd been crispy fried by acidic blood.

The monsters had picked off the rest of the Marines one by one.

Then Nickole said, "Do you know what happened to Hsu?"

"He's dead like everyone else," Washington muttered.

"Did he make it to the communication room? He was supposed to send a message."

"The fuck point is there in a message?" Rashad asked. "Ain't nobody gonna hear shit for two weeks. By the time they even *know* we in trouble, we'll be *dead*."

"Because they have to *know*!" Nickole said. "This is why I was sent on this assignment, don't you get it? The company *knew* about these things and they didn't tell Pradhuman's people *or* you guys!"

Rashad shook his head. "Maybe he did, maybe he didn't, I got no fuckin' clue, and the comm room's got a big-ass hole in it that Hsu and Big D made. Took out six'a them fuckers with 'em, for all the good it did."

Washington was staring down at his motion detector, and he suddenly cried out, "They're coming!"

Nickole reached over to Stepanyan's holster and removed the pistol. "I'm sorry, Step. Guess it really was your last mission."

She got up and stood next to Washington, taking the safety off the pistol.

Washington looked down at her. "You know how to use that?"

"We'll find out, won't we?"

He snorted. "Yeah. Guess I ain't gonna get that novel finished, huh?"

"Nope." She aimed the weapon over the barricade. "I just hope Hsu was able to get my last story out."

———

ME: So what's the novel about?

PVT. WASHINGTON: Well, it's about these two people who meet for the first time on Luna, and then they get separated when her parents get reassigned to Earth, and they both live crazy lives, only to find each other again when they're both in their nineties, and they pick up where they left off.

ME: So it's a love story?

PVT. WASHINGTON: Kind of?

—transcript of raw footage of interview of Private Malik Washington, Colonial Marines, J Company, conducted by Nickole Kejela

———

Hiromi Hasegawa read over the transmission that had been sent from LV-418 two weeks ago directly to her queue. The sender code belonged to the Colonial Marines, but the ID was Nickole Kejela's.

Based on what she read, Nickole was probably dead, along with the rest of J Company. But not before she uncovered the story of the century.

The files appended to the message proved once and for all that Weyland-Yutani had deliberately hidden the existence of Xenomorphs on LV-418.

Hiromi shook her head. "I knew you were talented, Nickole. Well done."

Then she deleted the entire message.

She put a call through to General Emilio Cruz on his personal line. Cruz was in the Philippines right now, so it was four in the morning, and he'd probably be asleep.

Sure enough, in a bleary voice, Cruz asked, "Hiromi, do you know what time it is?"

"Yes, Emilio, I am fully cognizant of the time. But I didn't think you'd want to wait to hear that I was right. Weyland-Yutani *didn't* cover their tracks well enough. One of my reporters almost exposed the Xenomorphs on LV-418."

Cruz's eyes went impossibly wide, and sweat already was starting to bead on his forehead. "Are you—?"

"Calm yourself, Emilio, I've already killed the story, and the Xenomorphs have done the same for my reporter—and J Company, by the way."

Waving an arm Cruz said, "I'm sure they died heroically. It's what they're supposed to do." He blew out a breath. "Good work, Hiromi. I'll let the Weyland-Yutani board of directors know. I'm sure they'll compensate you well for this information, as usual."

"Good." She smiled. "Sleep well."

EMPTY NEST

BY BRIAN KEENE

When Lance Corporal Lombardo finally found the hive, the woman seemed more terrified of him than of the aliens swarming around her. She knelt there in the nest, trembling amidst hatched eggs, desiccated facehugger carcasses, and the cocooned corpses of her crewmates. She gaped at Lombardo, eyes wide, her mouth a taut circle, screaming without sound.

Lombardo knew how she felt. Just a few minutes ago, he'd been screaming, too.

In truth, he'd been screaming for the last hour, pretty much from the moment their platoon had landed on Taurus Seven. So had everyone else in the two deployed rifle squads. In fact, the only people not screaming were Commander Maffei, Lieutenant Kennedy, and the synth technical advisor Dylan, all of whom were safe back on the UD-4 Dropship, and Thomas,

225

the platoon's other synth, who was currently ensconced in the driver's seat of the M577 Armored Personnel Carrier parked outside. Lombardo knew they weren't screaming, because their voices echoed sporadically in his helmet's headset, demanding status updates, or more accurately, wondering just what the hell was happening inside the supply depot.

The fact was, Lombardo didn't know what the hell was happening. He'd heard the other rifle squad's screams over the headset, same as his command had heard. There had been no contact with the other squad since then. He suspected they had been killed, probably in all manner of horrible ways. The only thing he knew for sure was the rest of his own squad— Blazi, Heimbuch, and Antonio—were dead. Their blood was splattered all over his body armor. He could have reported their fate back to the Dropship, but that would have left less time for screaming.

He glanced from the woman to the Xenomorphs, and then back to the woman again. Neither she nor her captors moved. The nest occupied what had formerly been the air filtration control room, located in the center of the supply depot, accessible only by a narrow service tunnel and a hatch-like door. Lombardo stood in the doorway, puffing out his chest and shoulders in an attempt to fill the hatch frame and make himself appear larger and braver than he really was. Right now, he felt neither of those things. He was scared and nauseous, and jittery from the adrenalin coursing through him. His M41A Pulse Rifle had never felt heavier than it did at this moment. He desperately wanted to glance behind him, just to verify that no alien was creeping along the corridor, but he was afraid to take his eyes off the ones in front of him.

The control room was dark, and there was movement in the shadows, just out of clear sight. Obviously, more aliens lurked in the darkness, impossible to discern due to their muted black and blue coloring. He caught a glimpse of a massive egg sac hanging from the ceiling, suspended by a thick, strong, organic resin. The presence of the sac meant there was an alien queen hiding somewhere in the room. Luckily for him, the queen's mobility would be limited due to the sheer weight of the sac. He remembered that from training. The queens couldn't move while the sac was attached to them. She'd be dependent on her drones.

Lombardo turned away from the shadows and focused on what he could see instead. He counted four visible combatants, plus the woman. She looked rough. Of course, anyone who had been captured by a hive of Xenomorphs would appear that way, but this was something else. She looked sick. Lombardo judged the woman to be in her forties. She was beautiful, despite the grime and blood, but too skinny. Her clothes hung from her frame. Her hair seemed thin and limp, and her skin was like alabaster, almost glowing in the darkness. A series of ugly purple bruises covered her arms and neck. He wondered why she wasn't cocooned like the rest of the supply depot's staff. The woman offered no explanation. She just continued to stare at him. The Xenomorphs did the same, as if awaiting a command. The silence was somehow more unnerving than the aliens themselves.

"I'm not getting paid enough for this shit," he muttered.

"Say again, Lombardo?" Thomas's emotionless synth voice sounded even colder when channeled through the headset.

"Can't talk right now," Lombardo whispered.

The aliens responded to his voice, skittering and hissing. They glanced at each other, tilting their cylindrical, elongated heads, and then turned back to him. It was clear they were communicating, but Lombardo wondered how. They had no facial features, save for their horrific mouths. No eyes or ears. And while they could screech and hiss, it didn't sound like a language to him. So how were they able to communicate? Was it telepathy? Some sort of pheromone? Or maybe the clicking and hissing sounds they made really were some sort of fucked-up language?

He wondered if a Xenomorph could scream, and what that might sound like.

His thoughts returned to the rest of his squad. Heimbuch had been the first to fall, barely five minutes after they'd entered the depot, impaled through the back by a Xenomorph's bladed tail, which had punched through his M3-1 Pattern Personal Armor like a knife through a swath of cheesecloth. Lombardo frowned, recalling the big speech their commander had given them about the armored vest. How the manufacturer, Armat Battlefield Systems, had specifically designed it for use when engaging in combat with Xenomorphs. How it was supposed to be lightweight and comfortable while still offering maximum protection. How it was manufactured with layers of titanium and boron carbide resin bonded to graphite-composite carbon fiber. How it could withstand bullets, shrapnel from grenades and explosive, lasers, and energy blasts. How it had been coated with an acid-resistant compound specifically to protect against the aliens' toxic blood. And how none of that had fucking mattered when that tail speared Heimbuch and lifted him up off the floor. He'd tried to scream, but when he opened his mouth, blood poured out. Instead, he dropped his rifle and grasped at the slick, blue-black appendage jutting from his body. Then, with one whiplash move, the creature had flicked its tail, sending Heimbuch crashing into a bulkhead. Quivering and sobbing, he'd died trying to shovel his intestines back into his abdomen.

Lombardo shuddered at the memory. He suspected that somebody from the Colonial Marine Corps should see about getting a refund from Armat Battlefield Systems.

Blazi had died next, mere seconds after Heimbuch's demise. Despite all their training and their previous encounters with the aliens, he'd panicked and done the one thing you were never supposed to do when fighting a Xenomorph in close quarters— opening fire with his M56 Smartgun while the creature stood just a few feet away from him, Heimbuch's blood still dripping from its tail. Blazi shouted curses, grinning as the rifle shook in his hands. The corridor had thrummed with the vibrations.

The huge weapon shredded the alien where it stood, smashing through the monster's carapace, severing appendages and pulping its innards. Deafened by the noise, their ears ringing, Lombardo and Antonio barely had enough time to scurry backward out of range before a rain of acidic blood fell like mist, enveloping the still cursing Blazi. His enraged cries quickly turned to screams as the lethal substance went to work on his exposed skin. Lombardo had to give the folks at Armat Battlefield Systems credit. That special acid-resistant compound had worked like a charm. The liquid toxin slid harmlessly off of Blazi's helmet, vest, boots, and padding. But the rest of him sizzled and bubbled as the alien's corrosive blood melted him alive. The corridor filled with the combined stench of burning meat and something that had reminded Lombardo of the way the air smelled just before a thunderstorm—an electric tang. The M56 slipped from Blazi's grasp. Blind and fumbling, he reached for Lombardo and Antonio, mewling helplessly as his face sloughed off, revealing the pitted, smoking musculature beneath. His eyes boiled in their sockets. The flesh on his hands dripped like hot wax. When he opened his mouth to scream, Lombardo noticed in horror that his tongue was dissolving. Blazi took one step toward them before toppling to the floor and exploding with the consistency of an overripe pumpkin. Steaming chunks of him splattered across the bulkheads, leaving behind a noxious reddish-pink stew.

But Antonio's screams—those had been the worst of all. It was fair to say that both men had collectively lost their shit after seeing Heimbuch and Blazi slaughtered in such a gruesome fashion. Neither Lombardo nor Antonio were strangers to combat. Both had been witness to—and participants in—the horrors of war. They'd battled lone Xenomorphs a half-dozen times, been involved in riot control on Rigel Nine, squashed the terrorist attacks on both the Lasalle Bionational space station and the Europa reclamation project, put down the rebel uprising on New Titan, and fought in numerous skirmishes during the silent war between Weyland-Yutani and the Globe Corporation. Despite all that, they'd panicked after one Xenomorph had dispatched two of their fellow squad members in such a quick and grisly fashion. It was one thing to see your friend—a friend you'd known since basic training—get shot or blown up. It was quite another to watch them be turned into soup.

Lombardo and Antonio had pushed ahead, going further into the supply depot, ignoring the conflicting commands shouted over their headsets. They'd charged on, breathless, fueled by adrenalin and fear, gunning down anything that moved—and a few things that hadn't. They didn't stop until they found the cafeteria, and then, it was only to check their weapons and gear and catch their breath.

"You okay?" Lombardo had asked.

"Fuck no," Antonio replied. "I've got Blazi all over my boots. And you've got a little bit of Heimbuch on your nose."

Scowling, Lombardo wiped his nose with the back of his hand. When he looked down, his hand was smeared with blood.

"Did I get all of it?"

Antonio shrugged. "Now it looks like you've got war paint."

Lombardo glanced around the cafeteria, checking the corners. "This is fucked."

"I remember when we were all recruits," Antonio had replied. "Heimbuch enlisting to get that Weyland grant money, and Blazi all patriotic and shit."

"And you and me," Lombardo agreed. "That judge gave us the choice, remember?"

Antonio had nodded. "Life in prison or life as a Colonial Marine. But I never thought—"

His words were drowned out by a loud, metallic clang, and then a Xenomorph yanked him up into a ventilation shaft in the ceiling. Lombardo couldn't tell how big the creature had been. All he'd seen was a blue-black blur of movement, and Antonio's legs kicking and thrashing as he was jerked upward. Then both vanished from sight, and the sounds began. The ventilation shaft echoed with thuds and bangs, and Antonio screamed. The alien hissed and warbled, and Antonio shrieked. Then there was a soft crunching sound, and Antonio squealed—one long, high-pitched, muffled plea, wordless and yet communicating all of the pain and fear in the world. It ended abruptly and then there was silence. Blood dripped from the ventilation panel. Lombardo had pointed his rifle at the ceiling, thumbed the selector from single shot past four-round burst and all the way to fully automatic, and then opened fire. The ceiling disintegrated, panel by panel. His arms grew numb from the significant recoil and his chest began to ache, but he kept shooting. The Xenomorph's carcass tumbled onto a cafeteria table, leaking toxic blood all over the ceramic surface. He kept shooting, the readout on the side of his weapon dutifully counting how many shots he had remaining. He didn't stop until the ceiling collapsed upon him.

Coughing, he had crawled out of the wreckage and stood up. His ears rang, and the room was filled with swirling dust. He found what was left of Antonio, but it was impossible to determine how he had died. All Lombardo had to go on were the Marine's final screams.

He heard ghost echoes of those screams now, standing here in the hatchway, facing off against the Xenomorphs in the air filtration control room.

"We should have picked life in prison," he muttered.

One of the aliens inched forward, creeping toward him. Its talons clicked like hailstones on the steel-grated floor. Lombardo knew from previous briefings that while Xenomorphs primarily preferred solitary ambush tactics, they would occasionally swarm when in larger groups. His previous encounters with them had always been with no more than one lone creature. Luckily, the other three aliens held their positions, seemingly content to let the lead Xenomorph proceed. The creature took another step, and chittered softly in its throat. Its segmented, blade-tipped tail swished slowly back and forth. Lombardo cringed, remembering once again what one of those tails had done to Heimbuch.

"That's far enough." He gestured with his M41A. "You stay right where you are, smiley."

Ignoring him, the Xenomorph inched closer. Judging by its body language, the creature was gearing itself to charge. The other three also shifted positions, perhaps emboldened by their companion's cautiously aggressive behavior. It appeared to Lombardo that they were trying to flank him—a move that would prove unsuccessful given his current placement in the hatchway.

"Stupid fucking bugs. You need to brush up on your tactics."

His voice echoed back to him, sounding very small. Lombardo breathed deep, trying to steady himself, and smelled his friends' remains, drying on his armor.

The woman was still staring at him. Lombardo did his best to sound reassuring, even though he felt anything but.

"Don't worry, Ma'am. It's going to be okay."

Slowly, she shook her head back and forth and mouthed, "No."

He stepped backward. The Xenomorphs edged closer. He took another step, and they did the same.

"That's right, you shit bags. Follow me." Keeping his eyes on the enemy, he whispered into his helmet microphone. "Thomas, you still there?"

"I'm here," the synth confirmed. "Just waiting on you, Lombardo."

"Command? You still on the line, too?"

"That's affirmative, Lance Corporal," Commander Maffei replied. "What's your status?"

"My squad is dead. Looks like I've got one civilian still alive."

"And the rest of the civilians?"

"Still cocooned," Lombardo reported.

"And their status? The atmospheric feedback is playing havoc on our sensors. Can't read their life signs."

"They're all dead," Lombardo lied, hoping like hell that he

wouldn't get caught. He didn't want to stay here any longer than necessary. "Like I said, just one survivor. A woman. Requesting permission to fall back immediately, sir."

"Do you have the woman with you?"

"Not yet. I'm working on it."

Lombardo paused when he was about halfway down the maintenance tunnel. He kept his weapon pointed at the open hatch, and thumbed the selector back down to the notch for four-round bursts. One by one, the aliens stepped into the tunnel, creeping warily forward in single file. They didn't rush him, obviously suspecting some sort of trap. He waited until they reached a point where both he and the woman would be out of the splash range of their blood, and then inched his finger just in front of the rifle's magazine, where a second trigger was loaded. He squeezed it, lobbing his last grenade. The rifle jumped in his hands. The projectile sprang from the under-barrel and arced toward the clustered aliens.

"Get down," Lombardo shouted, dropping and rolling, hoping that the woman understood that he was talking to her.

The Xenomorphs shrieked, and then the sound was lost beneath a concussive WHOOMP. Lombardo's ears popped. The tunnel shook. He rolled to a stop, sprang to his haunches, and raised his rifle. There was a smoking hole where the aliens had stood only a moment before. Acid blood dripped from twisted metal. Debris and severed body parts filled the corridor. The tunnel, however, was still structurally sound.

Or at least he hoped it was.

Springing to his feet, Lombardo worked his jaw, trying to get the pressure in both ears to subside. When he reached the debris, he cautiously stepped around the still-sizzling pools of acid, and took care not to brush up against any of the metal shards. Then he re-entered the air filtration control room. The woman lay on the floor, face down, hands over her ears, quivering. Lombardo started to call out to her, but then realized she was probably just as temporarily deaf as he was. Instead, he crept forward, eyes darting around, watching for any further aliens. The shadows were empty now. Perhaps the explosion had scared them away. He swept his rifle back and forth, tense and ready. Still, nothing moved. He hurried over to the victim, still cowering on the floor, and reached out a hand.

"Are you okay? Can you stand?"

The woman didn't respond, or even look up at him. Lombardo tapped her on the shoulder. She jerked her head up, gaping at him, her expression crazed. She began to scurry backward, crab-walking across the metal grating. Lombardo pointed his rifle barrel at the ceiling and held up his other hand, palm out.

"It's okay," he yelled. "I'm here to help you. We responded to the distress call."

She paused, blinking. When she spoke, he could barely hear her over the ringing in his ears.

"The grenade." He pointed at his ear. "I can't hear you. Are you hurt?"

The woman blinked again, and then pointed to her own ears.

Shaking his head, Lombardo held out his hand. She stared at it as if he were offering her a dead fish. Then, slowly, she took it. Her palm was cold. Grunting, he pulled the woman to her feet. She wobbled back and forth unsteadily, grasping her abdomen.

"Easy," he shouted, close to her ear. "Just take it slow. Can you walk?"

She nodded.

Great, he thought. *At least we can hear each other now.*

"I'm Lance Corporal Michael Lombardo, Colonial Marines. What's your name?"

She paused for a moment, licking her lips and glancing around the room. Then she focused on him again. "Alice."

"Okay, Alice. Are there any other survivors that you know of?"

He hoped she'd say no.

Alice shook her head. "Just me. Everyone else... they hatched already."

Lombardo realized that he could hear her more easily now. The ringing in his ears had subsided.

"You're lucky I got here when I did," he said. "I suspect you would have been next."

Alice turned away from him again, her eyes searching the shadows, as if looking for someone.

"No," she whispered. "It's just me. No one else left."

"I think you might be in shock."

Alice grinned, glancing off into the darkness again. Lombardo followed her gaze, expecting to see another alien or perhaps even the queen lunging out from behind the equipment, but there was still nothing.

"Command," he called.

"We copy you, Lombardo," came Kennedy's reply.

"Be advised, you might want to have Dylan on standby. I think she's suffered some emotional trauma."

"Copy that."

"Alice? Can you look at me, please?"

Slowly, she turned back to him, still smiling. The expression made Lombardo shiver, but he didn't know why.

"Alice, there's a transport waiting for us outside. All we have to do is reach it. So I want you to stick close to me, okay?"

Shrugging, she nodded.

"Do you know where the rest of the aliens went? Did you see them flee when I fired the grenade?"

"It's just me now."

"Okay." He paused, considering their options. Then he bent down, undid a Velcro strap on his multi-cam trousers, and pulled a combat knife from one of the six concealed pockets. He held the hilt out to her. "Here. Take this."

Nodding, she accepted the weapon without a word. Lombardo knew that if they encountered any more Xenomorphs, the knife would be useless in actual combat. He hoped, however, that it would help the shell-shocked woman focus, and give her the courage to follow him. He turned back to the hatchway.

"Stay close behind me," he warned, "and be careful of the rubble in the maintenance tunnel. There's sharp metal, some of it hot. And there's little pools of acid on the walls and floor. Trust me. You don't want to step in those."

If Alice understood him, she gave no indication. Sighing, Lombardo started forward, ducking through the doorway. After a moment, Alice followed along behind. He showed her where to step when they came to the blast site, and helped her navigate around the debris. Then he led her down the hall, and out into the main corridor. He paused, trying to remember which way he'd come. He'd been running at the time, gunning down Xenomorphs before they could reach him.

"Which way is the exit?" he finally asked, embarrassed.

Alice pointed to the right. "Don't you have people who could tell you? I heard you talking to them before."

"The atmospherics are messing with the equipment. Very hard for them to get a read on anything down here, other than communications."

"This way, then." She stepped around him and started down the hallway.

Lombardo grabbed her arm, noticing her wince in his grip. He eased up, surprised that he'd hurt her. He hadn't squeezed with that much force.

"Sorry. I didn't mean to hurt you."

"It's okay. I'm... it's not your fault. I'm sick."

"Sick? Sick how?"

"Don't worry. It's nothing contagious. I've got cancer."

"Oh." He paused, unsure of how to respond. "I'm sorry to hear that."

She shrugged. "It's been killing humans pretty much since we crawled out of the oceans, right? We can travel galaxies, colonize planets, clone people, replace organs, download our consciousness—but we still haven't found a cure for cancer. I've made my peace with it."

"Is it... are you...?"

"Yes, Lance Corporal. I'm afraid it's terminal."

"I'm really sorry."

"I'm sorry, too. Sorry you went through all this trouble to save a dying woman."

"Well," Lombardo said, starting forward again, "you're not dead yet, Alice. And you're not dying on my watch. Just let me take the lead, okay? If we come across more aliens, I don't want to accidentally shoot you."

"We won't." Her tone was matter-of-fact. "They've all pulled back now."

Lombardo frowned. "How do you know that for sure?"

Alice smiled sadly. "Because all the others hatched. The Queen's in hiding now. They emptied the nest when you were approaching. The rest of the aliens will be guarding her now."

"But I saw an egg sac back there in the control room."

"She had already detached from it. She'll grow a new one and start the whole process over again. But that will take time."

"Well, it's time she's not going to have."

He paused at the next corner they came to, and peered anxiously around the wall. The corridor was clear. He led her onward.

"Do you have any family you want us to contact? I can radio my command."

"No," Alice replied. "There's nobody. I'm alone."

"No partner? Kids?"

"I had a daughter. She… died."

"I'm sorry."

"It was a long time ago. She was stillborn. I carried her for nine months and everything was fine. She was alive. We watched her on the monitors. But during the birth, she… she didn't survive. I thought about having another, when the time was right. But then I ended up here, and… well, you know the rest."

Lombardo bit his lip, unsure of what to say. What the hell could he have said? What possible words did he have to console her? She'd been captured by aliens, seen all of her friends and co-workers die, was dying herself of terminal fucking cancer, and to top everything off, had lost her only child.

He paused at another corner and glanced both ways. A stenciled arrow on the wall pointed to the cafeteria. "I came from that direction. Is there a closer way to the exit?"

"Yes. Turn to the left."

Lombardo followed her instructions, and continued down the dark hallway. The only sounds were their footsteps and their breathing. He glanced at the LCD display on the side of his rifle, checking to see how many rounds were left, and how much battery life remained. Heimbuch had always covered his readout with black electrical tape, so that snipers couldn't focus in on the glowing screen. But Lombardo had never done that, preferring instead to know his weapon's status at all times. Satisfied with his findings, he used the manual cocking handle, making sure a round was chambered. He knew that psychologically, he was only doing these things to stay focused, but it made him feel better—the same effect he'd hoped the combat knife would have on Alice.

At the next crossway, he saw a red sign, glowing in the dark. It marked the exit. Lombardo sighed with relief.

"See?" Alice said. "I told you it wasn't far."

"It can't be this easy," he murmured. "Would they really just let us go?"

"They're not following," Alice replied.

Lombardo shuffled toward the exit. "But how can you know that for sure?"

"Because they sent me instead."

He paused, and was about to turn around when he felt something cold against his throat. Out of the corner of his eye, he saw a metallic flash. Then it was gone. Suddenly there was pain, and his neck felt hot and sticky. He heard a sound like gurgling water. Stumbling, he slammed into the wall and glanced at Alice. She clutched the combat knife in one hand. The blade was red with blood.

That's my blood, he realized. She...

"This was my last chance," Alice told him. "Don't you see? The queen, she's smarter than the rest of them. She understood my intent. I wanted to be a mother again, before I died. I wanted to feel it one more time—that life, kicking and growing inside of me. It was perfect."

Lombardo tried to raise his pulse rifle, but the weapon felt as heavy as stone. Instead, he let it slip from his fingers and brought his hands to his throat. He moaned as his fingers grew wet.

"You..." he rasped. "You... what...?"

"I was happy." Alice's smile turned to a scowl. "But then you had to come along and ruin things. You had to mess everything up."

Sputtering, Lombardo tried to talk. He was starting to feel very cold. He slumped against the wall, sliding downward, staring at her in disbelief.

"I won't let them take my baby," Alice said. "And I had to stop you from leaving here. I had to protect them, you see?"

Lombardo fumbled at the floor, blood-slicked fingers clawing, trying to grab his rifle. When he looked up again, Alice had knelt beside him with the knife. She started to speak, but then gasped softly, as if in pain. Her eyes glazed for a moment, and when she turned back to him again, her expression was rapturous.

"It won't be long now," she said, patting her chest.

He stared, eyes wide, as her shirt bulged just below her breasts.

He was dead before the birthing pains began.

DARKNESS FALLS

BY HEATHER GRAHAM

"You didn't hear the screams."

The words seemed to fall on the sunlit day like a sure and steady sweep of ice. Angela Hall didn't look at the tall, intense man who spoke them. She had been working in her garden—proud of the amazing tomatoes she was managing to grow. She had, in fact, just bit into one, adding a touch of salt from the small shaker in her belt. It was delicious. So good. Such a miracle.

She shoved her trowel into the ground and stood, dusting her hands together and staring up at the sky. It was so beautiful.

"Did you hear me? I can play the security footage for you."

Angela still failed to react. She couldn't. She couldn't let go of the terra-farmed earth, and the sky. Blue, with just wisps of clouds. Glorious—and unbelievable.

It was a *created* world.

Planet Oleta in the Upsalon Trident had proven to be a true oasis of welcoming hospitality in an area of the Andromeda Galaxy most people had considered to be completely uninhabitable. It was also so far removed from most known civilizations that—at the moment—it was a pristine and wonderful place to live.

Silver mining was the main occupation on Oleta. Angela wasn't a miner, she was a farmer—with degrees in agriculture and animal husbandry—but she had always liked miners. She had come across them often enough when she'd been Captain in the Colonial Marines—a part of her life she had worked hard to put behind her.

She wanted it to stay that way.

She had told no one here about her experiences; where she had been in her life, what she had been—or what she had done.

But this man, Police Chief Warrick Tarleton, apparently knew.

Because he had come here. To her. With his fantastic tale.

"Did you hear me?" Tarleton asked quietly. "If not, hear this!"

He stretched his hand, forcing her to see the screen on his communicator. She tried not to look. There wasn't much to see, she thought. Darkness, and shadows, and then... a splatter of crimson on the lens, something flying... limbs.

And the screams. The screams of the dying that didn't end until the crimson flooded the lens, and the dying were the dead.

She turned to stare at him, feeling as ravaged as the flesh of the victims in the caves.

"Yes, Captain Hall. They opened a new silver mine. There were opening ceremonies, a picnic, bands... and then screams. Four dead were discovered in the newly opened shaft; two children are missing."

"I'm not Captain Hall anymore! So, some other company idiot thought he could create a weapon and smuggled eggs onto this planet. When will we ever become a race without assholes as dangerous as the beasts?" Her voice was a monotone. "You need to call in the soldiers; you need the military authorities to handle this. If it can be handled. I can't help you; no one knows who I am!"

No one knew! Not being a marine was part of her beautiful new world!

"I've called the soldiers; they're coming," Tarleton said, staring at her so intently that she wanted to scream. "The thing is… the recruits out here are raw. They've never had to face any… anything like what… what we saw on the surveillance tapes."

"There are no experts who know how to handle this."

"What you have to understand is that… there are two children down there."

"I—I can't help you," Angela whispered.

And I am probably telling the truth. I will never forget Planet 8 in Star Magnolia in the Milky Way galaxy. That was where we'd come across the Xenomorphs, the ones who had used the condor dragon reptilians for their gestation, the creatures that ripped my company to shreds, consumed them alive one by one. I was powerless, caught in the rocks, watching, while they'd taken Daniel, torn into him…

Just seeing the surveillance tapes, brought back the fear—paralyzing fear!

"Okay. You're under arrest," Tarleton said.

"What?"

"You don't want to volunteer your services; you can just come with me anyway. You're under arrest."

"For what?"

"Failure to cooperate in a criminal investigation."

"That's not even a legitimate charge!"

"It is now," Tarleton assured her grimly. "You're it—you're all that I've got. You survived the condra-morth attack on your platoon. You're the only survivor. You killed a queen."

Because I'd been desperate; I hadn't thought, I'd run, and I'd hidden myself, and somehow… yes, I'd survived. When no one else had been left even recognizable as a human being.

He lifted an arm, indicating his hover-car. She looked up at the beautiful sky once again. Man created such wonders;

technology had taken a barren piece of rock like Oleta and turned it into a haven.

Man was also capable of gross stupidity. Someone had somehow brought alien eggs, Xenomorph eggs, to the planet. Someone somehow determined that they would create a work force or a weapon, something magnificent, where others had failed.

They just never got it.

And maybe, she was destined to never get away from the beasts.

"All I could see on your comm was shadows," she said, after taking a seat in the passenger's side of the bubble-shaped vehicle. "I realize that silver is the main substance being mined for here, but, I understand they're also mining for precious gems and rock salt. I—I haven't been involved in any of the mining operations. Which mine?"

"Silver mine," Tarleton said briefly. He glanced over at her. "Does it matter?"

"Everything matters," she said.

"I need to see the footage again," she said.

He passed her the communicator. She studied it briefly, then hit in the proper place to roll the footage again. She forced herself to stare at the screen.

"What are the indigenous life forms in the mine? Are there any? The planet was a barren rock, by my understanding, when they started the terra-farming and oxygenation."

Tarleton looked over at her. She'd met him a few times before; she liked him. He didn't talk too much. He was a big man, tall and muscular, with dark red hair and steady blue eyes. While the military controlled the mines, Tarleton was head of the civilian police.

"You're quite right. There are no indigenous creatures in the mine."

Wincing, Angela played the footage again. She watched the shadows. Whatever had cast them on the walls of the cave seemed to have a multitude of arms.

"There was some life form in the cave," she said. "At best, someone managed to smuggle in eggs, but that's only the first stage for these beings. There had to be a host—we know that the host can be human, or just about any kind of creature found on any planet. But, the creatures must have a host." She looked at him, frowning. "Why have you come for me? This happened at the mine."

"Yes."

"That's military jurisdiction from the get-go," she said.

"Yes."

"Then—"

"They're assholes," Tarleton said flatly.

"But, they're—"

"Headed by Lieutenant Colonel Simon Nicholson. Nicholson came from a posh military school. Never saw any action in the field whatsoever. He was assigned here because his family has an interest in the mines. He's claiming that the personnel down there went crazy because some kind of gas slipped into the oxygen system. He says we're just seeing them tear each other apart."

Angela looked at him incredulously.

"So Simon Nicholson is in charge here—with dozens of colonial marines at his beck and call. They'll go in; they'll find out what really happened."

"You know what really happened."

They'd reached the mine.

Tarleton parked and jumped out of the hover-car. Angela followed.

The remnants of a band shell remained, along with barbecue pits, picnic blankets, and more. But, the revelers were gone; men and women in their military apparel hurried about, gathering weapons, lining up.

There was a command station set up between two large military trucks. Tarleton was heading that way.

Angela hurried after him.

The first man she saw was young, perhaps in his mid-twenties. He had a wide-eyed look of panic about him, but he was doing his best to provide a blustering authority. "Alpha Company, stairs to the second level down; Betas will take the elevators. These are, we believe, our own people under the influence of a mind-altering substance; take care, preserve life at all costs—that includes your own lives!"

"Yes, sir!" The company captains—one a young woman of about twenty, the other a man who might have been just a few years older—acknowledged the order, adjusting gas masks over their faces.

"What are you doing?" Tarleton asked.

"My job!" Nicholson said.

"Our people are dead, Nicholson—what are you, an idiot? There is no gas—there are creatures down there!"

Nicholson appeared as if he was about to explode. "How dare you, Tarleton! Arrest him!" He told one of his men.

"Like hell—I'm Chief of Police."

"Civilian police."

"This isn't a military operation," Tarleton began.

"It is now," Nicholson said, quickly cutting him off. "I'm declaring martial law—times of need."

"Lieutenant Colonel Nicholson!" Angela said quickly. She'd been military long enough to know that rich boys who went to academies and came out officers would die—or let just about anyone else die—before they'd let their college-earned titles be ignored.

She even managed a smile.

"Sir, I'm Angela Hall, retired military. And I—"

"Yes, I know about you, Miss Hall. Everybody knows who you are! *Ex-fighter!* Thank you for coming by, but you're no longer in the military and this isn't a Xenomorph situation."

He was studying a map of the mine. He barely looked up.

"I beg to differ, sir, if you'll look at the footage you have—"

"I can place you under military arrest as well," Nicholson said curtly.

Then it started again. The screaming. Commanders calling out to one another. Screaming, screaming, screaming... Blood splaying over a lens until the viewers were blinded again... blinded by a sea of crimson blood.

"Next units!" Nicholson shouted. "Be alert!"

Marines scrambled and hurried over to the opening to the cave—all adjusting their gas masks.

"Asses!" Tarleton exclaimed, hurrying over to join the marines.

"Stop that idiot!" Nicholson said, snapping out the order to those soldiers. They rushed after Tarleton; too late. The man had pushed his way past the marines, and into the caves.

"Let him rush in ahead and get himself killed," Nicholson muttered. He shook his head. "Where are the air guys? The scientists are supposed to be here—if they just get the contamination under control!"

"Sir!" One of the men standing by him seemed uneasy. "Sir! They whisper in town about these caves. About the noises they've heard from around here. People do believe that there's some kind of creature down there."

"Joe, stop! Just because you're my cousin, you have no right to test my authority!"

"But, Simon—"

"Shut up. Hey! Who's a marine! Hoorah! Hoorah!" Nicholson said.

Men and women with their masks obeyed; it didn't seem to Angela that they moved as quickly as they had before.

"Lieutenant Colonel—" Angela began.

"There is no Xenomorph!" Nicholson snapped. "You need hosts. This was a barren rock."

At his side, Joe cleared his throat.

Angela stared at him, frowning. Cousin Joe looked terrified.

"Watch those people die," Angela said quietly. "There is

247

some kind of Xenomorph down in the caves."

Nicholson looked up at her impatiently. "I'm trying to pay you respect for past service, Miss Hall. You were a marine; you survived a lot. But, you need to clear out and let me handle this situation. The government assured us that the last of the Xenomorphs were destroyed more than a year ago; they can't be on this planet. Terra-farming was just begun in the last century. There's no way that a Xenomorph could be on this planet!"

"There are children down there!" Angela said. She inhaled and caught her breath. Tarleton had run into the caves.

He was probably as dead as the others.

Except Tarleton knows that they had a Xenomorpha situation!

Nicholson was telling her to leave.

I can run! I don't have to be here. I don't have to face this nightmare again...

There were children in the caves.

And there was no running. Depending on the Xenomorphs, they could kill every single marine on the planet—and then finish off the civilians.

"Simon," Joe said hesitantly.

"Lieutenant Colonel!" Simon Nicholson reminded him angrily.

"Sir..."

"What? What the hell is it?" Nicholson said.

Joe lowered his voice. "I heard your dad talking." He glanced at Angela nervously. "He believes that it was too easy to get into the mines. As if the tunnels had been... gouged out by something that was... non-mechanical and non... human. He thinks that the company arranged for giant Blue Moon centipedes to be brought here... just as the planet was oxygenated."

Angela felt as if a cold wave washed over her.

She couldn't believe it. She couldn't believe that anyone, even the most gung-ho and ambitious company man or woman out there, would arrange for giant Blue Moon centipedes and

Xenomorph eggs to be brought to the same place.

"Blue Moon centipedes. As Xenomorph hosts. Oh, God, help us, for we will need divine intervention!" Angela said.

"No, no, they wouldn't have brought giant centipedes here," Nicholson said, but he didn't appear to believe his own words. *Yes, Blue Moon centipedes might have been brought here; they were incredible tunnel makers—better than any digging equipment known.*

Nicholson spun around suddenly to accost someone. Angela saw a man she hadn't seen before that day—and yet had seen dozens of times before.

Because he wasn't a man, of course. He was an android, one called Tommy II. The newest model—they'd had one as their science officer when she'd last encountered Xenomorphs.

"Did the company bring eggs here? Centipedes?" Nicholson asked.

"No. Not that I know about. I am not… my programming, after events in the past, is now set to prevent me from lying," the android said.

"Centipedes. I can only imagine…" Angela said.

Screams sounded again; Nicholson's third round of marines. Angela couldn't help but stare at the screen.

Body parts—flew.

She saw the shadows of what looked like… great alien arms. A hundred of them—from a genetic splash between a centipede and an alien.

There was a sudden flare of luminescence; someone's flashlight shooting a huge arch.

That was when she saw the child. The little girl, hunched beneath an overhang of rock. She was just standing there, staring, in shock… screaming.

Chief of Police Tarleton suddenly appeared, making a beeline for the girl. He caught her and flew down behind one of the ragged boulders that lay to either side of the dug-out silver mine tunnel.

The light went out; she couldn't tell if the little girl and Tarleton had made it or not.

Angela winced… and looked back at Nicholson.

"Listen to me, Nicholson, and brighten up. I don't care what you say. You have Xenomorphs, hybrids that gestated in giant Blue Moon centipedes. You can take them out with a nuclear weapon. Probably destroy this planet, but if you don't kill them now, this planet will be destroyed anyway. There will be no one left alive on it. You can tell your men to quit with the gas masks—you don't need them. You do need greater firepower— flamethrowers. And don't send in small units one by one. We need a whole row of marines going in at once, firing at once with automatic weapons and the flamethrowers. The children, bless them, have survived somehow. You can see the little girl, hiding behind one of the rocks."

Nicholson just stood there, staring at her.

Angela let out an oath of impatience.

"What happened to 'hoorah'?" she demanded.

"You don't know what you're talking about," Nicholson said.

He is either incredibly stupid, or in shock. They obviously hadn't taught real-world blood and guts at his fancy school, she thought.

She let out an oath of impatience. He wasn't going to listen to her. She spun around and headed for one of the trucks. Luckily, weaponry hadn't changed much since she'd left the corp.

She found what had been branded as the "wooly mammoth," a flamethrower with a power and distance that was formidable.

Enough to take down giant centipede Xenomorphs? I don't know. But maybe I could at least get the child and get out and…

She wasn't alone; the android, Tommy II, had followed her. She looked at him suspiciously.

"I can't lie, and I can't kill," he assured her.

"Then you're a hell of a lot different from some of your predecessors!" she said.

"I'm different," he swore.

She didn't know whether to believe him or not. But then, she didn't know if she'd come out of the caves or not. She'd seen the little girl; there was no running. Except for into the cave; bearing her weapon, she turned, and she ran, heading in—the android behind her.

At the mouth of the cave, she stopped. The android was next to her and, as she paused, looking at the entrance and the stairs that had been cut into the earth and the elevator shaft, she saw that she had been joined by three marines, as well.

Almost the size unit of the company she had lost so recently...

She nodded briefly to them and spoke softly. "They can be very different, these Xenomorphs, as we know, depending on the host—giant centipedes, in this case—and whatever genetic interference might have taken place at the facehugger stage. One thing to remember—what they bleed is usually acidic. And they'll have an inner mouth—and it's the inner mouth that will be the most dangerous. Imagine the worst of what you've learned in a creature with a hundred or so legs... watch out. And you'll probably have the mouth, and the forcibles—what really 'bites' in a centipede..."

They saluted her, one short-haired, heavily muscled young woman, and the two men at her side.

"No elevator; we stand together."

"Yes, ma'am!" one of the marines said.

Creating a flank, they headed down the stairs.

Angela saw the first movement of a "foot." She froze for a moment.

It was worse than she had imagined; the legs were long. The creatures were long. She saw three of them. They had the huge, elongated head, and mouth, the mouth... the mouth on each already opening to allow that second mouth of razor-sharp teeth to protrude as they came toward them, hundreds of long feet waving, and, beneath the double mouths, the "forcibles" clicking away, ready to claw and tear...

"Fire!" Angela commanded.

And they did, as a team. They aimed for the giant heads

with the mammoth flamethrowers.

Yes, yes, fire is good! Fire decreased the acid dropping from the things; it burnt up in the flames, it enhanced them.

"Cover me!" she shouted.

She had come to the bottom of the stairs; huge tunnels existed, but castoff rocks and ledges surrounded them. She made a dive behind the rock where she'd seen the little girl. The child had ceased to scream; she had ceased to do anything but shake and stare in horror.

"Tarleton!" she screamed.

There was no answer. Neither did she see the man.

She didn't see any of his body parts, either. But then again, would she? The earth was burnt out and scorched from the acid and the flamethrowers; there was blood here and there... and pieces of colonial marine uniform... still attached to flesh.

Angela wrapped her arms around the child. She looked back to the marines and the android.

"Heading back!" she cried.

"Incoming!" the android, Tommy II, shouted, lifting his weapon. "Run!" he told her.

She did. Enough for their first excursion down. She was pretty sure that at least one of the three creatures they'd encountered was dead; the other two continued to thrash, legs flying about, teeth and forcibles clicking away.

She ran straight up the stairs, followed by the marines. As she reached the top step and the entrance to the cave, she burst out into the dying light of the day, the child still clutched in her arms, marines behind her, firing, firing...

She heard the sound, that awful sound the Xenomorphs seemed to make, no matter what hybrid creation they might be.

I know that sound, know it far too well, it had haunted far too many of my dreams!

Lieutenant Colonel Simon Nicholson seemed to have come to and gained back some of his senses since she—along with the android and the three marines—had gone into the cave. He was shouting out orders to a new wave of soldiers. "Flamethrowers, flamethrowers!" he ordered.

Angela held the little girl close as she raced toward his command center. When she tried to put the little girl down, the child clung to her. "Jake... Jake... Uncle Warrick went to find him... Jake... my brother, you have to get my brother, and my Uncle Warrick... please. Oh..."

The little girl started to sob.

Holding her, Angela blinked.

Uncle Warrick. So the cop who had come for her had done so with good—and personal—reason. The kids were his nephew and niece. But, he hadn't offered her up for nothing; he'd known what he was facing. And he'd known that she was a better bet than the Lieutenant Colonel who was still there blustering about...

"Okay, what's your name?" she asked the child.

"Dublin."

"Your name is Dublin?"

The little girl nodded solemnly. "They say it was a place."

"Yes. It was a place. A beautiful place, so I was told," Angela murmured. "Okay, you have to let me go."

The child's hold on her was so tight.

"Dublin, baby. You have to let me go, or I won't be able to go back in. I won't be able to find your Uncle Warrick, or your brother."

"What the fuck?" Lieutenant Colonel Simon Nicholson said suddenly.

Angela swung around; she'd just managed to set Dublin down.

She picked her back up.

The alien centipede-Xenomorphs had discovered the way out of the cave.

They'd killed one; she knew that they had killed one—but there were now several that had spilled out of the cave, great heads atop long bodies with those hundreds of long legs... and the rear of the creatures, seeming to whip around, as if they were scorpion-tailed. And the click-click-click of the forcibles in front of the bodies, beneath the giant heads with the double mouths, and the shimmering sharp teeth that dripped with the saliva of a constant hunger…

She wrenched Dublin off the ground and into her arms, running for one of the marine trucks. She thought about the way that the beings had been killed in the past…

So convenient when you could blast the acid dripping monsters into darkest space!

Think! She told herself, *think.*

Fire worked, but they needed so much of it!

Marines were running everywhere; fighting…

And dying.

Angela shoved Dublin into the passenger side of a marine trunk. "Stay! Don't move! Don't come out!"

Dublin nodded, and then screamed. Angela swung around in time to see one of the Xenomorphs bearing down on her.

She just had time to draw her heavy weapon, to send fire surging toward the creature.

The head caught fire; burned.

The thing screamed in a horrible dance of death just as she looked up; one of the marines who had so bravely followed her had just been skewered by at least four of the legs on one of the creatures.

"What are we going to do, what are we going to do, what are we going to do?" Lieutenant Colonel Nicholson demanded. He was by her side—trying to push by her to get into the vehicle along with the child, Dublin.

Angela ignored him; another of the things was coming toward her, forcibles clicking, teeth shimmering in the glow of the vehicle lights—night was coming fast upon them.

She turned suddenly, catching him by the lapels. "What's that other cave entrance? More silver?"

He shook his head, staring at her as if he had become crazed.

"Salt. Rock salt."

Salt. Rock salt.

She remembered being a child on a Milky Way planet similar to earth—and the neighbor boy who had thrown rocks at cats and dogs and enjoyed setting lizards on fire.

He'd also poured salt over centipedes and watched while they squirmed and died… Centipedes. Yes, at the heart of it all, they were vulnerable. She'd studied the creatures; she loved the earth, and farming, and animal husbandry.

"Salt!" She screamed the word. "Salt! Tons of it, salt and fire, salt and fire…"

"Yes, ma'am!" Tommy II called out.

The rear end of a centipede Xenomorph-thing was swinging around for her; she ducked and rolled, far away. She was headed for the rock salt cave entrance.

But then she saw him.

The little boy. He must have been a year or two older than his sister. His name, she knew, was Jake.

He had made his way to the entrance. He was alone.

One of the Xenomorphs was headed for him.

Did that mean that Chief Warrick Tarleton was dead? *Most likely,* she thought, and though she hadn't known him that well, she was saddened. He'd known the truth. He'd been ready to fight, no matter what the battle. She had been afraid. He had forced her to courage.

"Jake! Get down!" she shouted.

She could see one of them; it had been injured. It was missing several legs.

It still had enough. It was stumbling toward the boy.

Angela raced for it, firing away with her flamethrower. It made a horrible sound. She knew to aim for the head and the eyes. She kept her aim steady.

She almost had it down.

And then…

She ran out. Her flamethrower sputtered. The things were

not stupid—no matter what the host creature, they seemed to come out with a frightening level of intelligence.

It started toward her and the boy.

Well, that was it, then. She'd escaped once. And now…

She waved her arms at the creature, running to the left of the boy. "Run, Jake, run. See the Colonial Marine truck over there? Run, the shell is resistant to the acid and fire and bullets. Run, run! And you! Oh, my God, you are ugly! Come here, come here…

She waited. One of the legs would stab through her body any second. The leg would lift her; bear her to the chomping inner mouth of the repulsive beast.

Maybe it was just her turn…

"Go ahead, you bastard!" she cried.

Suddenly, fames whipped before, tearing into the thing. She heard it let out one of its terrible screams.

And she spun around. Chief Tarleton was there; he'd swept up a flamethrower, probably from one of the fallen marines.

"The salt is coming!" he cried.

She stared at him.

Salt! Will it work?

The marines were coming. They were minus their commander—and Cousin Joe.

They were accompanied, though, by the android.

Tommy II.

Tommy was hauling some kind of a massive machine with a great big nozzle. She stared at it, still somewhat in shock, as the man at her side burned down the Xenomorph that had been so very close to ending her life.

It was going down… but others were now peeking out the entrance to the cave.

"Duck!" Warrick called to her. "Duck, roll!"

She fell to the ground; he fell with her, forcing the two of them to roll fast and furiously away, far away from the opening to the cave. From there she saw that the marines had come up with tons and tons of the rock salt; they'd loaded it into the machine with the massive nozzle. The android, Tommy II, leapt up to the controls of the machine.

And he let loose…

Rock salt, hard, loose, started to fly.

And fly and fly and fly in a colorful rain, like hail, like rainbow infused snow flurries… so many minerals were part of the mined rock salt, the colors seemed to be endless. It was almost beautiful, large and small, like hair, like a delicate spray, it flew and flew…

It landed upon the creatures, and in the darkness, they seemed to catch those colors as they screamed in a crescendo, melting like the Witch of the West when she was doused with water.

The marines all about went still, watching.

The night sky seemed to take on the colors.

One by one, they went down. And when they were down, marines rushed over them in waves, burning the remains, chopping them to ribbons with their knives and guns and bayonets.

Tommy II didn't stop; he drove the machine to the front of the cave. He filled it with rock salt.

It was almost like fireworks.

She stood by the marine truck, next to Warrick Tarleton, and watched.

Bit by bit, the night came to an end.

Tommy II crawled down from the machine.

"Thank you. That was brilliant," Angela told him.

He smiled. "I can't lie. I can't kill human beings. I can't allow them to die, if it is in my power to stop them dying. You gave me the power."

She shook her head, waving a hand in the air. "No, no… you knew what you were doing. The marines are good."

She could go home, she thought. Home to the little house and lovely little farm she had going. They were far, far away from…

No. They were never far, far away from danger. She couldn't hide from it.

She realized it was over—and the marines were all staring at her.

"Nice, Captain! Nice," one of the young men called out to her.

"Hoorah!" went up.

She lifted her hands, flushing.

She'd lost what she'd had that morning, she realized. Her life of illusion, where she believed that she could hide, that she could find a world that was safe from all dangers...

Warrick Tarleton was there, too, nodding in grim acknowledgment of the marines—and her.

She turned and saw that there were many body parts here and there. Though a great deal of death had occurred before the creatures were stopped, Lieutenant Colonel Simon Nicholson was still alive and well—and whole.

She thought that he would immediately try to regain control; seize back his authority.

"I didn't do it! I swear I didn't do it!"

No, he wanted no control. And Angela believed him.

Chief Tarleton spoke, a protective hand on his nephew's head, another on his niece's head.

"Your cousin. Joe Nicholson. Your father brought in the Blue Moon giant centipedes. That would insure that the mines were dug out. But Joe couldn't let that be enough. You were the one in control—he might have been the better soldier, but you were heir to your dad."

"My dad... no, really, no..." Simon Nicholson said.

He didn't believe his own words.

"Maybe Joe was... eaten," Tommy II said. "I don't see him..."

"Here he is!"

A pretty young female marine walked up, dragging Joe along with her. "He's alive; he ran the minute the real action started."

"Don't... don't kill me, don't kill me, don't kill me..." the man blubbered.

Chief Tarleton wrenched him by the collar. "You're under

arrest. Sargeant," he said, addressing the young marine. "If you would see this man to the joint barracks? I believe that what he's done does call for banishment to a penal colony, but, hell. I'm not judge and jury."

"Yes, Chief!" the marine said.

Warrick Tarleton was staring across the space at Angela. She smiled crookedly as the marines went about their work.

They saw to their injured.

And their dead.

"Thank you," Tarleton said to her.

As if they been cued—which, of course, they hadn't, she would have seem them—the children rushed to Angela, putting their arms around her.

"Thank you! Thank you."

She nodded ruefully. "So—I'm not under arrest anymore?"

"I knew you'd... well, I knew you'd rise to the occasion. You know, they're probably going to try to talk you into coming back—into taking command here," Tarleton told her.

"Maybe... I could be a reserve," she said. She studied him. "I'm impressed. Joe Nicholson—good old cousin Joe. He got a lot of people killed. He nearly got the kids killed. And yet—you refrained. You didn't even give him a belt in the jaw. I might have been tempted to do that!"

"If I'd have touched him, I'd have killed him," Tarleton said. "And...well, I cling to whatever it is that makes us human, that makes us different. That lifts us above... above the creatures. I mean... well, we see evil in some of our own kind, right? Beasts lurk in all of us. But, so does something higher," he added very softly. "So. I'll get you home. I mean, the marines will get this under control. I wrenched you away from your farm."

Still studying the man, she nodded. She liked him. Really liked him. Him, and the damned android—and a lot of the marines. She hadn't liked anyone that way since...

Since Daniel had died.

But then, she hadn't known anyone who would take such risks for others since then.

"You're not moving," he said. "So, does that bode well for the future of this fine group of marines?"

"Maybe," she said. "But, you're right. We need some higher authority. For now…"

She ruffled the kids' hair and asked, "Are you hungry? I grow really great food on my farm."

"Hungry?" Jake said. "Starving!"

"If your uncle says it is okay…" Angela murmured.

"It's okay. I mean, I get to eat, too, right?"

"Sure."

They walked past the trucks and the fires, back to the hover-car.

"Pretty tricky, though. When you came to get me, you didn't mention that the children were your niece and nephew," Angela said.

He gazed over Jake's head and smiled.

"I try to be noble," he said, then he lowered his head, smiling, "and, of course, I try to avoid stupidity as well."

Angela laughed. Her beautiful world, created and false in so many ways, had nearly been destroyed.

But that night…

She thought that there was a new kind of beauty around her. It still existed in a created world. And yet…

It was beautifully real.

HUGS TO DIE FOR

BY MIKE RESNICK AND
MARINA J. LOSTETTER

"Xenomorph blood is one of the most corrosive substances known to Man, ideal for use in construction and cutting. Now that you've seen how the Company has perfected its procurement and retainment methodology, we think you'll agree that its employment here on your base is not only safe, but is indeed quite a boon," said Mr. Jones, the wide-eyed tour guide, skipping ahead of the small group with his clipboard in hand, eager to reach the final stop on their journey.

"Here we come to the pride and joy of our facility—where the root of the magic happens." Jones waved grandly at the floor-to-ceiling windows of the "Egg Lab" as they approached. White padded paneling lined the hall outside the lab, and two armed guards stood stoically at its entrance. General Amotz, along with her small security detail of two, nodded respectfully to the men as they passed.

She only half-noticed what Jones said at any given moment. His PR training had been thorough, but was completely lost on a marine of her caliber. Her superiors hadn't interrupted her leave for a tour of the half-constructed military space station because she needed a good dog-and-pony show. They'd called on her because the task was urgent, and she was the nearest high-ranking official.

Due to recent encounters elsewhere with Xenomorph populations, the Company's "perfected methods" had come into question, and the Colonial Marines had decided they needed a closer look at the systems being used to construct their base.

So they'd wrangled her an invitation, and assigned poor Ribar and Cortez—who'd also been on leave—as security. Marines on vacation were the only ones close enough which was the reason the base was being constructed here in the first place: there was simply not enough of a permanent military presence nearby.

Inside the lab, robotic arms slid back and forth on thick tracks mounted to the ceiling, operated and monitored by the technicians in the control booth, stationed a short distance away from both the lab and the adjoining "Egg Vault." They'd finished touring the booth only a few minutes prior, and having seen the contents of the lab on the array of monitors, General Amotz was eager to get a closer look at its contents.

As they drew up close to the windows, Amotz found herself squinting. The light in the hall was blindingly bright, while the bulbs within were dimmed. The black-metal arms moved with an eerie precision, and were jointed in such a way as to appear organic when not properly lit. The ends of several looked like hands, with elongated fingers. Others sported pincers. And one looked like a barbed extremity, flicking back and forth near the edge of the window, right where the hall lights created the greatest glare. It could have easily been a tail, ready to strike, to cut, to stab. It looked as though it lay in wait for one of the unsuspecting humans to draw closer, to lose it in the shimmer of the glass.

"If you'll all move closer," Mr. Jones beckoned, sidling up himself, nearer to the seam, nearer to that suspicious robotic arm.

Amotz caught her heart beating inexplicably fast in her chest. She was so eager to see one of these creatures in person, her mind was creating monsters where there were none.

With a burst of speed, the arm she'd been eyeing shot sideways into the room, out of its dark corner. It moved to a large tank occupying one-third of the space, tracing over the glass like a protective mother. Yellow liquid filled the tank, and the solution sat absolutely still. Not so much as a ripple fluttered through the murky film. But the tank wasn't empty; Mr. Jones had already explained that was where they kept the "neutralized" facehuggers. Hundreds of them.

She squinted again, trying to discern shapes in the preservation fluid. There, perhaps, was something that looked like the bony, pale fingers of an emaciated man. It twitched, or the light flickered, or her eyes refocused, and the phantom shape disappeared.

"Now," Jones began, "if you'll look to the right of the lab, you'll see—"

"Ma'am? General? Mr. Ribar? Sorry to interrupt…" The young aide with whom Ribar had left his son sidled up, looking sheepish, sliding her glasses higher up her nose. "Daniel is asking for you. He said it was time for his medication, but you didn't leave me anything."

Ribar looked annoyed. This had been a last-minute assignment for all of them, and he had tried to refuse because of having no one to place his son with. Amotz had suggested the kid simply come along. After all, this was only a milk run.

Ribar emitted a heavy sigh. "He doesn't take any

medication," he said. The aide looked confused. "He's messing with you," Ribar continued. "Ten-year-olds do that."

A too-wide smile flitted over the aide's face and away again. "Oh. Of course. I'm sorry."

"Who's with him now?"

The aide's cheeks blanched. "No one. I left him in the quarters we assigned you."

Amotz decided to intervene. "Go check on him, just to be on the safe side."

The woman hurried away.

Cortez bit back a laugh. "God, she's too easy!"

The tour guide seemed puzzled, looking for all the world like he'd just witnessed an exchange in a foreign language.

"I'm sorry, Mr. Jones," Amotz said. "Please continue."

"As I was saying: If you will focus your attention to the right, we'll start the neutralization process."

"To the right" was a large, dark cage, with thick struts and corrugated slats. It butted up against a thick, gray vault door, slashed in many places with claw marks. Beneath the door ran a length of conveyer belt, which ground into motion, groaning and screeching as its guide-wheels turned.

As the vault door slid upwards, a trap door at the end of the belt slid aside. A white-plastic and stainless-steel figure rose, hunchbacked, from the floor. It looked both ghostly and broken within the dark grasp of the cage. It was a mannequin in the approximate shape of a human, much as a poorly-wired skeleton bears that same approximate human shape. Its ovoid head lolled on its shoulders.

With a flick of some unseen-technician's wrist, the dummy came half-alive, lifting its head and opening its wide, devilish mouth, revealing whirling gears and clamps within. A small, blue pilot light glimmered behind its metal teeth.

Through the vault door slid a brownish-green egg, looking like the skin might flake but the tissues would give under one's touch—like a dried-out corpse. Only there was nothing *dry* about the ovomorph. Long strands of amniotic goo trailed over and around the egg like so much saliva.

Amotz unconsciously raised her hand to her throat, gulping down harshly.

"There are three known types of stimulants that signal to the egg and facehugger that a receptive host is nearby," said Jones, as though describing something as benign as a bake sale. "Not all 'huggers respond to the same stimulants, so we employ them all. One: movement of a warm body."

The mannequin inside the cage did a terrible parody of a dance.

"Two: mammalian pheromones."

The "tail" robot shot across the room, as if it meant to spear the ovomorph. Instead it spritzed a heavy mist over the quad-fold lips of the egg, which gave no signs of stirring. Amotz imagined that she could smell musk in the air.

"And three: Carbon dioxide emissions. It's the same way bed-bugs find their victims."

And with a puff of gas from another robotic extension, the pliant lips unfurled.

Amotz tensed as a single, bony leg inched its way above the folds, twitching once as if testing the air. In the next instant it sprang, leaping at the mannequin with legs splayed wide, like a giant, grasping hand.

The dummy welcomed it with a deranged grin, as the slimy, whip-like tail of the creature noosed itself around its throat. Moments later the 'huggers arms were wrapped around the thing's head, with its reproductive organs plastered grotesquely to the mannequin's mouth.

"*Watch!*" Jones insisted.

Seconds in, the creature began violently seizing, a few of its legs twitching away from the mannequin's head as though it longed to let go. From above, a thin beam of red sliced through the knot of the alien's tail, cauterizing the wound as quickly as it cut.

Facehuggers could not scream. They made only autonomic sounds. But it was clear from the way it thrust itself away, falling back onto the floor with its legs curling in the air like a dead spider, that it was in pain.

"We cauterize the proboscis—the tube that implants the parasitic cells which help morph the host tissue into a chestburster—and remove the tail. As you can see, robbed of its ability to complete its biological imperative, the 'hugger becomes docile and safe to work with."

As Jones droned on, a set of black-metal pincers entered the cage to retrieve the animal.

It twitched as the arm clutched around it, like a bug poked with a stick. It remained half-curled, still as death, until the arm was within reach of the tank. Sensing, somehow, that it was about to be imprisoned with the rest of its kind, the 'hugger jerked violently, again and again. Its claw-tipped legs scraped at the pincers, scratching long silver lines into the arm. The creature twisted and squirmed, and the technician tightened the grip.

Big mistake.

One leg pinched and tore, extruding a glob of yellow-green blood that foamed and sizzled as it sank into the softening metal. The arm gave an abortive jolt, still heading for the tank but now listing to the side. The technician lost control and it careened into the glass, cracking the side. The pincers popped open, dropping the flailing creature unceremoniously onto the floor.

Cortez and Ribar immediately un-holstered their side-arms, and the station guards at the end of the hall jolted to attention.

Simultaneously, a siren blared out and flashing yellow lights filled the space.

"It's all right," Jones said, holding out his hands, moving between the marines and the windows. "We have containment procedures. It's fine. We have to be prepared for accidents when working with animals. The lab's on lockdown. We've gone through this before. It's *fine*."

"Look, General!" Cortez pointed frantically at the tank,

where a handful of facehuggers had begun to swim at the crack. One after the other, they threw themselves at the weak point, but to no avail.

"It's *fine*," Jones wheezed.

It didn't *look* fine. Amotz' heart began to skip beats, thumping harder first in her ears, then her belly, as if it was clamoring for a way out.

More 'huggers joined the assault. More and more of the supposedly-docile, supposedly-incapacitated aliens banged themselves in unison against the crack, widening it, sending little spider-web fractures through the tank until—

The tank shattered, sending a great whooshing wall of liquid spilling into the lab proper. Hundreds of 'huggers scrambled through the flood, shaking themselves like dogs, their breathing flaps expanding and contracting lightning-quick to produce droplets of the preservation fluid.

Hundreds of them. *Hundreds*. All clammy skin and knobby joints with no desire but to *breed, breed, breed*.

"Still fine," Jones insisted, grabbing Cortez' wrist, yanking it away from his weapon. "They're contained, and you have to remember they've been neutered. They are harm—"

A wave of them rushed at the glass, sensing the warm bodies beyond. Their burnt-out reproductive organs thumped at the pane, smearing it with a combination of fluids. Their nails scraped like little rat feet at the glass and at each other. The pile grew as more and more of them leapt onto one another in a crazed push to get at the humans.

As the marines raised their guns, taking steady aim, the General signaled for the guards to join them. "You two, come on—and get more men down here! We're going to need all the firepower we can get!"

"General," Jones complained, "this is unnecessary, we are—"

She grabbed him by the collar, yanking him off balance. "If you say 'fine' again, so help me I will break your ratty little nose."

The pile grew and grew until all one could see was a

mass of legs, legs and more legs. Three facehuggers pinned themselves flat against the glass, sprawled out completely to extend to their full wingspan. They formed a triangle that looked... *deliberate.*

"Shit's going to happen real, quick," she spat at Jones. "I know strategizing when I see it, and those things aren't just some dumb bugs. So you better find a hole to crawl into." She dismissed him with an expression of total disdain.

He straightened his shirt. "I'm not going anywhere. I have full confidence in the Company, and in our lockdown procedures."

"Look around," she snapped. "You're the only one."

"If you shoot them, you will destroy this facility. Their blood will eat through everything!"

"I'm not the one who thought it was a good idea to bring sentient acid-bombs aboard and then *piss them off!*"

Cortez shouted as the three splayed 'huggers were simultaneously speared through by their comrades. The creatures tore at their legs, their backs, their breathing flaps. In moments, the sacrificial aliens were obscured by the volume of blood splattered across the massive swath of window.

The glass fell away like so much melting sugar, leaving nothing but dead air between the humans and the horde of angry parasitoids.

"Fire!" commanded the General, gesturing for everyone to back away down the hall as they shot. The high-pitched *crack!* of a hand gun was underscored by the bass-booms of the guard's rifles. Creatures leapt into the air, their legs outstretched, clamping down wherever they landed. Others scrambled up the walls, and the rest darted out under foot.

Chaos reigned and everything blurred. There were so many bodies, so many legs. They carpeted the surfaces, pouring over one another, flowing like an eager sea of spiders—only much worse.

Mr. Jones literally wet his pants, and the rank scent of ammonia mingled with the sour smell of corroding metals.

Acid flew all around. Barrels flashed, ozone burned. Ribar cried out in agony as a long glob of yellow blood hit his shin, searing it down to the bone. As he stumbled Amotz took his weapon from him.

"Call the ship in," she commanded him. "We have to get out of here. Let them know it's an emergency evacuation situation." He opened up a link.

Their ship sat in orbit around the planet, waiting for their day aboard the station to be completed. It was supposed to take them all back to Earth. All of them, even—

Ribar's kid.

Shit.

"Don't let a single one out of here," she yelled. "We have to protect the rest of the base."

A facehugger leapt at Cortez, just as he emptied his clip. He flung his arms in front of his face and the alien latched onto his gun. He tossed it away.

A guard tripped and a 'hugger clamped around his knee, ineffectually trying to tongue at him with the cauterized stump of its probiscus. After a moment it pulled itself tighter, curling in, putting extra pressure right on his kneecap until—*crack!*

The man's screams echoed down the narrow hall.

Out of the corner of her eye, Amotz saw a new shape in the melee. It wasn't bony and knobbed, not heavy and fleshy. It was long. Like a whip. Like a—

Tail.

"They're not all neutered!" she breathed, sure no one could hear her over the racket of shots-plus-acid-fizzle. Some of the 'huggers must have burned their way into the egg vault— clawed their way into the unopened eggs.

One with a tail sprang from the floor two feet in front of her. "Watch out!" she yelled to no one in particular. The creature's target lay behind, over her shoulder.

She whipped around just in time to see it clamp down on Mr. Jones, his last words smothered by the coil around his neck and the tube down his throat. Whatever he'd been about to say, *fine* wasn't it.

Mr. Jones went limp, his body collapsing like a sack of loose bones. He hit the deck before Amotz could loose another yelp.

"Protect your mouths!" Amotz ordered. "We have live ones. *Live ones!*"

But it was no use. The newborn facehuggers were protected by their brethren. Wounded individuals took bullets for them. The group's imperative to impregnate drove them like a hive-mind.

First Jones went down. Then Cortez on her left. The capped guard on her right. The second guard turned to her, ready to shout something, when one leapt and caught the side of his mouth with three legs, yanking his lips wide before it burrowed in.

Amotz took the last mag from Ribar, determined to protect him.

"Daniel—" he choked, his fingers clawing at his bloodied leg.

"You'll see him again. *You will!*"

The facehugger numbers dwindled, but not because they'd killed so many. Holes littered the floor like perfect, bug-sized escape hatches. She could only watch in horror as many crawled down and away, disappearing into the inner workings of the space station.

"We have to get the hell out of here!" she gasped in Ribar's ear. "Can you walk at all on your own? The docking bay's not that far. The ship is on its way."

"But Daniel—"

"I'll get him. *Me.* You'd only slow us down."

As the last of the creatures wormed its way out of sight, she handed Ribar his service pistol.

"No, I have to—"

"You wanna play the hero, or do you want to give your kid the best chance of survival? I order you to get to the docking bay."

He nodded solemnly. "I'm sorry," he mumbled before

going. "It was supposed to be my job to protect *you*. To keep you alive."

"You haven't failed yet. Get your ass out of here."

He saluted, then was gone.

Minus a weapon, she inched her way toward one of the downed guards. The man's lungs still worked steadily, but as she came closer, the alien on his face tightened its grip.

"Easy, easy," she whispered at it, crouching down to snake the rifle from the man's fingers.

She checked the mag—half empty.

"I'm sorry," she said, echoing Ribar. She knew the guard couldn't hear her, knew he was dead already. The only thing he had to look forward to was a larval Xenomorph punching its way out of his diaphragm. "I'm sorry," she said again, backing up a safe distance to take aim at his head and fire.

She did the same for the other guard, and Jones, and Cortez, choking each time she pulled the trigger.

Plastering herself to the wall, eyes darting, she carefully slid out of the lab hall and into the open causeway. Just six corridors separated her from the kid—but it was thousands of cubic-meters in which Murphy's Law could have a field day.

———

Out on the causeways, all lay eerily still. Only the incessant emergency siren blared out, so constant and steady it was nothing but white-noise. She hunched as she moved, ready to fire or spring out of a 'hugger's path any second. Sweat dripped from her hairline into her eyes. She felt too hot and too cold at the same time, and her gaze was never steady. Every moment that passed had her more skittish than the next. What if she didn't make it in time? What if she got there and Daniel was already on the floor, a cold, eyeless mask of a creature covering his face?

Ribar would have every right to blame her.

She passed several such unfortunates on her way—bodies sprawled out, unwilling incubators for Xenomorph flesh. She didn't have enough rounds to put them all down, and her chest constricted every time she made the choice to move on without ending someone's pain.

Many of the hallways were cordoned off with yellow tape, and a few areas were swathed in opaque plastic, behind which amorphous shadows faded in and out of the light. The scent of hot metal mixed with some kind of sour astringent taint in the air. Every time she caught an extra strong whiff of the acidic smell, she jerked away, sure it meant a 'hugger was upon her.

Ten meters from her goal, one fully-functioning bug dropped from the ceiling. She dove for the floor, bruising her knees, but avoiding the clutch of long legs. Its nails sliced down her back in the miss, creating hot lines of pain.

Swiftly, unthinkingly, blood pounding in her ears, she rolled over and fired, clipping the creature square in the center as it leapt for her face. Its bony body shattered on impact, and a light splattering of acid singed her right cheek. The acid bore little holes into her skin, creating deep open wounds, but she made no attempt to wipe it away. She knew she'd only get an injured hand for her efforts.

It didn't matter that it would scar, didn't matter that she could feel it eating through to the wet flesh of her mouth. Nothing mattered—not pain, not time, not breath—until she reached Daniel.

It was her fault he was here. It was her responsibility to get him out.

The door, when she reached it, was locked. She wracked her brain for the aide's name.

"Miss—Miss Campbell? Open the door. It's General Amotz."

A feral screech came from within, but the door snapped open. Blinking up at her from the other side was Daniel. Quickly she shuffled the boy inside, pulling the door behind her.

Miss Campbell was curled in one corner of the square room, between a desk and a cot.

"Come on, we have to go—now!" Amotz demanded.

"What's happening?" Daniel asked, calm and clear-eyed.

"I have to get you to your daddy, okay? He wanted to come, but I gave him a job to do so he had to do it, understand?" She took his hand firmly in her free one, toeing the door back open and scanning the hall. "Take Miss Campbell's hand too."

"No," the aide said dully.

Amotz barely glanced at her, preoccupied with setting herself up for a sprint. "Fine, don't take his hand."

"I'm not going out there."

"You don't have a choice."

Campbell hugged her knees to her chest, burying her face against them. "I'm not going," came her muffled whimper.

"Look, I'm not in the habit of *convincing* people to do what I say. I give orders, marines follow them, it's as simple as that."

"I'm not a—"

"I know. So you get to choose: come with me, or die here."

A long pause followed. *Come on,* Amotz silently urged, *get up! I can't save you if you aren't willing to be saved!*

"I'll… I'll just wait here. Someone will come."

"*I* came. No one else is about to."

Campbell looked up, her gaze unfocussed, voice steady. "I said *no!*"

Amotz wasn't going to treat her like a child. Maybe a person with less sense and a bigger savior complex would have forced her on her feet, but not the General. She knew you couldn't make a flailing man swim, and you couldn't make a grown woman choose a death-push over hiding. Amotz respected that. But she also had an obligation to Daniel. They couldn't hesitate any longer.

Hell, maybe Campbell was right. Maybe someone else would rescue her. Amotz could only hope.

She squeezed Daniel's hand tighter. "You ready, kid?"

His wide eyes locked with hers as he nodded, looking half his age and twice as delicate.

"Don't let go of my hand, no matter what else you do, okay?"

"Okay."

"Ready? We're going to run real fast. You let me know if you see any critters, okay?" She took a deep, cleansing breath. "Three... two... one!"

Daniel stumbled almost as soon as they were out the door. She yanked him up by the arm, half dragging him along, but she could see that this wasn't going to work.

"I'm sorry, I'm sorry!" he gasped immediately, eyes watering. Amotz was sure Campbell hadn't explained to him what the sirens were for, but the kid wasn't stupid. He knew bad shit was going down. He was trembling and trying to hurry, but it wasn't enough.

"Hey, I've got an idea!" she said. "Can you hold on tight if I give you a piggy-back ride?" He was too big to carry on her hip, and she needed her hands free for the rifle.

He wiped his nose on his sleeve. "Yeah."

"Good. Up then." She crouched for him.

They weren't more than two meters away from the door, were moving too slow and making too much noise. Three facehuggers rounded a corner, sneaking out from beneath a flap of brittle plastic—two tailless wonders and one fully-functioning baby maker.

"Quicker, Daniel! Quick! Hold on! Hide your face! Whatever you do, don't look up. Head down!" She rose to her feet before he was fully in place, and his little shoes scrambled against her sides. "Hold on. Hold as tight as you can!"

The 'huggers legs stuttered against the pipes of the ceiling, tapping out a harsher staccato pattern the closer they came.

Amotz got her hands fixed on her weapon at the same time Daniel stopped squirming. She fired in rapid succession, taking all three out. Acid dribbled onto the deck as though from a leaky faucet, while the alien corpses still clung to the ceiling.

She skirted her way around it. The boy bounced against her back as they ran, and his forearm cut tight across her throat, making it difficult to breathe.

But their pace was good. They could make it. One hall down, then two. A few more corners and they were halfway to home.

"Hang on, kid!" she choked out, trying to sound as reassuring as possible.

Her breaths came high and tight, and a half-sizzle half-roar swelled in her ears—whether it was her veins throbbing or a side effect of hyperventilating, she couldn't say. The bow in her spine ached, and her knees wobbled, but she knew she could make it. She could keep putting one foot in front of the other and get Daniel to safety.

She came to the last corner, around which lay the lab-hall and the final stretch to the docking bay.

"Almost the—" The elation died on her lips as she skidded to a halt.

At the far end of the hall, wires and flex-pipes dangled out of the ceiling like vines in a titanium jungle. They swayed to and fro with the movement of dozens of facehuggers skittering up and down the ridged surfaces. Coolant leaked from several pipe-ends, forming a pool below that was quickly covering over with a temperature-induced haze. Most of the bugs were neutered, but a handful of healthy 'huggers climbed up and down the "vines" in double-time, walking over their siblings, using them as surer footing.

They created a curtain that spanned the entire width of the hall.

They know! Somehow those breeding, parasitic bastards know *this is our escape route.*

"Remember what I said, Daniel. *Don't look up.*"

Amotz thought back to when they'd first arrived. She'd taken a cursory glance at the layout of the station. Were there any other completed portions that led to the bay? Any at all?

Maybe. Yes. There was one, I think. It's a long way around, but—

But what other choice did she have?

Pivoting on her heel, her boots squeaking against the grates, she rounded the corner again—

And gasped.

"What's happening?" Daniel demanded.

The hall was coated in facehuggers. It was three-hundred-and-sixty degrees of writhing, pale forms, all hurrying in her direction. Collectively, they gave the impression of a giant, gulping throat ready to swallow her down.

So many.

Too many.

"You gotta trust me, kid. Please trust me."

He nodded against the back of her neck.

She spun again, sprinting for the vines.

The curtain of facehuggers quivered, excited shivers of anticipation coursing through them in communal delight. One of the breeders swayed, rocking the flexible pipe back and forth before it tensed, flinging itself at her like a rock from a sling.

Biting out, yelling behind her clenched teeth, she fired. She shot the sucker out of the sky, and kept firing. She blew hole after hole into the mass of dangling station-innards net, still running full force.

By the time her firearm was empty, a fall of acid and wire-scraps rained down across the floor, eating away the deck and creating a dangerous chasm. As the bits and pieces of the broken creatures that still clung near the ceiling oozed more acid, the hole grew wider. The gap in the floor stretched to eight feet across, then broadened to ten.

This is gonna hurt so—

Dropping the rifle, she swung Daniel off her back, swiveling his arms around her neck so she could clutch him to her chest instead. She kept sprinting. Another few steps and she'd have to dive or fall.

Three… two… one.

Her boot slipped on the liquidized floor, tripping her, stealing her momentum as she sailed over the gap. Acid sprinkled her back, searing her spine, burning her muscles from the outside just as panic and rush had burned them from within.

At the last moment she gave Daniel and extra shove, violently propelling him to the other side of the hole.

The edge of the melted floor struck her squarely in the midriff. Dregs of acid that still remained on the metal tore at her stomach, but she hooked her fingers into the grooves of the flooring grates and pulled, hauling herself onto steady ground.

Mind fogged, body aching, skin sizzling, all she wanted to do was stay where she was. To rest. For it to be over now. Shock tried to overtake her. There was too much pain in too many places. She shut her eyes.

But then there were hands on her shoulders and neck. Small hands and big hands. Shouts. Demands. Something like, *"Hurry, hurry, they're coming!"*

It was Ribar, and the ship pilot.

"Come on, get up!" Ribar demanded, his son now in his arms. "They're still coming!"

Amotz felt like all she could do was crawl. Now that the kid was safe, everything seemed worth it. They could leave her and she'd—

He slapped her face, right across her new acid-scars. "Damn it, General! It's my job to keep you alive and I haven't failed yet!"

One more push. You can do it. You're a goddamned General in the US Colonial Marine Corp. You can get up off your ass and stay alive.

She accepted the pilot's hand, struggling to get up. Her legs didn't want to work anymore. Acid on the back of her knees had burnt out the joints.

Ribar leant a hand, helping to drag her.

The skittering of facehugger feet drew closer and louder, nearly drowning out the emergency siren.

The bay door opened just as the first alien attempted to leap across the chasm. It landed stealthily on the other side. Five, ten, twenty followed.

Amotz kicked her useless legs, trying to gain some purchase, trying to go faster.

Daniel made it through the door, then Ribar, then the pilot. Ribar started closing the doors before the General's legs were through it. If the doors closed on her legs, they'd jam, and the facehuggers would have a way in.

The order for them to leave her was on the tip of her tongue. *Run, go! I'm already dead, you don't have to die!* Ribar had tried. She couldn't ask for more. He'd done his damned job.

A 'hugger grabbed her boot. The beginning of the horde had reached her. She registered the sharp crack of Ribar's service pistol firing long before she noticed the hole in her foot. Hell, what was one more bit of flesh gone? What was one more—?

Her body got tired of fighting. Tired of consciousness.

She blacked out.

When she came to, the half-constructed space station was in their rear window. Her ears rang with the new silence, and her body felt light. She'd been laid out on a surgical table. White bandages covered nearly every inch of her from head to toe. Every bit of her was numb. Whatever drugs they'd given her were damned strong and, she had to admit, damned effective.

Ribar sat nearby with Daniel on his lap. Both of the boy's arms were bandaged from where the acid had caught him when they dove.

"We didn't think you were gonna make it," Ribar admitted to her.

"Neither did I."

"So much for our 'quick tour,' eh? I would guess that we'll no longer be endorsing the Company's new construction techniques."

She managed a dry chuckle. "Yeah. And you know what else? I'm never going on a milk run again."

Ribar smiled. "No kidding. How are you feeling, General?"

She pursed her lips and set her jaw. She felt fuzzy, spacey, mad at the world, and very much like she knew too intimately how hotdog meat was made. She was glad to be alive, but also a little tired of actually *having* to be alive. She felt so many things at once, she couldn't pick one.

Amotz shrugged, let out a little sigh, and said, "I'm *fine.*"

She wondered what a lie detector would make of that.

DEEP BLACK

BY JONATHAN MABERRY

We came in low and fast, using the storm to hide us. Lightning crackled us and heavy winds tried to knock us down, but Lulu was on the stick and she could pilot a falling star through hell itself.

Was it a good landing?

No, but we didn't die, so put it in the win category.

I wanted to bring a full platoon with me, but during the mission briefing it was determined that a three-man team had a better chance than a platoon or even a squad. What they called a low-impact intrusion for surveillance and intelligence gathering with potential for targeted response. Typical military action-report language that basically meant we had to go in, see what was what, and either come out with intel or pull some triggers. No possible estimates of the risk levels because we didn't know what we were dealing with.

Fiorina "Fury" 161 wasn't our world. It didn't belong to the suits at Weyland-Yutani. Not anymore. Long time ago it had been a mining facility run by a W-T private prison firm, with the inmates doing hard labor mining raw minerals—mostly lead and iron—and then smelting, forming and shipping it off-world. When they found lead on seven hundred asteroids and dwarf planets, all of which had lower gravity and therefore less cost to put product into orbit, the big world-based mines got shut down. The Fury miners were mostly shipped out, but a group elected to stay. A bunch of religious assholes who'd found Jesus and wanted to wait for Jesus on a rock that was as close to salvation as a pimple on the Devil's taint. For some reason that made sense to them, but they were double-X losers so don't look too close at the logic or you'll hurt yourself.

After W-T dropped its claim, Fury fell even farther off the public radar. The lease expired. No one gave a boiled shit about it.

Until an escape pod crashed there ten years ago. That never made the news feeds. No sir. That was need to know and most people didn't need to know. The Company did, of course, but only select groups within it.

I never heard of it before last Tuesday. Not a word, not a peep. Until I needed to know.

I'd just brought my team in from a dirty little job on a dirty little floating lab orbiting a planet where the NeoNorse religious fruitcakes were building a new kind of hyperspeed torpedo for use against mercantile transports. Why they thought Odin would care about interstellar trade is beyond me. I was told to shut them down and we shut them all the way down. Didn't lose a man—or woman, for that matter—but we rained down hell on them. Good practice for some of my greener shooters, because the NeoNorse were pretty tough.

Not tough enough.

We got to the way station expecting a three-day pass and a serious assault on the alcohol stores, but they were waiting for us with orders. Go to Fury 161 and find out who had landed at the old mine and turned on the lights.

No one knew who was there.

All we knew is that it wasn't us.

So, fuck it.

We shipped out on a Starslip F-430. Yeah, one of the new ones. Looks exactly like a bullet. Big, blunt, ugly, fast. They loaded us into a launch platform and pulled the trigger.

When we woke up we were in orbit over the target.

Four people on the ship.

Three of us and a pilot.

Pilot was a synthetic named Sid who looked like my mother in guy's clothing. Not intended, just happened that way. Sid wasn't one of the chatty kind. He drove the boat, handled the wake-up call from hypersleep and handled the post-transit briefing. I was first on deck and had to answer the usual questions after waking up, just to make sure my brain hadn't turned to iced decaf.

"Name?" asked Sid.

"Alyn Harper."

"Rank?"

"Master Sergeant, United States Colonial Marine Corps Force Recon."

Went through the rest. Serial numbers, mother's maiden name, first pet.

Lulu Hoops and Bax Patel came out next. Both E5 sergeants; both old friends. We'd all walked through the Valley of the Shadow more times than I could count. Reliable, steady, lethal as fuck. Bax was the nice one—as far as that goes; Lulu was nasty as shit. They were our version of good cop/bad cop, but when it got real they were both marines, which meant they took zero shit from anyone on the wrong side of the line.

I'd picked them because we'd worked three-man gigs enough times to be halfway psychic with one another. Not really, but the way soldiers are. There's a thing that happens when people with the right training and enough practical experience can read each other with perfect clarity. A glance is a whole conversation. You know them all the way down to the marrow and you've been in so many dicey situations that you are one hundred percent positive you can trust them. Gets to the point where even in a firefight we're all so aware of each other that we're handing over a fresh magazine before the guy next to us fires his last round. Like that.

Once we'd shaken off the effects of the four-week in-flight sleep, we clustered around Sid and he briefed us on the latest intel. Our ship was in a wide and irregular orbit, making use of all the orbiting space junk left over from the mining days. The Starslip was the latest generation of stealth tactical craft, so unless someone knew how to look for us all they'd see is more junk among the junk.

"Certain elements of the mission have been marked restricted until we established orbit," explained Sid. "Here's what we know…"

And he told us the real backstory to the crashed escape pod. The story didn't start on Fury. It started long before I was born. It started with a mining ship called the *Nostromo* and it involved a horror-show alien species, a true Xenomorph. Sid told us about the only survivor of that ship, a flight officer named Lieutenant Ellen Ripley, a nobody who managed, somehow, to survive an encounter with a uniquely aggressive species. That was how Sid described it. Uniquely aggressive. I saw Lulu and Bax swap looks. We hadn't heard any of this shit.

Sid told us about Ripley destroying her ship after all of the crew had been killed and escaping in a life pod. He told us about Ripley being in hypersleep for fifty-seven years, about her getting found by a deep salvage team, about her being kicked to the curb by the Company because no one believed her insane story—especially after she blew up her ship. And then how the colony on Acheron LV-426 went dark, which is the exo-moon of Calpamos where Ripley's team had first encountered the Xenomorphs.

Then Sid told us the part that made my balls want to climb up inside my chest cavity. A team of Colonial Marines had been sent by W-T to Acheron to assess the situation. And, let's face it, to obtain the Xenomorphs. The bioweapons division guys must have been creaming their jeans at the thought of what they could do with one of those. But everything went to shit. By the time the expeditionary force got there the colonists were dead and the monsters were off the chain. Everyone died except one marine—a corporal named Hicks—a little girl who was the last surviving colonist, and—no shit—Ellen Ripley. And she nuked the whole atmosphere processing plant and turned a good chunk of that planet into a glow-in-the-dark back porch of Hell.

"This Ripley bitch likes blowing shit up," observed Lulu. "Kind of dig her."

Bax shook his head. "Why do I have a feeling that from now on, every time you blow something up you're going to be saying you're 'going full Ripley'?"

Lulu thought about it, shrugged, nodded. "Could happen."

Sid ignored them and told us about how the Xenomorph had somehow infected Ripley during hypersleep and because these fuckers had molecular acid for blood, the smoke from burning plastic triggered fire alarms and the life pods. The tubes containing the three survivors were transferred to a life pod and dropped into the atmosphere of the closest non-vital planet. Guess where?

Fury.

"Fuck me," said Lulu. "Is this a rescue mission for them?"

"After all these years?" asked Bax. "We're coming pretty late to the prom."

"No," said Sid, "Hicks and the girl were reported KIA when the pod crashed. Ripley was rescued by the prisoner miners, but there was at least one Xenomorph on the pod. It escaped and killed most of the prisoners and all of the staff."

"Fuck me," whispered Bax. "Just one?"

"Just one," said Sid.

"What about Ripley?" I asked.

"Dead, too. A Xenomorph impregnated her and she committed suicide to prevent the birth of a queen of that species."

"'Impregnated' how, exactly?" asked Lulu. "She get tired of blowing them up and decide to do the nasty with one?"

"I don't need that image in my head, thanks," said Bax.

Sid explained about the life process of the Xenomorph.

"Well fuck me blind and move the furniture," Bax muttered, and he looked a little green.

"Did Ripley blow up the mine, too?" asked Lulu.

"Not this time," said Sid, and he explained how she organized the prisoners to try and destroy the alien by entombing it in molten lead. It hadn't worked, but she killed it anyway. To prevent anyone from harvesting the queen inside her, Ripley had thrown herself into the lead. There was nothing of her left to harvest. There was one survivor from the prison, but he was a nobody and he vanished off the official record.

Weyland-Yutani sent three separate science teams to scour the area, but they came up dry each time. The file on Fiorina 161 was closed and filed away as an expensive waste of time and opportunities.

"So who's down there?" asked Bax.

"Unknown," said Sid. "The Company left some satellites in orbit and they started ringing bells."

"Squatters?" asked Lulu.

"Unlikely."

"Even so," she said, "how's this our gig? We roll out to protect civilians and protect W-T assets, but nobody who signs our paychecks owns a stake in Fury anymore, so why are we all the way the fuck out here?"

Sid said, "We're picking up heat signatures from the mine

and from a large supralightspeed craft. It has stealth sheathing that's almost good enough to hide it from our sweeps."

I grinned. *Almost* is a fun word. Stealth tech is rampant, and some of it's good enough so some of the rival planets and rival corporations can't find each other. We can find nearly everyone and no one—no-fucking-body—can find our birds. W-T developed it for the military, but they've been using it for their private ops, too. Like ours.

"The fact that someone is bankrolling an expensive operation means they've found something important on Fury. If it's important then it legally belongs to W-T."

"'Legally'?" echoed Bax, one eyebrow raised.

"Ethically, then," conceded Sid. Then he seemed to consider the weight of that word, too. "The Company never formally relinquished the planet and have since paid retroactive taxes and fees to fully reinstate their claim."

"They own it," I said. "Whose ship are we talking about?"

"It's anyone's guess as to *which* corporation put a ship down there," said Sid. "Whoever it is has money, though. No group of squatters could buy a ship like that."

"If they can afford that tech," said Bax glumly, "then they can afford shooters to protect it."

"Agreed," said Sid.

Lulu gave him a killer's smile. Thin, and hard and ice cold. "Fuck 'em."

Lulu drove the drop ship.

She always drives like she's running from a bank heist. Bax kept praying to Ganesha and I kept rechecking my safety harness. Stupid, I know, because if we crashed at the speeds she used all I'd be is a well-secured corpse.

There was an ice storm turning the region around the mine into a winter wonderland. Twenty-two below, with winds that turned snow into a fusillade of ice crystals. Lulu was singing some old-ass song about weed, whites and wine. She steered with the shifts of the wind so that if anyone was looking we'd fade into the background motion dynamics like a piece of blown debris. If we showed up at all. With storm winds there was always the chance of a shield panel flying off.

"Hold onto your sacks, boys," yelled Lulu, "'cause this is going to be a bumpy landing."

She wasn't joking. Or underestimating.

We hit the ground hard enough to make the impact suppression system cry out in protest. Everything rattled, from the deck bolts to the fillings in my teeth. When we deployed onto the surface I thought Bax was going to fall down and kiss the dirt.

Lulu grinned as she strolled out after us. "Pussies," she said.

"Kiss my... brown... ass," said Bax, but his voice trembled so bad there was no emphasis.

"Okay," I snapped, "cut the chatter."

I pulled up an area map on the tactical computer strapped to my forearm. Lulu and Bax touched theirs to mine to establish a dedicated team Wi-Fi and synch up the telemetry. We couldn't risk using satellite uplinks because of the danger of detection. We had a good path to the mine, and by good I mean it was a hardscrabble pain in the balls. The kind of path no one in their right mind would ever use, which made it a good choice for coming up on the blindside of whoever was here.

Took us five hours to go six kilometers.

Along the way we encountered rocks, more rocks, ice, more rocks, snow, and more motherfucking rocks. Once Bax saw a creature darting through a drift, but when Lulu popped it with a single silenced round, it turned out to be some kind of long-haired six-legged something that none of us had ever seen before. It wasn't a Xenomorph, though, so we left it in a bloodstained patch of snow and moved on. The winds were at our backs, which was some mercy because they were so strong it would have doubled the march time to walk into them. As it was they pushed us forward.

When we were half a klick out we stopped for warm water from our flasks and a full protein and electrolyte bar. Lots of calories, all the right nutrients, but they tasted like ass. Greasy, gritty ass, too. Small wonder they never caught on in civilian markets. We could feel the recharge, though, and after a fifteen-minute rest we were ready to rock and roll.

We crept to the top of a ridge of stone that rose from the shoreline of a frigid ocean and studied the tableau below.

"Yeah," said Bax, "definitely not squatters."

The mining building was vast. More like a medieval castle back on Earth. Huge towers of stone and iron that rose into the stormy sky. Ice seemed to reach up its sides like clutching fingers. There were snow-covered heaps of ancient trash and shapeless chunks of metal. Nearby, a ship squatted on eight powerful legs. It was a design I'd read about but never encountered. A *Bái lóng*-class exploration cruiser. Nine hundred feet, with a two hundred foot forward beam that tapered back to a slender tail. It was painted to look like its name, a white dragon. Teeth and all. Massive fusion engines, and an impressive and intimidating collection of gunports and rocket pods pointing in every useful direction.

I didn't like it, but now I understood it. Or, some of it, anyway. Outside the reach of planetary government or star-system alliances there was no real law. Everything beyond the core systems was run by whoever could afford to provide infrastructure and protection. The Weyland-Yutani Company owned big, gaudy chunks of that real estate, but space was— let's face it—really fucking big. There was plenty of room and plenty of resources out there to encourage competition and an entrepreneurial drive on an epic scale. After W-T there were some dozen next-tier corporations, and on the tier below that maybe three hundred smaller ones. The only company that offered any real competition to W-T was the Jǐngtì Lóng Corporation, based on New China. They had twelve star systems and business interests in everything from novelty genetically engineered pets to heavy metals mining to pharmaceuticals. Total number of employees was sixteen million, give or take. So, yeah, big.

They call their special operators *Wúgōng*, which means centipedes. Comes from the type of combat rig they wear that has a lot of extra extendible arms capable of using autonomous-fire weapons. I've gone toe-to-toe with some of their teams on disputed asteroids and planets. They buried some of my boys, and I buried a bunch of theirs. We failed to bond.

"Fuck me," murmured Bax, because he lost ten inches of intestine three years ago after a dust-up with a *Wúgōng* kill team.

"Sweet," said Lulu, because she didn't like anyone and was always turned on by the prospect of a fight with someone worth fighting.

I said nothing. This was a day on the job and they don't pay me to have opinions.

Beyond the ship was an area that had been cleared off by bulldozers and in the center of it was the squat, ungainly and clearly damaged hulk of a Type 337 EEV military lifeboat. It was one of those old-fashioned ones that didn't look like it was deigned to do anything but fall. Badly. Small portable field work-shelters had been erected and interior light made them glow.

We saw no one moving.

"Maybe they're all inside to get out of the storm," suggested Bax.

"Lulu," I said, "thermals."

She flipped down her visor and tapped the temple controls to cycle from ordinary vision to thermal scan. "Got 'em."

"How many and where?"

"Nothing in the lifeboat. Nothing in the work tents. But a shit-ton in the ship."

"Give me a count."

She chewed her lip. "Can't lock down a hard number. Some in the forward part of the ship. Call it eighteen, but most of the signals are soft. Like they're cooling. Some trace signatures, too. Dozens of those, but I can't get an active read on them."

"Could be the shielding messing with the sensor," suggested Bax.

"Maybe," I said. "What else?"

"There's a cluster in the engine room, but that's even muddier. I think they're clustered around the reactor."

"Clustered?"

"Looks like it. Jammed in so tight I can't count individual signatures. Best guess is ten."

I squinted at the ship. "That's a seventy-man boat."

"Big damn ship to land," said Lulu. "I'd love to see what they have under the hood."

"Where's the crew?" asked Bax.

"In the mine?" ventured Lulu, then she shook her head. "No. Even with interference from the structure I'd get something and it's stone cold dead in there."

It was a bad choice of words and she realized it as soon as she said it.

"What's the play, boss?" she asked to cover her words.

"We didn't come out here to be bystanders," I said. "We go down. Scout the ground and then see about getting onto that ship."

"Rules of engagement?" asked Bax.

I nodded to the lifeboat. "That came off a Marine Corps ship, which means it's *our* property. The mine and everything else belongs to the people we work for. Which makes everyone on that ship looters. Personally I do not play well with kids who try to steal my toys."

Lulu and Bax smiled. They weren't nice smiles. I doubt mine was, either.

———

We came down quietly, making maximum use of cover, guns up and out, taking turn running point whenever we changed direction. We went to the *Sulaco* lifeboat first and peered inside. I expected it to be a charred mess, but I was wrong. We paused to stare at what had been done to it.

It was a shell. Every piece of equipment, every control panel, every inch of wiring was gone. The Jǐngtì Lóng science geeks had done the most thorough job of stripping a ship that I've ever seen.

"I don't get this, boss," said Bax very quietly. "Why strip it out? The boat crashed, some of it burned. Nothing left inside was of any use even in a fire sale."

"Yeah," agreed Lulu, "long damn way to come to get used parts."

"Which means it's not why they came," I said. "Ripley got implanted with the alien embryo aboard that boat, and there had to be at least one of those face-hugger sons of bitches on board."

"Sure," said Bax, "but I thought W-T science teams have been all over this stuff."

"Maybe they missed something," said Lulu with a shrug.

"Or maybe they have better ways of looking," I said. "You know how Jǐngtì Lóng operates. They always take a weird left-field approach to everything. They've jumped the line in tech development a lot of times, so maybe they figured out how to do what the W-T nerd squad failed to do."

It was true enough. Even though Weyland-Yutani was the big dog in the technologies market, there was a good reason why Jǐngtì Lóng was constantly nipping at their heels. From what I'd read I figured it was an event split between really good R and D and really good corporate espionage.

Bax and Lulu looked at the boat, then at the mine and then at me.

"So what you're saying," Lulu began, "is that this whole thing is about these assholes trying to harvest aliens?"

"Xenomorphs," corrected Bax, but Lulu ignored him.

"Maybe," I said. "We don't know but I think we'd better

find out before they go and do something stupid."

As we moved off I could feel ice form in the pit of my stomach. Sid had told us a lot about the Xenomorphs and they were some nasty-ass critters. Hard as hell to kill, with that acid blood, some weird extendible mouth, strong, and apparently vicious in the extreme. If all they'd ever done was kill a flight crew on a cargo ship or the unarmed prisoners in a mine I wouldn't be too worried; but they'd slaughtered an entire platoon of marines on Acheron. Our mission parameters included securing any specimens—in whole or part—for return to the W-T labs. But what trumped that was to make sure no one else walked off with so much as a fingernail from the creatures. That would give the competition something our team hadn't yet managed to acquire, which would result in something a lot worse than stock drops when Jǐngtì Lóng developed it into a bioweapon. That could shift more than the economic balance of power. With Xenomorphs on the leash, Jǐngtì Lóng could start—and likely win—a war.

We used the heaps of debris to hide our approach but then Bax tapped my arm and nodded to the security cameras mounted along the sides of the Jǐngtì Lóng ship. The small sensor lights were all dark. I looked around. All of the work lights in the camp were still on, but there wasn't anything showing in the ship's few portholes.

"Is that good or bad?" asked Bax.

"Nothing's good on this rock," I said.

We did a complete circuit of the ship and found no trace of activity. The engine housing was still warm, but that would be on its own system because it takes too long to restart those babies and is easier and cheaper to leave them in idle. We ended our recon at the rear hatch and that's where we found the blood.

There was a lot of it.

Too much of it.

We stopped and stood at the edge of a wide puddle that could not have been made from what was in the veins of a single man. Six, seven, maybe. Lulu knelt and waved her hand to indicate hundreds of tiny islands in that lake of red. Shell casings.

There were lumps of meat, too.

I heard Bax mumbling a prayer. *"Om Gum Ganapatayei Namah."* It was a prayer of protection to Ganesh, the Hindu god who removes obstacles and offers protection. Lulu said nothing. She generally didn't believe in anything, but she knew this wasn't the moment to mock someone who was calling for support. No atheists in foxholes, especially on planets this far from home.

We looked at the rear hatch. It stood ajar, and through the five-inch gap all we could see was a black nothing. Except on the door frame, on which was a bloody handprint.

It was not made by a human hand.

We stood there, barrels pointed at the door, none of us speaking.

I was scared, I admit it. We all were.

The Chinese team had come here to find what the Weyland-Yutani guys had missed. An egg, maybe. A face-hugger. Some DNA. Something.

And they'd found it.

Or it had found them.

I tried to do the math in my head based on the mission intel. From the sketchy data collected so far, we knew the Xenomorphs grew fast. Real fast. The one on the *Nostromo* went from egg to infant to full-sized killer in under a day. Scary thought. Very scary thought, considering that there were seventy or more people on the Jĭngtì Lóng ship.

How'd they grow one, though?

Did they find an egg hidden on the lifeboat? Unlikely. Our boys would have found something like that.

Unless...

When Ripley was rescued from the crashed boat it was days before the killings in the mine began, and even longer before the first W-T team arrived. We knew that one of the face-huggers must have gotten to Ripley because she was impregnated. Or whatever we should call what happened to her.

There had to be a second face-hugger, because a Xenomorph began killing everyone in the mining facility.

Had there been a third? Or fourth?

How many had come down to Fury with Ripley, Hicks and the girl? How many had survived the crash? How many had escaped into the frozen wasteland of this world?

Was that what the Chinese worked out? Had they come here in the hopes of finding something that wasn't on board the lifeboat, but which had escaped from it?

That handprint seemed to be a mocking, ironic statement. It told us that everyone involved in this op was stupid. Suicidally stupid. Even knowing what we knew about these creatures, we had underestimated them. Time and time again. On the *Nostromo*, on Acheron. On the *Sulaco*. On Fury 161.

Mistakes every step of the way, because civilizations as technologically advanced as ours make those kinds of mistakes. What do they call it? Hubris? Something like that. Us thinking we're smarter than Nature, and when has that ever been the case? We should have learned that lesson in the twenty-first century when all those diseases they thought they'd beaten came back because people used antibiotics the wrong way. What was the death toll in the 2020s and 2030s? Sixty-five million? Something like that. The same for the first Mars colonies, when they thought they'd be able to do workarounds to the problems of radiation and bacteria in the ice there. I visited the graveyard once. Out of the first fifty colonists they sent, forty-eight of them died of cancer or infections from unknown bacteria.

We're fucking idiots. A lot of the time.

"What's the call, boss?" asked Bax, but I didn't answer right away. Instead I looked from that open door up to the clouds.

Our mission was to secure the location but to also secure any and all biological samples.

Of this?

"Jesus Christ," I said, and the others cut me sharp looks.

I kept my gun pointing at the line of darkness between door and hatch.

"I want you to listen to me," I said very softly. And I told them exactly what I'd been thinking. All of it. They stood their ground and listened.

"We're not on the policy level, boss," said Bax.

"I know."

"We're here to do a job," said Lulu.

"I know."

Deep inside the ship we heard a sound. A single human scream. Of pain. Of use and a terrible resignation, as if something was being done to body and soul that the mind could not escape but could not bear. Then the voice cried out something in Chinese that none of us could understand. Except that we did. Not the words, but the meaning. The intent. It was a prayer, screamed out so loud it was hard to tell if the voice belonged to a man or a woman. A piercing shriek that was way past the point where it was begging for mercy. It was begging for release. The scream rose and rose and then it disintegrated into wetness.

And then silence.

Absolute and awful.

Bax licked his lips. "And that's what they want us to take back to Earth?"

"Yeah," I said.

"God," he said.

"Yeah."

Bax held his gun firm but he took a single step backward. Not a retreat exactly. More like a statement. Lulu turned sharply toward him.

"What are you doing?" she demanded.

Bax didn't answer, but he took another step backward.

"We have a *job* to do."

"Yes we do," I said. Now she turned to me, frowning because of something she heard in my voice. She started to say something but there was a new sound from inside. A different kind of shriek. High, but not human.

No, not human at all.

We listened. It came again, and it was closer this time.

"Boss...?" asked Lulu, and now there was doubt in her voice.

Another scream, and another. No... two of them, overlapping. Not one creature. We listened. We heard them.

Them.

The screams, and beneath that sound was a scraping, slithering, clicking jumble of noises. Coming toward us from the deep black beyond that narrow opening.

"They want us to bring this back to Earth."

This time it was Lulu who spoke. Her voice was hushed. All of the bravado was gone. When I turned to look at her I saw that she had backed up and stood beside Bax.

"Yeah," I said.

"No," she said.

"No," said Bax.

I put the stock of my rifle against my shoulder.

"No," I said.

DISTRESSED

BY JAMES A. MOORE

Perkins was looking right at Callaghan when her head exploded inside the hard shelter of her environment helmet. Her eyes had an instant to bulge and then there were bits of her skull slipping down the interior of the visor along with the blood and grey matter.

"Fuck me!" Pho let out his usual battle cry and cut loose on the metallic demon coming their way. The PAR-320 fired hot pulses of burning plasma all over the bloodied limb that was even now trying to rip Perkins from the armor. She was already dead, but Callaghan couldn't stop hearing her screams.

Three hours ago they were en route to Liddiwell Habitat for R&R. Ten minutes later they had the distress call from the *Shiname Maru*. Being Colonial Marines, they responded, even though most of them were due for a rotation out of the stink of their armor. The suit from Weyland-Yutani, the company that owned the supply ship in distress, promised a bonus if the work was handled quickly. Never let it be said that credits couldn't grease a few gears.

From the outside the ship looked just right as long as you ignored the eye-aching lights coming off of whatever the hell had hit it. Not a ship of any known kind, but according to the captain, it was bigger than what they saw and at least half of it was spilling out light in spectrums no human eye could see. Those same lights were causing the pain. They couldn't be seen, but they could burn out a retina in under two minutes without protection.

The suit from Weyland-Yutani wanted samples of that, too. There would be bigger bonuses. Callaghan loved incentives.

All of which meant exactly shit when the thing from inside that vessel came for them.

Ten minutes away they got the skinny on the situation: Whatever had hit the ship had taken out command, intentionally or not, no one could say, but the piloting crew was likely dead, the command center was ruined and most of the surviving crew reported being locked in the back of the *Shiname Maru* along with the supplies to start terra-forming another planet. At least fifteen dead or missing and the ship was bleeding atmosphere everywhere that wasn't sealed away with the remaining crew.

The marines were going in hot and they were going in sealed in their cans. They were also going in without much visual back-up. The same lights that hurt their heads also fragged their helmet cams. Du Mariste, the ops station runner was doing what he could, but there wasn't much he could offer except what could be seen from outside the *Shiname Maru*. So far that was enough to let them know that whatever was out there was bigger than it looked.

Two minutes inside and all they saw was blood, broken bits of frozen corpse, shattered machinery and debris moving around inside the main deck. The artificial gravity was shot, and everything that wasn't sealed in place was bouncing around at different speeds. It was like being inside a madman's snow-globe.

Mag-boots kept them standing on the surfaces of their choice. Most took the floors just for familiarity sake. Fifty percent standard gravity, which didn't hurt when you were locked in environmental armor.

Perkins had tapped her portable workstation into the ship and was trying to assess all of the details when the metallic limb telescoped down the corridor leading to the breach and punched a hole through hardened armor and her head.

Pho, one of the biggest men Callaghan knew, had let out his fuck me and started shooting. And now seemed as good a time as any to join into the fray.

Plasma strobed down the corridor and fried whatever it touched. The bursts were small, they had to be in closed environments, but they did their work well enough. A stray shot melted Perkin's armor to her leg. She was too dead to complain, but whatever had hold of her didn't seem to care. The metallic limb kept pulling her down the length of the ship, toward the breach.

The *Shiname Maru* was nothing remarkable. Typical industrial grade freight hauler, with preformed walls in the areas where the crew lived and worked. The rest of it was metal and more metal with just enough insulation to protect the pipes from clumsy human hands.

The walls were white polymer shielding that flashed past as they ran after what was left of Perkins.

Captain Ogambe yelled through the com-link, "Don't get yourselves killed in the hunt, assholes! A little caution!" Ogambe was a soldier, same as them. They tended to listen, but whatever was taking Perkins away had killed one of theirs and that left a bad taste in Callaghan's mouth. Pho had been on over fifty missions with Perkins. The sergeant referred to her as "little sister," when he wasn't busy trying to get her naked.

Pho was beyond pissed.

He charged hard down the starboard corridor. The port side split from near the airlock and left a lot of room for sleeping quarters and mess hall. Starboard side was where the glowing thing had punched through the hull.

Their magnetic boots clanked with each step, but the standard sound was missing. The mags didn't lock down with a full gravity. They did about a half. Running was easier than it should have been. Pho came from a colony where the gravity was almost fifty percent higher than Terra-Norm. It was a wonder he hadn't smashed his head into the ceiling above him.

Behind them the rest of the squad was heading along, and damn near every one of them was pissing and moaning into the 'com about how badly they were going to fuck up the Xenomorph that had killed Perkins.

Callaghan did his best to stay chilled. Angry made for sloppy. A little anger was okay, it helped keep you alert, but more than that made you focus on the wrong things.

Pho caught a reminder of that when a second limb rolled out from the corridor ahead of them and tried to punch through him. He managed to slip to the side and got cut along his chest, but it was only a grazing wound. Still, the nanofibers in the armor started weaving the holes shut. Good thing or he'd be dead in two minutes from exposure and lack of atmosphere.

It sobered him up though. Took the rage down to a better place.

"Fucking hell," Pho grumbled.

"Easy goes it." Callaghan slowed down, looked his companion over and nodded. His armor was doing what it was supposed to do. Pho had painted several characters in Chinese on the armor. He'd be touching up a few of them. The skull he'd sprayed above his helmet's visor glared at Callaghan with as much fury as Pho's eyes offered.

"Go after her!"

"She's dead, mate." Callaghan shook his head. "We're

going after her, but don't rush so much. Cap's right. Getting killed won't do you any good."

He checked his clip and prepared a back-up. Ten rounds and he'd have to pull. It wasn't as easy in the bulky armor, but he'd practiced the maneuver for that reason.

Pho looked him up and down, his head moving behind the visor. "I'm good."

"Then let's go."

The others were coming up fast. If they didn't move they'd be called back into formation. Now they were dogs off the leash, but Ogambe wouldn't let them stay loose if he caught up with them. They would already get chewed up and spit out when everything was over, but the captain understood the value of not actively screaming at anyone who was acting out if they acted out in ways that benefited the company.

As far as Callaghan was concerned, they'd just volunteered to be scouts.

Pho stood up and shook it off. There was a little red around the edges of the new seals on his armor, but it was holding and he wouldn't bleed out. He wasn't stupid enough to try running if the injuries were too deep.

The magnetic boots rattled and clanked as they hauled ass, and both of them activated the flashlights on their helmets, giving them a better view of what was ahead.

It was enough to slow them down.

The corridor was wrong. That was the only way to put it. The preformed walls were distorted. There was something causing them to bubble and break down, so the walls close to them seemed normal but only a dozen feet away the material was expanding and bubbling outward like badly blistered flesh.

"Fucking walls have herpes," Pho spat.

There was still a lot of debris in the air. Most of it had been human at one point. It was cold enough to have frozen the meat and blood and bone, but the stuff was still careening around the hallway like a bloodied snowstorm.

It wasn't helping with seeing what they were looking for.

"Whatever took her is coming back. You can bet your credits on that."

"Why you say?" Pho looked his way, scowling.

"It took her for a reason. Whatever it wants, it cut up everyone it could and it tore Perkins apart. It's coming back."

"I got a grenade."

"Me too, but I'm not blowing the ship apart. Company takes that sort of stuff personally." Callaghan started forward again, trying to squint past the floating matter he didn't want to think about too carefully. "Besides, I want that bonus."

"Bonus don't matter if you're dead."

"Not planning on dying."

Lights flickered in the distance, the same sort that flickered outside the ship. Every bit of flotsam and jetsam in their way was highlighted by the strobes, turned black and white before it became Technicolor again.

"Messing with my eyes!" Pho squinted and continued on. Callaghan followed after him, letting his friend's bulk save his eyes from the worst of the lights. Even with Pho in the way the strain was immediate. He'd heard of visors that automatically compensated for extra glare. They were not standard issue. You wanted them, you paid. If the bonus was big enough…

The metal slammed down the corridor at high speed and both Pho and Callaghan ducked instinctively. There were joints to the thing, but it was mostly just a long run of metal with cables attached. Here and there along the entire length were spots where the metal seemed to vanish and others where the lights were too bright to see properly.

Pho shot at it anyway and punched three holes close enough together to sever the thing.

What had already gone past them ricocheted and wobbled as it filled the corridor. The part that was still connected further on down the hallway continued on.

Pho got up and Callaghan followed and they ran now,

hauling ass down the hallway to see what the limb was attached to. It kept coming slipping past them. It was close to a hundred feet in length if he was right.

From behind them more lights strobed. These were different. They knew the signature flare of plasma rounds when they saw them.

"Fucking hope they don't hit us!"

Before Callaghan could answer the thing came for them.

He knew parts of it wouldn't be seen by his eyes. That didn't help him out at all, because it was big enough to fill most of the corridor.

Whatever it was made of, it was covered in burnt blood and worse nightmares. There were too many limbs to count coming off the thing, most of them much shorter than the telescoping thing Pho had cut in half. They were all shapes and sizes and about half of them were ramming into the walls, cutting through the plastic to gain purchase as it humped and thudded its way toward them.

Rather than focus on the whole of the thing, Callaghan aimed for the parts that were lit up and started firing. Pho peppered the surface of the behemoth coming their way. Neither of them seemed to cause much damage, but it came at them even faster than before.

Every time it moved, more of the lights showed.

There was no symmetry to the thing. It had moving parts, but they made as little sense as the vast number of arms it used to shuffle forward.

Then one of the limbs pistoned out and cut off Pho's arm just below the shoulder. The metal blurred and Pho screamed and then there was fresh, warm blood spilling through the air even as a second limb reached out and wrapped three skeletal metallic fingers around Pho, pulling him toward the main mass. The armor Pho wore did its job again and the nanofibers started sealing the wound in the armor, likely sealing the source of the bleeding at the same time.

Pho didn't fire this time. The blood flow was too sudden and the damage too severe. He was either in shock or unconscious.

Callaghan looked around to see if back-up was there yet. "This fucking thing just took Pho! Where is everyone?"

Bendez and Ogambe came toward him at a trot. Ogambe spoke into the com-link. "The others are finding another route. We want to flank it if we can."

He took command that quickly and moved right past Callaghan with large strides. The captain was armed with a Hemming 450 assault cannon. He braced himself before he fired off ten rounds.

Ahead of him the metal thing shuddered and fell back as each round hit and exploded, taking parts of the mechanical beast off with each shell. Big parts. By the time Ogambe was done there were several new holes that had nothing to do with shining lights.

Ogambe looked back at Callaghan with a very pissed off expression. "You want to tell me where Pho is?"

"That fucker took him, that's all I know."

It came forward again, new lights flaring into existence as it moved. Both Bendez and Callaghan flinched at the pain. Ogambe kept going. His visor had gone dark. Somebody was smart enough to get the upgrades before they met the damned thing. The captain fired again, bracing himself and pounding out another ten rounds.

"One of you get up here and back me up! I have to reload!"

Callaghan moved forward, pulling his empty clip and slapping the replacement into the slot without hesitating. Ogambe took up a lot of room but not enough to fill the entire hallway. He leaned around the man and opened fire, aiming at a dark spot where the machine was already damaged. Each round lit the interior of the thing. He could see Pho's armor locked into the center of the creature, but it was too late to stop his plasma rounds. If Pho was alive, Callaghan killed him. He saw the plasma searing through armor like it was butter.

That seemed to be enough for the thing. It withdrew, sliding backward down the corridor toward the alien lights.

Ogambe was cursing. Callaghan just stared.

Pho. Damn everything. His body had burned right along with that armor. No two ways about the fact that he'd just murdered his friend.

As he was staring, the thing he'd ruined changed. It split open and pulled itself into three separate parts. Each had more mechanical limbs, and each separate piece changed shape. As easily as a master sculptor might rearrange clay, the sections smoothed out and sculpted themselves. The limbs were all toward the front now and most of them wavered in the air like bug arms as the separate, smaller parts came hammering toward all three of the men.

Past the glare of the lights Callaghan could see thick chords behind the main bodies, and mechanical pistons and gears that moved nearly too fast for him to identify.

There was no time to dwell on Pho. It was fight or die and he wasn't planning on dying.

The plasma rounds burned what they hit, but the damned thing seemed to be learning. It moved the main body of shifting parts out of his way until he had to readjust. Metal burned and a few of those insane limbs were melted out of shape but then Callaghan had to retreat as the entire thing came for him, a half ton of metal aiming to shred body and armor alike.

Ogambe opened fire again and blew the main body of the thing coming for him into fragments. It came forward anyway and what was left of it, mostly jagged blades of shattered steel, caught the captain in the chest and smashed him into the closest wall. The wall gave out. So did Ogambe's armor. The com-link picked up his grunt and the sound of his ribs collapsing in perfect detail.

Bendez did better. He was carrying a plasma torch instead of a pulse rifle. The cutters were designed to burn through hulls and he used his to cut the thing coming for him nearly in half. The force of the attack sent him spinning away, but the attacking module stopped, apparently incapacitated.

That just left two of the things to come at Callaghan.

"Back away! I'm throwing down!" Without another word he pulled the pin on his single grenade and hurled it down the corridor at the lights.

"Callaghan! Wait!" Bendez's words came too late.

Zero gravity made it look easy as the metal ball of the grenade rolled far further than he could have thrown in a gravity field. It made it all the way to the glowing lights that made his eyes feel like they were bleeding and then the glare changed nature. The light was just as bright but in the spectrum that his eyes could see. Everything down at the collision point was painted a bright white by that glare and parts he had not seen materialized just in time to melt under the intense heat. All three of the limbs that had telescoped from the main body were melted away for over half of their length and the remaining parts deactivated, floating in the zero-g of the ship.

"The fuck are you doing?" the screams came through the com-link. "Are you trying to burn us alive?"

Bendez said, "The other corridor, Callaghan. They were coming down the other corridor. Status check! You guys alive?"

"We're here, but I'm kicking somebody's ass when this is over!" That was Rollins. She meant it, too.

"Just hit this fucker!" He couldn't make out that voice but the result was immediate: Down where he'd melted half of the thing that was exposed and in view, a hail of plasma fire ripped into the alien machinery.

In a perfect universe the juggernaut they were blasting would take a hint and burn away. Whatever the damned thing was, however, it was designed to survive in the extremes of outer space. Some of it melted, true enough, some of it withered and slagged in the extreme heat. The rest of it reacted as if it had just been burned, and the whole of the thing spilled more of the lights that could only be partially seen and then it gave birth to something entirely different. A wave of thick fluids bled out from the thing, coating the walls of the corridor and running toward them.

Callaghan reached for Ogambe and hauled him along, heading back to the airlock and the corridor that led to their ship. The hairs on his scalp were up and his body felt a chill of gooseflesh. Whatever the hell was coming for them, it couldn't be good.

Ogambe was alive, but he was whimpering in pain. Ribs had been broken and there was a real chance he was bleeding internally.

Bendez was right behind him.

There is a time to fight and a time to run and when a tidal wave of shit is coming your way, it's time to retreat.

They made it to a point where the stuff had not reached and Bendez looked at his legs. "Shit got all over me."

Callaghan looked, too. "It's doing something to your armor. Get back to the ship and get out of that suit, Bendez. Take Ogambe with you." What had hit him was translucent, but there were fine fibers running through it. Where the goop was touching Bendez's armor, it was breaking down and being absorbed by the stuff. The armor wasn't melting exactly, but it wasn't going to hold air for much longer if Callaghan was right.

Bendez nodded and slid the torch off his arm. "Take that. Might help."

Callaghan nodded and pulled the torch along with him. Bendez moved.

Du Mariste spoke to him. The ops had been silent for so long he'd forgotten about him. "Whatever you just did, it pissed that thing off. It's spilling something all over the exterior of the ship. Whatever it is, it's doing heavy damage to the hull."

"It's eating the ship." Callaghan spoke softly, horrified.

"What?"

"That stuff. I saw it on Bennie's armor. It was changing the surface. I think that shit is eating the ship. Eating whatever it touches."

He looked carefully at the surfaces that had been touched.

Du Mariste spoke again, "What the hell is it going to do with it?"

"It's making repairs. I think it wants to rebuild itself."

Somebody screamed on the com-link. Rollins spoke up over the sound. "It's definitely doing something. We tried to clean it off of Moretti and it's too damned late." Her voice was inordinately soft.

The lights came back brighter and the thing that had already hammered at Callaghan came down the corridor again. There were alterations. It was adapting, to the environment. Instead of multiple limbs it had restructured much of the same material— he could see the burn marks from previous encounters—into a heavy carapace. Thick plates of armor came front and center as it barreled down the way, and it had armed itself. Parts of Pho were stuck in there too, melted and ruined. The only thing that wasn't hurt was the pulse rifle his friend had been holding. For one sick second Callaghan was afraid that damned thing might aim and fire at him. He had to suppress a laugh that was utterly humorless and bordered on insane.

From behind the mass that was coming toward him Callaghan saw the familiar flare of plasma fire. Half of the squad had to be firing to make that much light but he couldn't see them, only the end results of their assault. The burnt, broken and repaired thing coming to slaughter him shuddered and stopped.

Callaghan opened his mouth to speak but Rollins beat him to it. "It's stopping, but not for long. What the hell are we going to do with this thing?"

Du Mariste asked, "What do you mean?"

"I mean, Callaghan was right. It's eating the ship to repair itself. There are tubes sucking in whatever gets melted by the crap it puked up and those tubes are feeding right into parts that are being built. I don't know what the fuck we're dealing with but we need to get way from it."

"Callaghan?"

"I'm not seeing as much but I think we need to break away the main freight and let this thing either have the rest of the ship or blow it into dust! There is no way in hell we're going to stop it with the ordnance we have."

Rollins said, "Yeah, we already saw what a grenade did. It pissed this fucker off."

Ogambe responded, his voice strained and sounding winded. "Make it happen. Rollins, your team needs to meet with Callaghan and seal the locks. Make the separation clean."

"On it. Coming from the port side, Callaghan. Don't shoot us." Oh yes, she was going to kick his ass when this was over.

"Just fucking get here! I'm going to try to suppress this thing in the meantime."

A new clip of ammo got locked in place, but he kept the plasma cutter at the ready in case the thing got too close.

He saw the lights from the squad's helmets coming his way on his left. On the right, he saw the thing shudder and start waking up again. Whatever damage they had done it was quickly repairing itself.

Callaghan thought about whether or not he could get to it with the plasma cutter before it grew active again, but he didn't like his chances.

Rollins led the pack. She looked his way and he saw the rage, she was locking inside. "Why the hell are you standing there? You've got a torch. Burn the locks. We don't have time to set charges." She pointed at the connecting umbilicals that locked the *Shiname Maru* to the freight and the remaining crew of the ship. If they were severed security protocols would lock down the supplies and after that it was a matter of using the thrusters from either side to push ship and cargo in different directions. Even as they were speaking Patel was taking over the port where Perkins had been working earlier. The light off the screen hid Patel's face behind a reflection.

Callaghan nodded and moved for the starboard umbilical. The heavily insulated locks that held ship and cargo together would each take a minute or so to burn through. The torch's glare was enough to make him squint. The insulation melted quickly enough and, once he started the actual cutting, metal and rubber pooled and rippled into freeform statues as they were burned away from the whole and frozen in the zero-g environment.

"Get the fuck down!" Rollins was screaming, and Callaghan had to look. The same thing that had stopped before was coming for them and the squad was braced and firing.

No time. He looked away and kept cutting.

Du Mariste spoke up. "The Company would rather have the remaining ship left intact."

Ogambe came through. He hissed his words for a moment. "The company can have it, long as we get away." He grunted. "That thing comes for us, we're going to frag it."

Callaghan looked down at his handiwork and nodded as the final connections in the first umbilical were severed. "Half way there."

The lights from the attacking unit flared brightly enough to leave blue phantoms in front of his eyes, but he moved anyway, clunking his way over to the port side, away from the main conflict.

So he got to see the machinery coming their way from the other side. "Got more coming on the left!" This one was different, more fluid in design. It rolled quickly and smoothly and had some sort of array at the top.

The array looked like it might involve actual weapons. Ranged attacks.

Rollins was already barking orders.

Patel said, "On it," and a moment later a wall smoothly slid down to shut off the corridor. It was thick and hermetically sealed.

Callaghan breathed a little easier and started cutting away at the second umbilical, flinching automatically each time molten fragments hit his suit. Nothing had burned through yet, but you never knew.

The port side's new wall shuddered.

The starboard side was bathed in unholy light and more flares of plasma fire cast long shadows his way that were devoured by the torch. He wasn't a tech guy. He just cut through everything as quickly as he could.

"Go faster, Callaghan! We need to get back to the drop ship and fast."

"I'm working as fast as I can, Rollins."

"Work faster anyway!"

Walleston screamed out in pain and then cursed. At least the man was still alive.

"Got it!" The last wire burned through and he pulled back.

Patel said, "Let's go. I'm ready to blow the docking locks."

The wall on the port side was glowing and starting to melt near the top. It bubbled in their direction.

Callaghan didn't have to be told twice to vacate. He moved toward the sealed airlock. On the starboard side he saw how bad things had gotten. Two of his companions were injured. One was missing and two weren't moving. The other five were still firing and retreating.

Patel shoved past him and tapped the controls on the airlock. "Come on, people. Let's go! Let's go!"

Callaghan readied his weapons and looked at the port wall. Everyone needed to get away.

Rollins and the rest were coming, and dragging the wounded with them. Someone, he thought it was Murneau, had lost a leg. The environment suit had sealed the wound nice and neat, but that didn't mean much. The leg was floating near the battered and currently unmoving monstrosity that had already done so much damage.

Even as he watched, more of the thick liquids spilled from the walls around the broken machinery. The walls obligingly blistered and started to bubble out into whatever sort of building materials that fucking thing ate.

Patel thumped him on the shoulder. "Go!"

Callaghan listened.

They made their way through the airlocks and onto their own jump ship as quickly as they could. When they were all in place, Patel hit the keypad on the jump side and then sagged against the wall in his thick armored suit.

"We're ready, Du Mariste."

Patel spoke softly. The response was immediate. The ship moved, surging away from the interlocking umbilical.

As soon as they were far enough away, Patel blew the charges and the vast store of supplies meant to build another colony slid away from the *Shiname Maru*. Despite himself, Callaghan looked over at the company ship. Over half of the hull was blistering as whatever the hell was stuck to the ship continued to feast.

"We need to blow that thing up."

Patel looked his way. "Why?"

"It gets strong enough, if it rebuilds itself, it might try to follow us."

"The company wants it intact."

"They're bugshit crazy."

Bendez had all that stuff on his armor. Callaghan wondered what was left of the environment suit and what had been done with the liquid that had been absorbing it.

"Besides. I think they already got their samples."

Rollins was the one who answered him. "Yeah? Well, we all love incentives." She sounded as tired as he felt.

DANGEROUS PREY

BY SCOTT SIGLER

The protector hides in the shadows.

It is damaged.

It waits.

It listens.

Its cadre is gone, killed by the dangerous prey. The protector feels no familiar taps, hears no identifying sounds. The protector smells the scents of the cadre, but the individual signatures are hidden beneath the mostly uniform death-scent.

The protector hears and feels the presence of only a single being—one of the dangerous prey.

A host...

The *craving* to strike, almost overpowering, suffusing the protector. The undeniable *longing* to collect the host, carry it back to the colony. Drives so strong they threaten to push out everything else.

This is what the protector was made for.

And yet, the protector feels the twang of a simultaneous and equally powerful need, one that fights against the impulse to collect—two storms lashing against each other, each trying to devour the other. That second need: the compulsion to warn the colony.

The protector waits.

From the vibrations in the ground, the protector can tell the dangerous prey is also damaged. It makes bleating noises. The prey is crawling.

The protector listens for loud-stings. It hears none. It listens for the heavy, clomping steps of the dangerous prey. It hears none.

And still it waits, simple-yet-efficient mind processing this war of urges.

The protector is the sole survivor of its cadre. Instinct tells it to behave one way if in a group, another way if alone. When alone, the protector must be more cautious. If the protector is too aggressive, if it strikes and dies, the colony might not learn of the threat.

The protector stays crouched in the shadows. Hidden. Motionless.

The protector waits.

The dangerous prey is two things: a host, and a threat. A threat to other protectors, to the colony, to the Queen. A threat so serious none of its kind could be left alive. That was why the cadre pressed the attack.

This was the second time the protector responded to a call against this species. The first time, the prey/hosts had soft skins of different colors. The hosts were different sizes, too. Some were big, some were small. Some could loud-sting. Most could not. When the fighting was done, though, all of the surviving hosts made those bleating sounds of weakness, of fear. Those that survived were collected and taken to the colony.

This time, though, the hosts—this *dangerous prey*—they looked the same. All of a similar size. All had mottled green skin, with hard areas not that different from the protector's own rigid carapace.

The first time the protector faced this species, the prey scattered easily. They were then collected one or two at a time and taken back to the colony. The protector did not collect one—a primitive drive left unfulfilled.

The second time, though, the dangerous prey operated like a cadre themselves. They remained coordinated throughout the battle. This alone made them a kill-or-be-killed threat, even before the use of the loud-stingers that proved so deadly.

To defend the colony, the Queen, the cadre struck.

Early in the battle, the protector's arm took damage. Two loud-stings rendered it unusable. By the time the protector recovered enough to rejoin the fight, the rest of the cadre was dead, as were most of the dangerous prey.

All but one.

A damaged one that can only crawl.

The colony *must* know. A trail must be laid. Carrying the warning back home is all there is, the thing that must be done above all others—but there is also that basic, primal need…

…the all-consuming biological *demand* to expand the colony.

The protector waits.

The protector listens.

The protector feels.

Finally convinced that the crawling, bleating host is alone, the protector rises from the shadows and silently closes in.

The dangerous prey is too weak to fight. It bleats, louder than before. Will that sound bring more of its kind?

Two tidal waves of need crash together—*survive and warn… expand the colony.*

The protector will satisfy both urges.

With its one good arm, it clumsily lifts the bleating dangerous prey. The host feels so *dense*. Smaller in size than the protector, but heavier in weight.

The protector starts back toward the colony. As it walks, it drags its tail along the dirt and rocks, leaving a scent trail for others to follow.

The protector is incapable of being happy. Or sad. Or angry. It returns to the colony because that is what it is made to do.

Soon, it hears the colony's low-frequency rumble-buzz. The protector smells the "us" scent, the one that identifies the protector's colony as opposed to that of some enemy queen.

The protector knows it is slowing down. The damage is significant, and worsening.

It knows it will not survive that much longer, but it will survive long enough to deliver the warning—and deliver the host.

The protector carries the dangerous prey into the colony's main entrance.

During most of the trip, the prey barely moved, but now it struggles. It fights, but it is too weak. The protector can't understand why a creature that weighs so much has so little strength.

The colony is warm. Comforting. It is thick with scents: acid, waste, chitin, with pheromones identifying individuals, castes and groups. It is loud with noise: the low rumbles of sound produced by the folded air chambers within the protectors' long heads, the high-pitched hisses of close communication, the endless tapping of claws and tails radiating through the secreted material that makes up most of the colony.

Others notice the protector, notice what it is carrying. They flock to the host, touch it, smell it, sometimes taste it, listen to its strange bleating. The protector senses growing agitation and anxiety in the others—they need to go out, to collect more hosts like these and bring them back.

The protector presses its head against a wall thick with the dried secretions of its kind. It hums out a message. The low frequency vibration carries through the material, spreading through most of the colony. The message isn't a word, but it communicates a simple message that all understand: *new hosts.*

This message brings more others. Many more. They swarm in from a dozen openings.

The prey struggles against the hands reaching for it. It tries to turn its face away from those hands, but there are so many the face vanishes beneath a thick layer of twitching black.

The bleating... louder than ever before.

Others press in so tightly that the protector can't move, is held upright by the mass of bodies that want to know more about this host. Pheromones swirl, noise thumps, a swaying mass of black undulates with an unstoppable rush of *want.*

If there were words to be shouted, if there was a war cry to be screamed, the tunnels would shake with a single, maddening, phrase:

Expand the colony...

The protector's scent trail will lead the others back to the area of the battle, which is close to a host hive. But that scent trail signifies a path only—it doesn't communicate the level of threat. The protector emits low sounds from the long sound chamber that comprises most of its long head: five deep croaks to signify the five enemies the cadre encountered. The protector extends its secondary mouth, clacks it in a chattering pattern that signifies the dangerous prey can kill from a distance. The protector twitches its long head side to side, angles it sharply: the loud-stings produce vibrations that confuse the senses—the next cadre needs to be prepared for this. Finally, the protector emits mimicked identifying scents of its nine dead cadre mates, combined with the death-scent to communicate that they are gone.

The dead protectors will not be remembered. They are only referenced so the others know that the dangerous prey can kill in high numbers. The dangerous prey are a threat to the colony—they must be collected, or they must be eliminated.

The colony's activity intensifies. Agitation and aggressiveness toward this new threat combines with the overwhelming drive to collect more hosts. Others pack in close, they hiss and screech, they climb the walls, they skitter across the ceiling driven by a desire that mimics madness, they throng together with an orgiastic need so pure and intense it borders on madness.

This is what they were made for.

The others start to pour out of the colony, following the protector's scent trail toward the prey's hive.

The protector knows what it must do next.

It takes the wounded prey deeper into the colony.

The protector carries the host into the egg chamber. Two others are there, guarding the eggs.

No, the protector can't feel emotion, but there is an undeniable sensation at coming into this place. If that could be put into a single word, that word would be *hope*.

In this room is the future of the colony, contained in the eggs that dot the floor.

More scents. The protector moves to the part of the room that smells *ready*, where eggs have entered the final stage. The mature couriers inside the eggs seem to sense the presence of the host. The protector hears the rustling of little legs, the curling and contracting of tails ready to launch the couriers toward any hosts that passes by the moment the eggs open. The couriers also make small sounds, instinctively tapping feet together in patterns that call out *I am ready, choose me*.

But one egg does more than tap, more than shiver and twitch.

One egg *sings*.

A signature sound, the likes of which the protector has known only through vibrations in the walls and floor. This sound calls to the protector, draws it in.

Yes, this egg is the one.

The protector is weakening. Too much damage. It has enough strength left, though, to hold the host against the wall near the singing egg. The prey has stopped bleating, stopped struggling. The protector and the two others press pieces of hard material against the prey's limbs, then spit on those pieces. The spit instantly grows tacky. Almost as quickly, the spit hardens, locking the host in place.

The prey was dangerous. Now it is immobilized. Now it is *cocooned*.

Soon, the egg will open. The courier will join with the host.

The protector's legs give out. It stumbles, almost falls into another egg.

Too much damage.

The others in the egg chamber come closer. They touch, they smell, they taste. They secrete pheromones not of *concern*, but rather, of *finality*. The protector smells these pheromones, tastes them, and understands that the time has come for one last act, one final way to contribute to the colony.

———

Weak, unable to move any further, the protector is placed in front of the Queen.

This protector has never before been in the Queen's presence. Now that it is, the protector has a sensation of completeness. Of fulfillment.

The Queen is glorious. The Queen is *everything*.

And the Queen… the Queen is dying.

The protector understands: this final moment will help her survive a little while longer, and what helps the Queen helps the colony.

The Queen lowers her huge, beautiful head, touches it to the protector's. The Queen hums. The protector's body vibrates with that sound—with the *song*. In that song, the protector understands that the Queen *knows*. Knows the protector brought a host. Knows the protector left a path to more hosts. In that sound, there is pride. Acceptance. There is something else that the protector's brain isn't sophisticated enough to comprehend, but if it could, that something else might be called *gratitude*.

The protector has done well.

And now, the protector can serve the colony in one final way.

The protector has no concept of time, no concept of distance or space. There is no philosophy in its thoughts that it has lived a complete life, a life of selfless service. But there is a calmness, a sensation of peace.

It did everything it was made to do.

The pain will end.

The Queen's primary mouth opens.

There is no struggle as sharp teeth slice through the protector's carapace, one scraping bite after another.

As the protector's legs and arms and tail tremble and twitch, it feels and hears the Queen feeding upon its body.

———

The egg does not think. The egg does not feel. But the egg can *sense*. And, the egg *knows*.

There are three primary things an egg is engineered to recognize: vibrations that indicate movement and size, repetitive rhythms, the presence of a particular waste gas. Any two of these factors can combine to trigger muscle contractions, to peel back the lips that protect the courier deep inside.

The egg's specialized cells detect the presence of that gas: CO_2. Suitable hosts emit this gas. The egg doesn't understand this in any way, wouldn't know what CO_2 was if it even had a brain to understand anything, which it does not.

It detects no vibrations that indicate movement of a nearby host. The egg doesn't *listen*, but it does *feel*. The egg's skin is a sensory organ so finely attuned it can detect not only the steps of a potential host, but also something far softer—the steady rhythm of a heart.

Faint, but unmistakable: *bump-bump, bump-bump, bump-bump.*

A host is close by.

Waste gasses. A heartbeat.

Almost...

The heartbeat is erratic. Weak. If it were stronger, steadier, the egg would have already opened. The egg's genetic code programs for one specific command above all others—make sure the host is healthy enough to survive implantation and gestation. Because once the egg opens, the courier will soon die whether the embryo is delivered or not.

And the courier inside this egg, this courier above all others, it *must* deliver its embryo.

The play of impulses across the egg's nervous system feeds into an automated yet complex response analysis process. CO_2, yes, but the host's pulse indicates it might not live long enough.

Then, the erratic heartbeat steadies, becomes more rhythmic.

The host isn't healthy, but it is healthy enough.

With a soft squelch, the lips curl backward.

———

For the first time ever, air caresses the courier's skin. Nerves fire. Neurotransmitters flood the delicate circulatory system. Muscles that have lain dormant finally twitch and flex.

The courier doesn't think. It reacts. It responds. Evolution has ingrained a clock of sorts into the very fiber of its being—as soon as it is exposed to air, it must move quickly, for it will soon cease to function.

The courier is engineered to find the target that must be nearby.

It detects CO_2.

Then, a heartbeat.

If neither of these things were present, it would still react to nearby movement. Any of these stimuli are enough to drive it to complete its purpose, its sole reason for existence.

The courier stretches out eight long, quivering limbs. Limb-tips press against the egg's firm wetness. The courier slides from the deep safety of this womb. Its tail remains in the moist warmth, while the rest of its body feels the coldness of this world.

The courier focuses—CO_2, the rhythm of a heartbeat—and it turns toward those stimuli.

A courier's eyes are simple things. They detect movement, and also areas of light and dark. It is the latter ability that best helps it in targeting: across the universe, most advanced creatures have more than one eye. Usually two, but sometimes three, or even four. No matter how many eyes, though, all of these creatures have only one opening for the mouth.

The *mouth* is where the courier needs to go.

The courier scans the pattern of light and dark before it: two small darker areas, one large one.

Eight limbs tremble. Eight limb-tips press down. The tail coils, pushes against the egg's soft, firm interior.

CO_2.

A heartbeat.

Two small spots above a larger one.

The tail extends, hard and fast and instant, launching the courier through the air. Legs spread wide, ready to clutch, to *hug*.

It lands.

Limbs clamp around the host's head.

The tail coils about the host's neck, squeezes tight.

The host struggles; teeth gnash together, as if it knows what comes next. The courier's sensitive underbelly feels the host's lips, marks the location of teeth and jaws.

The courier's tail constricts.

The host's skin is warm, warmer than the air of the chamber.

The courier feels the host's heartbeat increase, faster and faster and faster.

The host struggles, resists, tries to endure, but it cannot

draw air. When its own biology betrays it, when the mouth finally opens for a desperate breath, bony curves extend from the courier's underbelly, hook under the host's upper teeth and over the bottom teeth. The courier's powerful muscles hold the jaws open, prevent the teeth from biting down.

The courier extends its proboscis into the host's open mouth, forces it down the host's warm, wet throat. The courier delivers lungfuls of air, keeping the host from suffocating. But the proboscis has another function, one just as important as delivering oxygen.

Deep in the host's chest, in the lower esophagus, the future of the colony begins.

———

This prey is dangerous.

This prey is a threat to the colony.

Such threats require absolute and overwhelming action.

The protector does not mourn the one who laid this scent trail. The protector is as capable of sadness as it is of fear, which is to say, not at all.

The protector is not intelligent, but it is also not *stupid*. The protector can count. In a rudimentary way only. It can't multiply or divide. It has no words or symbols for the numbers it knows, and yet it knows the numbers. The protector recognizes the identifying scent of each and every other in this new cadre, this *large* cadre.

One hundred and sixteen others.

The largest cadre the protector has ever known.

———

The scent trail ends.

The protector clusters with the others in the darkness.

Death-scent permeates the air. A battle happened here. Nine protectors died.

The hosts must be close by. The cadre must find them.

The protector crouches on the soil, places its palms flat on the dirt and rocks. The others do the same.

Through the ground, the protector feels the natural sensations of the nighttime landscape: a breeze blowing sand and dirt across the surface; the barely discernible tickle of nearby insects and small animals; the familiar cadence of another cadre moving across the ground somewhere nearby.

And then, the protector feels it. So very faint and distant—the rhythmic thump of something solid, heavy. Something on two legs, something not like itself… something *alien*.

The protector turns its head to face slightly right—the direction from which the vibrations come. It does not know how far away this threat is, but it is not near.

Silence is the constant rule, yet the protector is the de facto leader of this cadre—it risks a hiss. Just this protector, just one hiss, so enemies can't tell how many others there are. The sound wave spreads out, hits rocks and sparse plants, bounces back. The protector's echolocation maps objects in the area before it.

In that area, it detects no movement.

The protector stands taller. It hisses again, a little louder so it can "see" a little farther. When these sound waves bounce back, the protector senses something else, something very important: flat surfaces, thick forms rising high into the air.

A hive.

The protector silently stalks toward the hive. As one, the cadre rises and follows.

———

The hosts' hive is massive. It is made up of many mounds with unnatural, flat sides. The protector has never known anything so large. The protector's colony lies beneath the surface—this alien hive's tall mounds rise up to the sky. Many lights shine. It is night, it is dark, but in some places the hive is as bright as day.

The cadre doesn't approach right away. It holds position behind a slight rise. The protector is the only one looking above that rise. The others stay down in the darkness, so still they look like rocks.

Loud-stings finally give away the prey's location—rapid-fire flashes, coming from outside one of the hive's mounds.

This is the dangerous prey. The protector tries to count them, but they are behind small barricades and the flashes make it difficult to identify individuals. The protector's primitive brain first thinks *seven*, then *eight*.

Another cadre is attacking the dangerous prey. The hosts do not flee—they stand their ground. So many flashes, so many loud-stings. The protector watches as his kind fall, one after another. Some lie still. Some twitch. Some thrash in place. A few rise and continue the attack, only to be struck down again.

Even from this distance, the loud-stingers create painful shockwaves. The protector's body, the bodies of the others, evolved to sense vibration and sound—they all suffer from the concussive forces echoing sharply from behind the barricades.

The protector quietly calls out. Two others approach. These individuals aren't special. There is no "leader" caste. Protectors are almost identical to one another. These two responded to the call simply because they were closest.

The three protectors press in against each other. When their bodies are touching, the low-frequency signals made in their long vocal chambers are transmitted by conduction.

To call what happens next a "plan" is too grandiose a term. A plan would require forethought, analysis, strategy. What happens is far simpler than that.

The other on the protector's right drops back behind the ridge and scurries away to the right, thirty others following silently along with it.

The other on the protector's left also drops behind the ridge. It—and thirty more just like it—will rush toward the dangerous prey from this very spot.

Where there was one cadre, now there are three.

The protector drops down. Its cadre is small enough now for completely silent communication, no hisses to be heard, no taps to be detected. Its body shivers, stops, shivers, stops, a pattern that causes the others to cluster tightly around it. It joins hands with two others, who join hands with others next to them, and so on, until all are packed in close and connected by touch. The protector squeezes simple rhythms, sending messages. This is not a language so much as it is the communication of basic concepts:

This one goes first. Other ones follow. Quiet. Slow. At hive, cadre hides, waits. Silence. When this one strikes, others strike.

The protector drops to all fours and scurries off to the left.

Fifty-six others follow.

The protector crouches in the shadows near a hive opening.

It has watched. It has seen.

The desire to strike is almost overwhelming. The *need* to defend the hive, the *urge* to collect hosts, these instinctive drives pulse through the protector as strong and fast as its own heartbeat, glow like the strange lights that dot the tall hive-mounds.

But the protector waits, as does the cadre behind it.

The protector saw one of the dangerous prey come out of that opening, run to join the fight against the other cadres. The protector saw that the opening *closed*, by itself, a moving wall sealing it up.

If it opened once, perhaps it will open again.

Around the opening, piles of objects form barricades. The protector understands these barricades are similar to ones it helped make back in the colony—barricades that block, that protect, that channel an enemy into a predictable path.

Behind the barricade stands one of the dangerous prey.

It holds a loud-stinger, the biggest one the protector has seen yet. This loud-stinger seems to be a part of the dangerous prey, connected to it by an extra arm made of metal.

So *close*. A viable host, right there, only a short sprint away. To subdue it, to take it back to the colony… the compulsion to collect is *so* powerful.

The protector faces a difficult, reactive choice—collect the lone dangerous prey now, or continue to wait. This dangerous prey isn't part of the larger fight. It is guarding the hive opening… which means there could be more hosts inside.

Expand the colony…

The protector's every decision is a thing of pure logic, a mathematical equation free of creativity. The protector's brain evaluates variables, compares them in a pre-weighted system that was in place long before it was born.

Capture one host, or multiple?

Multiple.

The protector doesn't *decide* to wait, per se, it simply does not move at that moment.

A rumbling sound, high frequency and low frequency both. The protector feels something coming, something heavier than a cadre sprinting at full speed.

Then, the protector sees what is shaking the ground—a hive that moves.

The moving hive *roars*, lets out a cone of flame. The protector's body shudders with pain from the shockwave. A loud-sting, but so powerful it stuns the protector into stillness for a few moments.

Another roar as something explodes out among the cadre attacking the hive.

So much new information. So many new sensations.

The protector waits. It hisses, trying to see all there is to see on the battlefield.

Echoes come back, echoes of moving prey. Four… no, *five*, running quickly away from the attacking cadres.

Multiple hosts, running, *fleeing*. They are coming closer.

They are headed for the hive entrance.

The wall that sealed the entrance… it slides back.

The hive is open.

The protector rises. The others rise with it. Low and on all fours, the protector gallops toward the hive opening, the others close behind.

They instinctively move to three abreast, the protector front and center. The cadre understands loud-stings, how deadly they are. If fired upon, the three in front will act as a shield, taking damage so that the others behind them may get closer.

The long, fast-moving column of apex predators closes in.

The dangerous prey reacts quickly, lets out a sound of alert, turning to point the large loud-stinger toward the cadre. Flashes erupt from the end. The other on the protector's left is knocked backward. The other on the protector's right loses an arm in a blast of chitin, acid and flesh.

The protector launches itself high into the air just as more flashes from the loud-sting tear into the others behind it. The dangerous prey angles the loud-stinger up, but it is too late— the protector arcs over the barricade and kicks down hard, its full weight smashing the dangerous prey to the ground.

Others scramble over the barricade. They are met with a deafening cacophony of loud-stings. The protector smells pheromones of agony, of death. It suffers the concussive pains of the dangerous prey's loud-stings. The protector is so close to serving the colony in the best way it possibly can—the sensation triggers a rush of hormones that increase aggression. In just a few seconds of action, the protector is awash in a swirling ocean of input and sensation.

The dangerous prey with the extra arm makes bleating noises. It starts to rise. It is so *dense*, so *heavy*, yet for all that weight it is weak. The protector clutches tight with hands, feet and tail. It must neutralize the dangerous prey.

The protector opens wide its primary mouth—the two

kilogram secondary mouth fires outward at over twenty meters per second, smashing into the prey's thorax, denting the mottled green carapace. The prey shudders, but doesn't stop. It struggles to rise.

The protector has more strength than the prey, but not enough mass to hold the prey down. Another protector grabs the prey, then another, holding it in place. The prey fights. The protector aims for the head, then again strikes with the secondary mouth. The two kilogram weapon smashes into the prey's face at the same time the tiny jaws sink through flesh and lock onto cheekbone. Blood flies.

The prey struggles. The protector feels internal muscles contract, forcing fluid through two hollow teeth of the secondary mouth. Almost immediately, the prey slows, weakens.

The dangerous prey stops struggling.

Through the secondary mouth, the protector can feel the prey's heartbeat: slow, steady, strong.

This host is still alive. It is *healthy*.

Others are swarming through the open entrance. A few dangerous prey struggle on, but they are overwhelmed, buried under a wave of shiny black chitin and twitching tails.

The protector gathers up its host and quickly moves away from the hive. The others will search inside, collecting potential hosts, killing anything that is too dangerous to capture. From inside that hive, the protector hears loud-stings. Few and far between at first, then none at all.

The battle is over.

For now, at least, the colony is safe.

The protector finds the scent trail. The host it carries must be taken back to the colony—to the egg chamber.

The young queen awakens.

An instinctive process begins.

She must escape. She must break free. Legs—small but powerful—kick out hard. She feels her crown press against the host's sternum. Her entire body contracts, then expands all at once, trunk and tail and legs combining to deliver all of her strength to a few square centimeters.

She feels the restraining bone crack.

She coils again, explodes again, feels the crack widen.

The third time, she feels the host's bone splinter and its flesh tear. Her body makes it halfway out. The host's body twitches around her, shivering in its final death throes.

The new queen opens her mouth for the first time. She cannot yet see. She hisses... the sound waves that bounce back tell her she is not alone.

Hands lift her, pull her free. Gentle hands, *loving* hands.

She is carried. She feels protected.

The caring hands hold something to her mouth. She smells it, is instantly overwhelmed by the need to *eat*. She would eat anything she is given, but this particular food is meant only for her, only for queens-to-be.

At this stage of life, her body is impossibly dense. A small percentage of it consists of normal cells: muscle, brain, nervous system, a few temporary organs that will be gone in a few hours. Most of her, however, consists of millions upon millions of compressed cell that contain almost no fluid. These waiting cells are packed so tight they are a nearly solid mass.

As digested food spreads through her system, these compacted cells absorb moisture and nutrients—the cells begin to expand. The little queen is like a long-dry sponge finally exposed to water. Fluid swells within these dormant cells. Her density drops, but her size increases exponentially.

Were she alone, without the support of her colony, the little queen would eat whatever she could find. Her sharp, dense teeth can cut through almost anything, and almost anything she can swallow down her digestive system can process. With this specialized food, however, this sustenance specifically meant for the body of a young queen, her growth rate is launched into overdrive.

Her cells expand. They divide. Within a half hour, her skin grows too tight, so constrictive that crinkling lines form with flesh bulging between them. An hour after her birth, that skin splits—her body swells. She becomes longer, thicker. The newly exposed skin quickly begins to harden, to provide support to her body and new limbs. This skin will last only a few hours before she is again too large, and the process repeats.

Her protectors can reach full size in little more than a day.

She is much, *much* larger, yet it will take her less than a week to reach adult size.

Shortly after that happens, her body will begin to produce eggs.

The loving hands finally set the young queen down. She can almost stand on her own. Protectors help her stay upright. She smells/tastes their individual pheromone signatures. Her tail presses against the ground, but it is still too weak to hold her weight.

The young queen hears something: a low sound. A *song*, one that is made only for her, one that defines her.

That song is picked up by the protectors. They echo it, *amplify* it, so that it spreads throughout the colony.

In that song is the Young Queen's identity.

I am… I exist.

She has a sense of self. She is an individual—those around her are not, they are *extensions* of her.

All but one.

The Young Queen is finally able to see. She can hear, feel, she can detect vibrations. All of these senses are assaulted at once. The *smells*, the *tastes*, the *sounds*…

The *sight*.

Before her is her mother—a hundred times larger. Sprawling crown, shiny black carapace, thin arms, delicate trunk, long teeth.

The large queen leans her head over the smaller one. Thick

mucus drips down from the older into the mouth of the younger, who swallows it down, adding more specialized nutrition and precious fluid to her rapidly expanding body.

Old Queen is beautiful and precious, but there is also a scent coming off of her that is disturbing.

Because Old Queen is dying.

Hisses, taps, low thrums, pheromones... the two queens share something that the protectors could never know—a *conversation*, an actual exchange of information and ideas. The two queens don't have long. Old Queen knows she must pass on her knowledge before time runs out.

Young Queen listens, so very carefully.

Together, in the half-light, mother and daughter discuss the future of the colony.

———

The author would like to thank Chris Grall, MSG, U.S. Army Special Forces (Ret.) for his assistance with making cadre instincts and silent communication logical and consistent with proven tactics from elite military ground forces.

The author would also like to thank Gwen Pearson, Ph.D. in Entomology, for her feedback in eusocial insect communication and colony behavior.

The work of University of Missouri biologist Rex Cocrof was also instrumental in applying actual insect communication methods to the Xenomorphs.

SPITE

BY TIM LEBBON

"Let's get busy!"

Sprenkel's familiar pre-mission call echoed around the dropship's interior, but no one responded as they plunged into the huge habitat's weak atmosphere. A heavy vibration settled into the vessel, and Durand closed her eyes as her combat suit absorbed much of the impact. She always hated this part. Dropping into an atmosphere, however weak it may be, after weeks travelling through deep space was always a shock to the system—gravity taking hold, ship shaken and buffeted by atmospherics, and knowing that the end of their journey was near, as were the dangers that might face them there.

In this instance, there was little indication of what awaited them. The colony on Weller's World had fallen silent, and they were the nearest Colonial Marine unit on hand to go and investigate. The fact that they were on their way home from a two-year tour of Delta quadrant hadn't come into the equation. Major Akoko Halley had accepted their orders without question, selected the crew to take down with her on the dropship, and two hours ago they'd left the comfort of the destroyer *Ariel* on this final mission.

"My nuts are shaking loose," Nassise said.

"You've got no nuts," Bestwick replied. "I sliced them off when you were in hypersleep, you just haven't thawed enough to notice." Laughter swelled around the dropship's interior, then Major Halley's voice cut in.

"System and weapon checks in five minutes. I want you all green across the board before we hit the surface."

Durand sighed. She'd willingly follow Halley into the jaws of hell, but the major did little to shed her Snow Dog nickname. She was as cool and distant as they came.

Around the dropship's circular hold, the Colonial Marines went through their self-checking procedures. Durand interrogated her combat suit and came up all systems online and fully functional. Next she assessed her com-rifle, zeroing every reading so that levels were refreshed. Laser, plasma, and nano charges were all full. Finally she and her neighbor, the big guy Misra, confirmed each other's readings.

Everyone announced themselves fully prepped.

Major Halley nodded. Their vital signs would be displayed on her own combat suit's visor, and she turned her head slowly as she assessed her crew. Bestwick and Nassise sat to her left, Sprenkel and Eddols to her right, and Durand and Misra were across the hold from her. They were a good, solid team who'd fought battles together, faced danger and death, and dished out their fair share. Durand knew that the major was more used to leading large complements of the 39th Spaceborne, known as the DevilDogs, into patrol and combat situations, but Snow Dog also enjoyed these smaller, more personal missions.

Some said she was a former phrail addict replacing the

drug's allure with the thrill of combat. Durand had no opinion on the matter. And even if she had, she'd never share it.

"Four minutes," Huyck said from the cockpit. "I've picked up the beacon, no signs of anything amiss."

"Circle the facility," Halley said. "Durand? With me." They unclipped their harnesses and passed through into the cockpit, grabbing hold of storage strapping as the ship was buffeted by Weller's weak atmosphere.

The artificial habitat was huge, and looked like any one of a score of planets Durand had landed on over the eleven years of her time as a Colonial Marine. Blasted, bare, lifeless, this place was scarred and inimical due to the light atmosphere belched from the massive processors several miles to the east. Storms raged.

"No place to spend Christmas," Durand said.

"No place to be at all," Huyck said. "These assholes deserve every credit of their pay."

"Yeah, well, you don't always have a say in where the Company sends you," the major said.

"This is a Weyland-Yutani base?" Durand asked, surprised. They hadn't been appraised of that. All indications were that this was an independent facility. She'd thought maybe they were contractors earning a crust overseeing the atmosphere processors, or perhaps some sort of scientific base funded by one of the Institutes.

"Not exclusively," Halley said. "But the Company has interests everywhere, you know that, and I have orders. There's research being done here, and we're to retrieve it if at all possible."

"What about the base's crew?"

"Help them if we can. They're still the priority." She glanced away, and Durand thought, *The priority for us, but probably not the Company.*

"What's happened here, Major?" Durand asked.

"No one seems to know. But all comm systems seem intact, and from what I can see, there's no structural damage."

"Not externally, at least," Huyck said.

Durand was troubled. They'd been led to believe that this was a search and rescue, and now minutes before setting down, Halley was revealing more.

"Major?" she asked.

Halley smiled. It was a rare occurrence. "Durand, don't sweat it. My people always come first, you know that. Whatever the Company wants… if we can do it, we will."

"Yes, boss."

"You're my wingman on this," Halley said. "Got it?"

Durand nodded. They'd known each other a long time. She'd never had cause to mistrust her major, and she wasn't about to start now.

"Huyck, put us down," Halley said.

Fully suited due to the toxic atmosphere, all comm systems open, the six marines followed their major into the facility's eastern quarter. It was a large base consisting of a main central hub with four arms projecting from it, landing pad to the north, and external buildings scattered at various distances. It had the look of an older settlement—expanded, extended, with several trash sites and a surrounding landscape flattened and scarred from vehicle wheels. Records indicated the habitat was over two hundred years old, and Durand suspected that the base had been here almost from the beginning.

Misra was her double. In situations like this they always worked in pairs, covering each other's backs, placing their full trust in one another. They'd fought together many times before, and acting together felt as natural as breathing.

Inside the main doors, everything appeared normal. Bestwick closed the doors behind them and the air movement settled. Silence fell.

"Forward, slow," Halley whispered. They all heard through their combat suits.

The corridor was wide and low and scattered with litter, walls scraped and battered, all signs of it being a well-used thoroughfare. No traces of combat. No movement.

"Nassise," Halley said. Nassise held his motion detector ahead of him and moved slightly ahead of the group. His instrument's readings played across their visors, showing a rough schematic of the structure up to thirty meters ahead. Nothing moved.

"Boss, I can patch into facility communications here," Eddols said. She busied herself at a comm point on the wall, while the rest of the marines spread out in a protective pattern.

Durand tried to make sense of the place. The major had given no indication as to what research they were looking for, and perhaps she hadn't even been told. It was hard to discern from present surroundings just what this base's prime purpose might be. It was likely that over the years its use had changed, and now...

Now, something had gone wrong.

"Nothing," Eddols said. "I've scanned all channels. There's no chatter, and the comms haven't been accessed for over nineteen days."

"Whatever happened here was a while ago," Sprenkel said.

"Stay alert," Halley said, unnecessarily. The whole squad were on tiptoes. They knew very well that some of the worst dangers could stay dormant for some time.

They moved on, heading along the eastern arm's central corridor and approaching the first doors leading off into side rooms.

"Misra and Durand on the left, Bestwick and Sprenkel right," Halley said. "Take it in turns."

They worked methodically, scanning the rooms behind closed doors with a variety of instruments before entering—motion detectors, heat monitors, gas spectrum analyzers. They found offices, sleeping quarters, and storage rooms, but nothing alive.

No sign of whatever had gone wrong.

After fifty minutes they reached the base's circular hub. This was a much larger structure, several storeys high, and it would take a lot longer to search.

"Two squads?" Misra asked, but the major shook her head.

"I don't like this. It'll take longer, but I want us to stay together. We do this floor first, then work our way upwards. I want to see if—"

"Major, movement!" Nassise said.

Durand moved to the left and crouched, Misra right beside her. They aimed their com-rifles along the gently curving corridor, and Durand checked out the motion readings.

"Next floor up," she said. "Seems confused, like..."

"Like a swarm," Misra said.

"Nice choice of word," Durand said. "Thanks for that."

"Let's move," Halley snapped, and they followed her towards a nearby open staircase.

Senses heightened by the first signs of something active, they moved smoothly and quickly up the stairs, cautious on the half-landings, suits scanning ahead and relaying information to their visors and ear implants. Every marine was trained to keep one eye on reality at all times—suits could malfunction, data and displays could be misread.

It was Durand who saw the first movement before any suit system spotted it.

"Head of the stairs!" she said, aiming at the shifting shape. She didn't fire—it could have been one of the facility's staff, confused or injured, or afraid of what was happening. But her finger stroked the trigger, and she stared at the place where she'd seen the object.

"What was that?" Misra asked.

"Dunno." The two of them had taken point. By the time Halley crouched behind them, everything was motionless once more.

"Maybe a shadow," Halley said, and Durand grunted, because she knew better than to mistake a shadow for something it wasn't, and they all knew that.

"What's that stink?" Eddols asked.

Durand took in a slow, deep breath. "Burning," she said. "That's burning flesh."

"No," Bestwick said. "*Burnt* flesh. There's no heat left to it."

At the top of the staircase the corridor headed in one direction, and at its end, past heavy doors warped and broken from their hinges, they found the first of the large control rooms.

"Holy shit," Durand whispered. She tried to settle and calm her breathing, but she allowed in the shock, just for a moment. Denying it was not possible.

Everything was burnt. *Everyone* was burnt. The whole area was scorched black, swathes of soot coating walls, floor and ceilings, computer terminals ruined, furniture slumped down into strange sculptures. The dead were twisted into crisp statues, a few on their own, many more stacked against two emergency exit doors that had failed to open. These piles were grotesque, sprouting thin limbs and melted heads, with flesh burnt away to expose blackened bones, cracked and crumbled beneath the terrible heat. Metal structures had melted, and a platform halfway around the room had collapsed.

"Move in, but slowly," Halley said. "Sprenkel, Bestwick, count the dead."

"Seriously?" Bestwick asked.

"Best guess," Halley said. "There were ninety-eight personnel stationed here. We'll start keeping count. Eddols, locate the nearest staircase."

A couple of minutes later they moved on. Bestwick estimated forty dead in that one large room, and when they climbed to the next level they found many more. These were piled in three rooms, barricaded doors melted from their mounts, bodies contorted into terrible, agonized poses. Many corpses had become one. Durand was only glad there were few facial features to recognize, although she saw several smaller, wretched shapes which could only have been children.

"What the hell could do this?" she asked.

"Plasma weapons?" Misra asked, but they all heard the doubt in his voice.

"No weaponry we know," Halley said. "Structures are largely sound, superficial damage, not even flamethrowers would be this precise. Whatever did this was just after the people."

"I think we can say this is a done deal," Bestwick said.

"I concur," Sprenkel said. "No sign of movement or activity. No survivors."

"We should sweep the rest of the base," Misra said.

"We will," Halley said. She glanced at Durand, then looked away.

What the fuck is this? Durand wondered. *Were the Company experimenting with something that malfunctioned? Some new weapon?*

"We'll finish this wing," Halley said. "North wing next, then—"

"More movement!" Sprenkel said. "All around, and incoming!"

"That swarm again," Durand said, and she glanced at Misra.

"Got your back," he said.

"Positions!" Halley said, and there was no need for her to elaborate. They knew how to set up a defensive structure. Three of them faced one way along the corridor, four the other, and they could only wait as the motion detectors showed the swarm closing in.

They all saw them at the same time.

"What the fuck—" Bestwick said, her voice swallowed in the explosion of gunfire.

Durand opened up with short, controlled laser bursts. Her suit darkened its visor to the glare of exploding and flashing ordnance, but she still saw the flitting, streaking things, flying along the corridor towards them and erupting in flames as they were taken down.

They were slightly larger than her fist, airborne and moving quickly towards them. Her suit marked targets and she continued firing, switching rapidly from laser to nano-munitions when targets became too numerous. The creatures dodged and twitched, some of them escaping the marines' onslaught, many more not. They blew apart, crashed against the walls and ceiling, splashing across the floor as wet smears, and each one seemed to explode as if filled with compressed gas. The atmosphere here was not oxygen rich, so Durand assumed that these beasts had some sort of internal combustion source.

That made sense.

Those people had been burned to death.

As Durand switched her aim from creature to creature, terrible confirmation came from the other direction.

"Nassise, watch out!"

"Boss, duck, don't let them—"

"Eddols, out of the fucking way!"

"Oh, no…"

"Eddols!"

The scream was loud and sustained, and Durand risked a quick glance behind her.

Eddols had taken one single, deadly step towards the attacking throng, and now the things surrounded her, seeming to hover or drift close to her while she burned.

Fire erupted from their mouths. It streamed out like liquid flame, twisting in the air, pouring and floating in defiance of gravity, impacting against Eddols and melting through her protective suit as if it was hardly there.

Nassise tried to go to her aid, but Halley held him back.

Eddols screamed. Her voice was high and agonized. She thrashed, dropped her weapon, and then started running away from her companions.

"Eddols," Durand breathed, knowing that she was watching her friend die.

The beasts swarmed, still exhaling that strange, lava-like fire onto their vulnerable victim. As she ran through their midst, more and more were attracted to her conflagration. Black, oily smoke belched from her ruptured suit, and the stink of cooking meat filled the air.

"Grenade," Eddols croaked, her voice wet and hot.

Durand and the others realized her intention, all of them crouching mere seconds before the explosion. It ripped along the corridor, destroying a score of the fire-beasts and sweeping a blast wall ahead of it, knocking more of them from the air to bounce and skitter across the floor.

Durand jumped up, braced her legs, brought her com-rifle up into a firing position, and unleashed a stream of nano-munitions against the creatures still rolling and struggling on the floor. The resultant haze of small explosions killed them all. She shifted her gaze. Eyes wide. Breath light and fast.

Eddols was spread all over the corridor.

Durand had seen plenty of people die, a few of them friends. But she'd never seen someone she cared about go out like this. There was not even comfort in hoping it had been quick, because it hadn't. After the screaming, and the burning, the detonation had merely been the end point of a tortured demise.

"Motherfucker!" Durand shouted, and she fired several short laser blasts past the blood and flesh-spattered area where Eddols had died. The shots illuminated the corridor briefly, casting shadows of several creatures flitting rapidly away from the chaos.

Someone else took them down with several careful shots. Durand didn't even see who had fired. She turned aside and stared at the wall, then down at one of the dead creatures at her feet.

"Durand!" Halley said.

"Yeah."

The major grabbed her arm, tight, and turned her so they were face to face.

"I'm okay, boss," Durand said. Halley's stern face communicated strength, safety, and cohesiveness, and Durand looked past the major at the rest of the squad. She loved every one of them.

"We move on," Halley said. "A quick, thorough sweep, and

now we know what we're up against."

"Do we?" Sprenkel asked. He kicked at a creature's corpse and it rolled from his boot, striking the wall and slicking down in a dark, wet mess.

"Misra?" Halley asked. Misra was one of the DevilDogs' extraterrestrial experts, well versed in most of the species encountered during humankind's expansion into deep space. He'd told Durand that he'd once seen a Xenomorph, but it was from a distance, and he'd been glad it didn't come any closer.

"Never seen anything like this," Misra said. "Never heard of anything, either. I've accessed all the quantum folds I can think of, and there's no record of this sort of thing anywhere."

"Mean, spiteful bastards," Bestwick said.

"Fire spite," Sprenkel said. "Good name, yeah?"

Durand looked down at one of the dead creatures again, keeping one eye on her suit readings in case they returned. The thing was a little smaller than her head, pear shaped, with a scaly hide and four thin, membranous wings. It appeared eyeless, its mouth a circular pit ringed with stubs of what might have been blackened bone or exterior teeth. It was one of the most peculiar, grotesque things she'd ever seen.

She kicked hard and it landed a few meters away with a wet, heavy thud.

"You're sure?" Halley asked Misra.

"Seriously, boss?" Misra said. "A fire-breathing lizard-bird?"

"More movement ahead," Sprenkel said.

Durand looked at the major, expecting her to issue immediate orders, but she seemed distracted. She was staring at the mess that had been Eddols, frowning.

"Major, we should take off and sterilize the facility," Durand said. "There's nothing for us to save here."

"But we've only just finished one wing and the central hub," Misra said.

Halley nodded at Durand. "Yeah, nothing's worth this. There's no sign of survivors, everyone's dead, and as for anything else... screw that. Okay guys, back to the ship. We'll sheek-gas the whole fucking place."

"I'd say neutron bomb it to hell," Bestwick said, "but that's just me."

"I'll decide once we're airborne and safe," Halley said. "Move out."

"We can't go," Misra said. "Our mission's not complete."

"It's complete when I say it is, Private," Halley said.

"No," Misra said, shaking his head. Just as Durand saw the subtle movement of Misra's com-rifle, and caught a strange expression on his face, the fire spites attacked again. Without warning, without any sensors picking them up, they powered along the corridor from both directions, emerging from shadows and service ducts, melting through doors as if they weren't there at all. They converged on the marines with fire swirling before them.

Durand fired past Misra and took out a creature aiming for his back. It burst apart and spewed flame against the wall. Halley crouched with them and they all opened fire, while Nassise, Bestwick and Sprenkel confronted the enemies attacking from the other direction.

The corridor once more became a scene of chaos and destruction. Laser flashes seared the air and scored walls and ceilings, nano-munitions exploded in spreading flares, and an occasional plasma pulse was also unleashed, warping and melting the structure and frying a dozen creatures at a time. Durand's suit quickly registered an immediate spike in temperatures, both from the fire spites' assault and the Colonial Marines' high-powered weaponry. Her suit protected her, but she still felt the temperature rise.

"Where the hell are they coming from?" Bestwick shouted.

"Ease back this way!" Durand said. "We'll reach the blast doors back into the east wing, seal them up with a plasma burst, then run like fuck for the ship!"

"Good plan," Halley said. "Move out."

"We've got your back," Sprenkel said.

Durand, Misra and Halley began edging forward, stepping over sizzling, spitting fire spites, shooting more down. Molten metal dripped from the ceiling in places, and Durand felt her suit hardening when one drip landed on her shoulder. Designed to offer some limited protection against a Xenomorph's acidic blood, the suit worked well. Even so, her shoulder was now stiffer, its range of movement lessened.

The ceiling ahead of them collapsed. A surge of fire spites poured down through the flexing, dripping metal, the fire, the hazy gas, and Durand thought, *This is it, we're dead!*

She, Halley and Misra unleashed plasma shots at the same time. Her visor darkened and the combined blasts threw her back, suit hardening to protect her against debris and the wave of plasma-fire sweeping along the corridor. Systems glitched, and for a long few seconds her readouts faded to nothing. Even her own vital signs indicators zeroed, before receptors and transmitters flicked on again, recovering from the energy surge and bringing her and her weapons back online.

A hand grabbed her arm and pulled her upright. Halley. The attack seemed to be over, creatures fled or dead. But something was wrong.

Behind Halley, standing before the blazing ruin of the corridor and the burning fire spites, Misra was pointing his gun at them all.

"This mission is *not* finished," he said. "We haven't done a full sweep. Someone might still be alive."

"What the hell…" Sprenkel said.

"Misra?" Durand shook her head, dizzied by the firefight and plasma blast.

Halley took a step forward and the marine switched his aim to her.

"Sorry, boss," he said. "Sorry, but we have to—"

"Everyone's dead," Bestwick said. "You know that. We've seen the bodies."

"This isn't about the living or the dead," Halley said. "It's something else."

"What else is there?" Durand asked.

"I smell the Company on him," Halley said.

Misra's eyes went wide, then narrowed as he shifted his aim up to Halley's chest. One squeeze of the trigger and she'd be spread all over the walls.

But he'd also die. Durand could see that Misra knew that.

"There's research," Misra said at last. "We find it, retrieve it, we'll all be rich. *All* of us."

"This is such bullshit," Bestwick said.

"An operative from ArmoTech approached me," Misra said. "Said if we got here and things were gone to shit, he could promise me a big payday if I retrieved the research being done here. There's a lab, deep down beneath north wing. They've got something down there."

"Got what?" Durand asked.

"A Xenomorph," Halley said.

"You knew?" Misra asked, shocked. His aim shifted.

"Of course I knew," Halley said. "It was part of my mission. Seems they got to you as a bit of added insurance." She shook her head. "The fucking Company."

"We can still do this!" Misra said. His gun did not waver.

"I'm not risking the lives of my unit for another second. We're out of here, Misra. Everyone's dead, and the facility is already toast. That's the story we tell."

"You're stupid!"

"And you're a Colonial Marine! You've served in the DevilDogs for five years! You'd really throw all that away for–"

"For a million credits, yeah," Misra said, nodding hard. "Yes. *I'm* the boss now, boss."

"No," Halley said.

Misra frowned.

Halley turned her head slightly to look past Misra, and the marine's reaction was inbuilt, instinctive. He glanced back.

Halley, Durand and Bestwick all fired at the same time. Two laser blasts took him in the gut, the third sheared off the top third of his head, spilling him back onto the fire spite-spattered floor and splashing his scheming brains into the bubbling mess.

Silence fell, interrupted only by Durand's heavy breathing. She felt no remorse. Misra wasn't the first person she'd killed, but it could be that he was the most deserving.

"That didn't happen," Halley said, glancing back at the rest of her unit.

"*What* didn't happen?" Nassise asked.

"Let's move out."

They almost made it back to the ship.

Rushing back along the east wing, passing rooms and spaces already checked and cleared, Durand and the rest of the team were looking for danger from behind.

It came from all around.

The fire spites must have circled the facility and broken in from outside, drifting through empty rooms and waiting at closed doors for the marines to close in. Spitting fire, melting through doors, and dropping from the service-filled ceiling space above, their movement became apparent only moments before they attacked.

Durand was covering their retreat. She turned and faced back the way they'd come as the shooting began once again, com-rifle bucking in her hand, targeting grid guiding her aim. Her companions worked silently, so tight as a unit that they almost acted as one entity, instinctively dividing target zones and ensuring all angles were covered.

"Seventy meters!" a voice shouted, and Durand had never been so pleased to hear Huyck. "Follow my signal, out through a store room and exterior door!"

"Let's move it," Halley said. Even under fire she was cool.

Sometimes, Durand wished she was just like the major.

Someone screamed. Durand turned and saw a fire spite circling Sprenkel's leg, unleashing its flaming emissions against his limb. He fired at it but kept missing as it came in close. His suit was protecting him for now, but—

The floor bucked. Durand stumbled and fell, striking the floor on her side. Winded, she rolled onto her back and took out a creature dropping directly towards her head. Its wet, blazing hot innards spattered down across her face, visor darkening and blinding her to what came next.

The superheated floor dipped, then fell away completely, taking her with it. She shouted. She heard the others calling her name, but darkness swallowed her, even though the suit visor had cleared again. Twisting as she fell, she struck bottom on her right side... and kept on falling.

All sound was sucked away. Light flared and faded, flared and faded, as fire and laser bursts played above her.

Just like being in space, she thought, because she was floating and weightless.

Her suit glitched again, systems flickering, before all input fell to nothing. Darkness welcomed her down.

———

She couldn't have been out for more than a few minutes. When she came to, she was bobbing against a floor in the flooded basement level. Her com-rifle held her down. It was the last thing she'd ever let go of, even in death. Her hand was locked around the grasp, and she used it to anchor her as she looked around.

Her suit systems were dead. Perhaps an impact had taken out the CSU, or maybe she'd sustained some damage that allowed water to flood in and short the whole suit. It was only pure luck that had maintained her oxygen supplies to her face mask. Without that, she'd have drowned.

The ship! she thought. *I have to hurry!*

She pushed herself up, standing so that the water came up to her neck and looking around. The hole she'd tumbled through was three meters up, and illuminated by flickering flames. No more gunfire.

"Boss," she said. "Bestwick. Sprenkel. Nassise?" There was no reply, and she could not hear the tell-tale hum of an open channel. Her comms were as dead as the rest of her suit's systems.

"Fucking great," she said.

Cautiously, she waded towards the wall and started climbing, using metal rungs cast into the structure.

A heavy vibration shook the ground. She paused, then started climbing faster, heart sinking as she pulled herself up into the battle-scarred corridor. She emerged from the hole just in time to hear the dropship's distinctive launch rockets blasting it up and away from the base.

"Oh, no," she muttered. With her suit dead, her vitals would show that she was the same.

Hefting the com-rifle, she looked back and forth along the corridor. For now it was silent and still, but for the glow of flaming dead things and drifting smoke.

I'll message them! she thought. *Get back to a central control room, get comms working, let them know I'm still here!* The Colonial Marines never left anyone behind.

Yet here she was.

And there they were. Drifting closer from along the corridor, maybe fifty of them. She spun around and they were coming from the other direction, too. They seemed slower than before, more contemplative. Maybe they were afraid after she and her companions had unleashed such destruction on their blazing hot bodies.

Or perhaps they were more intelligent than that.

They know I'm stranded, she thought. *They're going to play with me.*

"Fuck that," Durand said. Checking her com-rifle's charge,

finding it sufficient, she hefted the weapon, and braced her legs
into the familiar firing stance.

"Come on then, you bastards!" she shouted. "Let's get busy!"

Her finger stroked the trigger, and the world caught on fire.

AUTHOR BIOGRAPHIES

PAUL KUPPERBERG is a writer of novels, short stories, comic books, and nonfiction, including *The Same Old Story* and *In My Shorts: Hitler's Bellhop and Other Stories* (both from Crazy 8 Press). He has written over 1,000 comic books, ranging from Superman to Scooby Doo, and is the author of the GLAAD Media Award nominated and 2014 IAMTW Scribe Award-winning young adult novel *Kevin* (Grosset & Dunlap), as well as the Harvey and Eisner Awards nominated Life With Archie series (including the controversial "Death of Archie" story line) for Archie Comics. Paul is the executive editor and a writer for Charlton Neo Comics (http://morttodd.com/charlton.html) and you can follow him on Facebook, Twitter (@PaulKupperberg), and at PaulKupperberg.com.

DAN ABNETT is a seven-times *New York Times* bestselling author and an award-winning comic book writer. He has written over fifty novels, including the acclaimed Gaunt's Ghosts series, the Eisenhorn and Ravenor trilogies, volumes of the million-selling Horus Heresy series,

The Silent Stars Go By (Doctor Who), *Rocket Raccoon and Groot: Steal the Galaxy*, *The Avengers: Everybody Wants To Rule The World*, *Triumff: Her Majesty's Hero*, and *Embedded*, and with Nik Vincent, *Tomb Raider: The Ten Thousand Immortals* and *Fiefdom*. In comics, he is known for his work for Marvel, DC, Boom!, Dark Horse and 2000AD. His 2008 run on *The Guardians of the Galaxy* for Marvel formed the inspiration for the blockbuster movie. He has also written extensively for the games industry, including *Shadow of Mordor* and *Alien: Isolation*. Dan lives and works in the UK with his wife Nik Vincent-Abnett, an editor and writer of fiction. Follow him on Twitter: @VincentAbnett.

RACHEL CAINE is a *New York Times*, *USA Today*, and #1 international bestselling author of science fiction, young adult, fantasy and suspense. Her works include the Morganville Vampires series (YA), Weather Warden series (Fantasy), Stillhouse Lake (thriller), and the Great Library series (YA). She's written more than fifty books and a hundred short stories so far. Find her at rachelcaine.com, Facebook at rachelcainefanpage, and Twitter at @rachelcaine.

YVONNE NAVARRO lives in southern Arizona and is the author of more than twenty published novels and well over a hundred short stories. Back in 1996, *Aliens: Music of the Spears* was her fourth published novel. Her writing has won the HWA's Bram Stoker Award plus a number of other writing awards. She also draws and paints, and is married to author Weston Ochse. They dote on their three Great Danes, Ghoulie, The Grimmy Beast, and I Am Groot, and a talking, people-loving parakeet named BirdZilla. She admits to having a framed, signed photograph of a young Michael Biehn in her art studio. Visit her at www.yvonnenavarro.com or on Facebook.

CHRISTOPHER GOLDEN is the *New York Times* bestselling author of *Ararat*, *Snowblind*, and *Tin Men*, among many other novels. With Mike Mignola, he co-created two cult favorite comic book series, *Baltimore* and *Joe Golem: Occult Detective*. As editor, his anthologies include *Seize the Night*, *The New Dead*, and *Dark Cities*. His first trip into the

Alien franchise was the novel *Alien: River of Pain*. Golden lives in Massachusetts. Please visit him at www.christophergolden.com.

MATT FORBECK is an award-winning and *New York Times* bestselling author and game designer with over thirty novels and countless games published to date. His latest work includes the novel *Halo: New Blood*, the *Magic: The Gathering comics*, *Captain America: The Ultimate Guide to the First Avenger*, the Monster Academy YA fantasy novels, and the upcoming *Shotguns & Sorcery* roleplaying game based on his novels. He lives in Beloit, WI, with his wife and five children, including a set of quadruplets. For more about him and his work, visit Forbeck.com.

RAY GARTON has been writing novels, novellas, and short stories for more than thirty years. His work spans the genres of horror, crime, suspense, and even comedy. His titles include the Bram Stoker Award-nominated *Live Girls*, *Ravenous*, *The Loveliest Dead*, *Meds*, *Vortex*, and many others. His short stories have appeared in magazines and anthologies and have been collected in books like *Methods of Madness*, *Pieces of Hate*, and *Slivers of Bone*. He received the Grand Master of Horror Award in 2006. He lives in northern California with his wife and is currently working on several projects. Visit his website at RayGartonOnline.com.

WESTON OCHSE is a former intelligence officer and special operations soldier who has engaged enemy combatants, terrorists, narco smugglers, and human traffickers. His personal war stories include performing humanitarian operations over Bangladesh, being deployed to Afghanistan, and a near miss being cannibalized in Papua New Guinea. His fiction and non-fiction has been praised by *USA Today*, *The Atlantic*, *The New York Post*, *The Financial Times of London*, and *Publishers Weekly*. The American Library Association labeled him one of the Major Horror Authors of the twenty-first century. His work has also won the Bram Stoker Award, been nominated for the Pushcart Prize, and won multiple New Mexico-Arizona Book Awards. A writer of more than twenty-six books in multiple genres, his military supernatural series *SEAL Team 666* has been optioned to be a movie starring Dwayne Johnson. His military sci-fi series, which starts with *Grunt Life*, has been praised for its PTSD-positive depiction of soldiers at peace and at war.

LARRY CORREIA: *Monster Hunter International*, despite being self-published, reached the *Entertainment Weekly* bestseller list in April 2008, after which he received a publishing contract with Baen Books. *Monster Hunter International* was re-released in 2009 and was on the Locus bestseller list in November 2009. The sequel, *Monster Hunter Vendetta*, was a *New York Times* bestseller. The third book in the series, *Monster Hunter Alpha*, was released in July 2011 and was also a *New York Times* bestseller. Correia was a finalist for the John W. Campbell award for best new science fiction/fantasy writer of 2011. *Warbound*, the third book in Correia's The Grimnoir Chronicles series, received a nomination for the Hugo Award for Best Novel in 2014. The Dead Six series started as an online action fiction collaboration with Mike Kupari (Nightcrawler) at the online gun forum "The High Road" as the "Welcome Back Mr Nightcrawler" series of posts. These works predated the publishing of Monster Hunter.

KEITH R.A. DeCANDIDO has written novels, short fiction, and comic books in a variety of media universes over a career that spans more than two decades, as well as original fiction in his own universes. Recent and upcoming work includes the *Marvel's Tales of Asgard* trilogy (featuring Thor, Sif, and the Warriors Three); the *Stargate SG-1* novel *Kali's Wrath*; the *Heroes Reborn* novella *Save the Cheerleader, Destroy the World*; the urban fantasy novel *A Furnace Sealed*; the high fantasy police procedural *Mermaid Precinct*; three serialized *Super City Police Department* novellas; and short fiction in the anthologies *Nights of the Living Dead, The X-Files: Trust No One, V-Wars: Night Terrors, Baker Street Irregulars, TV Gods: Summer Programming, Altered States of the Union, A Baker's Dozen of Magic*, and *Limbus Inc.* Book 3. Find out more at his cheerfully retro website at DeCandido.net, which is the gateway to his entire online footprint.

BRIAN KEENE writes novels, comic books, short fiction, and occasional journalism for money. He is the author of over forty books, mostly in the horror, crime, and dark fantasy genres, including *The Complex*, *Pressure*, *Ghoul*, and *The Rising*. He has won numerous awards and honors, including the 2014 World Horror Grandmaster Award, 2001 Bram Stoker Award for Nonfiction, 2003 Bram Stoker Award for First Novel, 2004 Shocker Award for Book of the Year, and Honors from United States Army International Security Assistance Force in Afghanistan and Whiteman A.F.B. (home of the B-2 Stealth Bomber) 509th Logistics Fuels Flight. He also hosts the popular podcast, The Horror Show with Brian Keene.

HEATHER GRAHAM is the international, *New York Times*, and *USA Today* bestselling author of over two hundred novels, novellas, and stories. The founder of Slushpile Productions, she hosts numerous venues with dinner theater and author rock bands for various children's charities. Heather Graham and the Slushpile also have a number of recordings available on I-Tunes and other venues. Creepy-crawly-scary things have long intrigued her. She has written horror, suspense, romance, historical fiction, and Christmas family fare. Find her on Facebook or at theoriginalheathergraham.com. She sincerely hopes you enjoy her entry here as she is an avid X-Files fan!

Michael Diamond Resnick, better known by his published name **MIKE RESNICK**, is a popular and prolific American science fiction author. He is, according to Locus, the all-time leading award winner, living or dead, for short science fiction. He is the winner of five Hugos, a Nebula, and other major awards in the United States, France, Spain, Japan, Croatia, and Poland, and has been short-listed for major awards in England, Italy, and Australia. He is the author of sixty-eight novels, over two hundred and fifty stories, and two screenplays, and is the editor of forty-one anthologies. His work has been translated into twenty-five languages. He can be found online as @ResnickMike on Twitter or at www.mikeresnick.com.

MARINA J. LOSTETTER's original short fiction has appeared in venues such as *Lightspeed*, *InterGalactic Medicine Show*, and Flash Fiction Online. Originally from Oregon, she now lives in Arkansas with her husband, Alex. Marina enjoys globetrotting, board games, and all things art-related. She tweets as @MarinaLostetter, and her official website can be found at www.lostetter.net.

JONATHAN MABERRY is a *New York Times* bestselling author, five-time Bram Stoker Award-winner and comic book writer. He writes in multiple genres including suspense, thriller, horror, science fiction, fantasy, action, and steampunk, for adults and teens. His works include the Joe Ledger thrillers, *Roy & Ruin*, *Vault of Shadows*, *X-Files Origins: Devil's Advocate*, *Mars One*, *Patient Zero*, *V-Wars*, and many others. He writes comics for Marvel (*Black Panther*, *Punisher*, etc.), Dark Horse (*Bad Blood*) and IDW (*Warrior Smart*, V-Wars). And he is the editor of several high-profile anthologies including *The X-Files*, *Nights of the Living Dead*, and *Scary Out There*. Several of his works are in development for movies and TV. He is a popular workshop leader, keynote speaker and writing teacher. He lives in Del Mar, California. Find him online at www.jonathanmaberry.com.

JAMES A. MOORE is the bestselling author of more than forty novels, including the critically acclaimed *Fireworks*, *Under The Overtree*, *Blood Red*, the Serenity Falls trilogy (featuring his recurring anti-hero, Jonathan Crowley) and his most recent novels *City of Wonders* and *The Last Sacrifice*. He is the author of *Alien: Sea of Sorrows*, part of a trilogy written with Christopher Golden and Tim Lebbon for Titan Books. He has twice been nominated for the Bram Stoker Award and spent three years as an officer in the Horror Writers Association, first as secretary and later as vice president.

SCOTT SIGLER is the *New York Times* bestselling author of seventeen novels, six novellas and dozens of short stories. His works are available from Crown Publishing and Del Rey Books, including his most recent *Alone* (Book III in the Generations Trilogy). He is also a co-founder of Empty Set Entertainment, which publishes his young-adult Galactic Football League series.

DAVID FARLAND is an award-winning, *New York Times* bestselling author in both the science fiction and fantasy genres with more than fifty novels to his credit. He has written novels for both the *Star Wars* and the Mummy series, and this story, he says, "My fanboy dreams have almost all come true. Now if I can just write a Mad Max novel."

TIM LEBBON is a *New York Times* bestselling horror and fantasy writer from South Wales. He's had almost thirty novels published to date, as well as dozens of novellas and hundreds of short stories. His most recent releases include the apocalyptic *Coldbrook*, *Alien: Out of the Shadows*, *Into the Void: Dawn of the Jedi* (Star Wars), the Toxic City trilogy from Pyr in the USA, *The Silence* (Titan UK/USA), the thriller *Endure*, the *Alien-Predator* crossover "The Rage War," and the forthcoming *Relics* trilogy. He has won four British Fantasy Awards, a Bram Stoker Award, and a Scribe Award, and has been a finalist for World Fantasy, International Horror Guild and Shirley Jackson Awards. Works for the screen include *Pay the Ghost* (starring Nicolas Cage), children's spooky animated film *My Haunted House*, his script *Playtime* (written with Stephen Volk), and *Exorcising Angels* (with Simon Clark). Find out more about Tim at his website www.timlebbon.net.